ELEMENTS BOOK I

A Whisper of Wind

Aaron Scott Wickel

ISBN# 978-1-941052-57-0 Trade Paper
ISBN# 978-1-941052-58-7 eBook
ISBN# 978-1-941052-59-4 Hardcover

Library of Congress Control Number:
2014939998

Cover Design: Brandi (Shai) Fathers

Pronghorn Press
pronghornpress.org

To my wife, Jordan, and daughter, Amelia.
May you chase your dreams
and see them realized.

A Whisper of Wind Pronunciation Guide

Ailyana: Eye-lee-ah-nuh
Alator Kilobaski: (first) Al-uh-tohr (last) Keelo-bah-skee
Altarian: All-tare-ee-an
Alympia: Uh-limp-eeya
Alympus: Uh-limp-us
Apaz: Eh-paz
Arinn: Ahr-in
Asariel Ylen Khiings "Ari": (first) Ah-sare-ee-el, (middle) ee-len, (nickname) Ah-ree
Aurok: Ahr-ohck
Barthol: Bar-tholl
Benazahg Khiings: (first) Ben-uh-zog
Bockratandem: Bock-ruh-tan-duhm
Caspien: Cas-pea-an
Corai: Cohr-eye
Coroth: Coh-rohth
Cronus: Croh-nus
Daemon: Day-mun
Diera Volf: Deer-uh Vohlf
Elutha: Uh-loo-tha
Eta: Ay-tah
Ettias Khiings: Et-tie-us
Genotl: Jen-oh-tel
Gertry: Gehr-tree
Gruegen Gang: Groo-gen Gang
Instellitent: In-stel-ee-tent
Javelar: Jav-ih-lar
Jehora: Jeh-hohr-uh
Karia: Kah-ree-uh
Kehndrig Voelker: (first) Kayn-drig (last) Vohl-ker
Kilindrel: Kill-in-drehl

Kinara Katari: (first) Kee-nah-rah (last) Kuh-tah-ree
Luci'oan: Lucy-owen
Lycaon: Lie-kay-on
Maialyn Khiings: My-uh-lynn
Parnikus Khiings: Par-nick-us
Povine: Poh-vine
Sejm: Saym
Tarris: Tar-iss
Tendir: Ten-deer
Teora: Tay-oh-rah
Tor'qi: Tohr-kee
Trentir Savvage: (first) Tren-teer (last) Suh-vahj
Zaelek Khiings: (first) Zay-leck

A Whisper of Wind

[illegible]

CLASSIFIED
[illegible] KYR

OPERATIVE: CRONUS

[illegible] WAS REPORTED DEAD ON SCENE BY [illegible] TRENTIR SAVVAGE IS RESPONSIBLE FOR [illegible] BY MEANS OF [illegible] I'M SURE YOU ALREADY KNOW [illegible] IS DEVASTATED. I RECOMMEND THAT SHE BE [illegible] UNTIL CLEARED [illegible]

IT IS ABSOLUTELY CRUCIAL THAT [illegible] DOES NOT DISCOVER THE [illegible] DOCUMENT. SHOULD THEY DISCOVER [illegible] THEY WILL [illegible]

Secrets upon secrets. Lies upon lies. Whatever the Council and their elemental warriors are up to, whatever they know, it will all come to light soon enough. One way or another, we'll all find out about it. Do I know when? No. Though I can promise you that when we do find out, it's going to shape the course of history.

—Sindera Barbendas, *Creet Times*

A Whisper of Wind

1

At The Gold Kilindrel Casino, Creet...

I showed the picture of my fiancé to the uniformed clerk at the front desk.

"Have you seen this man?"

The clerk nodded toward one of the card tables. "Last I saw, he was over there."

I looked back to the gaming tables but didn't recognize anyone. I don't know why I expected anyone to give me a straight answer in a grimy, smoke-filled casino notorious for illegal trade. Most people would think me harsh for jumping to the conclusion that I'd been lied to, but I knew that there were security cameras everywhere, and the front desk had access to them.

Someone behind me grabbed my shoulder. I snatched their hand, twisting it as I spun. Alator's face slammed into the bar counter.

"Kinara! It's me!" he yelped.

I released him. "Where have you been?"

"I've been following a lead."

"What lead is so important that you can't send me a message to tell me you're okay?"

He massaged his wrist and shook his head. "Do you always have to be so intense?"

"You should know better than to sneak up on me."

"Fair enough." He lowered his voice. "Someone dropped an anonymous tip about Trentir Savvage."

Trentir Savvage? What would Alator want with one of the wealthiest merchants on the planet?

"What kind of tip?"

"You know I can't discuss cases with you until I solve them."

I hated it when he shut me down like that, and he knew it. All Guardian Investigation Task Force guys were the same. Whenever the G.I.T.F. needed a Seeker, they didn't hesitate to share sensitive information, but not before. It annoyed me because Alator and I had been partners on quite a few cases. Of course, that was when their department needed my help.

A few of those had been what they call "high profile" and had opened my eyes to how dangerous his job could be. It worried me that much more when he didn't tell me things. Alator could handle himself, and I knew that, but sometimes he dealt with extraordinarily vicious criminals. I'd feel better if I could permanently have his back, but our two departments operated so differently, that wouldn't happen.

I turned away from him and huffed in frustration. He took my hand and spun me back around. His amber eyes glinted as he smiled, and his tone softened.

"Come on, Kinara, don't be like that."

"Be like what?"

"You know." His hand tenderly brushed the hair out of my face, and my heart fluttered.

"Stop it. I'm trying to be angry with you."

Alator grinned. "I'd better tread carefully then."

That stupid grin got me every time. Not only that, but his perfect teeth, his stubble-covered square jaw…Alator pulled me in and kissed me.

I withdrew gently, focusing on the warm fire in his eyes. "It's disgusting how charming you can be."

He smiled and kissed my forehead. "I won't be too much longer. Meet me at home?"

"Fine, but be careful. Please."

"I promise."

I walked out of the extravagant, gold tower-like casino and took in the brisk night air that came with spring. The breeze carried the potent scent of vegetables sautéed in butter and the soft hum of hoverports overhead. In all my years living in Creet, I still felt like a tourist, just one with a unique perspective. I couldn't help but marvel at the sheer height of every building. Sometimes it felt like standing in a maze of glass mountains covered with neon signs.

I smiled to myself, remembering my frustration with Alator. I pulled the compact tablet out of my pocket and pressed my finger to the screen. I tapped the "Air Ride" app and pinged my location.

Within a minute, an air shuttle exited the Skyway and landed next to me. The side door released and swung upward.

"Where to?" the driver asked.

"Four-twenty Bligenville Way," I answered.

The shuttle's thrusters powered up, the landing gear retracted and we entered the Skyway. We merged into the express lane, careful not to spend too long in the launch zone. The Skypatrols were sticklers about shuttles being in that lane for an extended time.

When we finally landed in front of my apartment building, I transferred the credits due, leaving a small tip before passing through the glass doors that welcomed me home every day. They swung open as the doorman greeted me.

"Ah, Miss Katari, welcome back."

"Thank you, Kohr."

The elevator doors slid closed behind me and opened seconds later on the eleventh floor. At the end of the hall, I gazed into the security system's retina scanner, a click sounded, and the door slid into the wall.

The lights flickered to life as I hung up my jacket. I decided to cut Alator some slack and order takeout even though it was his night to make dinner. Hopefully, he wouldn't be longer than an hour. My stomach was threatening to eat itself.

I washed my face, threw my hair up in a quick kilitail, then changed into more comfortable clothes. Light glared off the picture frame on the dresser that held a photo of my deceased parents. I studied it, then my reflection in the mirror. Uncle was right; I looked almost identical to her. A pang of sadness struck my heart before I forced myself to refocus on the problem at hand: dinner.

The couch's cushion *floofed* as I sat, sending a slight puff of air up my back. The news channel came up on the wall screen, covering various feel-good stories.

An hour passed, but still no sign of Alator.

"Come on, Alator. Where are you?" I muttered as I returned to the kitchen to find something to nibble on. I grabbed a manafruna and peeled it, gazing at Alator's sword sitting beneath mine on the rack mounted next to the door.

The stand had been a gift from my father, yet another reminder of my parents. He'd always said, "One day, you'll get your sword, then we can hang our swords as a family." That dream was no longer attainable. We buried their swords with them in the Ceremony of the Fallen, and tradition dictates that a Guardian's sword stays with them to enable them to conquer trials in the afterlife.

The door clicked. "Sorry, that took a little longer than expected," Alator said.

"I have been starving for the last hour," I whined dramatically.

"Uh-oh. We'd better get started on dinner then. I know how you get when you're hungry."

"I thought we could get something delivered."

Alator stopped rummaging through the refrigerator and looked my way. "Can we afford that?"

"I think so. Most of the costs for the wedding are accounted for, and you've picked up quite a few double shifts this month."

"What about the trip to Heritage after the wedding?"

"What about it?"

"Don't we still need more credits for the resort?"

"No. Remember? My uncle gave us that early wedding gift to go toward it."

"Oh, right! What do we want to order then?"

I pursed my lips and thought for a moment. Anything sounded good at that point. "I don't know, you pick."

Alator looked at me skeptically. "Seriously?"

"What?"

"Every time I pick something, you tell me no!"

"I do not!"

He laughed and threw a dishtowel at me. I swatted it away before it hit my face. Alator shook his head, "What about Friga's?"

"We had that last week," I groaned.

"Kaltoren Deli?"

"Lame!"

"Woman, you'll be the death of me!"

I always enjoyed our playful banter. Alator made me laugh. "Okay, what about Litue's?"

"No way."

"Look who's being picky now!"

"The chief took my crew to lunch today. That's what we had."

I rolled my eyes. "Gilispet?"

"I could do Gilispet."

Alator navigated the big screen's search, opened a menu from the restaurant, and scrolled down. "You want the fried duplerings and trepais, right?"

I nodded with a smile, pleased that he knew me so well. He took a minute to weigh his options, then added his choices. The screen stated that our order would arrive in five minutes. Not bad for a weekend. *They must be slow tonight.*

The screen returned to the news channel. A special on the recently deceased senator, Yulden, aired. She'd been well-received in the community. Most people had adored her during her term.

A beeping came from our oven to let us know the food was conveniently being delivered straight to the rack inside. Alator took his hand off my upper thigh and retrieved our meal. The food smelled heavenly. The savory sauce on the duplerings mixed with the grease from the breaded trepais made me salivate.

Alator slid my food across the small table between us and the big screen.

I looked at him. "Did you forget the utensils?"

He sighed. "Yeah. I'll grab them."

"No, no. I got it."

I opened the drawer in the kitchen and retrieved what we needed. He watched me suspiciously, as if expecting me to throw them at him. I wouldn't do that. I liked his eyes too much.

We ate in silence as we watched the documentary.

"This is a nice tribute to old Yulden," I said.

"I was thinking the same.... Hey, when it's over, I have something to show you."

"What is it?"

"I'm not going to tell you! It's a surprise."

Our program froze, changing the screen to an urgent alert. A newswoman stood outside the city's capitol. The noise from the gathered crowd forced her to shout.

"This is CRS News coming to you live from the capitol in Creet. Behind me, you can see a man standing on the monument dedicated to Cronus, a highly decorated operative in the Guardian Forces. We can't be sure what his intentions are, but…"

An explosion vaporized the people surrounding the statue. The news woman's body slammed into the camera, ending the feed.

My pocket vibrated, startling me. I checked the screen. Uncle Kehndrig's contact information came up. When the call connected, I swiped up, sending it to the big screen.

Colonel Kehndrig Voelker stared down at us from his office. "Are you two seeing this?"

Alator stared intently at the screen. "Yes, Sir. We see it."

"Kinara, I need you to check in with your squad leader. We need every seeker out there looking for those bombs."

"Understood," I said.

"Alator, your chief mobilized your unit a few seconds ago. I expect you'll receive the notification soon."

Alator's pocket vibrated. "Just got it, Sir."

"Good, you know what to do."

Alator grabbed his sword from the rack. Before he even started for the door, the broadcast was hijacked. A man in a mask addressed the people.

"Citizens of Creet, I speak to you on behalf of the organization known as Javelar. For too long, we have sat idly by and watched as our planetary resources grow closer to exhaustion. It's time we act. We have planted bombs like the one you saw at the capitol all around the city. If the United-Guardian Forces do not surrender control of Earth's portal in thirty minutes, we will detonate them."

The transmission ended, and my uncle reconnected. "Get out there. We can't afford to give up the portal…. Move!"

I ran to the bedroom, my clothes flying everywhere as I snatched my black leather uniform from the closet and squeezed into it. Alator opened the apartment door and allowed me to pass through before closing it behind him.

I jammed the elevator's down button and when the doors slid open, we rushed in.

My fingers rapped my leg. Even though the elevator was the fastest way down, it wasn't fast enough. When the doors opened again Alator grabbed my hand as I turned toward the building's exit.

"What are you doing?" I asked. "The exit is this way!"

Alator pulled me in the opposite direction. "There's no time to call transport. We have to take my cruiser."

"I can't ride with you! It's against regulations!"

"Yeah, well, to Styx with regulations."

We sprinted to the parking hanger where his cruiser sat in its familiar stall. The moment I sat down, Alator hit the accelerator. He pushed a button on the dashboard, and the safety harnesses sucked us into the seats. The hanger door leading to the Skyway opened as we approached.

Alator flipped a switch, activating the cruiser's sirens, and we merged into the late-night traffic. The vehicles in front of us moved to the side, creating an opening. Alator accelerated to an uncomfortable speed. Not even a minute later, a traffic jam clogged all lanes.

He cursed. "Hold on!"

He flicked another switch and the cruiser's nose dove toward the ground. I took a deep breath as my stomach churned. An odd sound came from the rear of the vehicle. We leveled off, then, like an amusement park ride, we surged forward.

I grasped the handle above my head as we wove through obstacles in our path.

"How does it look up there?" Alator asked.

The congested lanes above had unclogged. "You're clear."

The cruiser tilted up, and we rocketed back onto the Skyway. My tablet vibrated, conveying a message from my uncle.

"Change of plans," I said. "We're going to Kintar Plaza."

"Got it."

The plaza wasn't much farther. Whatever the reason for the change, I hoped we weren't too late. The plaza was a busy place, and thousands of lives might be at stake.

I sent a quick message to my squad leader as we landed next to the four other GITF cruisers already at the edge of the plaza. Before I could put both feet on the pavement, a burly man approached us.

He twisted a corner of his thick, black mustache and frowned. "You know you can't have passengers unless they're authorized ahead of time. The chief is going to kill you."

Alator smirked. "Let's hope she doesn't find out, eh, Gen?"

"When does she *not* find out?"

"You worry too much."

"The Colonel said you needed a Seeker?" I said.

He nodded toward the fountain in the center of the plaza. "Talk to Malz. He can tell you more."

Malz would be easy enough to find. The man stood six and a half feet tall and weighed close to three hundred pounds. I spotted him standing next to the bomb squad truck talking to a technician. He saw me and jogged over, making his well-formed muscles ripple under his tight, black leather uniform.

Malz grinned. "I hope Alator didn't drag you into this mess!"

"Nope. That would be my uncle's doing."

"How is the old Colonel?"

"Stubborn as ever."

He laughed, and after a brief pause, I said, "I was told you'd fill me in."

"Right. Save lives now. Catch up later. We received a tip on a bomb in the area. So far, we've found nothing, but that doesn't mean we won't. Squads two and three are searching the last quadrant as we speak."

"Mind if I look at the other quadrants?"

"Be my guest. They're marked by poles five through eight. Five starts by the concrete wall in the northeast corner of the plaza," he pointed to the right.

"Thanks, Malz."

I strode over to the marker stuck in the grass. The GITF had extensive experience with these things, but it didn't hurt to double-check, especially since Seekers were the only Guardians that had sense enhancement.

I closed my eyes. *Concentrate*. I took deep breaths to help focus my senses. It would be impossible to sort through all the surrounding sources. Touch and taste wouldn't help much in this case. Relying on sight alone could hinder the search, so I started with the most logical choice: smell.

Every scent intensified. Even the faintest smell in range came to me as if my nose hovered inches above it. I committed each scent to memory before moving to the next. The smell of freshly cut grass, blooming flowers, and other flora came in droves. A wave of body odor caused me to cringe. *Is that me? I really need a shower.* I shook my head. *Focus.*

A minute passed before I had sorted through the scents, and nothing out of the ordinary caught my attention. I opened my eyes and saw the world much more clearly. Colors were more vibrant, edges were crisper, even the darkness seemed lighter. But despite these advantages, the ground still revealed nothing that might point me in the right direction. A gentle hiss pulled my attention away from the concrete below, growing louder with every step I took.

When I located the noise source, I couldn't move fast enough before the projectile hit the ground. A wave of pressure and heat slammed against me like a bag of bricks. My feet left the ground as the air around me became an inferno.

I forced the breath from my lungs and drew in as much oxygen as I could. The flames from the blast pivoted as I redirected the inferno into my mouth. Warmth filled my lungs, and the orange light's glow faded. I landed on my feet and skidded to a stop.

Blood from my nose dripped onto the back of my wrist. *That was close.*

My legs trembled, and I fell to my knees. I cursed under my breath. We had walked into a trap.

Alator rushed to my side. "Are you hurt?"

"I'm fine, but I can't absorb another one of those."

He looked back at Malz and pointed to the truck. "Get a barrier up, now!"

Malz retrieved a portable shield generator from his cruiser and placed it by the fountain. He hit the device's head with his fist. A brilliant blue flash of light exploded, temporarily blinding me. I knew better than to look at the light, but my thoughts were a bit jumbled.

When I could see again, the plaza had been enveloped in a blue field of energy that would protect us from any inbound projectiles.

Unfortunately, organic material could still pass through, and the shield would open slightly to allow it to do so. If the attacker brought the fight to us, things might go differently.

"That was close. Good thing it hit you and not the squads. You're the only Inferno on the field."

"Yeah, lucky me," I muttered.

"You know what I mean. An Aquarian would have…"

"Lieutenant, we've got incoming hostiles!" Malz called out.

My heart pounded. With my head spinning and my energy still recovering, I would be vulnerable. Alator drew his sword and stood to face the barrier.

"Get ready, here they come!" he shouted.

A human form burst through the barrier, followed by at least twenty more.

"Go. I can take care of myself," I insisted.

He nodded and surged forward with incredible speed. I cleared my mind once again, knowing that I only had to make one jump. I released the enigma building inside me and opened my eyes, focusing on Alator's cruiser.

Instantly, I materialized near the passenger door and leaned against the cold metal with a shiver. My body had lost a lot of functionality, and it would take at least ten minutes to recover. I had no choice but to watch the battle from the sidelines.

Alator had taken out three of the assailants but soon found himself being pushed back. There were too many for him to fight alone. It wasn't like him to be so reckless. What was he plotting? Shards of rock surrounded him like a cocoon. I'd never seen Alator use his element defensively. Was that his plan?

A few seconds later, the cocoon of rock exploded. Projectiles went everywhere. They ripped two enemies to shreds, but another Stone Guardian intercepted the others. I looked at Alator in awe. A suit of sturdy metal armor covered his body. His blade had transformed into a silver lance, and a large metal shield hung from his left arm. *When had he unlocked his elemental armor? Why didn't he tell me?*

Alator charged the opponent's stone wall, struck the center with his lance, and broke through. The stone turned to sand and fell to the ground, revealing the opposing Stone Guardian as he dangled lifelessly from the lance. Alator thrust the weapon forward. The tip extended twenty feet from the cross-guard of the weapon, then stopped. He spun, catching one opponent with his shield and others with his lance.

More adversaries rushed into the plaza shouldering devices I'd never seen outside of textbooks: Spectral Cannons! The opposition took aim, and my breath caught in my throat—bursts of green energy shot from the legendary weapons of mass destruction. Every man and woman the rounds struck exploded into a cloud of pink mist, leaving behind a five-foot crater where they'd stood. Malz, Aurorai, Teanya; it had wiped out the entire platoon of law enforcement officers in seconds. Tears clouded my vision. Many of those men and women had been my friends.

When the dust settled across the pockmarked plaza, only Alator's rock shell remained. Somehow, Alator had withstood the attack, but he couldn't take another volley. His defenses crumbled as the enemy forces closed in. I tried to stand, but my legs wouldn't cooperate.

"Alator!" I screamed.

I watched helplessly as a group of men pummeled him. Each blow Alator received sent searing pain through my chest. I could barely breath as the rage built with every surge of emotion. Once he had been subdued, they dragged him away, disappearing through the blue energy field.

A group of enemies turned toward me, aiming before releasing the green energy from their weapons.

I closed my eyes, watching my comrades turn to a pink vapor on repeat. Would it be painful? I hoped not.

A few seconds passed, but nothing happened. When I peered through one eye, a large man stood in front of me. His red hair flowed to the top of the black cape hanging from his shoulders.

Walls of water had formed to the left and right of us, but not to the front. Had he blocked the enemy shots? *No, it can't be! Those blasts are too powerful!*

The man's gentle voice addressed me with the slightest hint of familiarity. "Don't worry. I've got you."

"How did you…?"

"Survive the blasts?" he laughed softly.

"Only an Alpha…" I paused, "Cronus?"

The man raised his sword into the air, then swung down—both walls of water shot toward the enemies. The walls joined, turned horizontal, then cut the entire group in half. Cronus vanished. His movements were so fast I couldn't keep up with him. The only way I kept track was by following the bodies he dropped. It was a massacre. His destructive power sent shivers across my skin, yet watching him slaughter those animals held a twist of satisfaction.

When the last enemy had fallen, Cronus stopped moving long enough to send a two-fingered salute at me before he disappeared. The sound of trickling water from the plaza's shattered fountain and distant sirens magnified the realization that I was alone. Javelar had wiped out an entire Guardian Forces squadron in under a minute. With those weapons, who knew what defenses they had? And now, they had Alator. How was I supposed to get him back without my friends? I was the only one left.

As the paramedics walked away I pulled the blanket tighter around my shoulder. The flashing purple and red lights irritated my sensitive eyes. I couldn't bring myself to return my senses to normal, at least not yet. Fear of being surprised by another attack forced me to stay alert, even if my enigma had been mostly spent.

The paramedics said I was lucky to be alive, but all my thoughts were focused on what Javelar might do to Alator.

A black transport touched down next to the emergency vehicle. Uncle Kehndrig, stepped out, his short salt and pepper hair spiked as usual. When he turned, the light caught the bright white scar running down his face.

He rushed over to me. "Are you hurt?"

"No."

"Where's Alator? I thought he'd be with you."

I shook my head. I couldn't force out the words.

"Well," my uncle said, "Where is he? I need to…" he paused when he noticed my expression. "Kinara, sweetheart, what happened?"

"The Javelar took him," I said bitterly.

Uncle Kehndrig sat down next to me on the loading ramp and wrapped me in the safety of his muscular arm. His head rested against mine, and he whispered, "We'll get him back, I promise."

His promise didn't ease my worry. The Javelar organization was known for its brutality. Maybe the public didn't know, but the Guardian Forces did. I distinctly remember one video that they forced us to watch during training. One of our operatives had been captured while out on assignment. The Javelar strung her up and sawed her legs off just below the knee and left her to bleed to death. She was found a few days later with the footage of the horrific event strapped to her corpse.

I just hoped we could find Alator before his interrogation began.

2

At the Planting Season Festival in Corai...

The festival attraction's frigid pool water rushed over me as I fell in. Breaching the surface, I gasped in shock, glaring up at the second obstacle that had sent me into the water. I ran my fingers through my wet hair. I had grossly underestimated the difficulty of the course.

My twin sister, Asariel, was laughing at me from where she stood watching outside the enclosure.

"Give up, Zaelek!" she called from below. "You're wasting your money."

The attraction manager opened the glass door above me and lowered a ladder. I climbed the rungs, each step bringing further shame. When I reached the top, he offered me his hand. I ignored it.

"Want to try again?" he asked.

"Zaelek..." my sister began.

I scowled. "Shut it, Ari."

Maybe if I'd gotten farther this time, I'd give it another try. But this marked my fifth attempt, and I didn't want to blow all my money for the festival in one day. I gazed longingly at the attraction, debating whether or not to try again. *I couldn't even make it past the second obstacle. The next two will be even harder.*

The supervisor joined in on the laughter. "I told you, kid, Cronus himself couldn't beat this course! In my twenty years operating it, I haven't seen anyone win!"

That's because it's a cheating load of schleet, I thought as I made my way down the steps where my younger brother, Benazahg, waited with Ari.

She flicked her blonde hair over her shoulder. "You could have spent that fifty credits on dessert," she said.

"You know that not everyone wants to stuff their face like you do, right?"

Ari stuck out her tongue. "Please, I can afford to eat what I want. I'm in way better shape than you, Sparky."

"Don't call me that."

She was right, though. All of us were fit from working the farm, but somehow she stayed the fittest.

"You two are ridiculous," Ben said. "How can two twenty-year-olds be so childish?"

"Ben," Ari snapped, "stay out of it!"

"Hey," I said, "leave him alone."

Though three years younger than Ari and me, Ben had me by at least three inches. Also, he almost doubled me in size. But as brothers we shared the same brown hair and brown eyes.

Dad called us the anomalies of the family because of our hair. Mom and Ari were blonde, while Dad and Parnikus had red. If Ben and I didn't look so much like our father, people might have thought they'd adopted us.

"You want to defend him now?" Ari huffed. "Weren't you the one giving him a hard time about buying that stupid watch before we got here?"

All three of us bickered back and forth for the next five minutes. That is until Ari jabbed me in the side.

"Ow, what was that for?"

She pointed with her chin, and I followed the gesture. Our mother and father rounded the corner of another game booth and walked toward us, hand in hand.

Ben cocked his head. "What's wrong with you two?"

He turned and saw why we had fallen silent. Mom and Dad smiled when they saw us. It surprised me that I hadn't seen them when Ari did. Dad loomed over the crowd. Had it only been my mother, we might not have noticed until she stood next to us.

Dad grinned, his deep voice easily carrying over the distance. "Where have you kids been? We've been looking everywhere for you."

Ari thumbed the silver moon-shaped pendant my mother gave her for her sixteenth birthday. "Sorry, Zaelek was wasting his money on this stupid game."

Mom looked at the booth next to us. "What game?"

"Just a stupid obstacle course that even Cronus himself couldn't beat."

My father raised an eyebrow. "That's a pretty bold statement."

"Those are the supervisor's words, not mine."

"Did you at least give it a run for its money, Zaelek?"

"Not even close," said Ari.

Mom shook her head. "Asariel Ylen Khiings, he wasn't asking you. Twenty years old, and you still haven't developed any manners."

"Twenty years old, and you still treat me like a child."

"Stop acting like one, and I won't have to," Mom fired back.

Dad sighed. "...and we're fighting again. Great. How much does this game cost anyway?" He looked at the pricing board and gasped. "Ten credits a play?! How many times did you play?"

I looked down, my cheeks burning. "Five."

"What could you possibly win that's worth that much?"

"There's a Cronus card I want to add to my collection."

"I thought you had them all."

"No. They printed only twenty of those. It's super rare. If I collect it, I'll have all the cards. Then I can trade them in for a replica of Cronus' sword."

"A replica? Cronus would probably sell you his own sword for how much you'd spend playing this."

"The replica is worth half a million credits."

Dad's jaw dropped. "Half a million? How could a fake be worth that much?"

"It's made of genuine guardian metal, and the decorations are all precious gemstones."

Dad was probably assuming I intended to blow the money on random junk, but that wasn't the case. I planned to save half and invest the other half in our farm. This year had been rougher on my family than any year I could remember, and we needed some extra credits to fix a few of the pricier farming machines.

"And that's the last card you need?"

"Yep."

My father thought for a moment, stroking his red goatee. "Let me give it a go."

Everyone looked at him in surprise.

"Seriously?" I asked.

"Seriously."

Dad approached the booth's supervisor. The man's eyebrow rose as he looked my father up and down. No doubt he considered my father's worn jeans, faded flannel shirt, and tattered work boots before a crooked grin spread across his gruff face. He laughed and took Dad's money, then bowed toward the staircase leading down to the start. I moved closer to the glass wall that gave the crowd a view of the course.

The con artist explained the rules to my father. We couldn't hear anything from where we watched, but I knew what he said. The only rules were don't touch the glass or fall into the water. Make it to the end and win the card.

Dad gave the supervisor a thumb up, and the man slapped the green button on the console. A countdown started. When it reached zero, "go" appeared on the console screen, and the attraction shuddered to life.

Dad jumped up and grabbed the bar above him. Small notches worked their way up a slope leading deeper into the course. This part of the course was the easiest. Dad swung his legs and lifted the bar out of the socket, climbing with ease.

The supervisor's eyes widened. He'd probably assumed Dad wouldn't make it past the first trial. It was the rest of the course that worried me.

Dad landed gracefully on the platform at the end. The next challenge required strength and agility to avoid a giant fan's foam arms. He stopped and watched the machine spin.

"What is he doing?" I asked my mother.

Mom grinned as she replied, "Just watch."

He dropped as the foam arm passed, grabbing the platform's edge. Dad hung there momentarily, then let go of the side with one hand and dangled from the other.

He swung again and again, then released. His fingers found a small edge on the fan's metal base, and he hung from that. Using his feet, he shuffled around the bottom, then jumped upward to grab the opposite platform's edge before pulling himself up. It was a brilliant move that had never even crossed my mind.

The supervisor gawked, "Never saw anyone do that before!"

Mom laughed. "You'll find my husband is full of surprises."

Dad faced two flat metal walls hanging from the ceiling. He cracked his neck and smirked. Like a drug-enhanced pounzerlion, he bounced between the walls and landed on the platform at the end.

"He'll never get through the next one," the supervisor said.

I looked at him. "He made it through the last ones, didn't he? Besides, there's only the walkway left."

The man laughed and turned his attention back to my father.

Come on, Dad, just one more.

My father stepped on the walkway, and a low-pitched siren sounded. Bright white lights strobed from the wall, almost blinding me. I could only imagine how my father felt. He took a step forward. Out of the sidewalls came two spinning fans with foam arms that intersected the walkway at every rotation.

Dad surged forward, jumping, twisting, turning, and avoiding every sweep from the machine. When his foot hit the end strip, the attraction stopped moving. A loud bell rang, and fireworks shot high into the air. My jaw dropped. Dad had actually pulled it off on his first try!

I was so focused on Dad's progress through the course that I hadn't even noticed the sizable crowd that had gathered to watch my father. Now the air was filled with cheering, and people rushed to the exit to congratulate him. I looked at the attraction supervisor, who stared in disbelief.

Dad wore a massive smile as he walked toward us. "I'll take that card if you don't mind."

"How…?" the supervisor asked.

"Beginner's luck."

The supervisor retrieved the prize from its glass display and reluctantly handed it to my father. Dad then gave it to me and winked. I looked down at the card, speechless. Now I could trade it in for the replica.

Mom kissed my father on the cheek. "Still a showoff."

Three days later, I sat at the end of the bar in a quiet rundown pub. The shaken palomino I sipped burned like flames.

I listened intently to the conversation in the booth behind me as the gray-haired man said, "The boss won't like it."

"Couldn't we at least pitch the idea to him?"

"No. You know what he'll say. It's the same as last time."

Their conversation went back and forth like that for at least ten minutes. I had been stuck in Tendir for the past week chasing down a lead for local law enforcement, yet every time I thought I had something, it turned out to be another dead end. Perhaps this time would be different.

A breaking news symbol flashed in the mirror, catching my attention. As I turned to the screen, the barkeep raised the volume so we could all hear. A picture of a masked man appeared behind the news anchor.

"We apologize for this interruption," she announced. "The organization known as Javelar has launched yet another terrorist attack against the people of Creet. This attack makes fourteen since Kintar Plaza's destruction. At this time, the United-Guardian Forces refuse to comment on their progress in finding Lieutenant Alator Kilobaski, who went missing during the first attack three days ago."

One man in the booth snickered. "No surprise there. They never comment on anything."

I'd kept one ear tuned to the group in the booth and now turned my full attention back to their conversation.

"Focus," the woman in their group said.

"Sorry. You were saying?"

"The shipment arrives tonight at the Holling Pier. Be there for the unloading."

"Same time?"

"Same time."

The group rose and headed for the door. I sighed with relief. *Finally, a piece of information worth my time. Not a moment too soon, either.*

I waited for a few minutes, paid my tab, then went outside. The brisk night air made me shiver. Distant vehicles added a gentle note to the hum of the busy city but were quickly drowned out by the bullet rail's brakes squealing on the tracks above me. My contact sat in an unmarked vehicle across the street, waiting for my report. I strode over and tapped on the window. It rolled down, revealing a young, unfamiliar law enforcement officer.

"It's going down tonight," I said. "The shipment arrives at the Holling Pier."

"Nice work," the young man replied.

I nodded, and he pulled away. My part of the investigation was over. Typically, I had nothing to do with information gathering. The Tendir law enforcement didn't care though. Due to a lack of staff, they took any help they could get.

I still wasn't sure why they'd accepted help from a civilian consultant. Desperate times, I guessed. I'd understand if they needed me to sit in on an interrogation—that's my usual job, thanks to my unnatural talent for reading body language—but this sort of undercover work was new.

It bothered me that the sheriff had chosen me. Typically, I only worked part time during the planting season, but I hadn't been home for the past week. Waving, I signaled for an approaching taxi, its brake pads squealing as it came to a stop. I climbed in the back and settled on the scuffed leather seat.

The driver asked, "What can I do for you?"

"I need a ride to Corai."

"That's quite a distance. It's gonna cost you extra." His tone of voice made it obvious this fare wasn't what he'd hoped for.

"Not a problem."

If the fee were coming out of my pocket, it might have been an issue. In this case, however, my home station covered travel fees, as long as I remembered to get the receipt. Now my contract assignment had been completed, I could work on trading those cards in. I could almost feel the weight of that sword replica in my hand.

3

On the Rail-X train, headed for Tendir in Alympia...

My pale eyes stared back at me from the reflection in the window of the swiftly moving train. "Ghostly," came to mind. It mimicked the way I felt: only half-present as my concern for Alator consumed me. I fidgeted with the shimmerore band on my ring finger.

It had been three days since Alator was captured. There were no leads, I had exhausted the limited resources I had access to, and since the battle at the plaza, I'd slept a grand total of four hours. My head rested against the seat's head rest and I exhaled deeply. *How did an organization vanish without a trace? Wouldn't they have at least left something behind during the attack?* We needed to hurry. Alator would never give up information, but how long would his body take the interrogation techniques? So many questions plagued my weary mind that I feared I wouldn't sleep until Alator was found.

I pulled the small, heart-shaped locket from my blouse and opened it. A picture of my parents smiled out at me. They'd been gone for twelve years. Everything about that day when my uncle knelt down and scooped me up to tell me that my parents were never coming back still gave me chills. I was nine years old. I remember his body trembling and seeing the tears run down his cheeks as he said, "Kinara, sweetheart, there's been an accident."

I shuddered and pushed the darkness away. My hand rested on the worn baldric of my sword where it lay on the seat next to me. I'd meant to replace the strap before I left, but my search for Alator had kept me from many things I'd expected to be doing, wedding planning now the least of them.

The train finally came to a stop. I gathered my belongings and stepped out into the warm, heavy air seeping with skin clinging humidity. A slight breeze carried the distinct smell of farmland. I much preferred the city over this primitive, unevolved continent. Even Alympus, the crown city of Alympia, didn't compare to the smallest of our cities back home. The difference in technology alone testified to that. I guess it didn't surprise me. Alympia was the most impoverished nation in the world.

The man at the ticket booth looked up from whatever he was reading. "Good evenin', Miss. Welcome to Tendir."

I nodded toward the pickup area behind his booth. "Are the transports running this late?"

"Yes, ma'am. I'll send a request right away."

He smiled when I thanked him, then returned to his work. I found a small bench and waited almost fifteen minutes for my ride to show up. Waiting so long for simple transport seemed absurd. *Maybe demand for immediate access doesn't gain enough momentum here.*

When the transport stopped andI opened the door and slid my way onto the seat. The driver looked at me through his rearview mirror. "Where to?"

"Corai, please."

"You got it. It'll cost you extra though."

"That's fine."

The transport rolled onto the road, heading away from Tendir. I'd spent the past two days chasing down every lead myself, with no success, while we awaited official reports from the intelligence agency. At the same time, after nearly driving myself insane trying to figure out where I had heard Cronus's voice, I remembered: That voice belonged to Ettias Khiings.

Ettias and my uncle had served together and remained friends. Both men were fifth generation Guardians, something that was common in the Forces, especially for lifers. I remembered Ettias telling me when

I was younger, "Serving pretty much courses through the blood of a Guardian, and seeing a *fresh blood* is pretty rare." Uncle had spent almost as much time with Ettias and Maialyn as he did with his own family, and he typically ended up bringing me along when he came to visit so I could play with Zaelek and Asariel, the Khiings twins.

By the time we arrived in Corai, my watch read eleven hundred hours. My stomach growled; I had skipped dinner last night to make my flight and then catch the train. In truth, I hadn't been thinking about food but now my hunger was making itself known. The driver pulled to the curb next to the city hall. I paid him a hundred credits.

"Keep the change," I said.

Corai wasn't much to look at. A single traffic signal sat at the intersection in the center of town. I had no clue why they needed it since there were no vehicles in sight. Small family-owned businesses lined the street. If I wanted to get directions to the Khiings estate, I needed to start with one of those. My stomach growled again. *Why not start at the local café?*

I wandered the sidewalk until I came across the place my uncle and Ettias had taken me to many years ago. The thought of something fried and smothered in sweet sauces teased my taste buds. Upon entering the small restaurant, I picked up the scent of svinen bacon, triggering a wave of nostalgia. It hadn't changed a bit. The same faded paintings of farm life hung on the walls, and the other rustic decorations were the same too. A middle-aged woman waiting on a table of older gentlemen looked up and smiled at me.

"I'll be with you in just a moment," she said.

Once she'd topped off both men's drinks, she put the pitcher down, grabbed a menu, and guided me to a small table.

"What can I get you to drink, honey?"

"A cup of kaffee, please."

"Been traveling all night, huh?"

I laughed. "How could you tell?"

"You look it. We don't get many Guardians around these parts." She pointed to the sword strapped to my back.

Sometimes I forgot it hung there. One gets used to the weight when it's always present. "Ah, I don't imagine you do."

She smiled. "What brings you this far out?"

"Just visiting some friends."

"How lovely! Do you know what you want, or should I give you a minute?"

"Do you still have your villanti cakes?"

The woman placed her free hand on her hip. "We do. You must've been here before."

"A few times."

"Those are tomorrow's special, but since you've come from so far, I'll give them to you at that price."

"Oh! You don't have to do that."

"It's nothing, sweetie!"

I smiled as she walked away. I'd always been fond of Corai, the people were delightful, and it was the only place in Alympia I wouldn't mind staying, mostly because of the wonderful memories. I grinned, remembering the time Zaelek had fallen into the river trying to show off for me. His mom had been so mad when he ruined his brand-new pants! Had I not met Alator, maybe Zaelek and I would have had a different relationship, something more than a friendship. *I wish Alator was here with me. He would love to see the farmlands.*

The waitress returned a few minutes later with the piping hot villanti cakes and a small jar of morincai sauce. I thanked her, then poured on the thick brown syrup until it thoroughly covered the meal. My fork punctured the golden surface of the stacked cakes and scooped a piece into my mouth. The sweetness of the syrup blended perfectly with the buttery villantis.

When I had cleaned the plate and finished my kaffee, the waitress returned. "How was everything?"

"Amazing, thank you."

"Of course, thank you again for coming in."

She turned to leave, but I needed one last thing from her. "Excuse me, ma'am?"

"Yes?"

"Can you tell me where Zaelek Khiings is living? I haven't seen him in quite a while, and I'm not sure if he's moved out of his parents' house."

"You're friends with the Khiings family? Why didn't you say so before? Breakfast is on the house!"

"It is?"

"Yep! Ettias and Maialyn lent us some money last month to help repair the storm damage. Bless their hearts, if it weren't for them, I think we would have lost the place. Zaelek even helped put the shingles back up. He's such a nice young man."

"That he is…hey, I get a bit turned around out here. Could you point me in the right direction?"

"Not a problem. If you go out to the intersection and take a right, the road will lead you straight to their dirt road. Take a left at the first mailbox and you'll see their house in no time."

"Thank you so much."

I left the restaurant and followed her directions. If I remembered correctly, the Khiings lived a few minutes out of town when traveling by vehicle. It wouldn't take much longer for me to get there on foot. I concentrated and released a burst of enigma, shuddering slightly as it worked its way down from head to toe. My body surged forward, and the town became a slight blur. The day's heat changed to the sensation of cool air drawing across my skin as I bounded. Within thirty seconds, the outskirts of Corai came and went.

Soon, the Khiings mailbox came into view, and I made a sharp left turn. Down the drive, the large blue farmhouse peeked through the tree line. Nothing had changed. The two-story home was as warm and inviting as the last time I visited, the feeling of homecoming amplified by the smell of freshly baked yendorfruit werbles. I disengaged the void bound before I crashed into the stairs of the spacious porch.

The steps creaked as I climbed to the porch and a wave of nostalgia hit me when I reached out to knock on the red wooden door. Uncle used to let me be the one to knock whenever we came here. He thought it was cute how excited I got about it.

I rapped on the softwood. A deep thud resounded off the walls and ceiling of the porch.

Maialyn's voice called from inside, "Zaelek, please get that."

I waited patiently as his footsteps approached. The door cracked, and Zaelek stared at me with his deep brown eyes.

"Yes?" he asked.

"Do you really not recognize me, you idiot?" I asked.

"Kinara?"

"There you go."

"Wow! You look so different! Mom! Dad! Look who's here!"

He opened the door, as Maialyn stepped into view. A broad smile spread across her face.

"Kinara!" she cooed. "Look how you've grown! For a second, I thought I was looking at your mother! Ettias, get down here!"

"I'm coming, I'm coming." Ettias stopped halfway down the stairs, his eyes widened when he saw me. "Kinara?"

"Hi, Mister Khiings," I said.

"What are you doing here? Is Kehndrig with you?"

"Nope! I'm here alone. I thought I'd take a few vacation days and come visit!"

"Well, don't just stand there! Come in, come in!"

I took off my shoes and left them and my sword next to the welcome mat. Maialyn excitedly guided me into the kitchen and sat me down on one of the island's bar stools. Zaelek followed and took the chair next to me, his stare making me slightly uncomfortable.

"You good?" I asked.

He blinked rapidly, then looked away. "Sorry…I…I just can't believe it's you. You've really filled out!"

Maialyn reached across the countertop and slapped him upside the head. "Zaelek Khiings! That's no way to talk to a lady. Were you raised in a barn?"

"Technically…"

"Don't even start with your Hades driven remarks!" Maialyn scoded. "I'm so sorry, Kinara. I promise I raised him better than that. It must be his father's side."

"Hey!" Ettias said as he joined us.

I tried my best not to laugh. "I believe you, Mrs. Khiings."

"Please, you must call me Maialyn. 'Mrs. Khiings' makes me feel so old!"

Zaelek snickered. "I mean, aren't you?"

"Zaelek! Get out of my kitchen!"

He scrambled from the room, knowing full well what would happen if he didn't listen. Same old Zaelek. He always had something witty to say.

I laughed. "I'm surprised he's lived this long."

"What?" Maialyn asked.
"He hasn't changed a bit, has he?"
She laughed, too. "No. Not really."

4

At Khiings Estate...

The sun peeked over the tops of the trees sending pink streaks across the sky. I rolled a small stalk of flograss across the bottom of my lip to the other side of my mouth. The soft fabric of my shirt brushed against me as I leaned on the wooden fence.

"Zaelek," my father said behind me, "did you let the kilindrels out to pasture?"

"Yep."

The six-legged beasts preferred hanging out by the tree line at the end of the field. They were most likely on the other side of the small stream running through our property, and we wouldn't see the creatures until we fed them around mid-morning.

Dad placed his large hands on the fence. We stood side by side, silently watching the sunrise. My hair ruffled when a slight breeze announced the coming of the day's heat. I took a deep breath, taking in the farmland's scent with it. The sweet smell of blooming glindenhay and potent animal odors might be abrasive to Kinara, but to me, it smelled like home.

The early light shimmered on the dew clinging to the born again flograss. It almost looked like a field of gemstones.

"Dad. I didn't see Caspien this morning when I opened the gate. Did he come in with the others last night?"

"Good question. I wasn't paying much attention."

He licked his lips, then let loose a piercing, high-pitched whistle. In all my life, I had met no one that could whistle as loudly as my father. A whinny sounded from the other side of the pasture.

"He's there," Dad said.

"How could you possibly know that was him?"

"I just do. Maybe someday you'll understand."

My dad had an unbreakable bond with that kilindrel. Caspien had been around since before I was born and probably would be until I died. Kilindrels could live up to two hundred years. They were a symbol of protection. It's said that they choose a family to watch over, and considering how intelligent the animals were, I believed it.

"Good morning, you two!" Kinara called from behind us.

Dad turned and smiled. "Morning, Kinara. You're up awfully early for someone on vacation."

"Yeah, I thought I'd come out and enjoy the sunrise. I don't see them as often as I'd like back home."

"Well, there's plenty of fence here for all of us."

I wanted to ask Kinara about being a Guardian, but there hadn't been an opportunity for me to speak with her in private. There were so many questions to ask her, but where to start? Was she really so busy that she couldn't enjoy a simple sunrise? What did it feel like to wield an elemental force? Did she get to use it often?

Kinara placed one of her boots on the lowest section and leaned in. Her vibrant blonde hair flowed in the wind, and I looked away before she caught me staring at her again.

I couldn't believe how much she'd changed; I had barely recognized her. If I remembered correctly, she would have turned twenty-one last fall. My birthday is next month, making her only about six months older than me.

"Isn't this the kilindrel pasture?" Kinara asked.

"You have a good memory," Dad said.

"It's been forever since I rode one. I think it was the last time I was here."

"You heard the lady, Zaelek. Why don't you kids go for a ride?"

My heart pounded in my chest. "I don't know, Dad. It's been a while since..."

"Please?" Kinara asked.

Hades take her and those beautiful eyes. I couldn't refuse her when she looked at me like that, and she knew it.

I sighed, "Fine, I'll catch a couple for us after breakfast and saddle them up."

She slipped an arm around my waist and gave me a squeeze by way of thanks before she turned back to the house. Her strength surprised me. My father looked at me with a hint of amusement.

"She's cute, isn't she?" he said, watching for my reaction.

"She's engaged, Dad," I replied.

"What? No way!"

"Did you not see the shimmerore band on her finger?"

"I must have missed it. Styx," he cursed, "I thought I'd be able to set up the two of you. She's much prettier than Tiane."

"That's so rude."

"But it's true," he smiled with a wink. "I'd better get breakfast started, so you two can get out of here."

I shook my head as he walked away. It was a low blow, coming after the girl I fancied like that. *Nothing is wrong with Tiane.* Sure, Kinara had her beat in looks, but looks aren't everything. Tiane had a lot of personality. She was smart, funny, and seemed to get me. What's not to like?

By the time I finished my morning chores, Mom had rung the bell on the side of the house, meaning breakfast was ready. I came in the back door and found everyone at the table, waiting for me.

Ari glared at me. "Took you long enough, Sparky."

I scowled at the nickname. "I'm sorry my chores are harder than yours."

"What? That's kilindrel schleet!"

Mom shot her a nasty look. "Language! And what did we tell you about calling him Sparky? Only your father can call him that."

"Sorry, Mom," Ari said.

Being my twin, Ari had a special way of getting under my skin. However, I knew what set her off too. I shot her a triumphant wink as

I made my way to my seat. Her eyes narrowed at the gesture, and she quickly stuck her tongue out at me while Mom wasn't looking.

Kinara stopped scooping the scrambled cluckoo eggs. "What's with the nicknames?"

Mom sighed. "When I got pregnant with Parnikus, Ettias and I had a...*disagreement* about the children's names. I wanted them to have elegant names, while Ettias wanted something more common. Long story short, we compromised. We decided I would choose the names, but Ettias got to give them nicknames."

"So how did you choose Sparky?"

Dad chuckled to himself, and I knew where things were going. I suppressed an embarrassed groan as Dad began telling the story I always hoped would never be told again.

"Back when Zaelek was, oh, I don't know, three? He needed to...relieve himself while we were out feeding the animals. So, he walks up to the povine fence for some privacy and drops his trousers. Little did he know, I had electrified the fence earlier that week to keep the herd's escape artists contained. Well...let's just say he learned a painful lesson that day. Thus, I've called him Sparky ever since."

Kinara nearly spat out her milk with a laugh. "Poor guy!"

I sat next to Kinara, humiliated. I hated when Dad told that story, although I was grateful he toned it down this time. Usually, the story had more than enough detail to make a grown man blush. But I did notice that Kinara seemed to brighten a bit. There was something about her—sadness? Concern?—I wasn't sure what, but she seemed a little less "clear" than I remembered.

After breakfast, I set out to the barn to saddle the kilindrels. Catching a couple would be easy. They were already lined up by their stalls to be fed. The hard part would be finding Kinara a suitable match. I thought for a moment, then decided on one of the older kilindrels, Trilda, not wanting to send Kinara back to Kehndrig broken.

I grabbed a lead rope from the box sitting next to Caspien's stall. With a little luck, Trilda wouldn't get fussy about delaying her meal. I opened her stall and draped the rope around her mahogany neck to form a loose loop. At first, she protested, knowing full well what my intentions were, but she calmed after I gave her a treat.

I patted her broad shoulder, watching the short hairs fill the air.

They hadn't been brushed in quite a while, so I hoped Kinara didn't mind getting a little hairy. The rope halter slid over her leaf-shaped ears and secured her to the thick wooden beam of her stall. Now, I needed to fetch Fenrir, my kilindrel.

Kinara startled me when she called my name from the entrance to the barn.

"In here," I replied.

She made her way around Trilda, coddling the kilindrel's snout as she passed. Ever since the first time I showed Kinara the six-legged creatures, they had fascinated her. I might have found it charming if I wasn't being forced to take her on this ride. It annoyed me.

"Is this one mine for the day?" Kinara asked.

"Yep. That's Trilda."

"Hey, Trilda. You're so pretty!" Kinara ran her hand down Trilda's back, then patted her side. "Can I help in any way?"

"Sure. If you want to brush her before we go, you might get less hair on you. There's a brush in the box over there."

Kinara smiled at the opportunity to pamper her newfound friend. She retrieved the brush and ran it down Trilda's neck, and the kilindrel snorted in disgust.

She pulled the brush away and looked at me with wide eyes. "Am I doing something wrong?"

"Kilindrels prefer being brushed against the flow of their hair. Don't ask me why."

She gave my advice a try and laughed softly when Trilda's back leg kicked rapidly, like a dreaming canine. I retrieved Fenrir from his stall and led the pure white creature out to saddle him, careful not to put the kilindrels too close. They tended to be claustrophobic, and I didn't feel like getting kicked or bitten today.

Dad entered the barn. "You put Kinara on Trilda? Good call, son. I would have given her Milky, but Trilda is the better choice. You're sure Ari won't mind?"

"What she doesn't know won't kill her," I replied.

Kinara stopped brushing Trilda, who protested with a soft whinny. "If this is Ari's kilindrel, I can take another!"

I walked under Fenrir's neck to check his other side. "No. It's fine. She doesn't ride her anyway. The ole girl could use the exercise."

Dad retrieved a rope halter from the box. "Speaking of exercise

…Mind if I join you? Caspien would appreciate the opportunity to stretch his legs a bit."

"Be my guest."

He opened the stall gate and Caspien shook his red mane. Dad hadn't ridden him much this year either, and I'm sure the animal wanted out of the pasture.

Dad helped me saddle the kilindrels while Kinara brushed them down. With a little teamwork, we were riding into the forest within fifteen minutes. Kinara seemed to handle Trilda well enough. I, on the other hand, was experiencing difficulties with Fenrir.

"Did I cinch him up too tight?" I asked my dad.

He slowed Caspien until we were side by side. Caspien always had to be the group leader, no matter what, so Dad always led. Dad reached over and pulled the strap near Fenrir's flank.

"No. Strap must've slipped when you mounted. You should be good now."

The kilindrel ceased being fussy. I had taken up the rear of the formation in case Trilda threw Kinara. Our kilindrels were well trained, but that didn't mean they were immune from getting spooked by something on the trail. In a panic, the animals might rear up or try to throw their rider.

I looked up at the canopy of blue-green leaves. Tiny cracks of sunlight broke through, creating a beam where the dust had been kicked up. There was nothing like being out here on a warm spring day.

I returned my attention to Kinara. Maybe it was the way her hair bounced with the movement of the kilindrel or the way her light blouse fell over her skin-tight pants, but Kinara looked good in the saddle. If I didn't know better, I might've been convinced that she grew up riding kilindrels.

5

In the forest east of Khiings Estate...

I re-situated myself and squared my posture. Things were about to get ugly, and I regretted confronting Ettias about being Cronus in front of Zaelek, but I couldn't wait any longer. With every minute that passed, the risk to Alator increased, and it wouldn't help to bide my time waiting for the perfect moment.

I took a deep breath. "Ettias, I know."

"Know what?" he asked.

"You're Cronus."

Caspien stopped, but Ettias didn't move. I swallowed the lump in my throat and said a silent prayer that our relationship would keep him from killing me right here. His identity was so classified that only a select few could know. I'd even heard rumors that anyone who found out had been killed to keep the intel from getting out.

Without turning around to face me, Ettias asked, "When did you figure it out?"

"A couple days ago."

He sat in silence, looking into the canopy. I saw Zaelek staring at him out the corner of my eye. He was dumbfounded. He couldn't even utter a word, and I could sense the gears spinning in his head.

Ettias sighed. "You're lucky. Usually, I kill whoever finds out, but I won't kill you."

Relief flooded over me.

"Not yet."

In milliseconds, my emotions switched back to terror. What did he mean by *not yet*? Not yet as in "I haven't decided yet" or not yet as in "I'm going to interrogate every answer I can out of you, then kill you"?

Zaelek's jaw dropped. "Dad! What in Styx?!"

Ettias ignored him. "You know how classified my identity is, Kinara, and I know I can't lie to you as I might someone else. You're too smart for your own good."

I twisted the ends of my reins nervously. "I'll be honest with you, I'm not here on vacation. I came to ask for your help."

"You're incredibly brave or incredibly stupid to confront me about my identity, especially with only a day to think about what your plan was. Whatever you've come for must be important to you."

"He is."

"*He?*"

"Yes, Sir. Javelar captured my fiancé the night you saved me."

Ettias looked over his shoulder, piercing my soul with a look I'd never seen from him. "So, you'd risk your life for him?"

"Any day. He's the most important person in my life."

"I see. That's noble of you, but also reckless."

"Please, all I want to do is get him back."

"There are things in this world you can't comprehend, Kinara. It is far more evil than you realize."

He paused, seeming lost in thought. It made me nervous not knowing what he was thinking. I couldn't anticipate the thoughts of Cronus, not like I could with the man I thought I knew.

"They took your fiancé from the plaza?" Ettias inquired.

"Yes, Sir."

"If it was Javelar, your fiancé is most likely dead. It's unlike them to keep prisoners for longer than a few days."

My heart slammed against my chest. I had played through the

scenarios in my mind to prepare myself for what he might tell me, but it didn't help. The fear of losing Alator hit me with renewed potency.

"I just need to know if he's still alive. Please, Ettias."

Ettias turned Caspien around and rode past us without looking at me again. "Come on, kids. It's time to head back."

6

Classroom 102,
Zenja University of Veterinary Practices, Alympus...

I gazed out the window, hoping to see something more entertaining than the lecture slide's content. A few kids played a variation of voidball in the small grassy area nearby, but nothing else caught my eye. The breeze ruffled the canopy's leaves above them, providing a slight reprieve from the city heat. Days like this made me miss the farm's open range and the fields beckoning to me to slack off for a little longer. I could almost taste the clean air. *Just a few more days before I get to go home.*

This semester had been brutal. My classes' workload barred me from doing much of anything else, and I had no desire to return home just to study even more because I'd put my homework off.

My desk partner elbowed me sharply in an effort to to get my attention. "Parnikus..."

"...Mister Khiings?" the professor said.

I returned my focus to the front, taking in the fragile, elderly man. "I'm sorry, could you repeat the question?"

"Can you tell us the resting heart rate of a kilindrel youngling?"

"Two beats per second."

The professor's eyes narrowed, but he nodded with approval. "Very good…Well, students, I think that is enough for today. Don't forget to study the kilindrel birthing chapters again. That will be on the test."

I scooped my books up and dumped them in the new backpack Dad had gotten me before I left. *Just a few more days….* I missed the kids more than I cared to admit, even though Ari could be a handful sometimes. Poor Mom. She and Ari clashed more when I wasn't there to be the mediator. Zaelek usually made Ari's schleety attitude worse with his comments, and Ben tried to stay out of conflicts more than Dad did, though Mom told me he's been trying to help more lately.

It would be a couple of years before I graduated from veterinary school, so I hoped they learned to get along before I finished. Of course, I wouldn't be moving back to the farm, but I could still help even if I lived a few minutes away. I planned to open my own practice somewhere in town and would be free after five on most days unless an emergency came up.

When I stepped into the bustling university halls, a petite brunette barely missed me with her impressive stack of textbooks.

"Sorry!" she said.

"You're okay. Can I help you carry some of those?"

"No, I think I can…"

The stack of books scattered as she tripped over her own feet and fell.

"Woah!" I knelt down next to her. "Are you hurt?"

"No, I don't think so."

I tried to help her to her up, but she quickly sank back to the ground with a wince.

"Uh...looks like you sprained your ankle," was my diagnosis.

"This is so embarrassing."

"It could be worse."

Her green eyes studied me. "How do you figure?"

"I dunno. You could've been in your underwear or something."

She blinked a few times before bursting out in laughter. *Anything in the world and I go with underwear? Nice Parnikus.* No wonder you're such a hit with the ladies, I thought sarcastically. *Man, that's totally something Zaelek would say to a girl.* I had once wondered why Zaelek had such a hard time getting Tiane to notice him. Now I knew.

"You're silly," she said.

"So, where were you headed?"

"My dorm."

"Can I at least help you to your room?"

She cocked her head to the side. "Only if you tell me your name first."

"Parnikus."

"Well, Parnikus, I'm Amaya. Pleased to meet you."

I gathered all the books, wrapped her arm around my neck, and gave her a wink.

"Ready?"

7

Back at Khiings Estate...

Dad pushed the back door of the farmhouse open. Kinara and I followed him in before the door slammed behind us.

Mom came out of the living room."Ettias," she said, "what have I told you about slamming that door?"

Father pulled her aside. Their whispers intensified until Mom's face flashed surprise.

"Ari, Ben?" she called.

Ben poked his head over the stair railing. "Ari went out to the west field. I think she said she lost one of her gloves this morning."

"Go help her look for it, please."

"Okay, but then can I go over to Traiton's? He wanted to scramble today."

"That's fine."

Ben rushed to the back door, slipped on his boots, and was gone. Mom turned her attention to Kinara. I knew that look, and it terrified me. Kinara had "pulled the kilindrel's tail," and I didn't want to get involved in the ensuing chaos. I had enough to wrap my head around with Dad being Cronus.

"Kinara," Mom said. "You spilled classified information in front of my son?"

"Zaelek doesn't know about his…?" Kinara's surprise faded as she trailed off.

"Know what?" I asked.

My mother ignored me. "Of course he doesn't! What in Styx do you think 'classified' means? How could you be so irresponsible?"

"I'm so sorry, Maialyn! I thought he knew."

What was I missing? This seemed like so much more than Dad being Cronus—as if that alone weren't enough!

"*Sorry* isn't going to cut it, young lady. What was Kehndrig thinking when he allowed you to come here knowing that?"

"He doesn't know that I know."

That flabbergasted my parents. Dad pinched the bridge of his nose. "Anything else you want to tell us?"

"No. I think that about sums it up," Kinara said.

I stepped in. "Can I go anywhere but here? I don't see…"

"No!" both parents shouted at the same time.

It finally hit Kinara. "Oh. He really doesn't know…"

"Know what?!" I asked. A noticeable pause followed.

Dad said, "Son, do you remember what you told me you wished for on your tenth birthday?"

"To be like Cronus when I grew up."

"Do you remember what I said to you?"

"You told me that it was impossible because I don't have the Guardian gene."

My heart raced. *Did* I have the capability of becoming a Guardian? If that were true, that would mean…

"Mom? You're a Guardian, too?" I looked to my mother, desperate for her to tell me something—anything to keep me from believing that she had lied to me my entire life.

She looked away. "Yes."

"Why would you lie to us about something like that?"

"If Trentir Savvage found out about your father, Javelar would use you to get to Cronus. We wanted to keep you safe."

I leaned against the counter for support. My life had been a lie. I could have pursued my lifelong dream to be like Cronus, my father. It felt like they had robbed me of my very being.

"Were you ever going to tell us?"

Shame was reflected on both their faces. "Not if we could help it," Dad said.

A wave of disappointment and anger washed over me. The two people I trusted the most had betrayed me. If I couldn't trust them, then who *could* I trust? They had lied straight to my face, and the betrayal sickened me.

"I need to be alone."

I turned my back on them and left the house. How did they expect me to keep this a secret from my siblings? I had to tell them. If I didn't, that would make me as much of a liar as my parents.

"Zaelek!" my mother called.

I ignored her.

Standing beside Maialyn and Ettias...

"Should I go after him?" I asked.

"Let him be, Kinara," Ettias said. "He needs space to process."

Maialyn turned to her husband with uncertainty in her eyes. "Should we have told them, Ettias?"

"It's too late to change the past."

"What can we do?"

"We'll have to figure that out later. For now, we have other matters to attend to."

I really hoped those "matters" didn't include killing me and disposing of my body—a lump formed in my throat. In hindsight, perhaps this hadn't been the best plan. I don't know why I expected anything less. The Guardian Forces were a military force, and they took their secrets seriously.

"Are you going to kill me?" I squeaked.

Ettias pondered this for a moment before he seemed to make a decision. "That's not my call. Follow me."

Beyond the staircase Ettias pushed his hand against the center wall. A green light flashed, and the wall slid into the floor, revealing another set of stairs that led into a basement. Ettias gestured for me to go first.

The room was empty, aside from two glass cases, each holding a Guardian's sword. I assumed they belonged to Ettias and Maialyn, though which was whose, I couldn't say. Maialyn flipped a switch on the wall. A soft hum resonated from the floor.

Tiny digital particles exploded throughout the space, circling the room twice, like a swarm of flying insects, before stopping in the middle. They hovered for a moment, then formed into multiple cubes. Ettias touched the center one.

The other holographic parcels shattered and fell to the ground, spreading digitized materials over the tiles. The gray walls and floor of the room turned black, leaving us in perfect darkness. A small, glowing white orb replaced the remaining square box, then floated to the ceiling. Rays of light shone around us.

A female voice filled the room. "Good afternoon, Cronus. How may I be of assistance?"

"Good afternoon, Nadia. Please put me through to Colonel Kehndrig Voelker," he replied.

The glowing orb spiraled down to scan Ettias's entire body before a confirmation chimed. Words formed in the air a foot away from him that read: *Connecting...*

My uncle's voice came through. "Ettias, old friend, I wasn't expecting to hear from you today. Do you want to room share?"

"I think you'll want to see who's with us, so why not?"

A request to room share appeared and Ettias confirmed. The walls rippled, making sections of the space twist and turn in cubed waves, then suddenly, we stood in my uncle's office. I couldn't tell what happened or how.

Ettias looked at my dumbfounded expression and laughed. "No, we haven't left the farm. You've never experienced H.I.V.E?"

My uncle walked out of a room in his office I didn't know existed. Multiple expressions crossed his face in seconds. Had I not been the target of those angry expressions, I might have laughed.

"Kinara?"

"Hey, Uncle," I replied.

"What's the meaning of this, Ettias?"

Ettias chuckled to himself. "Don't look at me. Your niece clearly has a mind of her own. Maybe she should explain it."

I spoke up, "Uncle..."

"Choose your next words carefully. You'd better have an exceptional reason for standing where you are."

"I figured out that Ettias is Cronus."

His eyes widened. "How?"

"I recognized his voice when he saved me at the plaza."

Uncle Kehndrig pinched the bridge of his nose and groaned. I knew I'd put him in a difficult situation. Alphas' identities were never to be revealed to Guardians without the proper clearance. In the past, people had extorted the sheer power of Alphas by threatening someone or something they cared about, and the resulting carnage wasn't pretty.

"I guess that brings me to my next question, and I pray it's not what I'm thinking. *Why* are you there?"

"Alator," I replied.

"Mercy's breath, Kinara! If you had waited a few days, the grid search of Alympia would be finished."

"Alator might not have that long!" I paused. "This was the only option I had left…"

"Aside from asking me for help?"

The magnitude of my mistake felt like a punch to the gut. *Uncle Kehndrig isn't upset about my going to Cronus for help; he's upset because I didn't give him a chance.* Embarrassment, shame, and guilt slammed against a wall of confusion.

"I…"

"I don't want to hear it," he sighed. "Ettias, punish my niece as you see fit."

The transmission ended, and the room went dark. My heart fluttered, and my breath felt like someone had sucked it from my lungs. Silence. That's all that stood between two of the most powerful Guardians on the planet and me.

The ceiling lights flickered as they hummed to life. No one moved. Ettias and Maialyn stared at the wall ahead. It felt as if the tension alone would suffocate me.

Without a word, Ettias walked to the case holding the sheathed sword. He opened the glass pane and retrieved the weapon. As the blade slid from the scabbard, perspiration trickled down my neck.

Ettias's gaze lingered on the sword for a moment before he broke his silence. "I couldn't tell you how much blood this blade has spilled."

Maialyn locked my arms from behind. I tried to free myself but couldn't contest her strength. Ettias placed the tip of his blade in my navel. One wrong move, and I'd be gutted.

"Don't do this, please," I pleaded.

No expression disturbed his stone-like face. His eyes were cold. "Let me be perfectly clear, Kinara. If you breathe a word of my identity to anyone, I'll kill you without a second thought. Do we understand each other?"

"Yes, Sir," I squeaked.

When Ettias withdrew the blade, Maialyn released my arms. I slowly took a breath.

She sighed, "You kids are going to give us heart attacks one of these days."

8

That night at Khiings Estate...

The sound of chirping insects filled the night, as if trying to drown out the multitude of questions in my mind. The moonlight shining through the window cast gentle squares of light on the floor of my room. Sleep had come and gone, leaving me with little to do other than stare at the ceiling. Questions, scenarios, and possibilities plagued me. Though I hadn't told my siblings what I learned, I still mulled over the pros and cons of doing so.

A soft knock came from my open door.

"Zaelek, get dressed," my mother said softly.

"It's four in the morning," I groaned.

"Hush. You'll wake your brother and sister. Meet me in the backyard when you're ready."

I slid out from under my warm blankets, wondering why in the world I even considered this madness. Then again, my parents were a mystery anymore, so how could I know what they wanted? The cold wooden floor made my toes ache as I quietly dressed, leaving my boots off until I got downstairs. When I stepped out onto the porch, I saw my mother, father, and Kinara waiting for me.

"What's going on?" I asked.

Dad smirked. "We have a proposition for you. Keep your Guardian nature from your siblings, and your mother and I will train you. Deal?"

My eyes narrowed as I contemplated the proposal. I wanted to tell my siblings, but I also wanted to see exactly what my parents were offering. What harm could it do to keep their secret a little longer? Besides, if I ended up going to the Guardian Forces, they would put the pieces together themselves.

"Deal."

Mom and Dad smiled at each other with a mixture of relief and amusement. We walked for what seemed like an eternity before reaching our property's farthest field. Dad pushed the gate open and allowed my mother and Kinara to pass through ahead of us. I trailed behind them for another ten minutes, ending up somewhere in the woods.

It seemed unusually cold this morning, even for spring, and the crisp air burned the inside of my nose as I inhaled a faint sweet scent. The tree line broke, revealing a hidden field, one I hadn't seen before. Scarecrows stood silent watch from their posts, making me nervous. Was this part of our property? I didn't know if I wanted to discover the answer. When I shivered, the hairs on my arms stood on end.

My father sat, crossing his legs, and resting his blade on his thighs. "Zaelek, your mother and I decided to give you some training to enable you to decide if you want to pursue becoming a Guardian or not."

I looked at my mother, but she remained silent. Her uncharacteristically sullen demeanor over the last twelve hours had caused everyone discomfort, including my father though it seemed to be only toward the three of us and not my brother or sister. My sensitivity to others' emotions doubled the feeling of despair lodged in my chest.

Dad nodded to Mom. She closed her eyes, taking in a deep, gentle breath and tilting her hands. The slight breeze rustling the trees ceased. I looked to Kinara for answers but found none in her expressionless face.

That's when I heard it. A faint howl seemed to roll into the meadow from the trees. Another sounded to the right, then the left. The putrid stench of sulfur settled on the prairie.

As if the creatures had awakened the trees, their bark bulged and shrank like a wave. A branch extended from near the base of the tree and touched the ground. I shook my head, hoping that what I was seeing was just a figment of my imagination.

From the tree's trunk a deira volf appeared, one of the most fearsome beasts of the forest. Few people lived after encountering them. The four-legged creature shook its majestic brown body, making its thick fur fluff out. It stretched, then let out a yawn. The prominent canine teeth of the beast protruded a few inches past its bottom lip.

Two additional volves, identical to the first, came into view as they stalked toward my mother. I took a step back in fear.

"It's okay, Zaelek," Mom said. "They won't hurt us."

I hadn't noticed how rapidly I had been breathing until she attempted to comfort me.

Dad remained sitting. "These manifestations," he said, "are called Summonings. They aid your mother when she needs their help."

"They…belong to you?"

"Not quite," said Mom, "They're more like a type of guardian spirit." I started to ask a question, but Mom held a hand up. "I know you want to ask more about them, but we don't have time right now. For you to fully comprehend, it would take a month."

Dad stood, "There are two types of these creatures: Summonings and Daemons. Summonings do not have a permanent physical body. They feed off their summoner's strength; the stronger a summoner is, the more powerful and destructive a summoning will be.

"Daemons, on the other hand, are a permanent manifestation of elemental energy. They can cross between the Ethereal world and this world. In a way, they're almost like a storage vessel for elemental power. Daemons possess the ability to transfer energy to their counterparts, the wielder. Their strength, however, is substantially less than a Summoned creature."

Dad whistled the familiar pitch he used to call Caspien. Far in the distance, I heard a whinny. Caspien broke through the tree line and proudly trotted to Dad, coming to a stop before snorting at my father.

"Yes, Caspien. The time has come."

The creature snorted again.

"You did not."

Did my father just speak to a kilindrel? I had to be dreaming the most vivid dream ever. Caspien whinnied and blew air out of his lips before looking away from Dad.

"All right, fine. You didn't guess the right kid, though."

The kilindrel shook its head, almost as if annoyed.

"You speak to him?" I asked.

"It's one of the unique traits of Daemons. Summonings can't communicate on a verbal level."

All this time, Dad had been having conversations with Caspien, and I hadn't ever picked up on it. Sure, sometimes I saw him steal a glance at Caspien with an emotion that didn't fit the situation, but I thought it had just been an odd quirk. It never crossed my mind that the two were conversing.

Caspien shook. His short brown hair receded into his body, leaving behind a blue, semi-transparent, liquid-like skin. The once thick, red mane hanging from his neck became a cascading waterfall that fell to the ground. Caspien shuttered again, and the waterfall mane froze into icicles.

I reached out to touch him but stopped and looked at my dad. He nodded in approval. I placed my hand on Caspien's liquid hide. It came as a surprise that his skin felt warm to my palm.

"Caspien can regulate his body temperature to fit the needs of the situation. Try touching him again."

I did as instructed and found that the kilindrel's skin had gone from warm to ice cold. The phenomena left me in awe.

"Kinara, can I see your Summoning or Daemon?"

Kinara smiled softly, "I'm not strong enough to have one yet."

Before I could ask, Mom stepped in. "There are seven ranks of Guardian. Alpha is the strongest, and Eta the weakest. Somewhere between Gamma and Beta, a Guardian's Summoning or Daemon will manifest itself, if they have one. It depends on the Guardian."

"Doesn't everyone have a Daemon or Summoning?" I asked.

"No. It depends on the family's bloodline."

"Bloodline…what rank are you, Mom?"

"I'm a Beta."

"And Dad?"

"Alpha. He is the only one left we know of. Only a handful of

Guardians make it to Alpha, even though they may train their whole lives," she paused, and her eyes locked onto Kinara. "Kinara, if I'm correctly picking up your enigma levels, you're a Zeta, right?"

"Yes, Ma'am."

"I assume you have the void bound mastered."

"Yes, Ma'am."

"Excellent. I think this would be a wonderful time for you to learn the art of instruction. Why don't you teach it to Zaelek?"

Kinara's eyes widened. "Me? Wouldn't it be better for one of you to teach him?"

"We'll step in if need be, but it's simple enough that you should be fine."

Kinara hesitated for a moment, then agreed. "OK, Zaelek. Void bounding is like a type of enhanced running that Guardians use." Kinara then explained how the process of void-bounding worked, sparing no detail. Multiple times, I had to pinch myself to stay awake.

Though it was a lot of information, I got the gist of it. Per Kinara, experienced bounders could go for nearly ten hours before tiring in the slightest.

I frowned. "Seems easy enough, but when do we get to start elemental training?"

My father laughed. "Why don't we focus on the basics for now, Sparky? You'll see, there's a little more to it than just *manifesting* elemental power."

"What do you mean?"

"We'd need to get a Locksmith out here to unlock your element, and they are few and far between. The Guardian Forces only have a handful, and there's no way I could ask Kehndrig to send one to Corai."

A tinge of disappointment crept through me. They tell me all this and then tell me I have to wait for the good stuff. It wasn't fair.

"Ready to give bounding a try?" Kinara offered. "I'll show you how it's done once, then it's up to you. The trick is to focus on your concentration. We call this process *thought reaping*. You'll know you've reaped correctly when the lower half of your arm hairs stand on end. Think of how you feel when you get shocked, but without the pain."

A soft crack followed by a brief burst of wind rushed over

me. Kinara seemed to take only four steps before she stood at the other end of the clearing. Her speed took me by surprise. Was this how Guardians traveled? I couldn't wait to try it.

Clearing my mind of everything else, I focused. A ferocious blast of energy surged through my body. I ran through the clearing aimlessly. Nothing happened.

"Did I do something wrong?"

"Probably," Kinara said with a smirk. "Try again."

I tried and failed for a half-hour. Kinara guided me through the entire trial-and-error period. On what seemed to be the hundredth try, my arm hairs tingled, and a small burst of speed propelled me forward briefly before I lost it.

"Kinara, did you see?"

"I saw. Nice work. Now try to run the entire clearing."

My face was covered with sweat, and I panted heavily. "Can I take a break first?"

"No! Get out there and get it done."

I sighed. She was going to be the death of me. At least now that I knew what the microburst of energy after reaping felt like. The power flickered inside me, and I rocketed forward. The wind whipped through my hair, and energy raged inside my body.

Excited, I looked back at Kinara as I flew past her. "I'm doing it! I've got it."

My foot tangled in some long grass, and I slammed into the ground. I skipped across the dirt a few times before skidding to a stop. My feet were still above my head when Kinara reached my side.

"You all right?"

"Ouch."

"Yeah, that looked like it hurt. Anything broken?"

"I don't think so, but my head hurts."

"I bet! You're getting the hang of it though!"

Mother soon dropped out of a bound next to us. She inspected me for injuries my pride might incline me to hide. I'm sure she thought I was acting tough in Kinara's presence. Not that it would have mattered. Her overprotective mothering—more like smothering—destroyed any hope I had of impressing Kinara.

I could hear my father laughing from where he waited by the largest tree at the edge of the clearing. It didn't surprise me that he found my clumsy attempt amusing, but I felt my cheeks burning with embarrassment.

Kinara had me practice a few more times before she smiled at my progress. Once in a while, I caught her giggling while I ran. She said I looked like a newborn kilindrel learning to walk for the first time. I didn't find her comparison as humorous as she and my parents did.

Determined to master it, I improved over the next couple of hours. Though exhausted, I now had a legacy to live up to. I wanted to be like my father more than anything, now that I knew that my parents' strength was in my blood.

Around noon, Dad stopped the training. "We need to head back. The other kids might suspect something if we're out all day."

Mom and Kinara agreed. Relief flooded over me. I didn't know how much longer I could have continued. My legs felt like a gelatinous dessert at this point. Tomorrow would certainly bring the familiar ache of sore muscles with it.

9

In Khiings Estate's hidden training field...

"You can sit this one out, Kinara," Ettias told me when I started to rise for the next set.

I sat at the foot of a giantwood tree while Ettias conducted Zaelek's lesson this time. Today marked the second day of Zaelek's training. I couldn't help being slightly envious that "Sparky" was learning from two of the greatest Guardians in history, but they were, after all, his parents.

I could name a dozen recruits from the academy who would have killed for this kind of opportunity. Styx, the whole Guardian Force would probably kill to be in Zaelek's place. Considering Ettias could be the most powerful Guardian the world had seen, I'd say Zaelek had a decent chance of attaining Alpha with his help.

The ever-waving flograss prickled my palms as I closed my eyes and lifted my face to the sun. The warmth was soothing. A slight breeze carried the sweet scent that the trees and grasses released before they transitioned to their summer form. I activated my seeker senses and allowed myself to appreciate nature, something I rarely got an opportunity to do in the city.

Maialyn had stayed home to throw Zaelek's siblings off our trail and to wait for word from Ettias' contact. He had called in a few favors to help streamline the search for Alator—that alone was something I could never repay.

Ettias halted Zaelek before he could start another void bound. "Hold up. I'm getting a call from your mother."

Zaelek looked at his father. "How are you getting a call all the way out here? The mobile is at the house."

Ettias tapped his wrist twice. A V-12 bracelet uncloaked from its invisibility function. "I'll tell you more about it later."

He touched the watch face and a call symbol projected from it. Maialyn's voice came from the V-12's internal speaker.

"Hey, handsome," she said, in such a way that I could almost see her flirtatious expression.

Ettais smiled. "I take it you heard from Johanous?"

"I did. He'd like you to call him as soon as possible."

"Okay, we'll head your way. Love you."

"I love you, too."

Back at the house Ettias opened the door for Zaelek but barred my way before I could enter.

"I think it would be an excellent learning opportunity for you to be my second on this."

His words surprised me. "You're going to let me come along?"

"He's your fiancé."

He had a point.

Maialyn and Zaelek convinced Ari and Ben to accompany them to town for dinner. Once they had gone, Ettias led me down the passageway again to the bunker where a small tinge of fear crept through me. Near-death experiences have a way of playing with your mind.

Ettias booted up the H.I.V.E. system and made the call. The room changed once again, but this time we stared into a dingy apartment. An array of papers littered the burn-marked carpet, and the smoke from a still-smoldering cigarette billowed from an ashtray on a tattered table. Beside it sat a middle-aged man with his fingers laced. The man's well-groomed grey mustache turned down as he frowned.

"Cronus. Don't we usually meet alone?"

Ettias gestured to me, "Johanous, this is Kinara. She's an old family friend."

"You know I don't like surprises."

"I'm aware. Kinara will be my second for this mission."

"Training them young, I see. She must have some serious firepower to be hanging around you."

"Something like that. My partner told me you have some information for me?"

"Ah, yes…" he rummaged through a stack of papers on the table next to him. "The young G.I.T.F. Officer you're looking for."

I was sure my heartbeat could be heard a mile away. Had this man found him?

Ettias brought up another screen with a number pad in the right corner. "Before you ask, I have the FundTrans up."

Johanous smiled. "Very good. You'd do well to watch your mentor closely, young Kinara." He paused, "The price is high for this information, Cronus. You understand?"

"Of course. How much are we talking, ten, fifteen thousand?"

Fifteen thousand credits for information?! Was Ettias prepared to pay that money out of pocket?

The man laughed. "Not this time, old friend. Fifty thousand credits for this one."

Despair washed over me. There was no way Ettias could afford that. The Guardian Forces certainly wouldn't reimburse him for it. Sad as it may be, informants couldn't be paid more than a couple thousand credits for their services. Most likely for this exact reason.

Ettias cracked his neck, probably as a way to remind himself to hold his tongue.

"Why so expensive this time, if you don't mind me asking?"

"Crossing Trentir Savvage is a risky business. If he finds out I infiltrated his organization, I'll be dead by nightfall. Not to mention he would slaughter the entire platoon responsible for safeguarding his new plaything, just to ensure he'd dealt with the traitor. If you ask me, it's a real shame to lose such valuable resources. Regardless, I figured the legendary Cronus would be good for the money, so I stuck my neck out in good faith."

"Very well…" Ettias punched a code into the number pad. A

red *50,000* appeared above his head, followed by a green plus above Johanous. "Your credits are in your account."

"Thank you for your business, as usual, Cronus."

Johanous pulled a stack of papers from the pile as the fingers of his other hand poked through the air. A documentation upload request slid down from the roof in front of Ettias, who touched *accept*. Johanous' room disappeared.

"What happened?" I asked.

"Don't worry, this is normal. Johanous is just breaching their security system."

Our room shifted, and almost as quickly as the place had changed, an entire dossier floated around us in a circular motion. Ettias scanned the documents. He touched one, and the room changed again.

We now stood in what appeared to be a warehouse. From the ground up, data compiled itself until people formed.

I was stunned. "This is incredible!"

"These are the toys you'll get when you make Alpha."

"You mean *if* I make Alpha."

"I think you have a good chance, But let's focus on this for now, though."

He reached up and pulled a menu down from the bar in the corner. When he selected the "Crystallize" option, every person in the room looked three dimensional, as if we stood there with them. Chains came down from the ceiling, suspending Alator inches above the ground. I rushed toward him, only to have Ettias' iron-like grip stop me.

"Remember," he said, "this isn't real."

I composed myself, embarrassed. "Is he alive?"

Ettias swiped another option on the menu, and everything began moving in real-time. He zoomed in until Alator's broken body hung directly in front of him. The amount of blood on the ground made me ill.

"Nadia," Ettias said, startling me.

The A.I. responded with, "Yes, Cronus?"

"Run Diagnostics on the man in front of me."

A green grid encased Alator's body. After a moment, a large rectangular overlay extended from the grid. All kinds of data populated until it reached the bottom where it read "Diag. complete."

"Completed, Sir," the A.I. said.

"Display the results."

Another box appeared, reading, "Subject alive."

"He's alive!" I cried out.

An unfamiliar man walked into view, holding a whip. Panic pierced me like a blade.

Ettias ended the feed, "It's better you don't watch what might happen next."

He brought up a schematic of the warehouse in the feed. I barely heard a thing he said for the next ten minutes until Ettias noticed and snapped me out with, "I know it's hard, but you need to focus. It's the only way your fiancé has a chance."

Once we'd read the report, Ettias retrieved his sword. He instructed me to get what I needed and meet him on the front porch. It didn't take long.

"The intel said Alator was in Tendir," I said.

"Correct."

"It will take forever to get there! We need transport…"

Ettias cut me off when he pointed up. "I'm surprised a Seeker of your caliber hasn't heard it yet." I focused and heard an aerial vehicle approaching from the east. "I called in a favor from an old friend of mine. We'll get there much faster this way."

Before I could stop myself, I wrapped my arms around Ettias. "Thank you."

"You're welcome. Load up. We need to get to Alator."

The transport landed in the field next to the farmhouse with a soft thud. All six rotary blades protruding from the top of the vehicle slowed as we approached. A small ramp extended from its side, leading to the bay door.

When we strapped into the black cargo net seats, the ramp retracted, and the door shut. Ettias gave the pilot a thumb up, and the transport lifted off the ground.

Even though our flight only took about thirty minutes, my mind spun with a thousand possible scenarios. There could only be one outcome: bringing Alator home alive. I wouldn't be able to live with myself if something happened to him. If I had to, I'd face off against ten other blades to get him out.

10

The Zenja University of Veterinary Practices' dorms...

The transport exited the Skyway and descended to Amaya's dorm building. When I had helped her home days before, I hadn't expected to stand in her doorway for over two hours talking. If I hadn't, I probably wouldn't have gathered enough courage to ask her out today. It's funny how life brings people together.

I opened the transport door, looking back at the driver as I stepped out. "Mind hanging around?"

"No problem. How long should I expect to wait?"

"Not long. I'm just grabbing my date, and we'll be right out."

Amaya and I had agreed to meet in the lobby, so I couldn't imagine it taking more than five minutes. I entered the cramped revolving door and shuffled into the lobby. Elegant but antique-looking decorations filled what counter or tabletop space available and cracking paintings lined the walls. Like my dorm, the place appeared rundown and borderline abandoned. The memory of stepping into my dorm's lobby for the first time flashed through my mind. I remembered thinking it had to be a mistake. Luckily, I'd given the place a chance before dismissing it. My room was smaller than I would've liked, but they had remodeled it into a stunning living space.

I searched the lobby for any sign of Amaya but didn't see her. Strange. We had agreed to meet at noon. *Maybe I'm a little early.* I checked the watch Dad had given me when I started my first semester. It read a minute past noon. So where was she? I pulled the small tablet from my pocket and sent "*I'm here*" to her.

By ten after the hour, I began to wonder if she'd bailed. I was convinced there no way she would have bailed. She seemed just as excited about this as I was. Maybe I had misread her. Although I would never admit it to him, Zaelek could read people much better than I, and I couldn't help pondering how he would've interpreted the interaction. But matters of the heart weren't his strength, so maybe he wouldn't be much help here either. *Styx. What should I do?*

The elevator produced a *ding*, and the doors opened to reveal Amaya. Her thick, wavy brown hair cascaded over the front of her narrow shoulders and down her back. I'd found her attractive when we first met, but now I had to keep myself from gawking.

She approached sheepishly. "Parnikus…" She noticed my expression. "What? Does my outfit look weird? I knew I should have gone with the other pants…"

"Not at all! I think you look stunning!"

Amaya nervously twirled a lock of her hair between her fingers and looked away. "Are you sure you're not just saying that?"

"You're perfect."

"Well, you don't look too shabby yourself."

"Thanks!" I nodded toward the door. "Ready?"

"Yes! Sorry, I took so long…I couldn't decide what to wear."

"Don't worry about it. We still have the rest of the day," I said as we headed to the transport.

"Think you can handle me for that long?" she said with a wink.

"How hard could it be?" I said as I opened the transport door for her, and she stepped in.

She turned and laced her fingers in my tie and pulled me close with a playful smirk. "We'll see." She ruffled my shoulder-length red hair, then pushed away to sit.

I can't figure this girl out.

Hours later, we sat on a small park bench in the darkness. Amaya pulled her jacket tighter around her shoulders, then snuggled up to me, laying her head on my arm.

"What are we doing here again?" I asked.

"You'll see. Be patient."

I stared at the city lights reflecting off the manmade pond's surface, wondering if it would be weird to ask her if she'd like to come to the farm this weekend. Sure, we'd only been on this one date, but the more I spent time with her, the more I liked her. I found myself wishing we'd met sooner. Then it wouldn't be weird. I was sure Mom and Dad would really like her, too. *Maybe next time.*

The lights on the pond flashed once.

"Get ready," she said.

Music sounded from around us, and hundreds of water streams shot into the air in harmony with the beat. The lights changed from white to light blue, then cycled through various colors.

I stood, looking back at Amaya before returning my attention to the water show. "This is amazing!"

She rose and laced her fingers in mine. "Right? I discovered this place a few days after I got here. I'm glad I found someone to share it with."

I stared into her emerald eyes that reflected flashes of color from the water show. All I could think about was the way my heart fluttered. The chemistry between us coursed through me like water down a spillway, bringing with it a feeling previously unfamiliar to me. The aching in my chest and a longing to be closer to her prompted me to lean in until her breath warmed my skin. Our lips met, and I tasted the fruity hints of her lip balm. Amaya's hand caressed the back of my head, and she gently pulled me closer.

11

Tendir outskirts, Alympia...

My heart pounded in anticipation. Today was the day I would hold Alator in my arms once again. Everything had led to this moment, this mission, and I couldn't allow it to fail. But despite the living legend standing next to me, I was unable to shake the feeling that we were headed into something much more sinister than a warehouse.

Our transport touched down in one of the many fields on the outskirts of Tendir. Ettias gave a two-fingered salute to the pilot, then hurried me down the cargo hold ramp. My hair whipped as it took off.

Ettias tapped the display of his V-12 bracelet. A map of Tendir floated from the device's projecting system.

"The warehouse isn't too far from our position," Ettias said, double tapping a purple square.

The map zoomed in on the building and marked the surrounding street names.

"I didn't know the V-12 could do that."

"They can't. This is the V-16."

"The twelves were just released this year. How did you get one that's four generations ahead?"

He slid his finger down the interface, closing the map. "We need every advantage we can get against Javelar. They are far more dangerous than most give them credit for. Come on, we need to hurry."

I followed Ettias through a subdivision on the outskirts of the city. A few blocks in, we turned into an industrial area with heavy machinery and factories scattered about. Rather than head straight for the warehouse, Ettias led us into the building next to it.

The man at the desk looked up. "Good afternoon, how can I…"

Ettias sent a concentrated blast of water through the man's skull, painting the wall behind him light crimson.

I jumped in surprise. "What are you doing?!"

Ettias reached over the counter and pulled out a sword from the storage area, then pointed to a logo on its case. "He's Javelar."

"How did you know it was there?" Then I noticed the circular mirror in the corner of the room behind the counter. "Oh."

He frowned. "You need to be more observant."

I looked down at my feet. "Yes, Sir."

Ettias looked through the rectangular window at the end of the hall. He tried the door, but it didn't budge.

"Kinara," he said. "I need you to teleport into the other room and unlock the door from that side."

I concentrated. When I materialized on the other side, I stared at a group of men in the corner playing cards whose attention was drawn by my movement.

"Gentlemen," I said.

They drew their swords as they rose from their chairs. When I twisted the door handle and pulled, a blast of air rushed past me that led to muffled screams with groaning metal and splintering wood. In seconds, the men's mangled corpses were lying at Ettias' feet.

"At least we know we're in the right place," he said.

We climbed the staircase to the roof of the building. I looked over the edge.

"Are we scoping out the warehouse?"

"Nope."

"Then what?"

"You'll see. When I give you the signal, teleport to the balcony on the warehouse roof."

Ettias leaped, landed gracefully on the balcony, then waved. I materialized next to him and waited for him to inspect the door handle. A small stream of water spiraled around his wrist, then entered the keyhole. After the click, he twisted the latch.

The water ejected from the keyhole and enveloped the hinges in small globes. They spun slowly in a clockwise direction, mesmerizing me with their simple elegance.

Ettias saw my confusion. "To keep the door from squeaking."

We entered and stopped just before the catwalk split.

"You go left. I'll go right," he said.

I skulked across the metal pathway. Below, in the center of the room, I saw Alator hanging, chains wrapped all the way up both arms. He looked so vulnerable, something that I wasn't accustomed to. It took every ounce of self-control I had to keep myself in position and not rush to his aid but I knew that if I didn't follow the plan I could get myself and Alator killed. Not to mention Ettias, who was making his way across the catwalk opposite me. Once in position, we would jump to the concrete below. From there, I would focus on freeing Alator. Ettias had insisted that my ability to teleport made me perfect for this job.

Four guards formed a square perimeter around Alator. Perhaps Savvage thought no one dared oppose him and only allotted the minimum personnel...or we were about to walk into a nasty ambush.

A change in environment drew my attention as the floor below became covered in frost. That was the signal!

I teleported and stood right in front of my fiancé. My heart broke at the sight of his torn flesh. It made me ill to see him suffering, and I wished for nothing more than to drive my blade through whoever was responsible. I couldn't believe Alator still survived despite the extent of his injuries.

He shuddered as my chilly hands touched his ribs. A soft smile formed on his lips. "I'd know that touch anywhere."

"Shhh…Try not to talk," I whispered after swallowing the lump in my throat.

I felt someone bump against my back, accompanied by the clang of metal against metal. Startled, I looked behind me to see Ettias in a sword lock with one of the guards.

"Get him out of here!" he shouted while reaching up and touching the chain.

Ettias' ice crept up the links until it reached the hook near the top. I drew my blade and encased it in flames. These chains were resistant to elemental attacks, but not immune to them. Focusing, I sent all my energy to the flaming blade. I only had one shot at this. The flames turned blue, and my sword grew white-hot, sending heat waves up my arm.

I slashed where the ice was thinnest. It shattered the link, and I caught Alator as he fell to the ground. Slinging him over my shoulders, I ran for the exit, unable to teleport another person with me. Suddenly, I was jerked backward as something wrenched Alator from my grip.

What in Styx? I rolled to my stomach and searched for whoever had a hold on the chain but saw no one.

Cronus dispatched the last enemy by removing her head, then rushed over. "Mercy's breath," he cursed

"What's wrong?"

"Search for a small yellow box about the size of your fist. They've bound the chain to a GravStone."

I didn't know what that was, but I didn't have time to ask. *Focus*. Alator needed me to be more centered and calmer than ever. My eyes closed, and I allowed my Seeker senses to take over. So many potent smells assaulted me that it caused me to waiver. Alator's blood, everyone else's blood, body odor, oil, sweat—it all threatened to overwhelm me.

I opened my eyes and allowed my visual senses to dull the smells. Debris lay scattered everywhere. I teleported back to the catwalk and searched.

There! It sat in a glass case next to the control room.

"Here," I called as I jumped down next to it.

I swung my sword toward the glass, but Cronus grabbed my wrist before the blade touched it.

"Stop. It could be rigged."

Metal gears cranked above us, and we looked up. A small beam of light touched the floor where Alator had been hanging. The chain, still attached to the invisible tether, whipped up toward the shaft of light.

"No!" I shouted. We had to get him out of there!

I rushed forward, but an arc of electricity zipped down the chain at the same time. Alator screamed as the current pulsed through his body. A long needle shot from somewhere to his left and hit him in the neck. The electrocution stopped, allowing Alator to sink back to the ground.

Panicked, I ran to Alator's side and checked to see if he was breathing. His breath came in shallow gasps. I looked back to Ettias and shouted, "He's still alive!"

I could see sadness in his eyes as he knelt to examine the deadly needle.

"It's full of Jehora serum. I've seen it kill more good soldiers than I care to admit. There's nothing we can do, I'm sorry. I'll stand guard while you say your goodbyes."

His words hit me like a carrier truck. *No*... Tears filled my eyes as I looked down at the man I loved, the man I had planned to spend my life with.

He coughed, spewing blood all over me. Alator could see the horror on my face. He reached up and placed his hand on my cheek, sending shivers of dread across my skin.

"Kinara," he said weakly.

"I'm here," I wept.

"It's okay."

"You're going to be fine! Just stay with me!"

"No, not this time. Promise me..." Alator's skin lost its color and his veins turned dark purple.

The whites of his eyes turned green, and blood dripped from his mouth. His hand fell to the ground as one last breath escaped his blue lips.

"Alator!"

I collapsed onto his chest and wailed miserably. *How could I have let this happen? This wasn't supposed to be the way our life together ended!*

12

In Khiings Estate's hidden training field...

"Why sticks?" I asked my mother.

"Zaelek, tell me, do you want to start your first lesson in sword training with blades?"

"No."

"I didn't think so. Now, every Guardian has a unique weapon. It's designed for them and will only reach its true potential if wielded by its master. Thus." Mom drew her blade from her sheath. She swung down, and a volley of rock shards shot from the blade's tip, startling me. "That's only one example of the many ways I can use my sword. Every Guardian has their own style."

"So every Guardian has a unique sword. Got it."

"Not quite. I said every Guardian has a unique weapon. Not all have swords."

"Then why are we training with a sword?"

"Genetics. Your father and I have swords. You will probably have one as well. Enough talk. For now, pick up the stick."

I did as instructed, and to my delight, the stick morphed into a replica of a sword.

"How did it do that?"

"*It* didn't do anything on its own. I used my element to transform it."

I examined the wooden sword in wonder. It seemed like a piece of art. Every detail looked like a real sword, aside from its color.

Mother laughed at my expression. "The first thing we need to do is work on your stance." She used her foot to guide mine into position. "You'll want a good steady base. That way, your opponent can't throw you off balance and cause you to stagger. In a fight, balance is paramount. Your father might disagree, but he relies on brute strength, something I don't have. If you combine our techniques, you could best either of us in a one-on-one battle one day. Perhaps someday you'll even be able to take us both at the same time."

Best my parents in combat at the same time? The idea seemed ludicrous. I couldn't imagine becoming skilled enough to do that.

Mom continued, "The next thing to master is your grip." She adjusted my hands, twisting and turning them until they were in position. "If you have a weak grip, your opponent will easily disarm you. It doesn't take a genius to know that is never a good thing."

"I have pretty strong hands from working on the farm, Mom."

She slammed her training sword into mine, knocking it out of my hands. The blade twirled in the air, then stuck in the ground ten feet away. I looked at her in shock. "That's not fair! You're one rank below an Alpha!"

"Life isn't fair. In fact, it's cruel in many ways. Any Guardian that has potential could hold on to their sword, regardless of strength. It may break their wrists, but at least they still have something of a defense."

"If it breaks their wrists, how could they still fight?"

"That depends on the Guardian. Some would give up after being wounded. Others continue to fight even after a fatal blow. You'll need to figure out what kind of Guardian you'll be. Will you fight to the bitter end, or will you falter under adverse conditions?"

"I'll fight."

"That's easier said than done. You won't know until it happens. Once you figure it out, you'll know how to proceed." She looked toward the edge of the clearing. "That's enough for today. You have some thinking and practicing to do. We'll pick up where we left off tomorrow."

"They're back," Ben called from the living room.

I rushed down the stairs, excited to meet Alator. From the porch I could see only my father and Kinara coming down the gravel driveway. Kinara looked like death. Specks of blood covered her gray blouse and fair skin. Something was different about her. Her face showed no hint of emotion, as if only a shell of the Kinara I knew remained. No greeting, no Hades driven remarks, not even a simple acknowledgment of my existence.

"Where's Alator?" I asked.

My father shook his head solemnly, using a rag hanging from the railing to wipe the dried blood off his hands. Kinara never looked up as she climbed the steps. I turned and watched her silently follow my father into the house.

As he passed, Dad placed his giant hand on my shoulder. "I'll fill you in later. Let her have some space."

I nodded. Dad knew I'd be inclined to press Kinara for answers and end up making things worse.

My mother wrapped Kinara in her arms. She wept so loudly that my heart broke for her. Ben peered around the corner of the living room wall, alarmed by her crying. He looked at me, but I shook my head. Without a word, Ben returned to his chair.

Ari bumped my shoulder with hers and whispered, "What did you do to her, Sparky?"

Before I could answer, Dad told her, "Outside, now." The tone of his demand moved her instantly and she followed him outside.

Usually, I would be delighted to see my sister get in trouble, but not this time. I just hoped Kinara didn't hear Ari's snide remark. I wathed as Mom slipped a blanket around Kinara's shoulders before taking her upstairs.

My mother soon returned to put water on for what I assumed would be an herbal tea. Mom's renown as an herbalist kept her little side business flourishing, but it had become more of a hobby than anything else. Whenever any of us felt sick, the concoction of a strong, warm drink would be her go-to remedy. It usually made a difference, though I didn't know how much it would help this time.

Ari opened the front door, her usual proud walk now an ashamed shuffle. She passed me, offering an apologetic look, then went up to her room. My father gestured for me to join him on the front porch.

Dad sat on the steps and looked out toward the setting sun. The wear and tear of the day showed on his face. He patted the wood next to him and I sat beside him.

I silently debated whether I really wanted an answer to my question, but I had to know.

"What happened out there?"

"We failed," he replied.

"I don't understand. You don't fail missions."

"I wish that were true, but I'd be lying if I said it was. Even the most experienced soldiers fail from time to time. Sometimes it's because of external factors, other times, it's because we make mistakes. That's just how it works, son. Today, there was a mixture of both, and because of that, the world lost a bright young officer."

"Alator?"

He nodded. "Yes."

"How?"

"I couldn't tell you even if I wanted to. Alator's death will become classified information. I told Ari that there was an accident at the terminal when we went to pick up Alator, and he didn't make it. That's what we'll tell everyone else, too."

"But that's a lie."

"A lie that prevents panic. Imagine how the families of the other officers would react if they learned the truth."

"They deserve to know!"

"Maybe.... That's not our call, though. Welcome to the world of being a Guardian."

He stood and went into the house, leaving me to come to terms with the necessity of the deception. I couldn't comprehend why we would lie about this. I wanted to trust my father, but it was proving more difficult than I cared to admit.

The porch's automatic lights came on the moment the sun dropped behind the trees. I heard a fresh wave of choking wails and took a deep breath. Seeing Kinara like this unsettled me. From the day we'd first met, she'd always been so tough.

I headed upstairs, intending to go to my room and mull over my thoughts, but as I passed the guest room, Kinara whispered my name. I stopped in my tracks.

"Could you come here for a moment?" she asked.

"Of course."

Kinara sat against her bed's headboard with knees tucked against her chest. She must have showered; her hair was wet and her bloody clothes were gone. She was in a nightgown, the blanket my mother had draped over her downstairs was around her shoulders.

Kinara's visible suffering hurt me more than I would ever show her.

She tucked a wet strand of blonde hair behind her ear. "I told your mom I wanted to be alone, but now I don't think I can be."

"Are you thinking about hurting yourself?"

"What kind of idiotic question is that?" she snapped.

I recoiled. "S…Sorry, I don't know why I asked that. I guess all the training at work…"

She gently cut me off, "No, I'm sorry. You shouldn't have to explain yourself for trying to help."

I hadn't dealt with someone in such a devastated state before. What could be said to make her feel better? I couldn't imagine the pain she must be feeling, and I certainly couldn't relate to her situation. My mother would be better equipped to talk to her.

"I can get Mom back up here. I'm sure she wouldn't mind."

She shook her head, "Not after I just asked her to leave. I've already been such a burden on your family."

I sat on the edge of the bed and squeezed her hand. "No, you haven't. We're happy that you came to us for help."

"Yes, I have. I revealed your dad's secret, I accidentally told you about your Guardian nature, and I took advantage of everyone's trust." Tears formed in her eyes.

Ah, Styx! Please don't cry. My silent wishes crumbled when Kinara burst into tears. Awkwardly, I placed my arm around her shoulders and patted her arm.

To my surprise, she slid down and nestled against my chest and wept even harder. My stiff back muscles threatened to explode. The discomfort increased when I thought of what Alator's reaction might have been if he saw us like this.

“I’m a terrible person,” she whimpered.

“Nothing terrible about trying to save someone you love,” I whispered.

We sat, with her in my arms, until she cried herself to sleep. Gingerly, I laid her head on the pillow and tucked her in. I retreated to the comfort of my room and shut the door, sure that this would be the longest night of my life.

13

Kinara's room at the farmhouse...

I don't think Zaelek realized he woke me up when he tucked me into bed, but that's all right. His willingness to stay with me until I fell asleep was sweet. Though he could be an idiot, Zaelek had a heart of gold.

I felt silly for asking him to stay. Ettias no doubt told him about the situation, so he probably had a lot on his mind, too. The sense of loneliness rooted itself even deeper in my chest, crushing me until I almost couldn't breathe.

Another tear slid down my cheek. Alator and I had been together for three years before he proposed to me last fall. I didn't know how I could ever recover from losing him. This pain differed from the pain of my parents' death; this felt like an entire half of my soul had died along with Alator.

For another thirty minutes, I tossed and turned, listening to the increasing intensity of the rain outside, then the memories crept in to haunt me.

My first assignment, I thought as I pulled the door to the GITF HQ open. I approached the front desk and rang the small bell on the counter. A crash sounded from the back room, followed by a string of curses. Soon, a short, obese woman with a large hairy mole next to her eye approached the counter, her repugnant body odor reaching me before she did.

"What is it?" she snapped.

"I'm here to speak with Alator Kilobask, a lieutenant here."

"I know who he is."

Her stubby fingers jabbed her small earpiece until the gargle-like ringer played full blast from the external speaker on her desk.

"Yes?" a male voice answered.

"Lieutenant, you have a Miss..." She looked to me.

"Katari," I stated.

"...Katari waiting for you in the lobby."

"Tell her I'll be right down."

"Yes, Sir."

She jammed the earpiece again, then pointed her untrimmed yellow nail toward a row of chairs against the wall. I took a seat, not wanting to give the old hildenslug another opportunity to verbally abuse me. A few minutes turned to thirty, then to forty, and I wanted to strangle this Alator guy. Just as I was about to storm out of the building, the elevator door opened, and a young man with swept up, black hair stepped into the lobby and called my name.

"Sorry," he said as I approached, "The chief called an emergency meeting before I could get into the elevator."

"That's fine. Your receptionist's charming personality kept me plenty occupied."

A captivating grin spread across his face. "Ah, yes, Helgah is certainly a charmer."

I laughed and rolled my eyes. "I think we have some business to attend to."

"I think you're right. How does kaffee sound?"

"Wouldn't you prefer to talk about this in your office?" I said in astonishment.

"I mean, we can, but I don't know if I want to spend another second cooped up in my tiny little broom closet. Come on, you'll be saving my sanity." When I paused for a moment, he added, "I'll pay."

"I suppose kaffee wouldn't hurt."

"That's what I like to hear!"

Sleep only found me when my exhausted soul could no longer bear the suffering, and before I knew it, sunlight was warming my face. I stretched my stiff limbs. Maybe ten seconds of sweet relief passed before I remembered Alator's death. It was a nasty reality check.

I walked into the bathroom across the hall to splash my face and puffy eyes with frigid water. Maybe it would help. I could hear the Khiings' family moving about downstairs. It wouldn't surprise me if I was the last to get up.

I could see the clock at the bottom of the stairs; it was nine in the morning, a lot later than I usually slept. It irritated me. Sleeping this late felt like a waste of a day.

When I came downstairs after throwing my hair in a quick kilitail, Maialyn beckoned for me to join her in the kitchen, then handed me a bowl of fresh fruit.

"Let me know if there's anything else you need. We're all here for you."

Her tone carried the familiar gentleness I had experienced before I told Zaelek about his Guardian heritage. It put me at ease and made me feel welcome in their home once again. I nodded gratefully, then retreated to the dining room to eat alone.

"Good morning, Kinara," Ettias said as he passed the kitchen.

I chased after him, "Ettias?"

"Yes?"

"I think I'm going to return to Creet today."

"Is that so? Are you sure you can't stay one more night? Parnikus is coming home from university today, and we'd love to have you at his welcome home party."

I forced a polite smile, sure Ettias could see how exhausted and miserable I was.

“I’d like to prepare for Alator’s funeral, and I’m almost out of paid leave. Thanks for the offer, though.”

“I understand. Would you mind doing one last thing for Zaelek before you go?”

“Of course. Anything I can do to help.”

Though I said it, I only half meant it, invoking a pang of guilt for being annoyed by his request, at the same time knowing I still had so much to do and not enough time to do it. I reminded myself how much I owed Ettias for his help.

Ettias fished a pair of keys from his pocket. “Would you take these keys to Toldwer’s Supply in Coltown? All you have to do is give them to the man at the front.” He dropped his voice to a whisper. “He’s storing Zaelek’s sword for me, and I want it to be a surprise.”

“You already have it? How?”

“It’s not the type you’re thinking of. This one is for training, and all I need is for you to bring it back.”

“That should be easy enough.”

An enormous grin spread across his face. “Wonderful! I appreciate it!”

I took the keys from him, then went upstairs to pack my belongings. Once I returned with the sword, I’d be ready to go. I just hoped the task wouldn’t take too long.

14

Later, in preparation for the party...

The simple ride into town for groceries had turned into an infuriating debate with my father about career paths. Only the soft rumble of the Singine's powercel engine disrupted the uncomfortable silence between us.

Dad said, "Zaelek, I really think you should at least consider attending the Field Medicine Academy."

I glanced his way, careful not to drive us off the road. "What's to consider? I'm not even interested in medicine."

My father ran his large hand through his thick red hair. We had been having the same argument for several days, and both of us were determined to emerge the victor. Stubbornness defined the Khiings family, and I blamed both of my parents for that.

"Well, what are you interested in then?" he asked.

"I want to join the Guardian Forces."

"You know how your mother and I feel about that."

How could I not know how they felt about it? They'd been against the idea since I brought it up after training with them, but I didn't care. That is what I wanted.

"I know. I want to use the money I make in the forces to buy a plot of land and start a farm."

"A farm?"

"Yeah, you know, a place to raise animals and grow crops?" I said sarcastically.

"I know what a farm is, you little schleet. You know what I meant. There are other ways to get the money you need to do that."

I couldn't believe my father continued to lecture me like this. He never listened to me.

"What's wrong with a farm? You and Mom bought one after you retired from the Guardian Forces, so why do you care if I do?"

"Retired isn't the word I would use. We still get called in for emergencies you know. And that's beside the point. Your situation is quite different."

"Oh, really? Please enlighten me."

Our bickering continued the entire way into Corai. The argument ended as we pulled into one of the parking stalls outside of Genotl's Supply. The shop was one of the many family-owned businesses in town, but Genotl gave my family the best discounts as a favor for supplying him with our produce.

My father slammed the door of the Singine and headed for the shop. The Singine's horn sounded when I locked the doors with the small authorization bracelet. Dad opened the shop door for me, then followed me inside.

His voice boomed, "Genotl, ole boy. How are you?"

Genotl jumped. The bald, chubby man must have been completely lost in his book. "Ettias!" he smiled, "Glad to see ya haven't worked yourself to death yet! I'm doin' fantastic, how about yourself?"

Dad chuckled softly. "If my kids weren't trying to give me a heart attack every ten minutes, I'd say pretty good."

"Uh-oh, trouble with Asariel again?"

"Surprisingly, it's not her this time." My father shot me an annoyed glance, but I ignored it.

"Oh, well, what are kids for? Right, Zaelek?"

I smiled politely at his jest. Why had I agreed to come with him? I could have stayed home to say goodbye to Kinara before she left for Creet. What if I don't get to see her again because she spilled classified information?

We hurried through the aisles, throwing some of Parnikus' favorite foods in the cart for his welcome home party, then made our way back to Genotl's counter.

My father leaned close to him, "What have you got in your private collection, anything good?"

Genotl's golden handlebar mustache lifted when he grinned. "I've got the perfect bottle for ya, my friend. Remember that smooth marshine you were tellin' me 'bout?"

"You didn't."

"Oh, I did. One of my out-of-county suppliers brought it in for me yesterday."

Dad shook his head. "And that means it must be pretty pricey…"

"C'mon, Ettias, ya know ya don't pay full price here. People come from miles to buy your crops from me."

My father looked at him hesitantly. "Are you sure?"

"Of course, I'm sure." Genotl disappeared through the doorway of the room behind him. My father smiled and winked at me, and I shook my head. Every time we came in here, he talked about how he wished he could get his hands on that marshine. Apparently, it was a rare brew, only made in small batches in the Isles of Kandar. Something about the logistics of shipping it to the "far corners of Alympia" made it difficult to get here.

After Genotl rang up our total, my father paid, and we were homeward bound. He remained silent, so I concentrated on the beautiful scenery as I drove. The majestic trees' large red trunks lined the road, creating a forest wall in almost every direction. Their bluish-green leaves had barely broken free from their buds with the change of season.

We pulled onto our dirt road. It had rained heavily last night, so a path of mud lay between us and the house. The Singine, however, came equipped to handle such terrain. I turned the dial on the dashboard, engaging all of the vehicle's six wheels.

Mud flew everywhere while the Singine effortlessly adjusted to keep us moving. As the wipers cleared the windshield I could see my mother waiting for us on the porch with a smile. She swept her blonde hair over her shoulder as my father gave her a quick kiss.

I made a gagging noise, and my mother laughed, "Oh, don't be dramatic."

"Me? Dramatic?"

She dismissed me with a playful wave nd turned to Dad. "Did you get the Telr Root?"

My father stopped smiling and looked down at his feet. "No."

"Ettias! That's the whole reason you went into town."

"Sorry. I'll just get some when I pick up Parnikus."

"What am I going to do with you? Your memory is deteriorating with age."

"Well, I can think of a few things that are still pretty good." He winked and pulled her in close.

My face crinkled in disgust. "Would you two please get a room?"

My father grinned wickedly. "We have one. Right above yours."

Ari rounded the corner of the house and stopped when she saw us. Her clothes and hair were covered in mud.

I laughed. "What happened to you?"

"I don't want to talk about it," she said sullenly.

Mom gasped when she saw the mess. "Oh, sweetie! Go get cleaned up." She paused, then turned her gaze to me. "And you, go change into something nicer, please."

I looked down at my clothes, then back to her. "What's wrong with what I'm wearing?"

"Nothing, if you plan on never dating."

"Isn't this a family party? Wouldn't it be kinda disgusting if I found someone here to date?"

"Zaelek!"

"What? I'm just saying…."

"I'll have you know I invited quite a few people over, including Tiane, so no, this isn't just a family gathering."

"Mom! Why didn't you tell me sooner?!"

I rushed into the house. Clothes flew from my closet in my search for nicer ones. When I had found an outfit, I looked at myself in the mirror. My hair swept upward in a tidy fashion. A brown leather vest and a tan shirt with blue pants—the outfit my mom said brought out the gold in my brown eyes. As I fussed with the buttons on the shirt, I realized that it disappointed me that Kinara wouldn't be here tonight. If only she would just stay a few days more.

I shook my head. What was I thinking? She needed time to grieve and process, not to deal with *my* feelings, which in that moment were purely selfish.

There was a knock on the open door and I turned to find Parnikus leaning casually against the frame.

"What's up, little brother?" he said with a smirk as he surveyed my outfit.

His shorter-than-usual, flaming red hair surprised me.

"When did you get here?"

"Just a couple of minutes ago, I'm surprised you didn't hear the ruckus Mom was making."

"I guess I was a little distracted."

He chuckled. "Let me guess, Mom invited Tiane."

"How did you know?"

"Since when do you dress up and mess with your hair?"

"That's fair." He knew me too well. "How's school?"

"Better than expected," he laughed. "But I'll tell you about it later. I gotta go say hi to the other two."

Parnikus went across the hall to Ben's room, allowing me the perfect opportunity to slip away and get the gift I had for him. I'd kept it a secret, wanting to surprise him when he returned home. He would love it.

I ran downstairs to the back door and grabbed my coat. My mother poked her head out of the kitchen when she heard me. "Where are you off to?"

"I'm going to the barn. I need to get Parnikus' gift."

"Well, stay out of the mud and be quick about it. Our guests are about to arrive, and I need you to help me set the snacks out."

"I won't be long, promise."

I opened the back door and jogged toward the barn. Clouds covered the two full moons, but the yard's vibrant lights and a thick layer of gravel kept me from mucking up my boots. I lifted the wooden latch that barred the massive doors, their hinges creaking as they opened.

The barn was empty. My father hadn't called the kilindrels in yet. He liked to leave them out to pasture as long as possible, deeming it unfair for them to be cooped up inside, but now I wondered if that was because of Caspien.

I hurried to the stall used for storage, having to wade through a mountain of farming tools to get to my hiding spot. Dust flew when I pulled off the blanket covering my treasured gifts. I scooped up the wrapped sword and the polished, dark red, wooden box containing a set of beautifully crafted throwing knives.

With the items tucked under my arm, I sprinted back across the yard to the edge of the forest, placing the gifts at the base of a big tree where we'd built ourselves a tree house when we were kids. At just the right moment, right before we set off the fireworks, I would present them to Parnikus.

"Oh good, just in time," Mom said when I returned. "Come grab this pot of stew."

"I thought you said they were snacks?"

"Okay, so there's a little more . Big deal. Get in here."

I shook my head in disbelief. My mother was always trying to fatten up everyone who came through the door, I swear. I grabbed the stew and placed it on the set table next to the bowls. Hopefully, Mom wouldn't nitpick my placement of it like she usually did.

My father drew back a curtain in the dining room and peered out, "It looks like our guests are…Maialyn,can you come here for a second?"

Parnikus, Ben, and Ari joined us in the dining area.

Parn looked at Dad with worry, "Everything all right, Pops?"

Still holding one of the empty platters, Mom joined Dad, and watched the headlights coming down the road. Then the dish dropped to the ground, shattering.

"Ettias, how did they find us?"

"Get our swords," my father said.

A blast of air rushed past me and I heard, "Kids, stay inside," as my mother disappeared.

Mom rejoined us, swords in hand. She tossed one to my father, and he drew it from its sheath. Swirling shadows slowly danced across the blade's dark blue metal.

A man's voice called from the front yard, "Cronus, a moment if you would."

My father cursed, then stepped out onto the porch. From the window my siblings and I watched the stranger with brown, shoulder-length hair

"Get off my property, Savvage," said Dad.

Savvage? As in Trentir Savvage? Was the man responsible for so much death standing on our property talking to my father like they knew each other? What business could he possibly have with us?

Savvage stroked his well-groomed beard and smiled. "It's time to come home."

"I have no interest in helping your organization with its twisted agenda."

What? This *is Dad's home. Why would Savvage say differently?*

"I wasn't asking."

My father brought his blade up so fast I didn't see it. Sparks shot all over the deck as he held Savvage in a sword lock. *I didn't even see Savvage move! How did he close that much space so quickly?*

Savvage grinned wickedly. "It seems you haven't lost your touch after all these years."

My father surged forward, shoulder checking Savvage and sending him flying. Savvage skidded across the grass, then stood tall. Troops swarmed out of the transports parked in our driveway as my mother void bounded forward and locked swords with the man.

Savvage punched her in the face, catapulting her back toward the house. My father caught her in his arms, absorbing most of the energy behind the attack. Seeing Savvage strike my mother sent a heat wave of rage through me, but I knew I would just get in the way if I acted on the feeling. Dad would avenge Mom.

A soldier raised his hand, and half of the garden rose into the air. He extended his palm, and the huge chunk of ground hurtled toward the house.

My father jumped into the path and sliced the projectile. It turned to mud at his touch and fell to the ground, creating a small berm between Savvage and us. *He made that look so easy!* This had to be the power of an Alpha and why they were so revered.

Dad reached toward the man who'd launched the attack. The soldier screamed as dark red liquid poured from every pore in his body to form blood icicles. My father snapped his fingers. To my horror, the shards exploded outward, shredding the man and the two soldiers next to him to pieces.

Savvage turned to his troops and shouted, "Bring the kids to me. Alive."

Mom stepped in. “You won’t lay a hand on them.”

Savvage launched another attack, slamming his blade into my father’s while pivoting to kick my mother in the stomach. Her body struck the wall next to us, causing the entire dining room wall to collapse. She picked herself up and shook her head to clear the hair from her face.

I ran to her, “Mom!”

She pushed me aside gently. “Don’t worry about me, I’ve had far worse. Go, get out of here, now!”

“What’s happening?”

“Parnikus, get them out.”

Parnikus rounded us up and pushed us out the back door while my mother composed herself. The smell of sulfur permeated the air, and I knew Mom’s volves would soon join the battle.

We barely made it outside before the entire house exploded. The blast sent us flying nearly to the barn before we hit the ground. I covered my face as purple flames shot everywhere. *This is insane!* Having no weapons to fight back with didn’t help the gripping panic forming within me.

Sparks danced in circles around us before my father and Savvage settled a few feet away. I couldn’t even see them moving because of their speed. A purple ball of flames landed on Ari’s leg. She screamed.

My father’s shrieking whistle pierced the night. Caspien, Dad’s kilindrel, emerged from the tree line, its six sturdy legs rippling as he ran. Caspien’s body transformed into blue, semi-transparent liquid. His thick red mane became a cascading waterfall as he ran to Ari’s side and used his mane to extinguish the flames.

Savvage laughed with delight. “You know, you are the only person on this planet that has put out my flames, so far.”

My father slammed his fist into Savvage’s cheek with a nasty right hook, then they disappeared. They reappeared a few hundred feet away with my father on top of Savvage. Savvage rolled backward and kicked up, sending my father into the air. Sparks once again lit up the night sky, and I looked to where the farmhouse once sat.

My mother was keeping Savvage’s entire force at bay. Rocks and other debris flew in a dizzying array of attacks, leaving flames, puddles, and ground chunks everywhere. One of Mom's volves had seized a trooper, ripping his flesh to ribbons with his sizable claws and teeth before moving to his next victim.

Parnikus grabbed the back of my shirt and rushed us toward the tree line. A man blocked our path and readied a ball of water between his hands. Caspien got between us, snorting angrily.

The man screamed, "Stupid Kilindrel! Get out of my way!" He launched water at the animal, but when it touched Caspien's liquid hide, it absorbed into his body. Caspien tapped the ground with his hoof. A monstrous tidal wave rose from the ground and engulfed the man, taking the barn with it. The water stopped its forward momentum, then rose into the air, creating a perfectly still ball.

Caspien whinnied, and the ball spun rapidly around the man. A whirlpool formed over the attacker's head, creating a small bubble of air. Without warning, all the debris caught in the vortex ripped through the man's body from every direction. Blood filled the water, blending into a deep scarlet hue. The sphere fell to the ground, leaving bits of the man scattered about with the rest of the debris.

An explosion from the forest threw us all back into the conflict. I picked myself up from the stone path, desperately searching for my mother and father. Mom appeared in front of me, flooding me with relief. *We're safe.* I started to move closer to her but froze when a sword with no visible wielder pierced her chest, stopping only when its cross-guard reached her breasts. Mom gingerly placed her hand on my cheek and smiled. The sword shattered into a million sparkling pieces that floated to the ground. Blood seeped from the corners of her mouth as she fell, and in the distance, I heard my father call out to her. The two volves next to her howled in agony before exploding into wisps of smoke and sparkling motes that slowly drifted to the ground.

I couldn't make a sound as grief stole my breath. Savvage took the opportunity amidst the merciless chaos to plunge his blade through Father's chest. Instantly, Dad appeared a few feet from my mother's lifeless body, seemingly unconcerned with his own wound. He crawled toward her, but Savvage shoved him into the mud with his boot.

Savvage removed his blade, "Stay down."

Dad tried to push himself up but collapsed with his eyes shut.

Parnikus bellowed with rage and charged. Before he'd moved more than two feet, Savvage shoved his face into the ground so fast that he probably didn't know what hit him.

Savvage turned to his troops. "I think our Etas can handle taking the three boys into custody, yes?"

One man stepped forward. "Yes, Sir."

"Excellent! The rest of you, with me. We've planning to do."

As he passed Ari, he drove his blade through her stomach, never bothering to even glance in her direction. A sharp pain in my own stomach that took my breath away. I watched her silver moon pendant fall to the mud as the light left her eyes. She hit the ground with a gentle *thud*. A sudden emptiness in my soul left me hollow as a world of loneliness set in. What would I do without my twin, the only person that truly understood me?

It wasn't a fight after that. We were so distraught that we lost the will to even stand. The men dragged us to the transports and bound us with rope to a tailgate.

Before loading the three of us, the guards decided to have a celebratory smoke while they laughed about how "epic" the battle was, Parnikus leaned over to me and whispered. "Ben and I are going to cause a distraction. Once we do, run."

I looked at him with disbelief. "What? No way! If anyone should go, it should be Ben. He's the youngest!"

"You're the one who knows the forest. Ben and I are both bigger than you. We can probably hurt a couple of these goons before they realize you're gone."

"Parn…"

"No! Listen to me. In my left pocket, there's a knife. Grab it." He lifted his hip close enough for me to grab the knife. I furiously sawed at my rope restraint until it snapped. He sighed with relief. "Okay, cut us loose. Hurry, they're coming back."

Their bindings snapped just as a couple of men rounded the corner. Parnikus and Ben tackled them to the ground. My brothers beat them senseless, but one managed to cry out for backup.

I wanted to help, but Ben shoved me away, "Get out of here!"

My feet pounded against the ground as I ran into the forest. All I had to do was get far enough into the woodland and onto a game trail, but the light from the two full moons was diminished by the thick canopy above. It barely allowed me to see five feet in front of me and I stumbled when my foot struck something in the path. To my surprise, Parnikus' gift box of throwing knives had tripped me. Sloppily, I cinched the leather belt holding the knives to my waist, feeling around afterward for the accompanying sword. It wasn't here, but there was no time to look for it. I had to move; they would be searching for me by now.

I wanted to go back for my brothers, but knew it would be futile. I could almost hear Parnikus' lecture if the Javelar caught me after they'd worked so hard to get me out. With a heavy heart, I forced myself away from my defeated family.

I paused briefly at the edge of a cliff that overlooked the farm. The fire burning my demolished home still lit up the land around it. I had to get to safety before I could rest. With one last look, I turned and moved back into my forest sanctuary.

Movement caught my eye; someone ran toward me on the trail. They had discovered me.

15

At the trucks beside the smoking Khiings Estate...

The air left my lungs as a man's boot slammed into my stomach, and a suffocating cramp took hold of my guts. I gasped, bracing myself for the captor's next kick.

"Parnikus!" Ben shouted.

"Stop!" the only female called. "He wants them in one piece!"

The gathered group backed off, leaving two others to haul Ben and me to our feet. I looked to the forest, seeing no trace of Zaelek. He was gone. *Good.*

"Wait. Weren't there three of them?" the largest man in the group asked.

I suppressed my grin. *Nothing you can do now. He's long gone*. Our distraction had worked, even if it had only bought Sparky a couple minutes. A couple minutes were all Zaelek needed to put some distance between us. I remembered spending some time with him in the forest, and his innate knowledge of the surrounding landscape astounded me. I told myself he'd be okay.

"Mercy's breath! Savvage is going to kill us all if we don't get him back."

"I'll go get him," said the big man.

"No," the woman replied. "Sevil is the fastest. He should go."

"But…."

"I said no!" she turned to the lankiest man of the group. "Go get him."

Sevil nodded. "Yes, Ma'am."

"The rest of you get the other two in the truck."

The men shoved us toward the cargo hold. Wide-eyed, Ben dug his heels into the ground and looked at me. I shook my head. The last thing we needed was to make them angrier. Ben relaxed, probably under the misconception that I had another plan to get us out. I didn't. Aside from jumping out of a moving truck, I had run out of ideas.

One man pressed his blade against Ben's neck while another bound us to the vehicle's interior. They both jumped out as the engine roared to life.

The angry woman approached. "What are you two doing? Get back in there!"

"Aren't we supposed to be using the gas? I don't want to be in there when it pops."

"I don't care what you want. We're picking up a few more recruits in the next town over. You don't want Savvage to know you lost all three of them, do you?"

"No, ma'am."

The two men loaded back up, taking seats next to Ben and me. I cursed under my breath. If they had been stupid enough to leave us alone, I maybe could've come up with another idea.

As the vehicle began to move the grim realization set in that the only two family members I had left to look after were Zaelek and Ben. Zaelek had escaped into the forest, but there was no guarantee that he wouldn't be captured by that Sevil guy. Dad would always tell me, "If something ever happens to me, it's your responsibility to look after your mother and the kids."

Ben sat across from me, but the future looked bleak for both of us, so what had I accomplished? Everything had fallen apart in the last hour. "I'm not ready for this task, Dad," I whispered. Some days, it felt like he put too much faith in me, even if I was twenty-four-year-old. With his newly uncovered secret life, how could I protect my family from this kind of danger? I'm not strong enough.

I took a deep breath and tried to get out of my head. These thoughts weren't going to help me out of this. There would be time to feel sorry for myself later. Ben needed me to look out for him. I could do this.

Though I recited the words, I didn't know if I believed them. This Javelar seemed to have no place for compassion in their ranks. The fear racing through me refused to let up. There was so much we didn't know. I'd still called Mom and Dad every day for advice. How could I get through this without their guidance? My chest and back stiffened.

Ben was going to be looking for answers. I didn't have any.

16

In Coltown...

I paced the stained carpet of the small hotel room. The Coltown shopkeeper had instructed me to wait there because Zaelek's stupid training sword had been shipped to another facility. The shopkeeper took those keys from me hours ago, and he still hadn't come back. At this rate, I'd be lucky to get home by tomorrow evening.

I cursed my luck. If I had to stay here overnight.... To make matters worse, the hours of loneliness had been filled with off and on grieving, leaving me wishing that the pain would go away or even ease up a little.

A knock at the door provided a distraction from my misery. I looked through the peephole, saw the shopkeeper, opened the door.

"As promised," he said, handing me the sword.

I took the blade and thanked him. Curiosity got the better of me, and I pulled the sword from its sheath. The gray blade glimmered, curving gently from grip to its tip. Strange symbols, similar to what had been on Maialyn's sword, flowed down the sides. However, the oddest feature was the sword's cross-guard. The top of the guard followed the blade's gentle curve toward the tip, but the bottom ran toward the pommel. I couldn't help but wonder what kind of training sword was built like this?

I sheathed the blade and strapped it to my back beside mine. If I hurried, I could still make the midnight transport to Alympus. It would put me back a few hours, but I would be standing in my apartment before noon tomorrow, preparing for Alator's funeral.

The taxi service pulled onto the dirt road leading to the Khiings estate around eight-thirty that evening. *Maybe I'll get to see Parnikus after all.* Ettias should have picked him up by now and the party would be in full swing. I could play it off that I'd simply arrived late.

The taxi broke through the tree line, but no house lights were on. *Strange, I could have sworn the party was here.* The headlights turned toward the house, and I gasped.

Pillars of smoke rose from what was left of the farmhouse. Bodies, weapons, rocks, shards of metal, building materials, and other debris littered the ground. "Mercy's breath," I muttered. *What in Styx happened and where are the Khiings? There's no way they'd lost this fight, so they have to be here somewhere.*

An old military-style truck sat on the property's edge, and the three men huddling next to it approached.

I looked at the driver. "Go get help. I don't think these guys are local militia."

I focused on the area behind the tailgate of the truck, then teleported. The brisk night air flowed across my skin as I materialized, and smoke assaulted my nose.

"State your business," one man barked as he confronted the taxi driver.

"I was told to pick up a client here."

"We've escorted everyone off the property. Go back to town."

The driver didn't argue, he turned and sped away.

The man to the left huffed. "How'd we get stuck babysitting the rubble while Sevil hunts down the kid? Tell you what, if he doesn't bring the boy back before morning, Savvage is going to be furious."

Savvage? If these guys are working for him...Javelar! Anger seeped through me. I teleported behind the rear guard and drove my sword through his spinal cord while blasting the man next to him with a white-hot jet of flames. The smell of burning hair and charred flesh overtook my senses. I wrenched my sword from the first man and pressed its blood-soaked edge against the remaining guard's neck.

With curled fingers, I willed a small flame into existence, feeling its warmth dance across my palm. The orange light illuminated his face, and I recognized him. This was the man who had wielded the whip used on Alator. Without hesitation, I slit his throat.

Killing him didn't make me feel better, but at least the world had three fewer scumbags in it. I calmed my breathing and closed my eyes. Mercy's breath, I thought as I realized I should have interrogated him. I had let my feelings get the better of me, and now I wouldn't know what had happened here.

Before searching elsewhere, I dug through the wreckage around the ruined guest room. I knew my bag had survived this fire. It had been specially designed to withstand the heat of my element.

My backpack's strap poked out from a debris pile under one of the support beams. I pulled it out and dusted it off. Now to find the Khiings.

Movement near what was left of the barn startled me, and I cautiously made my way toward the shadowy lumps on the ground. As I drew closer, I recognized who lay before me.

"Ettias! Maialyn!" I shouted, running to them.

"Kinara," Ettias said weakly. "Zaelek needs your help."

"Is Maialyn…" I stared at her blood-soaked dress. Shock, sorrow, and confusion hit me all at once.

His voice quivered, and he looked over at his wife with so much sadness that my heart broke for him.

"No, she's gone."

"What happened?!"

"Javelar…. Listen to me, you need to tell Khendrig that Savvage is an Alpha."

My heart raced. "An Alpha? Are you sure?"

"Yes, now go! Zaelek needs you."

"I can't just leave you here like this!"

Headlights coming up the dirt road breached the tree line.

"Quickly," Ettais said. "He went east up the ridgeline." When I hesitated, he grabbed my wrist. "That's an order!"

A Whisper of Wind

I teleported to the edge of the field behind the ruined barn and initiated a void bound, letting the wind wipe away the tears rolling down my cheeks. Finding Zaelek in the forest would be challenging enough, but in the dark? I wasn't sure even a seeker would be able to pull this off.

17

A few miles into the woods behind Khiings Estate...

I forced my weary body through the massive forest. *Come on, Zaelek, keep going*. But my knees hit the ground as I succumbed to fatigue. Every drawn breath sent sharp pains through my lungs. I hoped my pursuer was far enough behind me that I could rest, even for a moment. My eyes burned and were heavy from lack of sleep.

Sunlight glistened off the early morning dew below me. Carabells chirped from somewhere high in the branches above, and the morning breeze brought relief to my sweat-drenched body. I glanced down at the throwing knives strapped around my waist and allowed my clouded mind to wander.

An object flew past my face.

I launched to my feet, stumbling over the tangled undergrowth before scrambling behind a nearby fallen tree. *Mercy's breath!* He was closer than I thought!

I readied two throwing knives and braced for an attack. Several moments passed in terrifying silence. The knives' polished surfaces glinted in the sunlight, and I realized they could serve as makeshift mirrors. Cautiously, I held one blade out past the end of the tree. There was nothing except for the forest in their reflection. Whoever this guy was, he knew how to stay hidden.

Something knocked the knife out of my hand, sending sparks showering across the needle-littered forest floor. I yelped, as I snatched my hand back.

My knife and a metal disc the size of a tea plate lay beside me, just outside the cover of the tree. I listened for any disturbances, too frightened to move. Should I reach out and grab the weapons? I took a deep breath, and snatched them up.

The disc seemed weightless. Its surface held a dull shine and had been polished to extraordinary smoothness. I carefully slid the edge down my arm, watching as it shaved off the hair. The disc would sever a wrist if thrown even at a casual speed. As fast as the man had thrown it, I worried that the decaying tree behind me wouldn't stop a weapon like this. There had to be something else to take cover behind.

My gaze fell on a large boulder twenty feet away. The attacker most likely had prepared another disc, so running at this point would be suicide. An idea came to me: What if I trick him into attacking, then run while he readies another projectile? How would I get him to launch one, though?

I wriggled out of my jacket and found a stick. After tying the cloth to it, I eased it out, allowing the light coat to be partially exposed. A disc went through it, and I ran for the stone. Not wanting to lose one of my own knives, I twisted to the right and hurled the assailant's weapon. The disc flew off target. However, when he stepped out, it veered into his hand, surprising both of us.

The man let loose a string of curses as I dove behind the stone. For a moment, I looked down at my hands in confusion. It seemed like the disc knew where it needed to go. I didn't have time to think, I needed to run. The man's injury to his throwing hand would hinder his ability, and he would have to catch up to kill me. I started a void bound.

I still wasn't used to navigating while bounding, so I used it in bursts through straight stretches. My plan worked until a nearby cliff forced me to stop. I peered over the edge and squinted at the sunlight shimmering off the still surface of a lake. If I jumped, I just might have a chance of escaping.

My assailant grabbed my arm and pulled me away from the

edge. "You know, I was just going to capture you and take you back to the truck, but you messed that up, kid."

His fist slammed my stomach, taking my breath away. As I hunched over, he brought his knee up and caught me in the nose, sending me back toward the cliff edge. I reached up and covered my aching nose with my hands. Blood seeped through my fingers.

He kicked my stomach repeatedly. I tried to defend myself, but his attacks were too fast to block. The taste of blood filled my mouth as the assault continued. Just when I thought it would never end, he backed away. I got to my hands and knees, crawling toward the cliff edge. With one last kick to my face, he sent me over.

Stinging pain shredded through my back when I hit the water, forcing me to suck in a mouthful of the lake. I choked for a moment, then everything was suddenly peaceful. The sun broke through the surface of the water, illuminating the ripples above as I sank. It wasn't so bad. At least down here there was no Javelar, no assassins with disc blades, just the cool embrace of Dad's element. The surface shattered as someone dove through and followed the trail of my blood.

I could see blonde hair and a green shirt. *Mom?* The woman wrapped her arms around me, her soft hands much more delicate than my mother's.

Kinara had come to my rescue.

18

In the back of a truck. Location unknown…

The morning sun peeked through the dark clouds, casting golden rays of light toward the horizon. Our transport rocked violently, jarring me from my stupor.

"To Styx with these potholes!" The driver's muffled shout carried from the cab. "What does the engineering crew do all day? Tend to the Fields of Persephone?"

Parnikus righted himself, moving away from the older man next to him and trying to shake the confusion from his mind. I was trying to understand what had happened when the memory of being sealed into the cargo hold and gassed surged into my consciousness. I could've sworn that my throat still suffered from what felt like glass shards being crammed down it.

The transport made one final sharp turn and came to a stop, releasing a deep sigh of air. I didn't want to get out. None of us had an inkling of what awaited us beyond the safety of this truck, and that terrified me. Only a small snapshot of a vast weed-filled field was visible through the opened flaps at the rear of the vehicle. My head throbbed, and my mind still felt foggy, but that didn't stop half-formed questions from plaguing me.

Two more trucks passed by before I felt my restraints loosen from outside. The woman I recognized from last night dropped the tailgate, then stepped back.

"Everyone out," she barked.

Once Parnikus and I jumped down, a line of guards pushed us into a large brick warehouse where at least a hundred other captives were massed together in the room's center. *Mercy's breath!* Why did they need so many people? Were they building an army? My stomach churned, and sweat trickled down my spine.

A man with long, dirty-looking blond hair in an incoming group struggled against two guards who gripped his arms. "You can't do this!" he glared at those of us standing in the circle. "Come on, you cowards! Fight!"

"Enough!" a man's voice boomed from above.

Everyone in the room stopped moving, suddenly silenced. I located the commanding voice's source: a thin man, who couldn't be older than thirty, stood on a cargo crate near the large metal door opposite us.

His pale-yellow eyes zeroed in on the long-haired man. "Release him."

The guards swapped worried glances but followed the order.

"What are you doing, Gliv?" the woman from our transport asked. She was obviously irritated by the distraction

"Instructing."

He stepped off the crate and landed on the ground with a soft thud. I was surprised he didn't break every bone in his body. He looked so fragile.

"We don't have time for this," she said, impatient.

"There's always time to instill discipline."

Uncertainty and wide eyes had replaced the long-haired man's look of determination. Gliv stalked toward him, letting a muffled cough loose into his arm.

"Bleeding bioresin addicts," one guard muttered.

I'd heard about that before. Zaelek had told us over dinner that one suspect he interrogated was addicted to it. It explained what this guy's problem was.

A hunk of ice encased the long-haired man's legs.

Gliv sneered. "What's your name?"

"H-handall," the man stuttered.

"Well, H-handall," Gliv's voice mimicked Handall's voice and stutter perfectly. "What do you think we do with traitors who incite rebellion?"

"I…I don't know."

"That's right. You don't know. You don't know a thing about this organization, so what did you think was going to happen when you were shooting your mouth off? A heroic battle for your freedom?"

The Javelar personnel chuckled amongst themselves. I released the strangled breath trapped in my throat. Hearing Gliv's question made *me* feel stupid, and I wasn't even the target of his ire.

Gliv manifested a shard of ice in his hand before shooting it into Handall's leg. Handall screamed so loudly and with so much pain that my stomach rolled, threatening to spill the measly amount of food left in it. I flinched as another ice shard entered Handall's other leg, bringing with it a fresh new wave of screams.

"You see, H-handall, I'd be willing to wager that over half of this group don't have the Guardian gene, let alone have an element unlocked yet. Even if they did, I'm certain they wouldn't know how to use it. I'd also like to remind you that every Javelar soldier in this room has extensive elemental training. So, I ask again, what did you think was going to happen given that information?"

Another icicle passed through the meaty area between Handall's peck and shoulder, but this one differed from the rest. Gliv pulled his arm back like he still held the ice, and the newly formed ice hook embedded in Handall's ribs. Blood bubbled from his lips.

"Answer me!" Gliv shouted.

"I wasn't thinking! I'm sorry! It won't happen again!"

Gliv closed the gap between them and kicked him so hard that the chunk of ice around his legs shattered, allowing him to skip across the room. However, before Handall hit the opposing wall, Gliv yanked him back with the ice hook.

A familiar male voice reverberated from the walls. "Enough, Gliv. I think they get the point."

Gliv froze mid-swing. "Yes, Sir."

I saw Savvage leaning against the sixth wheel of a broken-down rover. The memory of him plunging his blade into my father surged through my mind, and I planted my foot on the ground to keep me from charging him. *Pull yourself together, Ben. You wouldn't even make it ten feet before they stopped you.*

"You two," he pointed, "Get this bloody mess out of my sight. Take him to the infirmary or something."

My revenge would have to wait until I stood a chance against him, though, how long that would be, I couldn't say. But I vowed the time would come.

19

On the shore of an unknown lake…

Kinara rolled me onto my side, allowing me to cough up the water in my lungs and gasp for air.

She let out a relieved breath. “Don’t scare me like that.”

I rolled onto my back, taking deep breaths as the sun beat down on my face. “How did you find me?”

“I’m a Seeker. It’s kind of my thing.”

“A what?”

“You’ll learn about job classes later. Come on, we need to get out of here.”

She extended her hand and helped me to my feet. I noticed two swords strapped to her back.

“What’s up with the extra sword?”

“Your dad sent me to get this training sword for you yesterday.”

The overwhelming pain of loss surged again, leaving me breathless. This sword was his final gift to me. She unstrapped the weapon and held it out to me.

“I…I don’t think I can,” I said.

“What do you mean?”

"I don't think I can take that sword." I didn't know how to explain to her that the sword would be a constant reminder of how much I missed my family.

"When I lost my parents, I considered throwing out their sword rack. I used to stare at it for hours, thinking about everything they had taught me. One night, I couldn't take it anymore. I figured once it was gone, their words would stop haunting me."

"Did you destroy it?"

"No. Before I could light the fire, I realized something. No matter what I did, everything would still remind me of them. The park with the small swing set they once pushed me on, the dessert shop down the road from the Academy, the library where my mom took me to get my first book. There was no way I could destroy everything that sparked a memory of them.

"So I sat there, looking at that beautiful sword rack. I couldn't bear to think about how hurt they would have been if I destroyed it when they were still alive. Now, it sits in my front room and reminds me of how excited they were when they first brought it home. I learned to celebrate their lives rather than dwell on their deaths." She held the sword to my chest until I wrapped my arms around it. "This is your legacy, Zaelek. Don't let it slip through your fingers."

Away from Zaelek...

I had put some distance between myself and Zaelek, not wanting to give my report of his parents' deaths in front of him. Though Ettias had been alive when I left him, his wounds were so extensive that he couldn't have survived much longer. It was a miracle he'd lasted as long as he did.

Once out of earshot, I rummaged through my backpack until I found my R.E.A.P.E.R.. I pressed on its singular eye and the palm-sized metal sphere shuddered to life.

"Drone, initiate contact with Colonel Voelker."

The device rose and hovered above my head. A low hum sounded as it confirmed the request.

My Uncle answered, “Good morning. Are you holding up?”

“Not very well, Uncle Khendrig.”

“I figured as much. Did you make your flight back to Creet?”

“No. I’m still in Alympia.”

“What? Was there a delay?”

With a slight pause, I uttered, “Ettias and Maialyn are dead.”

I heard my uncle’s roller chair shoot away from his desk sa he shouted, “What?!”

“Javelar attacked them last night.”

A moment passed before he muttered, “How in Styx did Javelar find them? And why didn’t you contact me immediately?”

“I was preoccupied by attempting to save Zaelek from one of Savvage’s goons.”

“What about the rest of the kids?”

“They weren’t there when I arrived.”

Uncle Kehndrig cursed. “Anything else?”

“Ettias wanted me to tell you Savvage is an Alpha.”

My uncle paused. “I have to inform the Council right away. Your mission is to escort Zaelek to Creet. I want to speak to him in person. Get him gear in Tendir first, then head west. Don’t go through any major cities after that.”

The call ended abruptly. That answered my question of what to do with Zaelek. How could I possibly get him out of the country quickly while avoiding major cities? I groaned just thinking about the amount of walking we were going to do.

When I got back to Zaelek, he was gingerly touching his nose.

“Zaelek,” I called out.

“What?”

“Come on.”

He cocked his head to the side. “What’s up?”

“The Colonel wants me to take you to the nearest supply depot and hook you up with some gear…not that you’ll need it. We’re just going to Tendir, and from there, we’ll take a Volishka Transport to the nearest airfield.

“An airfield, why?”

“He wants to talk to you in person. Whatever this is we’ve gotten ourselves into, we now have the attention of a Guardian Forces Colonel.”

"But…"

I held up my finger and turned to head west. "No buts. I have my orders."

Zaelek trailed me like a volf pup after its mother.

20

Approaching Tendir…

After two hours of clumsily bounding through the forest, Kinara gave in to my begging and stopped for a rest. The short nap I took didn't help much, but it provided enough energy to get me to the outskirts of Tendir.

Massive buildings stretched toward the sky, surrounded by thousands of different structures. Highways bustled with too many vehicles to count, and the streets were alive with all kinds of activities. We entered a crowded plaza on the outskirts. My eyes were on a massive tower so when Kinara halted I walked right into her.

"Why'd you stop?" I asked.

She pointed at the large screen on the side of a building. A picture of me took up the entire monitor with "Wanted" underneath it.

"We need to get you out of sight." Kinara pulled me into the alley and faced me toward the wall.

"Stay."

She disappeared, then returned, holding a white cloak which she held out to me.

I took the heavy garment and looked at it with despair. "I'm going to roast in this!"

"Stop complaining and put it on. We can't have anyone noticing you."

I took the cloak, slipped it over my head and pulled up the rough hood.

"What about my sword?"

"It's fine. People won't think twice about seeing two Guardians walking down the street. It's not uncommon for us to pass through this city."

"I'm not a Guardian."

"They won't know that."

She guided me back onto the street. I kept my eyes to the ground and followed, catching the smell of cooking meat, and remembering how long it had been since I'd eaten.

"Can we grab something to eat?"

"Are you kidding?"

"I feel like I haven't eaten in days." I paused, "Please?"

"All right, fine," she said reluctantly. "We have to be quick about it, though."

Kinara led the way to a small food vendor stationed between two large buildings. She ordered two parnums and drinks for both of us.

The vendor handed us each a plate with an odd piece of deep-fried bread on it.

I looked at Kinara. "What is it?"

She fished out drinks from the ice chest next to the counter. "You've never had a parnum before? Do you live under a rock?"

Kinara pointed to it, obviously wanting me to try it. It certainly smelled wonderful. I picked it up and took a bite. My mouth opened, and I breathed out, trying to relieve my burning tongue.

"Hot!"

She laughed and rolled her eyes, then took a bite of her own scalding parnum. "Baby."

How could she not be affected by the molten cheese? She had to have a mouth made of metal.

Ten minutes later, we entered what appeared to be an herb shop. Not a single customer picked through its goods, and I wondered why Kinara would stop to do some shopping when she had just hassled me about eating.

Kinara greeted the clerk. "Good afternoon, Sir. We were wondering if you had any *sentient* oils?"

The clerk smiled. "Identification, please."

"Four-three-seven-two."

"One moment." The man checked a small screen on the counter. "Ah, yes, here it is. It looks like the authorization for your guest came through as well. Follow me."

We followed the shopkeeper into the back room and stopped at a large counter against the wall. He placed his hand on the countertop, then stepped back. It split in the middle to reveal a staircase leading down. The door at the bottom led to a a metal-walled room.

As the door closed behind us a female voice said, "Kinara, it's been a while."

Kinara smiled. "Too long if you ask me. Zaelek, this is Admari. She's the Quartermaster here."

"Nice to meet you," I said.

Admari's red bangs bounced as she nodded to me. "Likewise. Now, all I need is your boot size."

Admari retrieved the items and had me try the boots to ensure they fit before asking me to sign a form stating I would return everything when I got to the Academy.

Admari turned to Kinara while I laced up my boots. "I have a bit of bad news."

Kinara eyed her apprehensively. "What?"

"With all this Javelar activity, more Guardians are deployed than I can supply, and I don't have any Reaper Spheres left. Someone drew my last one two days ago."

"What's a Reaper Sphere?" I asked.

Kinara ignored me. "He doesn't need one. We aren't going that far."

Admari shook her head. "I'm sorry, Kinara, Colonel Voelker ordered a full equip. You'll need to work with a third party to avoid any missing item fees. I heard Galara had some in stock this morning."

Kinara groaned, "You've got to be kidding me. Is *he* the only one that has them?"

"Afraid so."

"Come on, Admari, can't Zaelek just sign for it and get one at the Academy? You know I don't do well with Galara."

"I'm sorry, but rules are rules. I can't send the completed forms until he gets one."

Kinara looked away and huffed. "Fine."

Admari handed me a bulging backpack, Kinara thanked her, and we left.

"Kinara…" I said.

Hearing her name snapped her back. "Hmm?"

"Who is Galara? You don't seem too comfortable with him."

"It's fine. He's just…unpredictable."

By the time we reached our destination, the sun had set behind the sky-piercing buildings, casting a warm light in their shadows as it mixed with the neon signs. Kinara guided me into an alleyway once again and pounded on a rust and graffiti-covered door.

A sickly-looking man with a pale face and yellow eyes answered. I had seen eyes like his a few times while working for law enforcement and knew they were the trademark of someone who had been huffing bioresin. He stuffed his sweat-slicked hands into the pockets of his hooded sweatshirt and looked Kinara up and down.

"Kinara," he sniffed.

"Galara."

"I didn't think your ego would let you stoop low enough to visit Tendir."

"Nice to see you too, resin whore."

"You must be really desperate to be knocking on my door, Princess," he said with a sneer.

Kinara turned to me as she stepped inside. "Stay out here and don't do anything stupid."

I paced the alley, careful to stay out of sight. My thoughts turned to my brothers. Were they okay? Did the Javelar soldiers kill them for orchestrating my escape? I prayed that they were alive and unharmed, wishing there was some way to find out if I should be grieving or planning a rescue mission.

Ari's smiling face flashed across my mind. Again, the crushing loneliness threatened to consume me from the inside. Our relationship had been in a weird place for the last year. Before the sudden change in her demeanor, she always made time to hang around with me and just be a friend. I'd tried to draw out that side of her on a few occasions, but she wasn't receptive to it. This confused and frustrated me. Now, I would never get to see her again, and it broke my heart.

A few minutes passed in emotional agony. The sound of a metal trash can crashing to the ground clanged loudly at the other end of the lane. A group of men struggled with a cornered woman. One assailant twisted her arm behind her back and covered her mouth to muffle her screams while another groped her. The people passing kept their eyes to the ground, not lifting a finger to help her.

Where in Styx was Kinara when I needed her? Should I help the woman, or remain hidden? Dad would never tolerate something like this, and neither should I. I pulled my sword from its sheath and rushed to help her.

When the men saw me storming toward them, they panicked and released the frightened woman. She turned and ran. As I reached them their alarm faded, and one man laughed. "For a second, I thought you were GITF. Though, I guess a real Guardian would have been much quicker."

The other men were equally amused as they surrounded me, drawing their crude, sickle-like swords, the type most street gangs used to declare their support of anarchy. If I remembered right, they called the blades *jeekas.*

Surprised they had called my bluff so quickly, I sloppily slashed at one of them, but my sword clashed against metal. The man I attacked swooped my weapon away, and his jeeka pressed against my throat.

One of the other men shouted, "Wait!"

My assailant's snake-like eyes narrowed, and he looked over his shoulder. "Why?"

"Isn't this the kid on the wanted poster?"

The man pulled a lighter from his pocket and allowed the gentle flame to illuminate my face. He laughed with glee, "Well, I'll be. If we turn him in, we'll be rich." He grabbed my arm and started me toward the street.

Kinara suddenly materialized in front of him and said in a very threatening voice, “Release him.”

“Not a chance, sweetheart.”

“I’ll make you a deal: release him, and I’ll let you leave here in one piece.”

One man rushed her, swinging wildly. Kinara sidestepped, then backhanded the man, causing him to stagger.

“Marken whore!” he screamed and charged again.

Kinara punched the man in the nose with a flaming fist. “This is your last warning. Leave now.”

“Get her,” yelled the man holding me.

Once again, Kinara teleported. Thick, warm liquid sprayed the back of my neck, and the man’s sword fell to the ground as he collapsed. She moved so fast I could barely keep up with her as she annihilated the men.

I backed away from her in terror, stumbling over a trash bin. “You…you killed them!”

She was angry, shouting, “I didn’t have a choice. They would have opened their big mouths, and we can’t let anyone know you’re here. How did they find you?”

“They were assaulting a woman, and I…”

“Tried to help?” Kinara seethed, “I specifically told you not to do anything stupid!”

“I couldn’t just stand by!”

“So what? You thought you’d just pull your training sword and rush to save her? The city is crawling with scavengers much stronger than you. You could have been killed, or worse, captured.” She took a deep breath and composed herself before continuing. “Get in the building. We have to wait for Galara to retrieve that Reaper Sphere.”

I picked myself up off the ground. Anger welled inside me, both at Kinara and at myself. She shoved me through the door to the cluttered shop, then went to take care of the mess she’d made. I looked around while she was out, disgusted by how dusty and grimy the display cases were.

It wasn’t long before she returned and stood by the window watching the streets. While we waited, I thumbed through a few of the archaic looking books near the counter. Every page released the sour scent carried by aged paper.

Nearly thirty minutes passed in silence, and Kinara paced the room. "It shouldn't be taking this long. Something isn't right."

"Maybe he had to take care of another errand ..."

"No, I was very specific." The clinking of keys and voices outside the door interrupted her. She crept the curtain back. "Schleet."

"What?"

"Rogue Guardians. They must be after your bounty."

My eyes widened. "You said we could trust Galara."

"I never said that. Stay here, I'll check the alleyway." Kinara teleported in and out of the room, "They have both doors covered. We need to get to the roof."

I followed her through a door near the back of the room and we ran as fast as we could up the stairs. About halfway up, the door at the bottom of the stairwell burst open. The men called out to their comrades then pursued us. Two men with swords jumped from railing to railing, quickly gaining on us.

Kinara looked down, then grabbed my hand and pulled me over her shoulders.

"What are you doing?" I screamed.

"Saving your life. Now, shut up."

The ground below us rapidly moved away as she jumped. Even though we were moving much faster, the two bounty hunters were still gaining on us. I couldn't see any way we were going to escape.

Just as our pursuers were upon us, Kinara opened the roof access and tossed me through it. She closed the door behind us, reaching into the side pouch of her backpack for a small metal disc. She stuck it to the handle where it began to beep rapidly.

Throwing me over her shoulder again—which made me just as uncomfortable as the first time—she ran to the edge of the rooftop. An explosion erupted behind us, causing the entire roof to collapse. Her feet left the rooftop just as the shock wave hit, propelling us forward.

We hit the adjacent roof and tumbled to the ground. My face skidded across the concrete, taking some skin with it. I covered my face with my hand, attempting to soothe the burning pain, at the same time wondering why things like this kept happening to me.

Kinara looked back, "That won't hold them for long." She grabbed the back of my shirt and hurled me into the air. I screamed as I cleared the roof's edge and fell toward the street below.

Kinara appeared above me, grabbing my shirt again. The world flipped as she rolled us forward, putting my back to the sky. She released a torrent of flame downward, and with a forceful kick, launched me up and over the small concrete wall on the opposite roof. I bounced off the glass rooftop once before coming to a stop.

The glass cracked but didn't cave in, and I sighed with relief. Kinara materialized two feet from me. As soon as her feet touched the glass, it shattered and we fell about fifteen feet, down into an office, before my back slammed into a desk. I groaned in pain.

Kinara pulled me to the exit and into another stairwell. Her hands slammed my chest, and I rolled back over the railing. As I fell, my arms flailing wildly, she combined jumps and teleportation to keep me away from the other rails, then caught me at the ground floor level and put me on my feet.

I looked at her in panic. "Are you trying to kill me?"

"Shut up and put on your hood."

I felt like an infant having to rely on her this much. Regardless, I did as instructed. Kinara flagged down a transportation service outside. She hurried me in.

The driver turned back, "Where to?"

Kinara transferred him a hefty sum of credits, "Tarvel street. Step on it."

The driver nodded and put the vehicle in drive, "What's at the south end for you?"

"My sister just went into labor, so my husband and I told her we'd watch the other kids while she was at the hospital."

My heart fluttered when I heard her refer to me as her husband but I knew I was more like an annoying little brother than a partner.

Within fifteen minutes, we arrived at our destination. Kinara thanked the driver, then I followed her as we made our way to the city limits. From there, we ran as fast as we could into the forest. I stopped her before going any further, "Why didn't we take the cab to the airfield?"

"Because there isn't an airfield in Tendir, and local drivers won't go as far as we need. The only way to get there is a Volishka Rail. We'd definitely get caught waiting around for a railcar."

"So what do we do now?"

"Find a place far enough away from the city to camp."

21

At the Javelar soldier intake facility...

Parnikus and I stood behind a line of twenty or so other captives, awaiting our turn to sit in the makeshift barber chair. It hadn't taken more than thirty seconds to shave off each person's hair as the line moved forward. While we waited I tried to imagine what could two non-Guardian kids could offer an organization like Javelar. My thoughts turned to Zaelek, hoping he'd somehow escaped.

"I said next," the barber closest to me shouted.

A guard shoved me toward the empty chair without saying a word. I sat, not having time to situate myself before what felt like a knife tore across my scalp. Each pass of the clippers brought with it another line of sharp pain. The guards jerked me from the chair and shoved me toward the other newly shorn prisoners. I ran my hand over my bristly head to see if the process had drawn blood but found none.

Two guards standing at the exit grabbed my arms and threw me into a sizable box-like room. More guards pulled me to my feet, escorting me further in. They forced me to kneel next to another captive near the front of the room. Soon, Parnikus fell to his knees beside me.

"You okay, Ben?" he whispered.

I shook my head. "No."

"We have to be strong. We can make it through this."

"I don't know if I want to make it through this."

"Hey, don't talk like that. Everything will work out."

"How do you know?"

"I just do, we…"

One guard called from behind us, "Hey! Keep your mouths shut! This isn't social hour."

We focused on our knees. Parnikus and I knew what would happen if we didn't listen. We'd learned that lesson upon our arrival. Watching that poor long-haired guy get nearly beaten to death for running his mouth held enough terror to keep all of us in line.

The room filled with other prisoners until at least a hundred of us knelt in rows. Time crept by in silence. Somewhere in the crowd of prisoners, the sound of flatulence erupted. Previously, I would have found such a disturbance funny. Not here. Not now.

A group of guards seized a prisoner near the back and dragged him away, leaving a trail of liquid feces behind. Nothing about the situation was funny. That unfortunate man was sick, and they would kill him. It was clear they showed no mercy to the weak and afflicted.

Trentir Savvage entered the room, followed by an unfamiliar woman. He took his place in the center front. "Your processing has ended. However, that doesn't mean you will become part of Javelar's ranks. You must first earn your place among us through combat."

Savvage stepped aside, and the woman addressed us.

"Before I assign you a platoon, we need to unlock your elements." She pointed at the man in the front left. "You. Come here."

Once he stood in front of her, she grasped his wrist and slammed her palm into his forehead. The ground surrounding him turned to ice.

Savvage huffed. "Water class, ice branch."

The woman nodded toward the exit. "Serial number eight-two-two-five-six.... Next!"

An elderly man approached her, and again, she slammed his forehead. Nothing happened.

Savvage rolled his eyes. "This one's a dud."

He pulled his sword from its sheath and lopped the man's

head off. I could feel the room erupt in silent panic. One of the other prisoners ran for the exit but didn't make it more than a few steps before the guards killed him, too.

Despair overtook me. I knew none of us Kiings kids had the Guardian gene. Mom and Dad had told us that when we were growing up. They wouldn't have lied to us about something so important. *We are going to die here.*

Parnikus must have sensed my thoughts. His hand moved to my shoulder. "Calm down."

"But…"

"Keep making noise, and you won't live to even see if you have the gene."

I quieted myself, though inside me the grim wave of dread churned like the sea.

Savvage encased his sword in purple flames, drawing everyone's attention. "Any attempt to flee, resist, or cry out will result in death. Now, give us the next!"

My anxiety grew as a young woman nervously approached. When touched by the other woman, the girl levitated. She was given a number and then dismissed. The line moved faster as more people cycled through. Some made it through; others were killed and thrown onto the growing heap of bodies.

When my turn came, tears filled my eyes. My breath came in shallow spurts as I came to stand in front of the woman. I wished none of this had happened, that I was still in the safety of our farm. Her palm made contact. My worst fear was realized when nothing happened, and Ari's merciless death flashed through my mind. I heard Parnikus cry out as Savvage raised his sword to strike me down. Just before the blade touched me, a monstrous wave of water flung Savvage and the woman back.

I held my breath convinced this was the moment of my death.

Savvage broke out into delighted laughter. "That's what I'm talking about! A pure Aquarian Guardian! I'll be watching you, kid."

The woman called, "Number two-nine-six. Next!"

I made my way to the exit and leaned against the wall for a moment. My heart still raced, and that feeling of doom still consumed me. I peeked around the corner to watch Parnikus. The danger wasn't over yet. If he didn't survive, I didn't know how I would live.

Savvage took a step back before the woman slammed Parnikus' head. Fire exploded around him like a tornado.

Savvage gleefully laughed. "Two pure elements in a row! And an Inferno Guardian, too!"

The woman called Parnikus' number, but before I could congratulate him, someone grabbed my arm and pushed me down the hall to a much smaller room with four reclining leather chairs. Four people with odd-looking devices in their hands sat on a stools next to them.

Another guard forced me into the chair next to a brown-haired girl who cried out as an identification code was seared into her skin.

The woman next to me seized my wrist. "Okay, two-nine-six, let's do something different for you. How about we tattoo the numbers inside a stream of bubbles, like after you jump into the water?"

Bubbles? I don't want a tattoo of bubbles! A burning pain tore at my skin, drawing a startled yelp. The moment the ink-stained my skin, I knew I belonged to Javelar.

22

Five miles outside of Tendir...

Kinara's soft snoring was the last thing I heard before drifting off to sleep and falling into a soothing dream.. I stood beside a lake, its surface still. Across the body of water, towering trees lined the shore. Their red trunks created a wall that nearly obscured my view of the white-capped mountain looming in the distance. The blue sky above held no clouds, just a lonely pale-red moon.

A diera volf sauntered from the tree line, its thick white coat shimmering in the sunlight. It lapped gently at the water. Upon noticing me, the creature tilted its head back and howled, exposing saber-like teeth. When I howled back, the volf's ears perked up before it retreated into the trees, leaving me alone again. I kicked a small rock from the bank into the still water. The ripples gently spread across the surface, eventually blending back in.

Kinara shook me awake. "We have to get moving."

I groaned. "It's still dark."

"The longer we stay in one place, the more likely someone will stumble on our camp."

I attempted to wipe the sleep from my eyes. The dream had offered a brief respite from the grief, but now it flooded back in. Why was this happening to me? All I wanted was for everything to go back to the way it used to be. No Javelar, no Guardian genes, just the mundane chores of the farm. Ben and Parnikus were the only family I had left—if they were still alive. A part of me wished I had stayed with them, at least we would have been together, no matter what happened.

It didn't take long to get ready. I had everything I needed in the backpack Admari gave me. The sky was still dark and Kinara was strapping her sword to her back when I emerged from my tent.

"So, how do we take this down?"

"Behold, the power of the Instellitent," she said as she held up a foot-long string at the back of the tent, then gave it a pull. The entire tent, blankets, and all, folded itself into a tiny square box.

"How did it do that?" No wonder she'd had them up so quickly last night!

Kinara smirked at my baffled expression. "Beats me, I just use it. You're going to have quite the experience in Creet if you thought that was amazing."

"It's different?"

"Alympia is the poorest nation on the entire planet of Ulypus. Very backward in contrast to Eldorado." She noted my expression. "My apologies. What I mean is technology is extremely advanced outside of Alympia. Don't worry, though. I'm here to help you adapt to the changes as we go. You'll be up to speed by the time we get there."

It felt good to be moving again. For the first time I allowed myself to truly appreciate the surrounding scenery. The forest was alive with color. Occasionally, I would see a red belonsquirrel scaling a tree, then stopping to watch us. The moment we got too close, the small rodent retreated into its home amongst the branches. Carabells filled the canopy, producing an orchestra of chirps and whistles. The forest floor shimmered with drops of early morning dew. We walked for about an hour in reverence, careful not to disturb the abundance of life surrounding us.

The distant gurgling of a river became louder as we approached. In the crystal-clear water, I could see terpfrish lazily swimming downstream. Kinara reached in my pack, removed a canteen, and quickly refilled it, along with her own.

We walked on until we reached a dam of logs forming a pool that had to be at least a hundred feet across. Three medium, flat-topped rocks jutted up above the water like a giant's pathway to the other side.

Kinara turned to me with a grin, "Give me your pack."

"Why?"

"Just give it. I'm going to show you another technique. Remember when I taught you how to thought reap? That's where you start, but focus more on balance. It's the key to this, so spend a little more time with that." She jumped across the three flat rocks and landed on the opposite bank. "See? It's not that hard. Just focus. You should feel the same burst of energy shoot through you, then all you've gotta do is jump."

I looked at the stones doubtfully. Clearing my mind of everything else, I focused on balance. The energy surged through me, and I jumped.

To my surprise, I soared over the water, hitting the first rock and almost rolling into the river.

Kinara clapped. "Keep going. You're doing great!"

"Is it normal to feel like I just got hit in the stomach?"

"No. Try releasing less enigma next time."

I nodded, knowing that if I over-thought it, I would end up wet. I reached the last rock without issue, so I continued toward the bank. To my dismay, I came up short and fell into the frigid water. Upon surfacing, Kinara's howling laughter filled the air. The shock from the cold water kept me quiet for a bit, but soon I splashed her and was laughing, too. It was good to hear Kinara laugh again.

"Hey! I just fixed my hair!"

She offered me her hand. I took it and pulled her in. For such a petite body, she made an impressive splash. Her expression was priceless when she emerged from the dunking.

Kinara playfully tackled me and pulled me under. We wrestled in the pool for a moment before she shook her head, clearing a clump of wet hair from her face. I climbed onto the bank and lay there. Though I was sopping wet, I didn't mind; we'd needed a refresher.

Kinara stretched out beside me, then rolled onto her side to face me.

"I'm surprised you got so far on your first try. I was expecting you to fail on the first rock."

"Umm…thanks?"

She laughed and waited for me to empty the water from my boots before getting back to her feet. We fell silent again as we continued, only stopping twice for short breaks along the way. The humidity climbed to uncomfortable levels and I felt as if I'd never get dry.

Around noon we came to a large lake and followed its shoreline. The scenery looked as if we had stepped into a painting. Trees lined the opposite bank, and beyond them I could see the mountains. A few light yellow, fluffy clouds graced the sky.

Kinara followed my gaze and smiled. Her backpack landed on the ground with a thud, then she teleported. A splash from the lake revealed her floating on its surface.

Still gazing at the sky, she said, "We'll have lunch here, but I need to call my uncle first."

I dropped my pack and sat next to it. I wasn't used to traveling this much, and my muscles ached from the strain. Sure, farm work had made me strong, but this was different. Everything had changed. I was having difficulty adjusting to the fact that nothing would ever be the same.

Kinara's voice carried as she talked to the Colonel, but I couldn't get more than bits and pieces of the conversation. A few minutes later she appeared beside me, wringing the water from her still-dripping hair.

"The Colonel wants us to travel on foot to the capitol. Most of the nearby cities are on high alert searching for you."

Did Javelar truly have this much influence? I hadn't broken the law nor harmed anyone, so what interest did any authority have in me?

All I could ask was, "Why?"

"Not sure, I'm just a foot soldier, so the details rarely get passed to me."

"I wish I knew what was going on."

"Me, too. Maybe we'll get some answers once we get to the academy," she paused thoughtfully, "Ready for lunch?"

Kinara pulled out two oddly shaped containers and threw one to me.

I examined it curiously, "What is it?"

"A DMRE. We call them gut bombs."

"It smells awful," I said when I opened the meal.

"Add some water. It'll help."

I unscrewed my canteen and poured a small amount, watching as the dry flakes transformed into a heated soup. Its smell didn't improve much, but it tasted fine. I finished it off and understood exactly why they called it a gut bomb. The meal was so heavy, I felt like I was going to burst.

Kinara studied the map that her *Reaper sphere*, as she called it, projected into the air. I looked over her shoulder, as her finger touched an area near a blue dot on the map.

"We're here."

I frowned, shuffling my feet. I wasn't too familiar with map reading. How could Dad ever have imagined I had a shot with her? My expression must have been a clear giveaway.

She smiled sympathetically. "I'll do the navigating. It looks like we're still about two weeks shy of Alympus." She pointed to a four-ringed circle in the far-right corner of the map. "This type of circle represents the capitol."

"Two weeks on foot?"

"That's if we hurry, which we should. The forest is crawling with bandits, and I'd rather not fight anyone else. In the meantime, this is the perfect opportunity for sword training."

"You're going to train me out here?"

"Yes, I don't want a repeat of yesterday."

"If it will help us stay alive, then I'm game."

We'd been on the road for six days now but were behind schedule because of our training. I frowned at the new bruises on my arm. Every night we sparred with sticks, each session coming with a new and more complex lesson.

When morning came, I sat up in my cot and took an exhausted breath, exhaling slowly. No sweet dreams for me last night, nothing but nightmares of my murdered family.

The sun illuminated the fabric of the tent, and the songs of the carabells soothed me.

I changed my clothes, ate one of the DMREs in my bag, then strapped my training sword, which I had yet to use, to my back.

When I walked out of the tent, Kinara greeted me. "Good morning. Ready to hit the trail?"

"I'm ready if you are."

As we walked, Kinara taught me various things about wildlife and basic survival techniques. We also practiced my void bounding. I had improved substantially over the last few days and could now maneuver a bit when I bounded, though I'd already had a few painful lessons that motivated me to learn faster. Yesterday, I ran into a tree, nearly knocking myself out. The day before, I'd gotten tangled in a thicket of brambles and I still had the thorn marks to prove it. Today, my goal was to avoid repeating those events.

We stopped for a break and a small lunch around noon when a filthy, middle-aged man stepped out of the bushes ahead. His beady, amber eyes were nearly the same color as his disgusting teeth.

"Good afternoon," he said with a crooked smile.

Kinara eyed the man. "Good afternoon."

"I'm Munolt. Perhaps you could help me? I'm looking for someone named Zaelek Khiings. Perhaps you have run into him during your travels?"

The breath caught in my throat.

Kinara shook her head. "Sorry, but we've had little contact with anyone out here for a few months now. Someone in Tendir might have information."

The man fumbled through his pockets. "Maybe if you saw a picture?" He pulled out a small, crumpled piece of paper. The sound of crinkling broke the uncomfortable silence as he unwrapped a wanted poster. He looked down at the sign, then up at me.

"Oh."

Kinara drew her sword. I followed suit and shifted my feet to adjust my balance, just like she and my mother had taught me. Munolt whistled, and five other men came barreling through the vegetation.

"You're outnumbered," said Munolt.

"You know that none of you are Guardians, right?"

"We still have the numbers."

He charged me.

I blocked his attack and slammed my free fist into his face. He toppled over a stump, landing on his butt. Even the few hours I had spent sparring with Kinara every night had made a vast difference in my defensive skills, not to mention my self-confidence.

One of the other men tried to take me by surprise, but Kinara was too fast for him. He crumpled on the ground, unconscious. With a quick turn, she countered another attack, grabbed the man, and threw him into one of his teammates. She transitioned into the next attack and thrust upwards with a flaming fist, catching the man behind in the jaw. He was launched into a tree branch above us, which snapped as his limp body wrapped around it, undoubtedly breaking his neck and back.

Kinara slashed open the recovering man's arm with a backlash as he rose from where he was sprawled on top of his comrade. He screamed, holding the gaping wound in surprise and glaring at Kinara. Her throwing knife planted in his neck before he could move.

Munolt tried to sneak away while we were distracted. With a quick step, Kinara overtook him and knocked him unconscious with the pommel of her sword.

She looked over her shoulder. "Let the unconscious ones live to bury their dead. We need to get out of here."

She waited for me to grab my pack, then we bounded.

Nearly two-and-a-half hours later, we took a break. Kinara watched me as I examined my sword.

"When we get to the base, you'll get a customized blade matching your element," she said. "It'll meet specific requirements unique to you."

"Do you know what my element might be?"

"Hard to say until we get you back to the academy."

"Okay, so how many elements are there?"

"There are four primary elements: fire, water, earth, and wind. Usually, people only get one aspect of them, like the ability to grow plants or levitation. However, if you have a pure element, you control all the smaller elements falling under that main branch. It's rare to get one of the main four, but I was lucky enough to get pure fire."

I…." I hesitated, forming my question in different ways, but no matter how I structured it, I couldn't see a positive outcome. Styx, I didn't know if I wanted the answer.

"What?"

"It's nothing."

"It doesn't sound like nothing."

I didn't want to cause her any more pain. She had been through enough. I owed her a lot for bringing me along with her and keeping me safe. Asking her to relive past trauma for reassurance seemed selfish. Still, I needed to hear the answer.

"Are you sure?"

"Yes. What's on your mind?"

"Do you think what happened to Alator will happen to Ben and Parnikus?"

Her expression darkened, and she looked down at her hands. I knew I should have kept my mouth shut.

"I don't know."

"I'm sorry, I didn't mean to…"

"It's fine, really. If I were in your place, I'd probably ask the same thing. I wish I could give you an answer, but I don't have one. I'm sorry," she paused. "Let's save the rest of your questions for later. It's time to get moving."

The sun went down while Kinara placed what she called a *SmokSkreen* around the growing fire. According to her, it kept the sparks from escaping and absorbed any smoke threatening to give away our position. I leaned against a log and looked up at the two full moons in the night sky. A calm breeze swept over me, carrying the scent of distant rain and brushing the faintest chill over my skin. If I closed my eyes, I could almost picture myself stargazing with my family. I wished I could go back in time and give my dad a warning, then maybe none of this would have happened.

Kinara sat next to me and followed my gaze to the sky. She smiled then whispered, "Beautiful, aren't they?"

"Yeah, I haven't seen stars like this since…"

She studied me. "You still haven't told me what happened the night Javelar attacked."

She was right. Though it was constantly on my mind, it felt as if actually saying the words out loud would only deepen the pain I already felt. I'd hoped she would not ask me to recount the event, yet a part of me wanted her to know. Something from my story might give us a clue about why my family had been attacked.

"Should we set up the tents first?" I asked.

"Not tonight. We'll just sleep under the stars. I don't want to leave all our gear behind if we get attacked again."

I didn't mind that. The idea of sleeping outside soothed me. "Okay, I'll tell you everything I remember."

When I finished reliving the attack, a peace fell over me. The fire cracked, and the nocturnal life of the forest chirped and hummed with a soothing familiarity. I stretched my legs and walked to the edge of our campsite, leaving Kinara to mull over the information. The tall grass rippled in never-ending waves. A howl sounded in the distance, most likely belonging to a koyo gazing at the moons.

Soon Kinara silently joined me, lacing her fingers with mine, squeezing tightly. Her hair grazed my neck as she laid her head on my shoulder. Feeling her body heat through my shirt and across my arm soothed my broken heart. She inhaled deeply.

We stood there for a time before she spoke. "I'm sorry about your family."

23

Arena preparation area:
Javelar Headquarters...

Parnikus and I took our place at the back of the formation. I could hear cheering through the walls. Luto, our platoon leader, turned, his brilliant green eyes examining each of the thirty faces staring back at him. He cleared his throat, forcing the thick veins protruding from his neck muscles to ripple.

"I'd like to welcome our newest bodies to the pit. Like the others before you, I'm sure you have no clue what's about to happen. Let me fill you in." He pointed toward the metal gate ahead. "You're about to enter the place where you will either live or die, the greatest challenge you've yet been privileged to face.

"If you haven't already noticed, they've marked each of our shirts with a blue line. That means 'friendly.' If the stripe is red, kill the person wearing it. I don't think I can make it any clearer than that. The fight ends when every member of the opposing platoon is killed."

I nervously looked at Parnikus who wore the same nervous

expression as mine but quickly transformed into a reassuring smile once he noticed me. He wore that smile as a disguise, but deep down, I knew he was as every bit terrified as I was. How were we going to make it through this? *We aren't killers.*

"Newbie," Luto called. "Eyes up front." When he had my attention, he continued. "This will be my fifth fight. That means if I make it through this one, I'll be accepted into Javelar's ranks. If we win, Gertry, my second in command, will become your new platoon leader. She has two successful fights under her belt, which is a lot more than I can say for the rest of you."

I swallowed hard, trying to choke back the fear clawing its way to the surface. If Gertry had seniority at only two wins, that didn't bode well for the rest of us.

Luto moved to the rack of weapons on the wall. "Weapon choice is decided by seniority. After that, we'll file through by row, and you'll take the weapon handed to you."

Luto drew a long, slender sword from the rack. He nodded to Gertry, who chose a wooden staff with a large blade at its tip. He called two more names, then guided the front row to the distribution zone. Gertry handed out various types of weapons as each person made their way to her.

When it came time for Parnikus and me to receive our tools, only two pitchforks were left. A few of the fighters ahead of us snickered when they saw what we were stuck with. *A pitchfork? How can we fight with something that isn't even a weapon? We'll be destroyed out there!*

I joined the rest of the warriors near the closed, solid metal gate at the tunnel's end, wanting to run away from this fight, but painfully aware that I couldn't.

Parnikus nudged me. "We should stick together."

"Good idea."

A few minutes later, Luto and Gertry took their place at the front of the formation. They now wore armor in place of the tattered rags that were our usual "uniform." Luto's armor was a shade of gold, Gertry's silver, but each was marked with a blue stripe.

An obnoxious high-pitched siren sounded, and Luto turned to face us.

"One minute until the gate opens."

No one said a word, but the restless fidgeting in the ranks spoke volumes. I looked to my left and saw a boy that couldn't have been older than fifteen, and a pang of sorrow rippled through me. It made me realize how lucky I was to have experienced my full childhood before being thrown to death's door.

The metal gate opened, and Luto charged forward with Gertry at his side. Our platoon flooded into the arena. I lost sight of those ahead as the thick vegetation swallowed them up.

"Spears," someone called.

The head of a spear ripped through the chest of the young boy next to me before he could even see it. His head fell back as the shaft propped his body up like a sick ritual killing. My eyes widened, and my stomach contents traveled up my throat. Before I could vomit, Parnikus pulled me to the right by my arm.

"Come on, there's nothing we can do for him."

I followed my brother into a small ravine covered by a large fallen tree. Our feet crunched through the gravel. He slammed me against the dirt wall and covered my mouth.

"*Mhm hm mhm mh hm…*" I protested.

"Shh." He pointed to the log above us, and I heard it—the slight but noticeable thud of someone crossing.

A male voice fell from above. "What was that?"

Another male replied, "We should check it out."

Parnikus released me and whispered so softly I could barely hear, "Get ready."

My grip on the wooden handle of my weapon was so tight that a splinter pierced my skin as two young men landed in front of us, each bearing a red stripe on his clothes.

I thrust forward and felt the four prongs of my pitchfork enter the closest enemy's chest. A light spray of blood speckled my face as he coughed. Parnikus and the remaining foe jabbed at each other furiously. I placed my foot on my opponent's chest and wrenched the pitchfork free. His body collapsed as I turned and hurled my weapon. Two of the prongs pierced the enemy's skull and sank into the soft dirt wall.

Parnikus' eyes widened, and he said something, but I didn't catch it. I was too focused on not vomiting as I stared at the person I'd just murdered.

Parnikus shook my arm. "Hey, you okay?"

I shrugged him off. "No. I just killed two people!"

"They would have killed us had we let them. You did good."

"Good? What in Styx are you saying? Mom and Dad would be disgusted."

"Mom and Dad are gone, Ben. We can't be worrying about what they would think, we have to concentrate on the two of us getting out of this alive."

Though it sickened me, I knew he was right. We had to survive this. We *had* to.

24

On the prairie...

Something about Zaelek's side of the story disturbed me. How had Javelar managed to find Ettias? Where was Ari? Zaelek said Savvage had stabbed her, but I didn't see any trace of her. I wouldn't mention this to Zaelek because I didn't want to give him false hope that Ari might still be alive.

I couldn't help thinking that things might have been different if I'd been at the estate. Then again, I hadn't been able to save Alator; Could I really have made a difference? Thinking of my failure brought the pain and guilt rushing back. I took a deep breath and attempted to exhale the ache in my chest. *I'm so sorry, Alator.*

I silently vowed to do everything in my power to bring Savvage to justice. He'd pay for what he'd done to me and the Khiings family. I'd see to that.

A scream broke the quiet. I rushed to the edge of the camp, searching for the source. *What in Styx was that?* A brilliant light erupted in the sky, allowing me to see a man favoring his left foot a few hundred feet away. The man squatted, then stretched his hands toward the ground.

A shock wave nearly put me on my rear. The ground in front of the man ripped open, and I braced myself as the planet's crust shook. Flames shot from the hole, and sulfur assaulted my senses, burning my eyes and nose. This was a summoning!

Zaelek called from behind me, "What is that?"

A fireball hurtled toward us. I tackled Zaelek, feeling the searing heat pass over us. I rolled off him and ran toward the tree line.

"Run, Zaelek!"

He snatched up his bag as we darted for the safety of the trees. *We're too slow, and Zaelek won't be able to maneuver at night!* I stopped briefly to throw him over my shoulders, before initiating a void bound.

My maneuvering through the thick vegetation led to scratches all over my body. I heard trees snapping behind us and knew the summoning—whatever form it might take—was in pursuit. Abruptly, my field of vision opened as I burst through the tree line.

I stopped just before we fell off a cliff.

Zaelek wriggled uncomfortably. "What are we going to do?"

I looked down to the river below, then toward the jungle. We'd survive the fall, but it would hurt. A faint orange glow behind us grew to a raging inferno. Our only choice was to jump.

"Off we go!"

I jumped. Zaelek screamed. Everything happened at once. My stomach churned as we began to plummet toward the river. Huge jets of flames shot above us, incinerating the spot where we had been milliseconds before. A scaled, winged beast reared its ugly head, and with a mighty leap, flung itself into a dive. It let loose a ferocious roar, revealing its sword-like teeth. In that instant I knew what I had to do, but I only had one shot.

For a moment time seemed to slow. I raised both arms, enigma surging through me. A tiny spark appeared above the center of my palms, expanding into a large sphere of fire. It spun clockwise, and as its velocity increased, it flattened. Small flares shot from the fiery disc, singeing pieces of my clothing.

The disc rocketed toward the winged terror. Recoil from the launch thrust me downward even faster, and the tax of the attack hit me full force. I blacked out.

Falling above Kinara...

Seconds before I hit the water I saw Kinara's fire disc catch the creature between the eyes. The attack engulfed it in flames. Its wings buckled, and its lifeless body dropped from the cloud of smoke. Cold and pain rushed over me as my sword and backpack absorbed the shock of impact. My head reeled while sparks of light danced behind my eyelids. The water snapped me out of my brief daze and I was astonished to find I was actually still alive.

I broke the river's surface and gasped. Ahead, I could see Kinara floating on her back. I looked up, watching with horror as the creature's body plummeted toward her.

"Kinara!" I yelled as it crashed into the water and disappeared beneath the surface, taking her with it. *No, no,! This can't be happening!*

Another boom sounded, as the river bottom gave way at the point of the creature's impact, opening a gaping hole beneath the surface. The river's flow became a raging waterfall as it dropped into whatever lay below. I tried to escape the pull of the current but was swept over the edge, riding the torrent down to the frothing surface of still more water below. The force of the falling water pushed me under. I tried to claw my way to the surface but the flow held me down. My lungs burned, increasing my panic, but I managed to swim down and away, breaking free of the rush. When I surfaced, I coughed violently before I finally managed to gulp in a breath.

I was in an underground lake. Then I saw Kinara ahead of me, floating face down. I swam to her and flipped her over. She wasn't breathing! Tucking her in my left arm, I side-paddled to a flat rock jutting out of the water. I pulled her up and began resuscitation. Every compression came with the fear that she might not come to, every breath I shared felt like a prayer to breathe life back into her. *Come on!*

At last her chest rose and fell. She began to cough up water, and I turned her to her side.

After catching her breath, she looked at me. "Where are we?"

"Are you okay? Do you have any injuries?"

She gently pushed me away and sat up. “I’m fine, but I need to know where we are.”

“I have no idea. The water carried us down here when that… that *thing* punched a hole in the riverbed.” I glanced toward the surface. “Where is it? Is it dead?”

“Doubtful, its summoner probably dismissed it.”

“Why?”

“I don’t know, but whatever the reason, we should be grateful.” She picked herself up and examined the cavern, dimly lit by the light from the gaping hole above. “It looks like we’re in an old helixore mine. I’d bet there’s a way to the surface deeper in. Come on, we’ll have to swim to that archway over there.”

“What if it caves in?”

“Get in the water, Zaelek.”

I didn’t want to get back in the water, it had almost killed us once already. Kinara dove in, but I didn’t follow. What if that creature was waiting for us to come back into the lake so it could finish us off?

“Zaelek!” Kinara growled when she realized I was still just standing there on the rock.

I reluctantly followed, trying not to think about being crushed between those horrible teeth. Not knowing what else might be lurking below us terrified me. I swam a little faster, eager to find a way out.

Kinara led us through the archway that was supported by old wooden beams. The deeper we went, the staler the air tasted, and the more panic wrenched at my guts. The mere thought of getting trapped down here sent shivers down my spine.

Gradually, the tunnel opened into a huge cavern and we were able to stand and make our way to dry ground. Odd, glowing white crystals protruded from the rock walls, dimly illuminating the space and revealing a set of old mining tracks in the center.

Kinara examined the chamber. “Stay here. I’m going to scout ahead. Don’t touch anything.”

“You’re going to leave me here by myself?”

“You’ll be fine. Don’t be such a baby.”

Easy for her to say, she can defend herself, I thought. She vanished. I paced to try to keep warm, but it wasn’t helping. I silently thanked the heavens for the light-filled crystals. I wasn’t sure what I would have done if she’d left me in the dark.

Time crept by. It felt like Kinara had been gone for hours. I picked up a small rock and threw it across the cavern. A loud metal clang startled me. Something clinked, and the screech of grinding gears echoed off the glowing walls.

Bright lights flickered to life and I could now see two tunnels, one at each side of the area. Another screech of metal sounded in the tunnel Kinara had chosen to investigate. A mining cart zipped through the room and disappeared nearly as fast as it had come.

Kinara appeared in front of me. "What did you do?"

"I'm not sure."

"What did I say about touching things?"

"I swear, I didn't mean to."

She shook her head, then paused. "What if we rode in the mining carts?"

"Are you serious? That's a terrible idea!"

"Do you have a better one?"

"No…" I frowned. "But how are we going to catch a cart? They're so fast."

"Look at the tracks; there's a braking system there. All I need to do is pull that lever."

She walked to the post next to the track, pulled the lever, then hit the switch on the cavern wall. A cart came rocketing down the path and squealed to a stop near the entrance to the other tunnel. She hit it again and a second cart arrived.

"All aboard," I said.

We each took a cart and situated ourselves.

"Throw a rock at the switch," Kinara said.

I leaned out of my cart, picked up a rock, and threw it at the button on the wall. It missed.

"Oops."

"We really need to work on your aim when we get out of here."

She picked up a stone and hit the switch. The carts started off slowly but picked up speed. I hunkered down inside mine, not wanting to have anything take my head off. The tunnel opened into a giant rock chamber speckled in light crystals. Multiple tracks at different levels, supported only by wood, went in every direction.

Our carts sped on, taking us down a steep decline. A clunk sounded, and the path between Kinara and me switched, separating us.

"Kinara!" I shouted.

Kinara's eyes widened in horror as we rocketed down different tunnels. *No, no, no! Not good!* My path opened again, and as I rounded a sharp corner. I grabbed the edges of the cart as it made the turn on two wheels. There were so many turns I lost track of how many times I changed course. It was like some frightening, ancient amusement park ride. The cart lurched downward, gaining even more speed.

Just as I thought this ride would never end, my cart slowed and bumped into a caved in sectioned of a small room. I climbed out, falling to my knees when my feet hit solid ground.

A soft blue light glowed through a crevice in the wall to my right. I moved closer and a gentle breath of air brushed my skin. Maybe I'd found a way out. I wondered if I should wait for Kinara or go look for her, but decided I should keep moving until I reached the entrance. That would be the best place for me to meet up with her.

I inched my way into the crevice. It narrowed, and I had to turn sideways to continue. At the far end was an incomplete doorway with rusted hinges dangling from the wooden beams. I continued to follow the light.

Beyond the doorway was a flight of steps. As I descended, each gray stone of the stairway brightened until they were pure white. The moment my foot touched the last step, every stone on the path ahead lit up, urging me forward. I followed it into a vast room, the walls etched with ancient glyphs. Behind me a hidden wall slid closed, blocking the exit. Shattered bones lined the edges of the room and I prayed they weren't human.

The walls shook and then slowly began to move inward, threatening to crush me. I turned and pounded on the door, hoping it would open if it sensed someone was still in the room. I imagined this was the cause of the crushed bones and sheer terror gripped me, blurring all my thoughts into one chaotic stream. I turned, looking for another way out before sprinting for the other end, desperate to find an exit there.

When I reached the center of the room, the glyphs on the encroaching walls pulsed with light. Something sharp shot past, grazing my shoulder. I winced but kept running as blood trickled down my arm.

Upon reaching the end, I stopped before I hit the wall—no door or exit. *I should have waited for Kinara!*

The floor trembled, and the lit path split, revealing a narrow glowing pool shimmering below. With no other choice I dove in, and the warm water engulfed me. The canal of water burrowed deep under the back wall of the ever-narrowing room. I scanned the passage for any hint of an exit, but only saw a dead end. My mind raced, filled with a hundred thoughts at once: What sadistic person had built this? Why force me to escape into an underwater tunnel that offered a shred of hope, then rip it away with inevitable drowning. *Why?*

I swam only a few feet through the dimly lit tube before the water rippled in front of me. Was I hallucinating? I reached out and touched it. My hand pierced the veil of fluid, and I felt crisp air around my fingers.

I poked my head through the membrane. The water that should have clung to my head refused to pass the invisible barrier, leaving me completely dry as I surveyed the small room. Carefully, I pulled the rest of my body through. To my surprise, every drop of water stayed within the barrier, some mysterious force holding it in place. I slid my hand into the oddity again, watching in fascination as it produced the same results. The only time I'd seen water behave like that was when Dad demonstrated his skills. The memory of the battle between Savvage and Dad flashed through my mind as I tried to find an explanation for the phenomenon.

Whispers echoed in the room, startling me. I whirled around, trying to locate their source. The opposing wall split apart, revealing yet another room.

"Come, boy," whispers taunted from within.

I resisted the urge to follow, and a calming force pulled at my soul. I pushed back, making it recoil. Another feeling, one offering power, seized the other's place. It promised to vanquish my foes; it vowed revenge. The feeling toyed with my resentment and grief. I tried to clear my thoughts, to fight off the temptations, but they increased until they raged within me. Would it be so bad to accept?

Moving cautiously into the circular room I saw a shapeless mound begin to rise from the floor in the center, two pillars that began twisting around each other, gradually separating. When they stopped at waist height, a stone hand sat atop each pillar, in the palms of both hands was a small, beautiful crimson rose gemstone.

"Take them," the whispers tempted.

I reached for the stones.

The hands seized my wrists, wrapping around them as they came to life. A pillar of water shot up to the ceiling on my left, and a shock went through my body, forcing my hands open. The stone fingers interlaced with mine. I tried to pull away from the unyielding clutches, but I couldn't free myself. My heart raced, and nausea took hold. If the stone hands closed, they would shatter mine.

My palms burned. I screamed as a band of blue electrical energy encased my wrists. Another shock shot through me, rendering me paralyzed. The floor spun, giving me a clear look at the room I had come through. The veins in both my arms glowed fluorescent blue, and power surged through me. My heart pumped wildly, aching with each beat.

The force holding the wall of liquid dissipated, allowing the water to flood into the room. I sucked in a deep breath, waiting for my head to go under, but then the hand pillars rose until I hung above the sloshing waves. The column of water from before loomed in front of me, vertically flattening to reveal a near-perfect reflection of myself.

I watched as my eyes turned a bright bluish-white. *Am I going to die here? Are my eyes going to burn out of my skull to punish me for being greedy?*

Yellow streaks swirled where my pupils once were. Thin, blue lightning bolts danced around me, electrifying my skin with light. The energy flow's enormity pressed against my chest with such force that I couldn't breathe. Just as I was about to pass out, the pillars released me, unleashing a final blast of power, and thrusting me into the back wall. I bounced off and landed face down in the water, then sank into blackness.

25

In the arena: Javelar HQ...

Parnikus scaled the ravine's dirt wall and looked at his surroundings. I followed his lead when he gestured to me, stumbling over a root on my way up. We were still in a thick green place. Unable to see more than a few feet in any direction.

"We need higher ground," I said.

"Yeah, this vegetation is thick. Any ideas?"

I thought for a moment, then noticed a tree behind Parnikus with a staircase of branches. "Hold this."

Parnikus took my blood-soaked pitchfork and followed my gaze. "If you make it halfway up that without one of those branches snapping, I'll be impressed."

I grabbed the lowest branch and pulled myself up. "Shut up, I'll be fine." When I neared the top of the tree, I could see over most of the plant life.

"See anything?" Parnikus called from below.

"No. Just more trees."

A resounding crack from below startled me and sent a tingling sensation through my body. I inspected the branch I stood on for any sign of damage but found none.

"You okay up there?"

"I'm fine, I just thought…"

The tree shuddered and sank into the ground a couple inches. I wrapped my arms around the trunk. *What the…?*

Another crack sounded, louder, like a whip being snapped. The entire tree moved straight downward, forcing my feet off the branch. My muscles went rigid, and I clung to the trunk as it continued toward the ground.

"Ben, let go," Parnikus shouted.

Though I wanted to, I was frozen with fear. The ground swallowed me whole. I clawed at the loose dirt but sank even farther. A metal glove snatched my wrist and pulled me up.

Gertry stood above me. "That was close."

Parnikus looked to the sky with a sigh of relief. "Too close."

I analyzed our surroundings, which had transformed. Not a trace of vegetation was left on the red sand, and I could see the entire arena for the first time. "What happened?"

Gertry glared at the stands packed full of people all around us. "*That* was a terrain change. They do it for visibility when the fight nears its end."

I nodded toward the stands. "Who are 'they?'"

"Our loving brothers and sisters of Javelar."

Parnikus tossed me my pitchfork. "Looks like we don't have time for questions."

I followed his stony gaze and saw a group of red stripes approaching. They dragged a heap of bloody golden metal, all that was left of our platoon leader, Luto, behind them. That's when I noticed that only Gertry, Parnikus, and I remained. There were ten of them and three of us.

Gertry's armor clanged as she stepped back. "Get behind me."

"What?" I asked. "Are you crazy?"

"Just do it."

Parnikus and I moved. Gertry's pike lit on fire, and she hurled it toward our foes. The moment it hit the ground, an explosion decimated half of the opponents and sent the others sprawling. Gertry collapsed to the ground. I couldn't believe what I had seen. *How did she do that?*

"The rest is up to you two," she panted.

"How did you do that?" Parnikus asked.

"Survive first, questions later."

The remaining red stripes got to their feet, clearly enraged. They charged forward. Parnikus and I rushed in front of Gertry and braced ourselves. I jabbed my weapon at the approaching enemy. She sidestepped and slashed her sword downward. I leapt back, but the metal caught me just above my left knee.

My leg muscle flexed to stabilize me, oozing blood from the wound. I could still stand, but I didn't know for how long. Parnikus forced the woman to retreat when he grazed her inner thigh.

"Thanks," I said.

The red stripes regrouped and closed in, surrounding us. I went to lean against Parnikus for support, but as soon as our skin made contact, a strange feeling surged throughme, and a pressurized blast forced me in front of Gertry. As if acting on instinct alone, I thrust my pitchfork toward the enemy.

A water wall shot from the weapon's prongs, then formed a protective shell around Gertry and me. Both of Parnikus' arms ignited in fire, and, like a carabell pumping its wings, his arms shot forward.

Three volves of fire surged from the flames and ran circles around my aqua dome. Their speed increased until I could no longer discern their figures from the inferno's red streak. The streak expanded upward, forming a cyclone of fire. Steam poured off the shell of water, and the humidity it created felt as if I stood in a steam cave.

As quickly as the volves had appeared, the cyclone ceased, leaving nothing but scorch marks and charred bones on the battlefield. My wall of water splashed to the ground.

"Parnikus!" I screamed.

A slight flare hovered where Parnikus had once been. It spewed ash into the air, then widened into a ring. Parnikus' right half stepped through, and the ash swirled around him until his body was complete.

I let out a breath of relief. "Don't do that again. I thought you had died."

"Me, too," he replied.

Gertry laughed and sprawled out on the sand. "Looks like you guys have some spirits that don't want you to die. You two really are something else."

26

Deep in the helixore mine...

I deactivated my Seeker senses, feeling the slight wave of relief as my enigma flow returned to its resting state. It had been about thirty minutes since I teleported out of my cart in the unloading room, and my Seeker senses had been on ever since. Now, I stood in the middle of an abandoned helixore mine trying to back track enough to pick up Zaelek's trail. I wasn't succeeding.

I shook my head, disgusted at myself for losing him. There were too many rails to follow, and with the track routes crossing and changing, I didn't have any clues. Even with full enigma reserves, it would take hours, if not days, to bound down every tunnel. Still, I had consumed so much enigma taking down the summoning that I wouldn't be back to full capacity for at least a day. I cursed my luck. My uncle would have my head if something happened to Zaelek.

I spotted a crude banner that read "Gruegen Gang" hanging from a wooden beam and became more cautious. The Gruegen Gang were well known throughout Eldorado for dabbling in everything criminal. If this was one of their lairs, things could get complicated. Especially if Zaelek had been delivered to them via a mining cart. All I could think to do was recon their operation to see if Zaelek had been captured. If he had, I would form a plan from there. Getting him out would be difficult, as most Gruegens were rogue Guardians.

I bounded through the tunnels, occasionally stopping to peek around a corner. The tunnel opened into an ample space but to the left of the track a cliff dropped into an abyss. To the right, tucked away in a hollowed section of the mine wall, was a small encampment. Cages the size of small homes lined the wall next to it.

Two individuals huddled together in the closest cage to the camp. One of them was child-sized, and the other had to be an adult. I knew I couldn't just leave them there.

I cursed and slipped toward the cages, keeping close to the wall, and activating my seeker senses again. The Gruegens laughed and talked amongst themselves in their encampment, unaware of my presence. When I reached the nearest enclosure, I patted the ground to get the prisoners' attention. A woman looked up at me and held a young girl close.

"*Tiha comai*!" she said.

I gestured for them to stay quiet and grabbed two of the bars, concentrating. The metal emitted a dull orange glow once it got hot, but the woman soon pointed behind me and gasped, "*Seto Klia*!"

I whirled around and saw a group of men.

One man snickered, "Hello, gorgeous."

My blade slid from its sheath and I created a fireball in my free hand. The men laughed as they drew their weapons. *Schleet! They're Guardians.* Like the breath being pulled from my lungs, the enigma in my body dissipated, and the flames were snuffed out. *What?*

A different man spoke, "Hard to use your element, ain't it?"

"What did you do?" I hissed.

"First time with a Scrambler, I take it?"

I had heard rumors of that nasty ability that blocked elemental enigma. Still, it was extremely rare. This situation could only get worse. I tried to teleport but only got about ten feet from the cage.

"Look at that, boys! We caught ourselves a jumper!"

The men surrounded me. A stone slammed my sword hand, knocking the weapon free. I dove and gripped its handle. Someone grabbed my waist as another pinned my sword to the ground with a thick vine. I kicked and screamed as the man holding me pulled me up. The others grabbed my limbs, immobilizing me.

One man grabbed my chin and examined me. "She's a fiery one, ain't she? She'll fetch a high price on the market! Who wouldn't love to get their hands on this little tart?" I wrenched my head away and spit at him. He backhanded me before commanding the other men to open the cage next to the woman and child.

They threw me in, and a forcefield flowed from its roof, covering the bars. I slammed my fist against it. My body bounced off the walls, throwing me back and forth. I hit the floor, and the men laughed again.

"Bet you won't do that again," one said.

Another chimed in. "She even looks good gettin' tossed around! I'm a little jealous of whoever buys 'er."

The gang laughed, then shuffled back to their camp. I groaned in pain and sat up. This branch of their band must specialize in human trafficking.

The woman crawled to the edge of her cage. "*Li opar teh kiona.*"

"I'm sorry. I don't understand," I said.

"Ah, you speak Atlantean. My apologies, I thought my people sent you."

"Your people?"

"The Altarian tribe. I am Karia. This is my daughter, Teora."

Altarians? I thought they were just a myth Alympians used to keep their children from wandering the forests. As the story goes, Altarians will dismember and devour any child found alone in the woods. A gruesome tale, but effective, nonetheless. I didn't believe it, but maybe there was some truth to it, and that was enough to pique my interest.

"I'm Kinara."

"Tell me, Kinara. What brings you to such a place?"

"I'm looking for someone. We became separated in the mine."

"It seems luck isn't on your side today."

I tried to get a signal on my R.E.A.P.E.R. Sphere but had no success. We were too deep in the mine. I wanted to scream. *Zaelek is missing, I'm captured, what else can go wrong?* I sighed. *Think, Kinara! How can we get out of these cages?*

In another part of the mine…

When I regained consciousness, I stood somewhere in the mine with no memory of how I got there or any idea how much time had passed. My confusion intensified when I tried to turn to look at the surrounding cavern walls, but couldn't move any part of my body.

Something cold and wet dripped on my arm. I tried to wipe it off but failed again to move. The droplet slid down my skin, raising tiny bumps on my arm. My arm moved to wipe the water away, but I wasn't the one controlling the limb. Someone else was in control, and they carried me forward as if I were tied to puppet strings.

What in Styx? I involuntarily took a deep breath, catching the faint hint of sweetness in the mine's stale taste. Why couldn't I move?

A female voice echoed in my mind, "*Quiet, boy. You're breaking my concentration.*"

What the…?

"*I said, be quiet!*"

Who are you?

But the voice remained silent.

Answer me!

The invisible force moved my hand to the leather-wrapped handle of a throwing knife and ran the edge across my wrist. The cold metal sliced through my skin, and I exhaled loudly. The entity had felt it, too.

"*Each time you interrupt me, you'll get another mark.*"

You're hurting yourself, too!

I felt the blade slice into my skin again. "*In a manner of speaking, but it's not my body that suffers, it's yours.*"

Blood dripped from my fingertips. I wanted to scream but instead was forced forward again. Another deep breath. The sweet scent returned. We navigated the tunnels in whatever direction the smell guided us.

Eventually, the tunnel opened, and we stood in an ample space. A crescent shaped cliff ahead seemed to drop off to nowhere. Along the path sat a small encampment tucked away in a hollowed section of the mine wall with cages lining the rock outcrop next to it.

Three individuals occupied the cages—two in one, and the third in the cage next to them. We walked past without slowing, but the lone woman called out. I couldn't understand her, but I recognized her voice. It belonged to Kinara. She seemed to speak another language. I tried to seize control, but the entity held too tight of a grip on my mind and body.

"Help us!" a child shouted.

We stopped. Something about the young girl caught the entity's attention.

The Presence addressed the woman using my voice, "You are Altarian, yes?"

She nodded. A low-pitched siren echoed off the walls, and someone from the camp yelled.

"Hmmm...Sounds like we've been discovered. No matter. I've been waiting for a chance to stretch my legs."

I didn't know what she meant by "stretching" *her* legs, but I didn't like the way my body tensed when she said it. A group of men ran at the cages, weapons drawn. My lips involuntarily curled into a wicked grin, and I felt the intensity behind "our" gaze. I had a strong feeling I wasn't going to approve of her actions.

Within seconds, I found myself behind the enclosures, hidden from view. My hand stretched out, and a black cloud oozed from it. The Presence stepped us into the smog.

A strange sensation came over me, and I felt weightless. *What is this stuff?* The entity ignored me once again, and walked me back into the fray. We jogged through the black cloud and approached one man who had separated from the pack. The man slashed at the fog with his sword, almost hitting me, but the Presence sidestepped us just in time.

The entity's emotions fused with mine, filling me with excitement and an unfamiliar lust for violence. We skirted around the man, focused on his back. The tips of my fingers ripped open as claws replaced my fingernails. My gums felt a similar pain, and when I licked my lips, I could feel that my canine teeth had become fangs.

The man turned, his face growing more alarmed by the second. "What is this?!"

I caught a hint of my reflection in his armor, revealing two volf-like ears and a set of blood-red eyes. Together the Presence and

I laughed with glee, and the sound bounced off the stone walls. My hand went through the man's chest and his blood painted the ground. I clutched his still-beating heart and ripped it out, feeling the Presence revel in the brutality. His lifeless body collapsed.

Mercy's breath! I just killed someone!

"You haven't seen anything yet," the Presence assured me sarcastically.

The smoky cloud broke, allowing the others to see their comrade fall. It took only a few seconds for the warmth of our victim's blood to cool on my skin. In the space of those moments we maneuvered to our next mark. He fell, clutching a gaping sword wound in his neck.

"Stop!' I cried out in my mind.

We moved to where the men could see us. Tightening their grips on their weapons, the men charged. Unfamiliar energy pulsed through my veins, and with a surge, it released. A thin, flexible shell of pitch-black armor encased my body. The Presence sidestepped a few attacks, then retreated toward the camp.

The black cloak hanging from my left shoulder rippled before settling at my side. I tried again to seize control in the ensuing chaos, but the entity ferociously slammed back at my conscience. My head pounded. *Styx!*

"Stupid boy, are you trying to get us both killed?" she hissed.

You're the one taking on multiple opponents at once!

She huffed. *"So long as you stay out of my way, we'll be fine."*

The men charged again. A small spark grew in my palm but fizzled out when they surrounded me. A wave of annoyance flooded my mind. The men grinned and addressed me, but I couldn't understand their words.

Again the Presence slammed against my mind, *"Give me your memories!"* she demanded

I fought but didn't have the strength to keep her at bay.

One man stepped forward, and I finally could comprehend as he said, "Everyone's tough 'til they meet the boss. But scrambling always brings 'em down a notch."

"*So, that's what happened*," the voice seethed in my head.

"That's impressive," she voiced through me. "You must be proud to wield such power."

The gang leader smiled. "I'm not one to boast."

A smirk formed on my face. "Got you."

We drew our training sword and sprinted toward him. The circle of men closed in to defend, but the Presence stopped just short of the leader and changed direction. My feet hit the shield of a man to the right, using it as a base to leap to safety.

We headed for their camp, snuffing out every source of light on the way. Satisfied with the diversion, the Presence slipped us into the shadows. The musky smell of body odor and sweat kept us informed of the men's location as they searched for us. Soon, they split into groups of three to cover more ground.

One of the groups wandered a little too far from the others, so we stalked them, allowing the darkness to conceal us as we leaned against the corner of a tent. We waited for the group to pass, then drove our blade through one of them before disappearing again. The men looked around in alarm.

"Send up a flare, Dorik!" one said.

The man called Dorik raised his hand and launched a fireball from it. We charged into the light and slit the other man's throat while he looked up. Dorik's eyes widened as we grabbed his head and shoulder, pulled him in, and sank our teeth into his neck. We thrashed our head like a hungry volf attacking its next meal. His blood flooded into my mouth with a metallic taste.

An urge to vomit washed over me so vigorously that it stopped the entity in its tracks.

"Weakling!" she screamed. "Contain yourself!"

I wanted to scream. The entity allowed me this, and the cavern echoed with a low-pitched howl. I saw the men running toward me, and again, we dipped into the shadows. The leader barked orders when he saw the bodies.

Silently, we picked up a rock and hurled it into the weapons rack across the way. The clatter of metal drew the men's attention, and they began to vigorously search that area. My void bound activated, and before they had a chance to react, we'd lopped off their leader's head. Chaos erupted all around me.

A small spark formed a ball of white light in my palm. It levitated for a moment, then separated. The two pieces danced in a circle. We closed our fist, crushing them. Sparks shot up my arm, only stopping when they reached my shoulder. We extended our hand toward the men, then opened the fist.

A brilliant beam of energy disintegrated the top halves of two men and what remained fell to the ground. Burning flesh seared its scent into my memory. We retreated to the cages and prepared another blast. Before we could initiate a new attack, I felt a slight prick in my neck. We reached up and discovered a small dart.

"No!" the entity shrieked.

The world faded, and I blacked out.

27

In the Gruegen Gang cage…

A tremor shook the mine, ejecting chunks of rock from the ceiling. What were they doing out there? They would bring the entire mine down at this rate! The humanoid figure with the odd volf ears jolted back into view. He grinned, and his blood-red eyes focused on the settlement with an intensity that terrified me. The clawed hand of the stranger whipped outward, and a blinding sphere of pulsating light formed in his palm. Then he grabbed his neck, and both of his volf-like ears flattened against his head. He collapsed.

What just happened?

An additional group of shirtless men surrounded him while others dealt with the remnant of gang members.

Karia rushed to the edge of the cage. "*Sep, Elutha! Tel mobas lin gerat!*"

One man looked over, clearly alarmed. His bulky muscles rippled under his tattooed, light brown, hairless skin as he ran to the cage and fell to his knees. The man tenderly ran his large hand down Karia and Teora's faces. "*Karia, Teora, ner tola kei vaya!*"

Karia addressed the man. "Elutha, this is Kinara. She was captured trying to save us."

Elutha's kind, deep brown eyes focused on me, and he smiled. "Thank you for trying to help."

I nodded, though I didn't feel worthy of his gratitude. If I'd saved them, I'd feel differently. Elutha freed us when another man brought the keys to the cages. I approached the group of men who still guarded the stranger, curious to see him up close. When I saw him, I gasped. Zaelek?

It couldn't be. He looked so different: Shoulder-length black hair had replaced his short brown hair, and he now had a set of black volf ears. The thin shell of armor covering his body resembled an elemental armor. Had he unlocked his element somehow?

His black hair receded, leaving the ears to jut out. Elutha barked an order, and one of the men picked Zaelek up.

Panic filled me. "What are you doing? Put him down!"

Elutha rested his hand on my shoulder. "We mean him no harm. We're going to take both of you to our village where he can be studied further. You'll be safe there."

"What do you mean 'study' him?"

He gestured toward Zaelek. "Is this a common transformation with your people?"

"No! I've never seen this before."

"Exactly. We need to understand what happened here."

"This is ridiculous, you can't just hold us hostage!" I paused. "Drone…"

Elutha crushed the sphere as soon as it appeared. The aggressive move startled me.

"What in Styx?!"

"I can't allow you to transmit our location to anyone. Our people must remain hidden."

"So, you're taking us prisoner?"

"If that's how you choose to look at it, yes."

I looked desperately at Karia. "Please!"

Karia returned my gaze uneasily. "I'm sorry. I have no say in the matter. Elutha speaks on behalf of the Chieftess."

"Who?"

"Our leader," said Elutha. "I assure you she will be more than hospitable to you and the…man-beast." He nodded to one of the men, and the man seized me, binding my hands behind my back.

"What are you doing?! Get your hands off me!"

"Sorry. It's protocol when transporting outsiders."

The men surrounded me. I could teleport, but that would mean abandoning Zaelek, and I couldn't do that. I had no choice but to allow the strangers to escort me out of the mine.

Walking for a few minutes, we arrived at the entrance to the shaft. When we stepped into the light, I recoiled from the glare.

"Where exactly is your village?" I asked.

"Not far. No more questions," Elutha said. He put a gag in my mouth then nudged me forward.

I lost track of time as we walked through the seemingly endless forest. I thought we would never break through the sea of trees, but eventually, we found ourselves at the base of an extensive mountain range. Many cliffs lined the mountainside, sharp stones, and gnarled tree trunks protruded from the jagged walls.

Seeing the mountain brought on a mixture of despair and annoyance. The thought of clambering up the craggy face in my current state of exhaustion made me want to sink to the ground and go no farther. All I wanted was to be home, lying in my soft bed. No Javelar, no Altarians, just me finally having a chance to grieve for Alator in the comfort of my blankets and pillows.

Elutha stopped the party at the foot of the cliff. "We're here."

But there was nothing there, not even a measly outpost. Elutha approached the cliff wall and placed his hand on it, whispering to himself. His thick tattoos glowed white briefly, then faded back to black. I watched as a ripple appeared in the face of solid rock.

Green light about twenty feet above us crawled down the cliff until it reached the ground. A wall of golden energy replaced the rockface barring our way. The men at the front of our party stepped through and disappeared. I dug my heels in as the rest of the party pushed me forward into the energy's radiating warmth. It washed over me as I passed through, and I stood staring at what should have been the inside of a mountain.

A broad ray of sunlight shone down through the ceiling of the hollowed, rock dome and illuminated a massive tree growing in the center of the crater-like formation. A gleaming lake wrapped partially around the crater's edge.

The men took the gag out of my mouth.

"Cloaking technology?" I asked with wide eyes.

Elutha laughed. "Close, but not quite."

They led me down a cobblestone path and into the sanctuary-like city below. I marveled at the tan stone buildings lining the road, and their red, tiled roofs. People filled the streets, going about their business with the occasional glance our way. How had they hidden an entire city here? The Forces must know about this. Surely it was too large to have gone unnoticed.

A swarm of guards rushed up the path to intercept us.

Their leader addressed Elutha. "*Gulti mabori katayamondal.*"

Elutha bowed and handed us to them. They blindfolded me before escorting me to a holding cell. Once inside, the guards removed the cloth covering my eyes but replaced my restraints with a high-tech pair of handcuffs.

I paced the cell, wondering what would come next and what they thought they might gain by holding us here. Why go through all this trouble to conceal themselves, just to reveal their location to total strangers? None of this made any sense.

What felt like an hour later, a tall woman entered the room. Her straight black hair cascaded down her back, swaying back and forth as she approached my cell. I couldn't help but notice how her dark hair complimented her olive skin.

She said, "You speak Atlantean, correct?"

I looked at her suspiciously and nodded. "Yes."

"I am Ren'Za, second in command to Chieftess Ailyana. Before we consider you a guest of our nation, there are some things we must clarify. What organization do you and your party belong to?"

"The United-Guardian Forces."

"Do these Forces harbor any ill will toward the Altarian race?"

"We don't know anything about your race."

Ren'Za's beautiful sapphire eyes looked up from her electronic tablet. "Please answer the question with a yes, or no."

I sighed in frustration. "No."

"Who do you report to?"

"Colonel Khendrig Voelker."

"I see, and do you have contact with him?"

"No."

Ren'Za combed over whatever was on her tablet. A few awkward minutes passed before she returned her attention to me. "Excellent. The readings from your Khordrus confirm you are telling the truth."

"My what?"

"The restraining device on your wrists." Ren'Za called someone at the door, and a small group of female guards entered the cell. "There is one final process to complete." They grasped my arms then led me down a stairwell.

When we reached the bottom, we stood in an underground garden. A white tree with sagging branches grew in the center. The woman on the right spoke. "Once we unlock the Khordrus, you will remove all your clothing and place it on the benches."

I looked at her in horror.

"A proper search is required before we begin the final process. Resist, and we will not hesitate to kill both you and your companion."

I weighed the potential outcomes of a few tactical escapes, none of which had promising results. Taking a deep breath, I removed my clothing, shivering with discomfort as I stood completely naked before the guards and Ren'Za. Their hands groped my body as they conducted an intrusive search.

Ren'Za smiled when they found nothing. "You may put your clothes back on."

I did so with haste. My clothes were the only comfort I had left. The moment I had done up the last button on my blouse, the women seized my arms again and led me to the tree. Ren'Za walked to a small console at the edge of the concrete ring separating the tree's soil from the walkway.

The guards threw me to the ground next to the trunk and stepped back. Ren'za tapped the screen of the console. A transparent barrier of energy shot from the concrete ring, locking me inside.

I shouted to Ren'Za, "What are you doing?"

Ren'Za glanced at me. "We must erase the past seven hours from your memory. No one can know our location."

"Are you insane?!"

"Do not worry, your memories before that will remain intact. This tree is native to our homeland, Altaria. We planted it when we settled here. The tree responds to an electrical stimulus. The extent of memories erased depends on how much energy it absorbs.

"I must warn you, however. The experience will be unpleasant, but you won't remember the pain."

Ren'Za slid her fingers across the interface, activating the electrical current. I looked at the tree and saw it change from a faint glow to a bright array of colors. It groaned as its branches moved.

With fantastic speed, a branch wrapped itself around my left wrist. I tried to pry it off but another captured my free hand and forced my arms away from my body.

"No! Wait!" I screamed.

The tree lifted me a few feet. Even as I kicked at the branches, two more limbs immobilized my legs. A fierce blast of flames flew from my hands, but the branches were unaffected by the flames licking their white wood.

Ren'Za called to me. "Save your enigma. The tree won't be affected by any element."

I cursed. More branches extended from its trunk and wrapped themselves around my waist. They coiled up my body until they reached my shoulders, then split in two. One of the limbs continued until it clasped my neck, trapping it in place. I gasped for air as it began to tighten.

The other branch split again, producing two thin twigs at its point. They worked their way next to my ears. Abruptly, they entered my ear canals and stopped before rendering damage to my eardrums. Electricity erupted through my skull, traveling all the way down my body. I screamed as my body convulsed.

28

At the Altarian research facility...

I squinted as a bright light overhead blinded me. My head pounded, and my body ached. I was so disoriented I thought I was going to vomit. My hand went to shield my eyes but something restrained me, and I realized I was lying on what felt like a metal table.

I pulled at the restraint with all my strength. All it did was create a head-splitting clanging. I tried to move my feet and my other hand. They, too, were locked in. My breath quickened, and I struggled like a trapped animal.

A female voice called from the corner of the metal room. "Doctor, he's awake!"

The glass door to the left slid into the wall, and a man rushed into the room, "How long?"

"I'm not sure," the woman replied. "I was just going over the notes when he started fighting the restraints."

The doctor pushed the light away from my face. He held a finger up, then moved it back and forth. My eyes tracked the movement. I tried to speak, but a growl escaped my lips. *What in Styx?*

"Fascinating. I've never seen a transformation like this."

Transformation? What was he talking about? Then I remembered those stone hands taking hold of me. Something had obviously happened to me down in that mine.

The woman spoke, "What is it?"

"I don't know," the doctor said. "Let's see if he has any level of self-awareness."

The woman carried a small, book-sized mirror to the foot of the metal table. Clinking noises sounded from under the table, and it tilted until vertical. I looked at my reflection. Two large, volf-like ears sat atop my head. My eyes glowed red, and my fingers ended in elongated nails. I squirmed and hissed. My canine teeth were much more longer than they'd felt in the mine. What was happening to me? And what happened to that…*thing* in my mind?

The doctor scrawled something onto an electronic tablet. Pain rippled through my body as the beastly features receded into my skin. When the sensation finally stopped, I leaned my head against the table in exhaustion.

He looked up from his writing device and stroked the stubble on his face. "Do we have any data that might help us discern what causes the recession of the transformation?"

"No, Doctor," the woman said.

"No matter, I'm sure we'll have it soon enough." The doctor paused, then addressed me, "Can you hear me?"

His words took a moment to process. It sounded like he spoke in two different languages, yet somehow I understood both. "Yes."

"Incredible. Cypa, inform the Chieftess that our guest in the lab is concsious."

My head dropped as the words jumbled again in my mind, then I understood them. "Who?"

Surprise flashed across his face as he came closer. "You understand what I'm saying?"

"Yes."

"Elutha told me you only spoke Atlantean."

"You're speaking Atlantean," I said, convinced he was trying to trick me.

"We're conversing in Altarian."

The man jabbed my arm with something sharp, and I yelped.

"What are you…?" My body went limp, and I couldn't formulate the rest of my question.

"A paralytic to keep you from harming us, or yourself. Don't worry, it won't have any permanent effects."

The doctor unlatched the restraints and turned me to my side, accidentally lifting my shirt. He gasped. "You have the Mark." He paused, "Cypa, come here for a moment."

The woman's footsteps grew louder as she approached.

"Do you recognize this scar on his back?"

What scar?

"The leafless tree," she said in wonder.

A brief wave of panic washed over me. What were they seeing? I'd never injured my back!

"Do you know what it means?"

"No."

The doctor sighed, shaking his head. "Education simply isn't what it used to be. What do they teach you kids in history these days?" He cleared his throat. "Long ago, the Altarians fought the bloodiest civil war our people had ever seen. It lasted for over a decade. Still, after the eleventh year, whispers spread across the land of an independent party who was tired of fighting. Their leader, Asonna, was a gifted sorceress who could amplify elemental power.

"The amplification, however, left its mark in the shape of a scar. It soon became known as the Mark of Asonna. Only those who she deemed 'worthy' received this gift and were coined 'Champions of Asonna.' The Champions infiltrated both sides of the warring people and brought them to their knees from the inside. Once both sides had been subdued, Asonna implemented a new form of government, one we haven't deviated from since that time."

I hadn't even unlocked my element! How was it possible I'd been affected?

"How does it work?" his assistant asked.

"The Champions needed to touch an object that Asonna imbued with her power. Once the power entered their body, it stayed there. Where such an artifact would be found is beyond me, but the Chieftess must be informed right away."

The room spun in a blurred mass as my captors pulled me down the hallway on some kind of levitating table. Two skewed figures opened a set of massive doors, allowing us to pass into a large open room. I couldn't prop myself up, so I just lay there looking like a lopotrout out of water.

"What is the meaning of this?" a woman said.

The doctor addressed her. "Forgive us, Ren'Za, but we need to speak to the Chieftess."

"The Chieftess isn't back from the Ulinda Hunt. She appointed me to keep things in order while she is away. Now, why have you brought this…abomination before me?"

Abomination?

"This *abomination*, as you call him, is a Champion of Asonna."

"Impossible."

"I assure you, it isn't."

Ren'Za hesitated. "Then why does he look like *that*."

"This is a reaction to the drugs sedating him. Something must have gone wrong during the amplification."

"I'd say. He looks more beast than man."

"Don't worry, most of the traits go away once the drugs have run their course."

My heart slammed hard against my chest. *Most? Am I going to be stuck like this forever? I don't want to look like a lab experiment gone wrong!*

"Most?"

This time, the doctor hesitated. "The ears are proving to be more resistant."

With every passing moment, I loathed myself more and more for taking those stones. If Ari had seen me like this, I would never have heard the end of it. The familiar wave of grief washed over me when I thought of her, followed predictably by thoughts of my parents and brothers. I had to get out of here, so I could find out what happened to them. I didn't know how, but I would do everything in my power to find a way.

"Take him back to the lab and run more tests on him."

The doors behind us swung open, and multiple pairs of footsteps echoed throughout the room.

Another woman's gentle but firm tone came from the new group. "What's happening here?"

Ren'Za's blurry shape knelt. "Your Highness. I was hoping to have this *creature* out of the courtroom before you returned. The doctor was just about to take him back to the lab."

A man immediately rushed to my side. "Ailyana, this is Kinara's companion."

The Chieftess' calm demeanor turned to anger. "How did this happen to him?"

"Your Grace," the doctor interjected, "We were instructed to conduct humane research on him."

"This is a man, not a wild animal! What part of what you've done is humane?"

Ren'Za rose. "We weren't sure how to…"

"Get out of my sight, now."

The doctor and his assistant grasped my arms and started to lift me.

"No," the man who had identified me said. "Leave him there."

They gently let me down, then they and Ren'Za scurried from the room. Gratitude filled me. I didn't want to think about what might have happened to me if the Chieftess and her group hadn't shown up when they did.

"Elutha," the Chieftess said.

"Yes?"

"Take him to the public infirmary and have the staff flush the drugs from his system."

"As you wish."

Elutha's muscles rippled under the elaborate, thick, black tattoos on his bare back as he pushed open the doors of the infirmary. Sunlight spilled in, stinging my eyes. I squinted as I followed him outside and stared at the majestic city with clear vision for the first time. Dwellings of all sizes and materials stretched in every direction, divided only by the broad, improved roads running between them.

As Elutha guided me through the stone lanes, I saw many citizens in dazzling clothes bustling by. The scent of cooking meats and other foods filled the air. Shops lined each side of the streets, their owners attempting to sell goods just outside.

Elutha gestured toward the path with his chin. "Come on. Let's go find Aurok and Kinara."

It didn't take long to realize that the citizens looked at me as if I were a kilindrel in a povine pen, and it made me uncomfortable. Thankfully, we came to a circular plaza where everyone didn't need to be so crammed together. The assortment of goods being sold in its center kept the majority of attention off of me.

Ahead, I could see a distant palace sitting atop a hill. A tree the size of a small skyscraper loomed over it. Its green leaves shimmered in the brilliant sunlight. Chills shot across my skin just looking at it.

"Elutha!" a voice called from up ahead.

A man who must surely be his identical twin joined us with Kinara in tow. A sigh of relief escaped me. I didn't know what I would have done if something had happened to her.

Elutha introduced me. "Zaelek, this is my brother, Aurok."

I extended my hand in greeting. "Pleased to meet you."

Aurok looked at my hand suspiciously, then grasped it. An overwhelming force of enigma went through me. It was so intense my legs almost buckled and it left me wondering if that was normal here.

He laughed. "The pleasure is mine."

Elutha hugged his brother. The thick black tattoos on their arms, necks, and backs now formed a complete picture of two warriors crossing blades.

"I'm glad we found you! I thought you might be here."

Aurok nodded toward two other men standing awkwardly next to a fountain in the plaza. "Hey, I hope you don't mind, but I brought Tarris and Coroth with us."

"Not at all! The more, the merrier."

Kinara winked at me. "Glad to see you're…" she stopped. "Are those…volf ears still on top of your head?"

I reached up and was disappointed to find they were still there. Kinara approached me and flicked one.

I recoiled in pain, "Ow! What's the matter with you?"

"Interesting…. How did you get those?"

I recounted the events. Elutha and Aurok listened.

Kinara shook her head in frustration. "I tell you not to touch anything, and you do it anyway. It's like I'm talking to a wall."

"I think I learned my lesson."

"Oh, really? Because I thought you would've learned when you activated the mine. Now look at you! You have two extra ears!"

"It's not like I asked for them." I said, touching my normal ears self-consciously.

"You might as well have."

Elutha stepped in. "Okay, you two. That's enough. Why don't we discuss this more at dinner? I'm sure you both have questions."

Aurok laughed. "And we have questions for you, too."

Kinara nodded. "That sounds good to me."

"Then it's settled. Dinner and answers!"

Elutha led us through the lively streets of the village. Children crossed our path while they played a game involving a leather ball and sticks. It seemed the goal of the game was to keep it away from the two other children chasing it.

One boy bumped into me and smiled innocently. "Sorry, Sir. I wasn't watching… Woah! Are those volf ears? How did you get those?"

Tarris thumped the child on the head. "Don't be rude."

The boy looked down at his feet with regret. "Sorry." As he scurried away to rejoin the others, I thought about how strange Tarris' reaction was. I hadn't seen anyone discipline a child without having a connection to them. I wondered if it was part of their culture for everyone to act as a parent.

When we arrived at the tavern, we stood outside while Coroth arranged for seating. The building's broad support beams were carved in the shape of giant leaves and painted a dark green. People sat on wooden chairs at patio tables, lost in their own conversations. It reminded me of my hometown.

Coroth called to us, gesturing with one bulging arm. We followed him into the spacious building, trying not to push anyone out of their place in line. A wooden bar lined with stools sat to the left, but the room's right side opened into a seating area surrounding the massive hearth where flames danced within its fire pit. By the time we sat down at an empty table next to it, the host had arrived to greet us.

"Good evening, and welcome to Joro's. I'm Joro, and it is

my pleasure to serve you this evening. Coroth informed me that two special guests would be joining us tonight from the Atlantean speaking world. Undoubtedly, that would be the two fresh faces seated at the table, am I correct?"

Elutha nodded. "That's correct."

Joro waved two of the servers over. "In good spirits, my team and I have selected our most popular dishes. It's already been paid for, so don't worry about it. I'm hopeful that if we ever integrate into the outside world, your friends will recommend my humble business to their associates."

Integrate into the outside world? Why would they want to do that? They had their own secret piece of paradise right here. It seemed crazy anyone here would want to give that up.

The owner departed, disappearing into the crowd. The food arrived shortly after, and Tarris insisted on preparing our plates. He chose a variety of dishes, then set them down in front of us.

I pointed at a dish with odd tentacles poking out of it. "What are those things?"

Elutha finished slurping one down then replied, "Those are Kinbar Eel legs. They're a delicacy here."

I hesitantly picked one up and took a bite. The meat tasted like a povine steak. Its texture, however, reminded me a little of rubber.

Aurok laughed. "Good, isn't it?"

I nodded while chewing the rubbery flesh. Though it wasn't my favorite dish, Dad always taught us that everything was delicious when we were a guest in someone's house.

Elutha scooped another serving of a dish that looked like a yellow cloud onto his plate.

"So, Kinara, who were you trying to call back at the mines? I might be able to get you in contact on one of our secure lines."

Kinara finished chewing before replying. "Really? I was trying to contact my commander. I just need to report to him and tell him we're okay."

"Commander you say? What organization do you belong to?"

"The Guardian Forces."

"Hmm…seems reasonable enough. Let me see what I can do."

Kinara pointed to my ears. "The Colonel will want to know what's going on with Volfboy, too."

"Hey!" I protested.

I knew she was right, though. The whole situation at the mine had me desperate for answers, and I worried I hadn't seen the last of the Presence. It terrified me to think of that *thing* getting loose and rampaging through this hidden city.

Elutha chuckled. "I imagine he would, but we don't know what's going on, either."

I had been so preoccupied with the conversation and the meal that I hadn't noticed the beverage sitting in front of me until I dished up a second plate. The blue fruit atop the blonde colored drink danced across the surface as it bubbled.

When the liquid touched my tongue, I tasted a mixture of bitter and sweet. I drained the cup before a young waitress refilled it in passing. After the second glass, I noticed a profound fogginess falling over my mind.

Coroth laughed when he noticed my reaction. "Better slow down on those drinks! You'll be drunk before we get to dessert."

Nonetheless (though against my better judgment) I had a few more. I wasn't the only one, everyone else drained as many as I did and laughed as Aurok and Tarris told stories of their childhood.

At some point during the night, the staff introduced live music to the scene. The owner cleared some of the tables and chairs to make room for dancing. Kinara and I soon found ourselves dancing like fools. The rest of our party laughed hysterically and cheered us on as we embarrassed ourselves. Eventually, we convinced Coroth and Tarris to join us. Elutha and Aurok clapped from the table but seemed to be enjoying everything right where they were.

When the time had come for the pub to close, Joro instead threw a private party, inviting his multitude of friends to join us. We laughed, danced, and drank the night away. It was quite a change from recent events.

I woke in a soft bed at an inn, remembering that Elutha had requisitioned the rooms for us last night. I also remembered that he said we could stay here until we left. He called it a "peace offering" for how we'd been treated when we arrived.

My head pulsed, and I felt nauseous. The world still spun as I got up to shut the drapes. Sunlight poured through the window as mid-morning approached.

I slowly returned to my bed and eased myself onto it, trying not to increase the pain in my head. The second my eyes shut, there was a gentle knock on my door. I groaned and pushed myself up off the bed.

It was Ren'Za and she was carrying one of the strange tablets I had seen earlier.

"My apologies for disturbing you, but I have a message from the Chieftess. She would like to meet with you at noon today in the Royal Gardens."

I'd expected the Chieftess would want to talk to me eventually, but I wished the meeting had been scheduled for this evening. I didn't know if I would be at a hundred percent before noon.

"What time is it now?"

"Ten in the morning."

"Of course it is," I mumbled under my breath. "Alright, how do I get there?"

"Elutha and Aurok will be waiting to escort you."

"Thank you."

She curtsied and left.

I shut the door, then rummaged through my backpack for a fresher set of clothes. All of them were gone. A brief panic attack ensued before I noticed the note at the bottom of the pack. It read: *While you were out last night, we cleaned your clothes for you. You will find them hanging in your closet.*

The closet door creaked as I opened it. Hanging from the bar were my clothes, and underneath them sat my boots, now spotless. As I slid the hangers across the metal bar, I discovered a new set of clothing I had not brought. Another note hung from the shirt: *For your meeting with the Chieftess.* I laid the formal-looking clothes on the bed.

Not wanting to smell like a svinen pen, I hastily showered and brushed my teeth. I threw on the knee length pants and the pair of new-looking sandals, then moved to the black shirt. When I tried to put it on, I noticed how different it was: It had a hole for my head and one sleeve to put my left arm through. The piece of cloth only covered my left pectoral muscle and the left side of my upper back.

I looked at myself in the mirror, frowning at the sight of the two black volf ears. I looked ridiculous. I just wanted to throw on one of my own shirts, so I didn't give people another reason to stare. However, not wearing the clothes could insult someone, and I couldn't have that. I crossed the hall and knocked on Kinara's door.

She peeked through the crack and scanned me from head to toe. "You, too, huh?"

"If your clothing looks like mine, you might be in for an interesting stroll across town."

She grinned. "You wish."

Kinara pulled the door back, and I had to keep my jaw from dropping. A beautiful, white sleeveless dress hung from her shoulders and draped almost to her feet. Slits lined with gold went from the bottom of her dress to her mid-thigh, exposing her fair skin. The gold from her outfit complemented her eyes and slightly curled hair. It made me feel even worse about the ears.

"You look fantastic."

She blushed and smiled. "Don't get used to it."

We found our new friends waiting at the base of the inn steps. When they saw us, I knew from their horrified expressions that something wasn't right.

"What?" I asked.

Tarris and Coroth howled with laughter.

Elutha pointed to the shirt I was wearing and said, "Zaelek, that isn't a shirt."

Kinara tried to contain her laughter. I shot her a nasty glare, and she covered her broad smile with her hand. I felt the blood rushing to my cheeks. *She must think I'm an idiot.*

Elutha walked over to a well next to the inn and retrieved the hanging bucket.

"Get ready," he said. "This is going to hurt."

Before I could brace myself, he dumped the frigid water onto the fabric of the "shirt." Searing pain erupted where the cloth touched, and I gasped, collapsing to one knee. It took every ounce of self-control I had not to utter a sound.

The black fabric deteriorated, exposing my bare skin. It left behind a perfect tattoo that resembled Elutha's symbols but had its own unique style, almost like a shoulder piece for ancient armor. The art began halfway up my bicep and ended just at the base of my neck. It also covered my left pectoral muscle with its elegant design. The pain dissipated, but the area had turned red and swollen.

I didn't know whether to feel honored or angry about the tattoo. I rose to my feet. Everyone but Kinara knelt on one knee with their heads bowed and a fist over their chest.

Elutha slapped me in the back, sending jolting stings throughout the area of the tattoo. "Congratulations, Zaelek."

"Thanks, but why a tattoo?"

"Think of it as a gift from your Champion predecessors. Each one of them had these markings. The shoulder piece signified their prowess in battle and their status in the community. As they grew in strength, they would add their own unique design to form a complete sleeve. Come on, let's get you to the Chieftess."

It didn't take us long to reach the palace. The stone walls protecting the structure created a perimeter around the trunk of the largest tree I'd ever seen. Its size made the village look like a scene constructed from children's building blocks. Massive spires extended from the walls, ending in spiraled points hundreds of feet above us.

The large metal doors of the gate ahead were open. Two guards wearing heavy armor were positioned on opposite sides of the entrance. They slammed the ground with the butts of their pikes when we approached.

"Halt," one called. "State your…Elutha, is that you?"

Elutha waved. "Good morning, Sible."

The man saluted. "The Chieftess is waiting for her guest in the Royal Gardens, Sir."

Tarris led us through the gates, his large body looking tiny next to the scale of the surroundings. We followed the cobblestone path that led through the grounds, passing beneath vine-covered archways every fifty yards or so. The rampant vines had taken over the rails connecting the arches, creating in a hedge-like barrier.

I marveled at the palace's incredible architecture. It was nestled in a hollowed out portion of the tree's base. Its top section disappeared behind the wall of wood where the outside carving had stopped. Thick green stalks crawled up the perfectly chiseled stone blocks, competing to project their huge, beautiful cyan flowers.

The cobblestone path led to dark red, wooden doors. Colossal stained glass windows topped the entryway, depicting a Jintian wildcat holding its prey in its mouth. The enormous cat's elegant red mane and spotted body were depicted as matted with blood.

We turned at the end of the central courtyard and went through a stone archway. Tarris stopped us before we entered a large atrium with no roof.

"Zaelek, this is as far as we go. Kinara will stay with us. The Chieftess requested to speak to the Champion alone."

I didn't feel comfortable meeting the Chieftess alone. A million scenarios raced through my mind. *What if I make a fool of myself...again? What if I offend her somehow?*

"How do I address her?"

"Your Majesty, Your Grace, Your Highness. Take your pick."

"Can't one of you come with me?"

Coroth gently pushed me toward the path. "Go on. "

I took a few steps forward, then looked back. Elutha nodded to me in encouragement. Kinara's worried expression didn't make me feel any better.

"I'll see you soon," I said.

I admired the plant life as I walked, hoping that the lively garden's tranquility would soothe my anxiety. Carabells chirped from their perches, eying the pollen-carrying insects that flew between flowers. A few exotic susserflies fluttered by my face on their multicolored ribbon-like wings.

The path curved and followed a large, yellow hedge. I heard the faint sound of water cascading from the other side where there was an open area. In its center sat a three-tiered fountain made of white stone.

A young woman sat at the base of the fountain running her slender fingers through the crystal clear water. She wore a magnificent headdress made of dark blue and purple feathers. A snarl to my left got my attention as a Jintian wildcat prowled toward me.

The young woman brushed her midnight black hair back over her shoulder.

"Enough, Jhika. He isn't here to hurt me."

The large cat slunk to her side, never taking its golden eyes off me. She smiled. Her dark purple irises studied me, but somehow, her almond-shaped eyes put me at ease.

"You must be the Champion that I've heard so much about. I'm the Chieftess of the Altarian people."

I bowed. "It's a pleasure to meet you, Your Highness."

"Please, there is no need for such formalities. You may call me Ailyana," she stood to face me. "I hope you have been finding our home to your liking."

"Yes. Your people have shown us such hospitality during our stay. I wish there were a way I could repay you."

"No need. It is our honor to host a Champion," she paused, "Let us discuss why I requested a meeting. From what I understand, you and your companion came across our people by happenstance."

"Yes, Ma'am."

"I don't believe in coincidences. How absurd it is to think that a Champion of Asonna simply fell into our laps. No, I believe you were sent to us for a reason. Regardless of what that might be, I read the report from Ren'Za and discovered that you are part of an organization from the outside world."

"Not quite. Kinara is part of the Guardian Forces, but I haven't joined yet."

"But you intend to?"

"I do."

Ailyana pulled her headdress off and shook her silky hair out. The pitch-black color complimented her perfect, light mocha skin. "I see. Is anyone from this organization expecting you?"

"A Colonel who was close to my father."

"And this Colonel command your companion as well?"

"He does."

"Excellent. I have a proposal for him."

29

Waiting at the garden entrance…

Zaelek returned in the company of a young woman. I had to admit, I hadn't pegged Zaelek for a tattoo guy, but he pulled it off. The thick black lines of the drawn armor complimented his defined muscles. I chewed the inside of my lip, then purged the thoughts, feeling like these new emotions bubbling up were cheating on Alator.

The woman smiled at our group, and the men bowed. I quickly followed their lead. This must be the Chieftess, though her youth surprised me. For some reason I had imagined her to be an old lady.

She addressed Elutha. "Where might I find Kinara?"

My breath caught in my throat.

Elutha nodded at me. "This is Kinara, Your Highness."

"Kinara," the woman said. "I am Ailyana."

I bowed again. "Your Highness."

"I'm told you might be able to contact your commander."

"No, Your Highness. My means of communication got destroyed in the mines."

"You can use the system in our briefing room."

I hesitated, mulling over potential outcomes from contacting the Guardian Force from an unknown system. "Do I have a choice?"

"You always have a choice, but you don't always have control over the consequences. Though, if it makes you feel better, I only want to make him an offer. You have my word that you will be free to go if he declines, that is after we render you unconscious and leave you back at the mines."

I didn't like the way she'd slipped that subtle threat into her answer, but what choice did I have?

"I can request a meeting with my commander, but only if we allow them to use a private server separated from our main channel."

"Very well. I accept your terms." Ailyana turned to Coroth and said something else in Altarian.

Coroth touched his chest with his fist, then trotted toward the palace. Ailyana gestured for us to follow. The cobblestone path led to the building's wooden doors where a guard admitted us.

Beautiful dark blue banners hung from the grand staircase banister at the end of the enormous reception area.

A gorgeous maitan crystal chandelier graced the ceiling in the center of the room. As we followed the Chieftess through a stone archway, I admired the numerous painted portraits that lined the well-lit hallway.

Elutha smiled when he noticed my curiosity. "These paintings represent every generation of rulers that we've had."

An oddity caught my eye. "Why is that frame empty? And why are all these portraits of women?"

"If a Chieftess brings shame to our people, we strip her portrait from the frame. If you look closely, you can still see a scrap of the painting in the corners. As for your other question, the Altarian tribe has always been ruled by the eldest daughter as our tradition dictates."

Zaelek interrupted. "These women look quite old…"

"Zaelek!" He had to learn to think before he opened his mouth!

The Chieftess laughed. "It's alright, I find his directness refreshing," she paused. "The woman in the portrait next to me is my mother. She died while participating in the annual hunt when I was very young. I've been the Chieftess for a little over a decade now."

Zaelek's jaw dropped. "But that would mean you were what…? Ten years old?"

"Eight," she said, smiling at his astonishment.

I couldn't imagine what being a ruler at that age would have been like. I did find the idea of a contemporary matrilineal society interesting, especially one as successful as this one seemed to be.

Ailyana stopped at the last door in the hall and opened it. A light flickered to life. In the center of the room sat a large flat tabletop stationed on a pedestal.

"Anya,"she said, *Powenda upa eram HIVE system.*"

Ailyana's command piqued my curiosity. I thought only the Guardian Forces had access to HIVE Systems.

The Chieftess laughed at my baffled expression. "Kinara, your organization isn't the only one that has access to private companies. Besides, HIVE values discretion, just as we do."

The familiar hum of the system surrounded us, and the AI answered in Altarian. Ailyana responded, then the menu floated down from the ceiling.

Zaelek gawked. "This is incredible."

Ailyana turned to me. "It's ready for your authorization code. Just type it in on the console."

I entered my number on the touch screen.

A female voice answered, "Thank you for contacting the Guardian Forces. May I ask who is calling?"

I responded with, "Identification number 4372."

"Please enter your security code into the system you are calling from."

A request came up on the touch screen. I moved my body to block anyone's view then typed my mother's name, *Kamila Katari*."

The woman paused while she checked my credentials. "Thank you, Miss Katari. How may I help?"

"Please put me through to Colonel Voelker's office."

Annoying music played while I waited. I always hated calling the office on an indirect line.

The music stopped when my uncle answered. "Kinara? Where have you been? I've been worried sick."

It felt good to hear a familiar voice other than Zaelek's. "There's been a…situation."

"What *kind* of situation?" Uncle asked, with a note of disapproval in his voice.

"It's hard to explain. There's someone here who wants to talk to you."

Ailyana stepped in before my uncle had a chance to respond.

"Good afternoon, Colonel. My name is Ailyana. I am the Chieftess of the Altarian tribe."

"I was wondering when your people might decide to emerge from the shadows."

Shock flashed across Ailyana's face. "You know of us?"

"Not much gets past me, Your Highness. Though I'll admit, I haven't been able to put a pin in your location."

Ailyana fell silent as her fingers tapped against her leg. Clearly this information had surprised her.

"I see. Perhaps later we can discuss setting up an in-person meeting. For now, would you be willing to participate in a room share? I prefer to see whom I'm talking to."

A request to room share floated in front of Ailyana. She accepted, then the room became my uncle's office. I noted his less-than-pleased expression as he studied us from behind his desk.

"Kinara, Zaelek, good to see you're unharmed. Wait…why in Styx do you have volf ears, Zaelek? You look ridiculous."

I squirmed under his scrutiny as he looked to me for answers. This was the second time this month that I'd met him like this. I'd be lucky if he trusted me to carry out a mission ever again.

"It's a long story, Sir." Zaelek hung his head and continued to stare at the floor.

Ailyana cut in before any of us could speak. "Colonel, I wish to speak with you concerning Zaelek."

Uncle's eyes narrowed as he studied Ailyana's face. "Go on."

"During their travels, Zaelek came into contact with an Altarian artifact. Its power transferred to him, connecting him to our people. Our people refer to it as *Multendonda*, roughly translated to…"

"The rise of a Champion."

"You surprise me again, Colonel."

"I think you'll find I'm full of surprises. Let me guess…you want to keep Zaelek."

Zaelek shifted.

Keep Zaelek? I stared at Ailyana, wondering what she wanted

with him. This whole situation was making me nervous but surely Uncle Kehndrig wouldn't allow that to happen.

"Not exactly. Zaelek is linked to our people now, but I'm not naïve enough to think you would just hand him over to us. I would like to use this opportunity to create a bridge between my people and your organization."

Uncle rested his elbows on his desk and laced his fingers. "I'm listening."

"Our warriors awaken their elemental prowess much differently than your people do. Our process requires a more…*natural* touch. If one who undergoes this method completes their trial, a new breed of warrior is born. One that doesn't require a locksmith's skills to gain power past the Epsilon rank, or the third tier of strength in the way your warriors do."

My eyes widened. It had been my understanding that Guardians could progress through the ranks naturally. Why did she think otherwise?

"It's good to know that I'm not the only one here who does their homework."

I stepped forward. "Sir, what's she talking about?"

Uncle sighed. "The Council decides who passes the Epsilon tier. We don't tell future soldiers about it, so we can weed them out by their personalities. They allow only those Guardians to be promoted who show dedication and promise."

Weed them out? I couldn't believe what I was hearing. That would mean even if someone worked their guts out, there's no guarantee they would progress in rank. The Council had to deem them worthy, regardless of their dedication and hard work. The thought mortified me. In the first days at the academy, relentless self-improvement was ground into our heads. Why would they lie to us about progression? I'd seen so many Guardians burn out from chasing the Delta tier. "*Don't be an Epsilon lifer*" the cadre would always tell us.

"So, the Guardian Forces' *Pave One's Own Path* slogan is just a load of schleet?" The words flew out before I could stop them.

He laughed. "Pretty much. I'll explain later, but I believe the young Chieftess has more to say."

Ailyana nodded. "*We* will awaken Zaelek's element our way, then have him train under our Combat Master, Luci'oan. I can guarantee that we'll have him at Delta rank in two years, which is beneficial to both of us."

I blurted, "Delta in two years? That's impossible!"

She ignored my outburst. "In return, Zaelek will stay with us for a time and operate within our force."

"How long is 'a time'?"

"Three years after his training."

Uncle chuckled. "Why so long?"

"I understand your skepticism, but I have my reasons. The Champions of Asonna are a sacred order to our people. Letting them see a champion rise within our ranks would bolster morale and keep a piece of Altarian culture alive."

"I'll make you a counteroffer. You get Zaelek for the first year after his training, then we alternate from there. Also, Kinara trains with Zaelek to oversee his progress and report back to me. Consider her a liaison for the Guardian Forces."

I suppressed a groan. I didn't want to stay here for another year! The city was where I belonged, not in some unfamiliar country playing ambassador. Why couldn't I just go home and grieve for my fiancé in peace?

Ailyana thought for a moment. "I accept. Kinara and Zaelek will train under Luci'oan for the time being."

A wave of disappointment washed over me. I had hoped that Ailyana would decline the offer, and we could go our separate ways.

The Colonel glanced at Zaelek. "Excellent. However, there is one last thing we must consider."

"Yes?" Ailyana frowned.

"Is this what you want, Zaelek? You're only a civilian, so I can't order you as I do Kinara. The choice lies with you."

All heads in the room turned to Zaelek. For a minute or two, he just stood there, unsure what to say. Then he broke the silence. "It is what I want, Sir, but can I make a request?"

My uncle waited for Zaelek to go on.

"Will you help me find out what has happened to my brothers?"

"You'll be pleased to know that one of our recent reports

confirmed your brothers are still alive and training with Javelar. Ettias would haunt me until my dying breath if I left his kids in the hands of Trentir Savvage. I'll do everything in my power to help you get your brothers back if you agree to join the Forces."

Ben and Parnikus are training with Javelar? The news came as a shock to me. Was this because none of the Khiings children were contracted with the Forces? Did Savvage take them because they were the sons of Cronus? There had to be an explanation.

"Then, I agree," Zaelek said.

30

In a tent, awaiting whatever came next...

It took eight hours of mad scrambling for the Altarians to prepare the ceremony, giving me plenty of time to think about why two organizations were interested in me. It made me uncomfortable. Mom and Dad had always taught us to be humble, and this felt like the complete opposite. From the moment Elutha had stuck me in this tent and announced that I would be the Altarian's new Champion, I had been doted on like some kind of king. I hated it.

Sacred order or not, the people were putting way too much faith in me. What did they think naming me Champion is going to do? *I'm just a simple farm boy....* That made me smile. More like a farm boy *with volf ears!*

I didn't know if I could handle any more change in my life. The only thing holding me together was that Kinara and I were about to train under a legendary warrior.

Elutha opened the flap to the tent. "The ceremony will start soon. Are you ready?"

"Can I answer that after we get this over with?" I asked.

He chuckled. "Don't worry. You'll do fine. You should be honored. You will be the first outsider to partake in an Altarian ritual."

Aurok's head poked through the other flap. "Come, it's time."

I shook out my stiff arms. My hands were cold and clammy, and my heart raced. I couldn't help wondering what might happen if I embarrassed myself again in front of everyone…in front of Kinara.

I slapped my cheeks to help me focus and pushed aside the tent flap, gawking at the gigantic pillar of flames raging in the firepit. Spectators stood in a circle around the inferno, cheering wildly. The vibrations reverberated through my entire body when the large drums were struck.

Ailyana entered the circle, and the drums halted after two mighty strikes.

"Today, we welcome an outsider into our family. Let us show our new brother what it is to be Altarian!"

The crowd roared, then dropped their voices to a whisper. "*Imbalo.*" Their chant got louder with every repetition. Another kick from the drums sounded, then followed the people's rhythm. A shrill battle cry sounded from somewhere in the crowd, intensifying everyone's energy. Whoops and hollers came from every direction. I felt the power of the crowd's energy deep within my soul, and a spark of newfound pride that they were welcoming me into their culture.

Two Altarians wearing an assortment of pelts and feathers burst into the circle, dancing around the firepit with an intoxicating frenzy. Ailyana threw her hands into the air and looked to the sky. More dancers joined the first two until they all moved in unison around the fire. Elutha guided me into the circle with Aurok's help.

I grew more anxious with every drumbeat and it intensified when the dancers surrounded me.

"*Imbalo, Imbalo!*" the people shouted.

Then everything stopped, leaving nothing but the crackling flames and salty smoke. A guttural hiss echoed through the people as the multitude parted behind Ailyana.

In the newly formed pathway stood a lone figure garbed in beautiful purple robes. Grasses or some kind of fur surrounded his ankles and wrists, amplifying the sheer terror of his animal-skull mask as he ambled into the circle like a prowling volf. The gap in the crowd closed behind him and the people fell silent.

The masked Altarian slammed the ground with his fist, and as he rose, a wooden staff grew from the dust. He moved toward me, juddering the staff every few steps.

I heard terrifying, incoherent whispers from behind the mask. Another boom from the drums startled me, causing me to lose my footing.

"Come, child," the figure hissed. "It is time to show us your true self."

The Altarian threw his hands forward, releasing a cloud of spores into the air. Before I could catch myself, I inhaled them. My vision blurred, and vertigo forced me to my knees. I could barely make out Kinara's worried face at the edge of the circle before I realized I could no longer move. My breath came in sharp spurts. A bright white light overtook me before I fell through what felt like another dimension. The world began to spin.

I slammed into the ground and writhed in pain. It took me a moment to realize that the light of the fire had disappeared. The village had been replaced by a forest. While scanning my surroundings, I clambered to my feet. The trees weren't anything like the forest outside the village. Instead, they had thin green needles in place of the familiar blueish-green leaves, and their trunks were dark brown. A blanket of stars shone through a hole in the canopy, leaving me to wonder if Kinara even stood under the same ones.

The fallen needles crunched under my feet. Other than the noises I produced, I couldn't hear anything—no orchestral chirps from symphon bugs, no whistles from nocturnal carabells, nothing. The silence made me anxious.

I entered a clearing, wary of whatever might lurk in the moonlit grasses ahead. This had to be the trial Ailyana mentioned during her conversation with Colonel Voelker. Maybe I just needed to find my way back home. The stalks of the grass-like plants dully lit when I brushed them with my leg, and a cloud of luminescent insects retreated deeper into the forest. A slight breeze carried a resinous scent. The smell of it seemed off, like a cross between musk and urine. A branch snapped behind me, and I whirled but saw nothing.

I turned back, then saw movement ahead. Something rose from the ground. Clumps of dirt fell as a horrifically disfigured creature broke through the soil. The abomination had to be at least twenty feet tall with arms that dangled to its feet. It turned its pale, skinless white face to the sky, exposing its bare skull as it half screamed, half roared.

In an instant the creature materialized only a few feet from me and swung its arm, catching me in the stomach and launching me into a tree at the clearing's edge. The impact stole my breath and I exhaled blood.

I coughed violently, trying to gulp in the fresh night air. The creature moved forward, but its walk seemed labored, hindering its speed. Its fetid breath filled the night sky like a cloud of smoke. I scrambled away from it, tripping over my own feet. It appeared in front of me and backhanded me across the face, sending me skipping across the ground. I only stopped when I hit another tree. My vision faded in and out.

A streak of white flashed from the woods and rammed the lanky creature, sending the abomination across the clearing. To my surprise, a volf with a pelt as pure as the first winter snow stood before me, piercing my soul with its ice-blue eyes. It threw its head back and let loose a low-pitched howl.

Moonlight glinted off something falling from the sky. My sword landed next to me with its tip stuck in the ground. My newfound ally looked at me, expectantly.

I limped to the sword and pulled it from the soil. A tremendous surge of power flowed through me, coursing through my veins like a jolt of electricity. The vegetation around me flattened, and my clothes and hair whipped as shock waves emanated from the weapon. I was consumed by the conviction that it was time to end this.

The white volf charged the creature, and I followed its lead. I slid across the ground, barely avoiding another swiping attack from that rubbery arm. The volf leapt into the air and released a pressurized blast from its fanged mouth. Its wind hit the beast, making it stagger.

I surged forward and thrust my blade into the monstrosity's calf. It shrieked, then kicked me in the side before I could pull the sword out, leaving the blade jutting from its flesh. I flew sideways and landed on my back. I saw the volf skirting around the creature's legs until it found an opening. The white canine latched its jaws onto the hilt of my sword and wrenched it free. A stream of black slime splattered its thick coat.

It dodged another attack from the creature before flicking its head and throwing the blade back to me. I snatched it from the air and charged again. When I was only a few feet away from our opponent it spun, catching both me and the volf in its attack. We were launched across the clearing, landing a few feet from each other.

The creature materialized in front of us and got down on all fours. Its white skull hovered inches above my face. I could smell the putrid scent of rotting flesh. It opened its mouth, revealing chunks of its last meal and strings of saliva. Once again, the creature let loose a terrifying roar, driving the sound into my ears like a sharp knife. I couldn't die here. Parnikus and Ben still needed me.

I thrust the blade into its glowing green eye, forcing it to recoil and cover the wound with its human-like hand.

The volf launched himself onto its chest and kicked off, sending a blast of wind into the creature's sternum. As if a whip slashed the sky, a crack filled the air, and the nightmarish figure skidded across the ground, leaving a massive trench in its wake.

As it pulled itself to its feet, I saw movement behind it. Another volf with pitch-black fur and glowing red eyes stalked out of the trees. It jumped and latched onto the nape of the creature's neck. The volf shook its head viciously, drawing a pained screech from the beast.

Just when I thought the creature might fall, it grabbed the volf and threw it in our direction. The black volf landed gracefully next to us. Both volves looked back at me, their eyes holding an inspiring light of determination.

They surged forward. I initiated a void bound, slowing only when catching up to the volves. They each latched onto one of the creature's arms but didn't stop running. Their momentum threw the monster off balance, and it fell. I jumped, and with both hands, drove my blade deep between the creature's eyes.

31

In the crowd around the Altarian fire pit...

Zaelek, who had knelt unmoving, his eyes staring at nothing since the beginning of the ceremony, collapsed onto the ground. The Altarians uttered a hushed chant. I started to rush to his side but Elutha grabbed my arm.

"He'll be fine, Kinara, I promise. Let him be. This is part of the awakening process."

"What's happening to him?"

"He's facing his trial."

"What kind of trial?"

"That's hard to say. For some, it's a battle between them and their inner demons. For others, it's a puzzle or retrieval of some past relic. The process is unique for everyone."

"What happens if they don't pass their trial?"

"They return to us with their element unlocked, but they do not receive the *jimpomenkai.*" Elutha must have read the confusion on my face. "The blessing of the ancestors. It allows progression in strength without a Locksmith's assistance. This is one of our most powerful gifts, but it can have a price. In some rare cases, the person doesn't come back to us and will eventually die. That is why so many people come to support the ceremony."

His promise didn't reassure me. "Then how do you know he'll be fine?"

"Zaelek is strong. I can tell by the way he carries himself. He'll make it through. Now, come. We don't want to be standing next to him when his element awakens."

I hoped Elutha was right. And I did have faith in Zaelek. I'd seen him struggle, but he never gives up, and I knew he wouldn't start now, especially with his determination to find his brothers

I looked at my watch. A minute passed, then two. I chewed my thumbnail while Elutha whispered something to the Chieftess. Their expressions led me to wonder if Zaelek had been in the process longer than usual. *Three minutes.* Whispers began to creep through the crowd.

A thin puff of dust came from Zaelek's hand. Everyone fell silent. Like a line of fine powder trailing behind a stick, the dirt slowly circled him. His chest lifted off the ground and his entire body rose until he floated at least five feet above our heads.

The dust circling him spun, then intensified as it reached dizzying speeds. The circle tightened, then exploded upward, enveloping Zaelek in a furious cyclone. I covered my face as dirt pelted my skin.

Then, everything stopped. When I looked up, I saw Zaelek hover, then descend before collapsing once again on the ground. Elutha, Aurok, and I rushed to his side.

Ailyana shouted, "Pure wind!" and the crowd erupted into more cheers.

"Is she sure?" I whispered to Elutha.

He smiled, "There's no mistaking it."

Pure wind! There weren't many who got that strain, most only got a branch. I couldn't help smiling. *Zaelek really is the son of Cronus!* I knew his father would be so proud.

Zaelek didn't budge. He was breathing but there was no movement. I took his hand but it was completley limp. Concerned, I looked to Elutha.

"Is he going to be okay?"

"Yes, but for now, he needs to rest. He'll be as good as new in the morning."

The crowd slowly dispersed, speaking softly, respectful of what they had witnessed, but the energy still carried a subtle vibration of excitement.

I helped Elutha and Aurok carry Zaelek to his room at the inn.

"Shouldn't someone stay with him tonight to make sure he's all right?"

Elutha pulled the blankets over Zaelek. "This is normal, Kinara. Nothing has ever happened to anyone after they came out of the trance."

Aurok turned and winked at me, "Unless, of course, you're looking for an excuse to keep him company tonight."

I felt my cheeks get red hot. "Nope, I'll take your word for it."

The brothers laughed and then bid me goodnight. Before I left Zaelek's room, I checked his forehead for any fever—just to be sure—before I pulled his door shut on my way out and found my way to my own bed.

Sunlight poured through the window onto my face. I stretched my limbs as far as they would allow, feeling them tingle slightly. For a moment, I allowed myself to lie there and enjoy the peace of the morning. I bathed, got dressed, and then strapped my sword to my back, just in case we started training today.

Although staying here for an extended period annoyed me, I couldn't help but be interested in seeing how the Altarians trained. Especially when the sessions would be led by a combat master. Not to mention having a unique fighting style could prove useful in the fight against Javelar.

I walked into the lobby and found Elutha and Aurok waiting.

"Zaelek's not up yet?" I asked.

Elutha kept his eyes trained on the wooden carving of the kilindrel he had been working on yesterday. "He is. We knocked on his door a little while ago. Should be out any minute."

About five minutes later, Zaelek entered the lobby.

"Good morning," he said.

"How are you feeling?" I then noticed that the volf ears were gone. "And what happened to those ears?"

"Huh?" he said as he patted the top of his head gingerly. "Guess they disappeared…." He smiled. "Now I feel even better!"

"You don't have any adverse symptoms?"

"No, but is it normal to feel like everything is clearer?"

"Yes. Every warrior experiences heightened senses after their element is unlocked," Aurok said.

"Does it go away?"

"No, but you get used to it."

"Interesting." Zaelek seemed deep in thought for a moment before turning to me and asking, "But what about my element?"

"What about it?"

"Did you see what it was?"

Surprised by the question, I looked at Elutha for answers. How could Zaelek not know?

Elutha still didn't look up from the wood carving. "Pure wind," he stated.

"Pure wind?" Zaelek muttered.

Aurok stood. "Come, I think it's about time you got rid of that training sword."

32

Later, in the Altarian blacksmith's shop...

"Come, Zaelek," Elutha said, gesturing me through the doorway to a narrow shop. I inhaled the potent smell of metal and leather when we entered. It reminded me of the farm. Various weapons and armor cluttered the walls, hide banners hung from the ceiling behind the rough counter near the entrance.

Elutha spoke to a young man there and waited while he retrieved the blacksmith. When she finally came to the front of the shop, the light brown skin of her muscular arms was glistening with sweat. Her resonant voice surprised me when she said, "Let me see that training sword."

I handed it over, unsure why she wanted it.

She pulled it from its sheath and examined the blade. "Where did you get this?"

"It was a gift from my father. Why?"

She raised an eyebrow. "My great grandfather forged it."

Did Dad know about the Altarians?

"How can you tell?"

"The markings on the blade are from an ancient Altarian script called *Renkinda.* The text is part of a family heirloom that my grandfather coveted. He used to read it to me before he died. I'd recognize it anywhere."

Elutha interrupted. "If it was forged here, doesn't that mean he won't need a new weapon?"

"No. It isn't complete."

Her answer puzzled me. "What do you mean?"

"We forged the sword in its basic form. It still needs to bond with you, which I can help with if you want this as your weapon."

"I can keep it?"

"I'll make an exception. My grandfather would have been proud to have one of his weapons serve a Champion. Besides, I would just put it in a display case if it wasn't being used."

The generosity of the Altarians astounded me. This was a priceless family heirloom, and she was going to let me keep it.

"Thank you. I'm honored. What did you mean by 'bonding' the weapon to me?"

"Each Guardian has a unique set of attributes awakened when they access their elemental power. A Forgesmith, such as myself, crafts blades that complement those attributes." She handed it back to me and said, "You'll see. Follow me."

She led us to the back of the shop, to the forge, where a pit of white-hot liquid lay in the center. To the right sat a hammer and anvil.

"Draw your weapon," she said. I did as instructed, and the sword turned white before vibrating in my hand.

The blacksmith circled around me. "We forge much more here than simple materials, Champion. For generations, my family has served as conduits to natural forces beyond your wildest imagination. The great spirits guide this natural energy into the forge, then usher it into your weapon to encourage a bond with your element." She placed her hand on my shoulder. "You can let go of it now. Don't worry, it won't fall."

I released my grip and stared in awe at the hovering weapon. The blacksmith reached out, carefully gripping its blade. Her head shot toward the ceiling, eyes glowing cyan. Wisps of green smoke hissed from her fingers, encasing the blade in their vaporous touch. She set the weapon on the anvil and struck the edge with her hammer. The sword's glow surged. It slowly grew longer and more slender.

Sturdy black cloth wrapped around the hilt like a jik constrictor, leaving visible the small blue gems protruding from it. Its curved grip gently arced opposite the blade and ended in a small ring. Two strips of material grew from the loop like a vine.

Again, the sword surged, and a small ball shot into the pit next to us.

The blacksmith's eyes widened. "Another weapon?"

Bubbles broke the still surface of the liquid metal. From the pit rose another sword. She grasped the new weapon with her metal tongs and placed it on the anvil, watching with curiosity as the two swords stopped glowing. My training sword's blade had altered in color, shimmering a brilliant pearl-white. The second blade had the same shape as the original. Still, its color was black and sported deep red gems instead of blue.

After a brief delay, the weapons encased themselves in new baldrics, each matching their color. Strange new symbols wrapped around the cases.

She gestured toward the weapons. "Take them."

I wrapped my fingers around the grips, and the weapons lifted my arms above my head. They angled themselves down my back, then stopped. Multiple strips of fabric wove around my stomach, securing the casings to me.

Satisified, the blacksmith leaned against the anvil and whispered, *"Raiy'den."*

"What's that mean?" I asked.

"It's your sword set's name."

"It seems…fitting."

"Yes…I've never seen a person receive two weapons. It'll be up to you to discover their full potential."

Kinara examined the swords more closely. "How are you supposed to draw these from their sheaths? The blades are massive."

"I'm not sure I can," I said.

I grasped the swords, and the baldrics snapped open releasing them simultaneously.

Kinara took a step back. "Woah!"

The weapons themselves felt incredible, like a perfect extension of my arms. I slid them toward their sheaths, and the blades guided themselves into place. The cases snapped shut.

"That's incredible!" said Kinara.

"Yes," Elutha said, smiling. "Quite remarkable."

The blacksmith retrieved a tiny leather pouch from one of her shelves, then handed it to me.

"What's this?" I asked.

"A Kintaya stone. It's a shop tradition to give one to each of our customers."

"Do they have a special meaning?"

She laughed. "Inside each of these stones are a few seeds. If you put the stone in soil and water it every day, an Altarian tahrnic root will sprout in about a month."

I had no clue what she meant.

The blacksmith pointed to the counter where a clay pot housed a beautiful flowering bush. Its stunning dark blue leaves complimented the white and pink petals of its flowers.

"That's gorgeous!" Kinara said.

"Yes, but it's more than decorative. The fruits in the center of the flowers have medicinal purposes. Many of our healers apply a paste from the fruit to woundswhich will help fight off infection."

"Thank you," I said, extending my hand.

The same look that had crossed Aurok's face when we first met flashed across hers. She grasped the hand. Another overwhelming enigma surged through me, taking my breath away, just like before. When she released me, the enigma stopped and I took a deep breath. *Okay, seriously. Why in Styx does that keep happening here?* She smiled and nodded, then returned to the forge as Aurok snickered to himself.

I barely remembered the walk back to the inn. The wish that Mom and Dad could have seen this whole process occupied my mind. I couldn't even show my siblings. Would Ari have gotten something similar to me or something different? Anger billowed in my heart, and soon, the anger erupted into a burning resolve to free my brothers. We *would* be reunited.

Elutha and Aurok told us they had, "some matters to attend

to," and that they would see us tomorrow an hour before dawn. They encouraged Kinara and me to relax for the rest of the day and explore the village. Before leaving, Elutha gave both of us a purse of coins, courtesy of Ailyana.

I extended the Kintaya stone to Kinara. "Here, you have it."

Her eyes widened. "What? Why?"

"Plants aren't really my thing."

"Are you sure?"

"I'm sure."

Even though I lied about plants not being "my thing," the seed was a small price to pay to see her beautiful smile. Seeing her happy was enough for me.

Kinara insisted we use some of her money to buy some soil and a pot from a nearby agriculture shop before taking her newfound treasure back to her room. She wanted to get the seed into the soil before going out for the night. I sat on her bed and watched while she prepared the planter.

As she placed the stone in the soil, she paused and said, "I almost wish I was a Stone Guardian."

"Why?" I asked.

"I've always loved growing plants, but most of the time, I kill them." She laughed softly, and I glimpsed sadness in her eyes. "If Alator were here, he wouldn't let me anywhere near this seed. He used to tell me, 'Everyone knows plants don't like Infernos. Stone Guardians are the only ones they'll resonate with.' Of course, that was just him teasing me. He was one of the best green thumbers I've ever known. One time I asked him why he worked for GITF and not the greenhouses. He told me that plants didn't need other plants to look out for them, but people needed other people to do just that."

"He sounds like a great guy."

She smiled softly. "He was."

Once she had planted the stone, we went back into town. By the time I plopped onto my bed, I was ready to turn in. I closed my eyes, excited to see what tomorrow would hold and how my training would help me get my brothers back.

33

At the inn...

"Zaelek?"

A knock at the door woke me. Groggily, I got up and answered it, finding Elutha standing before me.

"Everything okay?" I asked.

"Yes. I just needed to wake you. We shouldn't make the combat master wait. He really hates that."

"I'll get ready and meet you out front."

I got dressed and strapped my swords to my back. When I opened the door open, Kinara was waiting for me.

Kinara winked. "Nervous?"

"Uh…not really. I'm more excited than anything."

That was mostly true, but I did harbor a twinge of anxiety about what was to come. Still, I wasn't about to show her that.

We met Elutha and Aurok outside. It was still dark, without the slightest hint that dawn might be on the way. Luckily, Elutha and Aurok had lanterns. They beckoned for us to follow and jogged toward the outskirts of the village, immediately outdistancing us. The fresh morning air invigorated me as we trotted down the stone path.

At the edge of the village Elutha brought us to a halt.

"The training grounds are outside the sanctuary, so we need to travel without light. We can't risk outsiders seeing us. Luci'oan will meet us there."

Aurok snuffed his lantern. "Watch your footing, the path to the grounds can be treacherous."

The guards nodded to us in passing before we slipped through the entry. We jogged for a time, then veered into the forest, weaving our way around trees and thick brush. I frequently stumbled on roots and unexpected holes in the ground while Elutha, Aurok, and Kinara had no trouble traversing the terrain. They had to wait for me to catch up at times, which made me more self-conscious than I already was about my abilities.

After what felt like an hour of stumbling through the woodland, we arrived. A small building with warm light illuminating its windows sat at the edge of a vast prairie. Elutha had us wait and approached the structure alone.

He returned shortly, then led us around the back to where Luci'oan's heavily muscled body leaned against the building. When he looked up, the light hinting at the impending sunrise caught the right side of his face, revealing a thick white scar running from the center of his forehead to his jawline. He pushed off the structure and walked toward us, his long black hair swaying. Sweat glistened on his dark skin.

He extended his hand to me. "Your first lesson will be how to gauge your strength against another Altarian warrior's. This gesture is unique to our people. Only those who have unlocked their element during the awakening ceremony can initiate it. You will only experience it here."

I looked at him, remembering the unpleasant experiences with Aurok and the blacksmith. *Mercy's breath!* I didn't want to make a bad first impression, but I really wasn't looking forward to experiencing that again. Realizing I had no other choice, I clasped his hand and felt the suffocating pressure as it took my breath away. When he released me, the enigma vanished. My entire body shook from the extreme power output.

Luci'oan brushed his hands off. "In our culture, the warrior is defined by the strength of the pressure you just experienced. When you greet another person in this manner, your power will either falter, overwhelm, or negate theirs. We refer to this phenomenon as a *soa'al presence*. This is how we decide where an Altarian warrior will be ranked amongst their peers."

He walked to Kinara and offered the same gesture. She took it, and I watched as she grimaced, just as I had.

Luci'oan nodded, then turned to Elutha and Aurok. "You're free to go. They'll be safe here."

Aurok and Elutha touched their fists to their chests. Elutha pointed toward the building with his chin. "We'll wait inside until they're done."

"Then I suggest the two of you take this opportunity to train. I won't have two of my former students getting out of practice."

Aurok bowed before leaving. "As you wish, Master."

Luci'oan turned back to us. "Today, our focus will be elemental manifestation." Kinara started to speak, but he cut her off. "I am aware of your capabilities. You would benefit from learning my way."

Confusion rippled across her face. "How do you know what I'm capable of?"

"You tried to take on my Summoning."

Kinara and I looked at each other in shock. The man we were about to train under had tried to kill us.

"You're the Summoner?" I asked.

"Yes, I mistook you for enemy scouts but quickly discovered otherwise. That's why I withdrew."

"When did you know?"

"When Kinara attacked my dragon. The Javelar scouts that pass through here are much stronger than either of you. Most of our lower ranking warriors could best you in combat."

His gaze zeroed in on Kinara, but she returned the look with just as much fire. It was obvious Luci'oan had struck a nerve. She took a moment to gather her thoughts and apparently decided to take a different tack.

"Where do we begin, *Master*?"

"With a history lesson."

I watched the annoyance flash across Kinara's face so clearly that I had to suppress a laugh. She looked like she was about to erupt.

The first half of the day consisted of content-heavy lectures. Luci'oan covered the origin of elemental power. He explained that our ancestors' discovery of their power had been an accident. The first Locksmith, Uranus, awakened the element of his dying comrade, Gaia. His emotions were so concentrated that when he touched Gaia, her element surfaced. The power it produced healed the injury she had sustained in battle. Gaia, the first Stone Guardian, had received the nickname Mother Earth.

Before starting on the physical portion of our training, we had a small lunch, a good thing since we'd never had breakfast and I was hungry. While we ate, Luci'oan gave an introductory lecture on elemental use. Afterward, we followed him farther into the clearing to a place where rocks formed a half-circle. He seated himself on the largest stone, directing us to choose other stones for ourselves.

Luci'oan plucked a stalk of grass and slipped it into the corner of his mouth. "Let's begin. Sit down and cross your legs. For the first part of this training, I need you both to close your eyes. Listen to my voice and open your minds. Focus on your breathing. Take a deep breath, then slowly exhale and observe where you feel the breath's movement."

His words were slow, inducing a state of deep relaxation as he continued.

"Now, I want you to listen closely to the environment. Take a few moments to hear the world. Feel how your surroundings interact. While you do this, notice how every part of your body connects to nature. Feel the breeze gently brush through your hair, how softly the air touches your skin, and the earth beneath you. When you turn your attention back to the environment again, you should hear your element."

So, mine will be like a breeze?

Kinara answered first. "I can hear mine."

"Good. What about you, Zaelek?"

I sheepishly replied, "No."

"Try again. Kinara, I want you to keep practicing until all you have to do is concentrate to hear it."

I tried again, repeating the process again and again with no success. It wasn't working.

Some time passed until Luci'oan asked me again.

"I don't hear anything," I said.

"Yet," he corrected.

I attempted the process for another hour but still came up short. Luci'oan instructed me to keep practicing until I succeeded and continued Kinara's training in another part of the clearing. By the second hour I grew even more frustrated with each failure. After the third, I wanted to punch something. How was I going to be ready to rescue Ben and Parnikus if I couldn't even do something as simple as this?

Luci'oan returned to check on my progress. "Are you making any headway?"

"No, I'm not sure what I'm doing wrong."

"It isn't a matter of right or wrong. It's being able to rid your mind of all the thoughts racing through it."

"Easier said than done."

"Yes, but I'm sure you'll succeed before morning."

"*Morning*?"

"You're not leaving this spot until you get it. Kinara and the others will head back to the village without you. Keep training."

Every muscle in my body wanted to go back to the inn and rest. "What if I can't get it by nightfall?"

"Then you won't eat or sleep until you do. You must first conquer the mind and soul. Once you do, you will have control of your body and not the other way around.

"I may starve by then," I mumbled in frustration.

Luci'oan chuckled. "I see you still have some humor left in you—'means you haven't given up. That's good." He turned and walked back to his hut.

Heading back to the village...

Elutha, Aurok, and I headed back to the village. I remained silent as we navigated through the forest, my thoughts muddled with questions about why Zaelek couldn't reach out to his element.

Elutha said, "You're concerned about Zaelek?"

I nodded. "I've never seen someone struggle with manifestation like this."

"Honestly, Kinara, I don't think I have either."

"Do you think he'll get it by morning?"

"It's hard to say. If not, Luci'oan has a backup plan. There's another combat master in the village whose power differs slightly from ours. Luci'oan seems to think that she might be able to help Zaelek."

I cocked my head. "Different how?"

"You're familiar with Daemons, correct?"

"I am."

"Sometimes, Daemon wielders need to use another method to communicate with their element."

"So, this other combat master might know what to do?"

"Hopefully."

As we entered the gateway and walked on toward the inn, I had to ask, "Could I use the HIVE system to send my report to the Colonel tonight?"

He dug through his pocket. "I almost forgot. The Chieftess wanted me to give you this communicator. It's programmed so you can call your commander's direct line." Elutha handed me a small metal rectangle.

"How do I use it?"

"Give the sides a pull."

I pulled the edges and watched as a small holographic screen extended from the middle. A green button appeared on the screen.

"So, I just push the green button?"

"Yep."

"Thank you so much."

Elutha and Aurok dropped me off at the inn. In my room, I threw my stuff on the bed, intending to call Uncle Kehndrig. Before making the call, however, I checked the windowsill and the pot of soil sitting there. I don't know why I thought there would be a sprout so soon, but checking it still excited me.

I watered the seed and opened the communicator. A dial tone sounded from the device's external speaker.

Uncle answered. "Hello?"

"Uncle, it's Kinara."

"I'm glad to see that the Altarians are holding up their end of the bargain. How's everything going? Was Zaelek able to get his element unlocked?"

"He did. Looks like he got the pure strain of wind."

"Pure wind, huh?" he chuckled. "I guess I'm not surprised, considering he's Ettias' son. Did you start training yet?"

"We started this morning, but Zaelek hit a snag, so he's still out there."

"What kind of snag?"

"He's struggling with elemental manifestation."

"I've seen that happen before."

Hope flowed through me, my worries evaporating like a bucket of water thrown on hot coals. "You have?"

"Yes, it's uncommon, but it does happen. Don't worry, he'll pull through."

I sighed with relief. "Master Luci'oan has the other combat master coming out to look at Zaelek in the morning."

"Smart. Sometimes another teacher does the trick."

"I hope so."

"Alright, sweetheart, I need to make another call before I go home for the night. I'll talk to you soon."

"Goodnight, Uncle. I love you."

"Love you, too."

The call ended, leaving me feeling homesick. I missed my apartment and having a place that was my own. A memory of sitting on the couch with Alator sent a shooting pain through my chest. I still needed to figure out what to do with his possessions. Throwing them out seemed disrespectful, but what else was I supposed to do? He had no family who might want any of it. I moved my belongings off the bed, then slipped under the covers, trying the best I could to push the thoughts of my fiancé out of my head.

34

Night, continuing to attempt elemental manifestation and failing...

I shook my head in frustration after failing the most recent attempt. With a sigh, I gazed up at the bright moons. *This is ridiculous. It shouldn't be taking me this long.* I stretched my cramping legs and leaned back on my hands, allowing the stars to soothe me. My eyelids grew heavy, and I began to drift off.

Something cracked me over the head. I yelped and grabbed the area throbbing in pain. Luci'oan stood over me, slapping a wooden stick against his hand.

Anger welled up inside of me. "What was that for?"

"Never let your guard down when you're exposed. I could have easily killed you."

"You couldn't just call my name?"

"Would that have gotten the point across?"

I huffed and crossed my legs. "Probably."

"You need to sense your element to access it, so figure it out."

"Why do you care if I sense it now or tomorrow?"

"Because Ailyana asked me personally to train you. I intend to keep my word, so stop moping and get to it."

Luci'oan sat on his stone to monitor me. Multiple times during the night, he enforced his point by smacking me with the stick. By the time the sun came up, my body was aching. Kinara and the others returned to the clearing just before dawn, but this time, someone else accompanied them.

"Who's that?" I asked Luci'oan, looking at the woman proudly striding toward us.

"That's Arinn. She commands the Altarian Special Forces. I had Elutha ask her to assist with your training."

Arinn approached, her dark brown hair swinging in a kilitail. The sun glinted off her silver armor and the swaying sword hanging from her left hip.

"I hear you're running into some problems, Luci'oan."

"It's taking abnormally long getting him to sense his element."

His response made me scowl. It sounded like I was deficient.

Arinn studied me briefly. "I'll see what I can do. You continue Kinara's training." She removed her armored glove. "Let's find out what's going on in there."

I flinched when she touched my forehead. "What...?"

"Relax."

Her presence pulled at my mind. It felt like the presence from the mine, so I pushed back with my conscience.

"Your mental defense is impressive for a newbie," she said.

"What did you do?"

"Discovered the issue. You're keeping something barricaded, which is keeping your element at a distance. Think about it like this: your element is like a living being. You must share everything with it to form a bond."

"How do I fix it?"

"You'll have to figure that out on your own. I can tell you what the problem is, but not how to solve it."

I mulled over the possibilities. Nothing popped out at me, and I certainly didn't want to ask Arinn for an example. I felt stupid. How could the son of Cronus—not to mention the Altarian Champion—be this weak and helpless?

I continued until finally, I felt the first whisper of wind brush my mind. The gentle sensation grew more profound in my consciousness, further confirming the suspicion that this was indeed what I had been searching for. Relief and joy flooded through my weary body.

"Arinn, I hear it!" I exclaimed.

"So, Luci was right."

"Right about what?"

"You and I are very much alike. Unlike Luci'oan, Kinara, and most elemental wielders, we communicate with our element. We require a bond with our power."

"I'm not sure I understand."

"Take Kinara: She draws her power from the planet and the environment. You draw your power from an internal source, like a battery. You'll see what I mean in due time. For now, keep reaching out to your element. I'll inform Luci about your progress and see how he wants to proceed."

Determined, I continued and soon felt my element reaching for me in return. We connected, and power surged through me. A blast of wind erupted from my body, ripping the surrounding vegetation from the ground.

The power left my body just as suddenly, and the rest of my enigma disappeared with it. I fell backward as my muscles gave out. Arinn materialized next to me and caught my head in her hands. Luci'oan peered above me, inspecting my body for injury.

Luci'oan looked at Arinn. "That's enough for the moment. We need to get him something to eat."

At first I couldn't sit up, so Arinn cradled my head in her lap until I could. Luci'oan brought food and monitored me as I ate.

"I think I should be his mentor, Luci," Arinn said. "I know how to train him."

Her suggestion caught me off guard. I had been thinking about it, but I didn't know she would offer.

"What about the Special Forces?"

"The Captains can handle things while I'm away."

"Very well. I'll continue with Kinara."

"Come with me, Zaelek." Arinn grabbed me by the sword cloth wrapping around my waist. "We need to teach you control." She led me back into the forest and to a small meadow with a massive rock in the center, then pushed me to the ground. "Sit. We're removing distractions. Now, locate your element, but don't connect with it. I'd prefer not to end up in the trees."

I searched my mind, and almost immediately felt it.

"Found it."

"Good. I want you to form your hands like this," Arinn moved her hands to her chest, then created a hollow between them, as if she held a small ball. "When I'm safe behind that rock, connect with your element, but don't take all its power. Take just enough to manifest your element between your palms."

A drop of liquid formed in the hollow space of her hands, growing until it touched her skin and remained immobile. She tossed it. I reached out to catch it and the sphere burst when it hit my hands, soaking me with frigid water. I gasped.

Arinn laughed. "Once you get the hang of control, you should be able to catch that."

She disappeared behind the large rock in the clearing's center, poking her head out just enough to watch me. I reached for the element and felt it reach back. When we connected, I tried to only take the needed amount, but the power overwhelmed me. Another blast ripped the surrounding vegetation from the ground. The enigma drained from me, but this time, I had enough strength to remain sitting.

Arinn peered from behind the rock. "Again."

"It'll take the rest of my enigma!"

"If you're unsuccessful, yes."

Reluctantly, I complied, reaching for the presence and trying to take an even smaller amount of enigma. A thick cloud of dust kicked up, making me cough. My body went limp, and my head hit the ground.

A few moments later, Arinn leaned over me with a slight frown. "What are you doing? Explain what's happening in that thick skull of yours."

"I reach for it, but every time I try taking a small amount, it overpowers me."

"Did you try telling it your intention?"

"Are you serious?"

"When you regain your strength, try again and see if it makes a difference."

The mere thought that I only had to ask seemed laughable. When ready, she went back to her cover and gave me a nod. This time when I reached for the presence, I consciously asked it for only a fraction of its power. The presence eased back, extending a piece of itself. When we made the connection, the sensation of a cool breeze on a hot summer day rushed over me. I looked down and found a small swirling ball of air had formed between my hands.

It didn't grow slowly like Arinn's had but expanded rapidly, forcing my hands open. A concentrated shock wave shot toward the rock and slammed into the stone face, obliterating half of it and sending shards everywhere.

I stared in horror.

Arinn appeared on the branch of a nearby tree. "Whew! Good thing I moved!"

"I am so sorry!"

"Don't be. At least we're on the right track. Try again, but try to explain what you're hoping to accomplish to the presence."

I reached for the elemental power and asked for less than the last time, explaining what we needed to do. It hesitated for a moment, not wanting to release any less than it already had. *Come on,* I coaxed, *all I need is a little. Just enough to mimic what Arinn did.* The presence extended a paltry amount of enigma to me. When I accepted it, a small cyclone slowly spun in the middle of my imaginary sphere. It danced as it grew to the width of my hands, then stopped.

Arinn came to my side and watched. She cautiously made her way in front of me, then formed her water ball. She tossed it to me, and I caught it. An idea popped into my head, and I could have sworn the presence giggled. I twisted my hands and watched with joy as the ball launched back at Arinn, soaking her.

She laughed. "I guess I deserved that." She twisted her hands, and a freezing veil of water drenched me from head to toe. A grin spread across her face as I gasped.

"Remember who can produce that water."

"I should have thought about that."

"Come on, let's head back to the others. I imagine you've had enough for today."

Later that night, I had the strangest dream. I sat on my bed but wasn't alone. A white Deira volf pup sat next to me and nudged my hand for attention.

I scratched behind its ears. "Where did you come from?"

The dream changed, and I stood in a field under the full moon. The white volf stood just ahead, but it was no longer a pup. Its ears perked, and the majestic beast whirled around. A low growl emitted from its curled lips, and the hair of its back stood on end. Its saber-like fangs were large, even for a volf.

The volf's head turned to the sky and let loose a terrifyingly low-pitched howl like it had when we fought the creature during my elemental awakening. Ominous black clouds crept across the moons. In the distance, I saw dark figures with glowing red eyes swaying back and forth. My burning farmhouse appeared between the creatures and us, and fear took hold of me.

The volf looked back, "Don't be afraid, Zaelek," he said in a soothing voice.

It calmed me for only a moment before a woman's scream filled the air. Both the volf and I surged forward.

When we were almost to the house, the volf shot a whirling blast of wind from its mouth. The wind ripped at the flames but didn't put them out, and the red-eyed demons surrounded us. I took my black sword in my right hand and slashed at them, but two more took the place of every monster slain.

The volf tore into one creature next to me, then shouted, "Draw from my power!"

I reached out as I had to my element and connected with the volf. Our connection brought with it a euphoric sensation, like we had known each other for years. A blast rippled across the field, pushing the demons back to the tree line. I turned to the house and watched it fall. The dream shattered.

I shot up in my bed and screamed in frustration. My vision blurred, and I fell back into blackness. The volf appeared again and licked my arm.

"Who are you?" I asked.

His bright blue eyes stared at me. "I am Lycaon. You called me, and I answered."

"You're a Daemon."

"Yes."

"Was it you who took control of me in the mines?"

"No. There are two of us locked within you, but the other is sealed far deeper than I. When you chose her presence over mine, the altar allowed her to temporarily seize control of your body."

I didn't understand. Did the altar imbue Daemons to me, or were they there all along? "How do I free her?"

"I'm not sure you want to."

"Why?"

The white volf turned and vanished.

At the same time, in Kinara's room…

I poked my head into the inn's hallway. *Is someone screaming?* Another scream from behind Zaelek's door startled me. I materialized into his room. Flames encased my fists in preparation to neutralize whatever threat stood between him and me, but I saw only Zaelek. I checked the closet, the bathroom, even under the bed but found no one lurking in the shadows.

It must be a dream. I tried to shake him awake. His eyes shot open, glowing red and wide with fear. I yelped as he grabbed my wrist with startling strength before going limp in my arms.

"Zaelek!"

The elderly gentleman at the front desk shouted in panic when I surged into the lobby.

"My companion needs medical attention. Elutha or Aurok need to be called immediately."

"I can't make any calls because of the passing storm."

"Mercy's breath! Any idea where I can find them?"

"I don't know. I'm sorry."

I cursed silently, then turned and slammed the front doors

open, nearly blowing them off their hinges. I needed to get to the palace. Now!

Rain soaked me when my feet left the front porch. The people in the streets barely had time to get out of the way as I ran. I cursed again. Bounding wasn't an option. It was too dangerous. A cart wheeled onto the road ahead, blocking the path. Enigma filled me and I jumped, clearing the startled driver.

The faint light of the palace gate glowed ahead. Reaching the barren pathway, I erupted into a void bound. The torrential downpour made it impossible to see more than fifteen feet ahead and I skidded to a stop so close to the closed gate I could have licked the wood.

Guards swarmed from the guardhouses at each end. "*Keto helm koment!*" one shouted.

I answered, "I need to find Elutha or Aurok! Please!"

Aurok stepped out of guardhouse. "Kinara? What are you doing here?"

"It's Zaelek! Something is wrong!"

He turned to the other guards. "*Jimop ken tiaran.*"

They nodded, then he returned his attention to me. "Let's go. I'll inform Elutha later."

We took a shortcut and arrived at the inn in a few short minutes. Aurok said something to the man at the desk. The man searched until he pulled out a tablet, then handed it to Aurok. I followed him down the hall.

Zaelek's door clicked open as the tablet unlocked it. Aurok flicked the light panel and looked at Zaelek with concern.

"How long has he been like this?"

"I heard him cry out and found him maybe ten minutes ago, maybe fifteen."

Aurok placed his hand on Zaelek's forehead. "He's burning up. We need to get him to the palace's medical wing."

"Will he be okay?"

Aurok's muscles rippled as he pulled Zaelek up onto his shoulders. "Go outside and shoot a fireball into the sky."

"Why?"

"You'll see."

I closed my eyes, focused, then teleported outside. Raindrops pelted my skin like miniature icicles. I balled my hand into a fist until the flames consumed my arm and threw my fire upward. A jet of flames trailed the ball of light like a comet. It hurtled upward and exploded, casting a warm orange glow across the village and reflecting off the puddles where water pooled on the ground.

Aurok surged past me in a bound. I followed, barely able to keep up with him as he traversed the city. Every Altarian on the street had moved to the edges of the road. *So that's why I launched a fireball.* When we arrived at the palace gate, the guards had it wide open.

Ailyana was waiting for us at the doors to the palace. "What happened?" she asked.

Aurok entered and continued across the foyer. "I don't know."

He led us up the stairs and through hallways until we stopped in front of a green door. Aurok rapped on the dense wood.

A bald, middle-aged man cracked the door, then opened it upon seeing Aurok. "*Gilsde morka den.*"

Aurok laid Zaelek on the hospital bed. "Kinara, stay with him. I'll retrieve Elutha."

I nodded but didn't utter a word as my gaze fell to Zaelek. I couldn't lose him, too.

35

In the training rooms of Javelar HQ.

"Benazahg! Again!" the instructor barked.

I focused my enigma and watched the water in my palm come to life. With a forward thrust, I launched the trembling ball into the ceramic target. Salen, the young man I had become familiar with, panted next to me. However, Salen wasn't the only one. Most of the Aquarian trainees struggled to hold their hand at chest level. The power drain started to plague me a few launches ago. Still, my enigma stores seemed to deplete at a slower rate than the other trainees. Was it because I'm a 'pure' Aquarian?

Another trainee's straggling stream of water fell short of its target. I looked out of the corner of my eye and watched a proctor scribble something on his tablet. Part of me wanted to know what it meant, but perhaps it was better to remain a mystery. The proctor continued pacing his regular route, slowing when he reached me.

"Stay here once we dismiss everyone."

I nodded, not daring to utter a word. Every time a proctor neared me, my skin slicked with sweat, and I had to remind myself to breathe. Something about them seemed off. I just hoped that I wasn't about to find out why they were monitoring us so closely.

For the subsequent two volleys, I fixated on trying to figure out why I had been asked to stay. Had I messed up the exercise? Is that why I wasn't as tired as the rest of the group? Maybe being a "pure" Aquarian had nothing to do with performance.

The instructor dismissed the class, but I remained, praying that whatever reason they kept me didn't have negative consequences. Salen and one other older gentleman remained as well, so that gave me slight hope. At least we wouldn't have to go through whatever this was alone.

"The three of you follow me," the proctor said.

I glanced at Salen, whose wide eyes told me he didn't know what was happening either. We were herded into a spacious room with concrete walls and a single glass barrier standing between us and what looked like a control center. A few men in white lab coats moved back and forth along a wall of screens and instruments of some kind. Behind us, a new group of trainees flooded into the room. I noticed Parnikus amongst them and slipped over to stand beside him.

Relief flooded his face when he saw me. "Have they told you what's going on?"

"No. Did they tell you?"

"No."

The other trainees wore the same confused expression as we did. Two more groups joined us, then the proctors nodded to one of the men behind the glass and left us. The door we had come in through slid closed with a resounding thud and a whirr of the machinery hidden in the walls.

"Good morning, recruits," a man's voice crackled through the speakers. "You're here due to your higher-than-average performance during training. As a reward for your exemplary efforts, you'll be receiving a gift to assist you in your next fight."

A gift? New weapons or armor, maybe?

The speakers clicked off, and small pipes extended from the walls. Pink gas spilled into the room. Multiple recruits ran to the door, pounding on it and begging for the proctors to let us out. No answer came from the other side.

My lungs burned. The room filled with coughing as we inhaled the gas. A few trainees closer to the walls collapsed, writhing in pain. It didn't take long before my stomach felt like it had been lit on fire, and then my legs gave out. I convulsed on the ground as the ripping pain settled in my arms.

Parnikus gripped my shoulder with wide eyes, his cough not as desperate as mine.

Bubbles foamed out of my mouth in place of words. *I can't breathe! I'm going to die!*

"Come on, stay with me, Ben!" Parnikus struggled to speak as he, too, was feeling the effects of the gas.

Another wave of burning pain tore through me. They were killing me!

The gas ceased pouring into the room, and I gasped, trying to purge my lungs of the poison. I blinked to clear the tears, but gagged from lack of oxygen.

The speakers crackled to life. "Congratulations. You've received your first dose of Ele-Stim. Over the next few hours, you'll feel a little disoriented, sore, and nauseous, but the side effects will go away. This is normal. You do *not* need medical assistance, so don't waste the medics' time with your concerns for the next day and a half."

An entire day of symptoms? What did they do to me? It didn't come as a surprise that they wouldn't explain it. None of the recruits seemed to know anything outside of what they'd told us. There were whispers here and there of what something might be, but no one actually knew.

The proctors opened the doors and filed us through to the cafeteria. I stayed close to Parnikus.

As the server scooped a heaping pile of brown mush onto my tray, I whispered to Parnikus, "Are you okay? You didn't seem as affected by the gas as everyone else."

"I'm still a little dizzy, but I think I'm fine."

"Good."

As I carried my tray across the cafeteria, the scent of the food became much more appealing. A deep rumble emanated from my stomach. I didn't remember being this hungry. Maybe I'd worked up an appetite during training. My vision flashed between what I was used to seeing and the same scene but with a new vibrancy in colors I'd never experienced before. I steadied myself as the colors swirled in my head. Then they abruptly disappeared.

"Ben," Parnikus said, "everything all right?"

I furrowed my brow. "Yeah."

"Then let's eat. I'm starving!"

My body ached as I lay on my straw bed in the cage that the Javelar called my living quarters. Even our kilindrels' dirt stalls back home were more comfortable—at least they weren't stone. I shifted, trying to get comfortable on the cobblestone supported "mattress".

Gertry poked me through the small slit in the bars.

"Hey, you alive?"

"I wouldn't be moving if I wasn't."

Her question, however, had some legitimacy to it. Only a few hours ago, Parnikus and I got our first dose of Ele-Stim. I still didn't know what purpose the ordeal served, but whatever it did, it hurt.

"You and Parnikus got the Ele-Stim dose, right?"

"That was it. How did you know about it?"

"Because I got it, too, a while back."

I had a hunch that we weren't the only ones who'd received the treatment, but didn't know for sure. It comforted me to learn that someone who had also undergone the process still looked healthy. Maybe this was how she got so powerful.

"Lots of fun," I huffed.

"Oh yeah, *loads*.... Is Parnikus okay, too?"

"Yeah. He reacted to it better than I did."

"Good."

I rolled over to look at her. "Do you know why they put us through that?"

"Give it a few days, and you'll feel better and stronger."

"I don't have a few days. The next battle is tomorrow, and I can barely walk."

"Hey, from what I hear, only those Commander Savvage thinks have potential to survive the trial are chosen."

"Chosen" is not what it felt like. Why exhaust the fighters

that have a chance to make it out? It sounded more like giving the enemy an advantage. The thought that Savvage, the man who killed my family, commended my performance and considered me an asset disgusted me. Mom and Dad would be horrified if they saw what we'd become.

"Is that supposed to make me feel better?"

She scooted closer to the bars. "Come on, don't be such a sourgrad. I need you and Parnikus for the battle. Without you, our chances of winning fall drastically."

"You sound a bit desperate, Ma'am."

"You would be, too, be if this was the battle that could get you out of this place."

It would be Gertry's fifth arena battle. If our platoon won this, she would take her place in the ranks of Javelar. It also meant that Parnikus and I would become the next platoon leaders. Few platoons had ever had two leaders.

I didn't like the idea that we would be in charge. We had only won two fights in total. What made us suitable leaders? Nothing but blind luck.

36

In the medical unit in the palace...

As I regained consciousness, I looked around the room and saw Elutha pacing near the far wall. Kinara was asleep in a chair in the corner.

"Where am I?"

Elutha started at the sound of my voice. "The palace infirmary," he answered as he came to my bedside.

"How did I get here?"

"Kinara and Aurok brought you in."

I stretched my stiff muscles. "Was I out for long?"

"Just over a day."

"A day?!"

Kinara stirred, then opened her eyes. Relief soon replaced her brief look of confusion. "Zaelek! You're awake!"

I started to sit up, but Elutha pushed me down. "Not so fast."

"But I need to talk to Arinn," I protested.

"There will be time for that later. I don't think Arinn will be too pleasant if you wake her in the middle of the night. For now, you need to rest."

"What time is it?"

"It's nearly midnight. Get some rest, then we'll talk about it tomorrow morning."

Elutha placed my clothes on the bed. "Are you sure you don't want to take the day off? I know Arinn won't mind."

I shook my head. "I need to talk to her." I closed the curtain hanging from the ceiling and changed into my shorts. My reflection in the mirror on the wall stared back at me. I ran my hand across the newly formed muscles of my body. They were more extensive and more defined than before. My tattoo had also expanded down my arm by three inches.

As I opened the curtain, Elutha stared at my arm. "Didn't your tattoo end just above your elbow?"

"That's what I thought, too," I replied.

Kinara ran her finger over my skin in awe. "Your muscles grew as well."

"Are you checking me out?" I teased.

She turned bright red. "No!"

Elutha laughed. "She was."

"I was not!"

As Elutha and I laughed, Aurok entered the room. "What did I miss?"

"Oh," Elutha said, "Kinara was just taking a good look at Zaelek's new muscles."

Aurok grinned. "Uh-oh. Better get that under control. Arinn's known for breaking up fraternizing warriors with cold water."

Kinara's fists balled in frustration. "To Styx with you guys. You're not funny!"

"Let's get the you to Luci'oan. They're probably wondering why you haven't shown up for training yet."

Arinn and Luci'oan greeted us when we arrived and then we split up. Arinn took me to a secluded section of the prairie. Once we stopped, I said, "I need to talk to you about what happened."

"I agree. Tell me everything."

I told her about the strange dream. She listened intently until I finished, then looked to the sky.

"I didn't expect this to happen so soon," she said. "Your Daemon has a…prominent personality."

"So, you know what happened?"

"I do, but I had to drag Aetos from my subconscious."

"What do you mean?"

"It's best if I just show you."

She whistled loudly and looked again to the sky. I followed her gaze and saw a giant golden cararaptor diving toward us. Before it crashed into Arinn, it unfurled its massive, feathered wings and stopped inches above her head. I shielded my eyes from the blowing debris produced by the creature's mighty thrusts. The cararaptor's huge talons dug into the ground as it landed next to Arinn. She stroked the beast under its beak.

"This is my Daemon, Aetos," Arinn said. "She is shy, so she avoids introducing herself whenever she can."

The creature squawked with displeasure and nudged Arinn with its massive beak.

"Oh, hush," said Arinn. "You know it's true."

I marveled at the richness of Aetos' golden color, surprised that the cararaptor didn't refract sunbeams. Arinn continued scratching under the beast's chin and mumbled something to her I didn't catch.

"My dad could communicate with his Daemon, so does that mean you can talk to yours?"

"Yes, but I am the only Tamer in the village who can."

"Tamer?"

"It's what we call those with Daemons."

"So, other Tamers can talk to each other's Daemons?"

"That depends. If two Tamers are equal in strength, they can communicate with the other's Daemon. We know this as *Kempotenkai*. Once the bond is established, they can communicate with the Daemon until there is a significant power difference. However, it is important to know that you will only be able to control your own Daemon, regardless of strength."

"I see. Please tell her it is a pleasure to meet her."

The cararaptor bowed and Arinn laughed. "She can understand you; you just can't understand her."

"When did Aetos appear to you?"

"I conjured her. Normally, I wouldn't rush this, but your Daemon is restless and might not help you unless you help it first. Now, follow my lead."

She outstretched her palm face up and drew a circle in the center. Once I had completed mine, she tapped the center of her palm. I followed, and the symbols we drew softly glowed. She held her palm toward me, and I pushed mine toward her. The glyph left my hand and floated six inches in front of it. It expanded, creating a ring the size of me. A fierce wind exploded from the ring, carrying the same low howl from my dream.

A small white paw poked through the dot in the center, then was followed by a second. The claws grasped the edge of the inner circle and struggled for a moment. A volf pup's head appeared, then the small creature pulled itself through, landing on the ground. It turned to me with its shimmering blue eyes.

Arinn moved closer. "So, this is your Daemon."

I squatted, inspecting the pup with curiosity. It was so much smaller than I thought it would be.

The pup shook its white coat, and its deep voice said, "It's a pleasure to meet you in person, Zaelek."

I faltered. It felt surreal that I could talk to something other than a human.

"The pleasure is mine," I didn't know what else to say.

"I'm guessing you're wondering why I'm not fully grown. Allow me to explain. As you get stronger, your power will become so immense that you will need someone else to help you maintain it. That's why I have a permanent physical body. It acts as a reserve for all that extra power you can't hold. As you develop, the reserve enigma will grow, requiring me to grow as well to accommodate it."

That explained why Aetos is so big. I'd never seen a cararaptor her size before.

Arinn smiled. "I couldn't have said it better. Now, let's continue. We'll do endurance training today, so I'll need you to exhaust your enigma stores before we begin."

"How do I do that? The last time I exhausted my enigma, it took me fifteen minutes to recover."

"Precisely. Every morning I'll have you do this, then we'll wait until you can stand again. Once you recover, that's when the real training begins."

"Mercy's breath!"

"Did you expect your training to be easy?"

"Well, no…."

"Then trust me. Form your element like you did a couple days ago, then release all of it into the sky."

I concentrated, taking a deep breath to stabilize my shaking hands. Unfortunately, I knew all too well what the burning tingly sensation felt like and didn't want to recreate it. I released a torrent of wind skyward, then collapsed to my knees. My muscles systematically gave out from my feet up.

It didn't take as long to recover as it had previously, but it was ten minutes before I could force my shaky legs to stand. Arinn nodded in approval.

"Okay," she said, "time to start void bounding."

"I can barely stand!"

"Lucky for you, we aren't standing. We're running! Don't worry. Your enigma will still recover even when bounding, but slowly. Now, go!"

My legs burned for a few hundred feet, then gave out, and I skidded across the ground. This was insane! How was I supposed to keep this up all day?

Arinn launched a medium-sized ball of ice at me. I rolled, barely escaping. "What in Styx?"

"This is how I'm going to keep you moving. The next one will be much bigger. Get ready!"

A gigantic ice ball formed above her, which she proceeded to hurl at me. I released a burst of enigma and darted away. Before coming to a stop, another attack came to intercept me, forcing me to slide under it as it passed over. Then, another ice ball rolled my way. I'd be lucky if she didn't kill me before this ended!

Training with Luci'oan...

Another ball of ice rolled across the plains. "What's going on over there?" I asked Luci'oan.

He placed a hand on his hip. "That's Arinn's way of keeping Zaelek motivated."

"Please tell me we're not going to do that."

"No. My training method differs from Arinn's. Our training has more of an…'elegant' approach." He smiled.

I let out a relieved breath. "So, what are we doing then?"

"You'll see. Follow me."

Luci'oan initiated a void bound, and I surged forward. We entered the forest and continued until we came to the base of a rocky mountain with little vegetation.

Luci'oan pointed to the peak. "Get to the top in less than twenty minutes."

I looked up at the looming behemoth. "Twenty minutes? There's no way!"

"Not with an attitude like that, there isn't."

"What happens if I don't make it in time?"

"You'll turn around wherever you are and come back down… so you can start again. Your time starts now."

Dust kicked up under my feet as I scrambled up the trail. About a quarter-mile up, the solid earth turned to sand. The resistance of the unfamiliar terrain winded me much faster than expected. With every step in my bound, my feet slipped back a few feet. It felt like running on ice.

Ten minutes in, the lower half of the mountain fell behind me. *If I maintain my pace, I just might have a shot at this.* I leapt off of rocks and climbed higher. The incline got steeper every few hundred feet until the trail collided with a cliff face.

I grabbed the nearest handhold and ascended. My legs and arms shook as I approached the cliff's rim, making it even more challenging to pull myself up. *Come on, you can do this. Just a few more feet.*

Luci'oan peered over the edge and extended his hand to me. "Time's up."

His words were crushing. Now I'd have to do this agonizing exercise all over again! I took his gloved hand, and he pulled me up. The harsh sun beat down on both of us, but the sweat pouring off me was suffocating.

"How long do I have for the next run?" I asked.

"Twenty minutes."

"No way! I just exhausted myself trying to get up this time, and I still didn't make it!"

"Try harder."

I wanted to scream. How could I try harder than I already had?

Meanwhile...

Lycaon watched with interest from the shade of the tree line as I trained. The dirt, grass, and everything else lying on the ground stuck to my sweat-covered skin. Even my drenched shirt had become a muddy grass mess. I dropped to my knees and panted as Arinn's most recent ice ball passed me. Rather than hurl another attack at me, Arinn strode over and smiled.

"Nice work," Arinn said. "I think that's enough for today."

"But it's only noon." I instantly wished I could recall the words that just slipped out.

Arinn laughed. "I'm impressed. You can barely stand, and yet you still want to keep going. Sorry to disappoint you, but I've used up my allotted training enigma for the day."

"You can only use a certain amount?"

"Yes, and no. It would be horribly irresponsible to use all of my enigma up, now wouldn't it?"

"I don't understand."

"Think about it. What if the village were attacked today, and I had used all my enigma training you?"

"I guess you wouldn't really be able to fight."

"Not at full potential." She gestured toward the forest. "Come, the physical body isn't the only thing that needs training you know."

Arinn led Lycaon and me into the forest. We walked for a little while, then stopped at a steaming pond.

"What is this place?" I asked.

"Luci's secret hot springs. They have healing properties that soothe an exhausted body. He doesn't like people to know about it, so try to keep your mouth shut for his sanity's sake."

"Won't he be mad about *us* using it?"

She chuckled. "What makes you think I care?"

I looked over my shoulder, expecting Luci'oan to be waiting there with a stick. A splash pulled my gaze back to the pond. Arinn's clothes hung from a low tree branch, and she sat at the rocky back edge of the formation with her arms resting on the ledge. I blushed as I saw her bare skin and looked away.

Her voice carried across the water. "What's the matter? Aren't you going to get in?"

"You're naked!"

"And?"

"I just…" I stopped in embarrassment.

"Oh, that's right! Your culture! Well, you're part of the Altarian culture too now, so get used to it. We'll be doing this every afternoon. The quicker you learn to be less awkward, the better. Now, get in here. I'll even look away."

Lycaon snickered when I hesitantly took off my shirt and hung it on the branch next to hers. The rest of my clothes, however, I hastily removed and flung myself into the pond.

Once I settled, Arinn looked back. "See? That wasn't so difficult, was it?"

My gaze fell to the water. "I guess not."

"For the first week, we'll just enjoy the springs. After that, we'll do some training here, too."

Lucky us. I really hoped she didn't plan on making us get out of the water for that.

37

At the Altarian Training grounds...

Arinn led Lycaon and me to our usual training spot. "It's time we start on your enigma transfer skills, Zaelek."

A week had passed, nevertheless, my muscles felt like they were going to fall off my bones. I had never been so sore in my life. Even so, Arinn did not let up. In fact, she appeared to be intensifying my training each day.

"No more endurance training?" I asked, hopefully.

"Not for the next few days. The body needs time to recuperate after enduring such abuse. Besides, you won't be much use in a battle if you haven't mastered elementals."

"Am I still going to drain my enigma?"

"Yes, but only half of it. We need the rest."

"Will it be enough?"

"Definitely not. That's the point of this lesson. You and Lycaon need to get used to coordinating with each other to maintain efficient enigma flow."

I raised my hand to the sky intending to release the enigma, then hesitated and put my hand down. "How do I know when I reach the halfway point?"

"Release a steady flow of wind until your fingers tingle for a moment. That will be the body's natural way of telling you."

My brow furrowed. "Why didn't I feel it before?"

"Because you were releasing it all in one shot."

I opened a channel of enigma flow at my fingertips. A slight breeze brushed the grass below, causing it to ripple.

"Like this?" I asked.

"You need to release more or we'll be here all morning."

My body shuddered as a light tickling sensation worked its way down to my toes. The wind pressure increased, flattening the vegetation to the ground. Arinn's hair and clothes whipped around her. I soon felt my fingers tingle, and I cut off the flow.

Arinn smiled. "Nice work. Now, for the fun part."

"Should I be worried?"

"I hope you didn't think all of your training would comprise me running you ragged across the field."

"It crossed my mind."

She dismissed my words with a flick of her hand. "Let's find out what you can do. Observe." She formed a ball of water, then floated it about a foot away from her. Her hands danced in a circle, and the water slowly rotated to the right. Its pace increased, and the sphere formed a tube-like shape.

"That's new," I said with a raised eyebrow.

"When you do this, I have a feeling it will turn out differently than mine. Go ahead, try it."

I formed my hands in a circle. A small cyclone swirled to life between them. My palms extended outward, and the miniature dancing tornado moved forward.

"Good," said Arinn, "Now, gently increase…"

My hands moved counterclockwise. The cyclone's size and speed increased a hundredfold. *Oh schleet!* The vacuum of wind sucked Arinn and me into it. Our bodies were tossed around in the vortex. Then, we fell. The tornado died down, and I landed with a thud while Arinn landed gracefully on her feet.

Lycaon stood a few feet away and shook his head. "You're lucky I'm here."

I pushed myself off the ground.

"How did you stop it?"

"I countered its direction with a similar force, neutralizing the rotation."

Arinn nodded in approval. "Smart."

"Sorry, Arinn," I said.

"I didn't expect that to happen either, so no need to apologize. We can apply this lesson to the next attempt."

My muscles seized. "I don't think that'll be happening today."

"Nonsense. That's why we have Daemons. Though, I imagine you'd only have two more of those with your current reserve."

"How do you figure? Lycaon just had to match that to stop it."

"Lycaon used his own enigma. Daemons can't use the enigma they store for you unless you allow it. We'll get to that, eventually."

"So, now what?"

"Reach out to Lycaon like you do with your element. You should feel the connection when he reaches back."

I concentrated, not knowing what to feel for. It felt like pushing a request out to the world, hoping that someone would reply. Lycaon's presence brushed against my mind like a headlight in fog. A surge of enigma filled me. Mobility returned to each muscle group, and I stood as if I had used no enigma.

Arinn smiled. "Very good. Now, we work on controlling the amount of enigma you take from Lycaon."

On the rocky cliffs nearby…

I crawled away from the edge of the stone face I'd just scaled.

Luci'oan sat on a rock just a few feet away. He clapped slowly. "Well done, Kinara. You got to the top in under twenty minutes."

I collapsed to the ground and rolled over onto my back, staring up at the blue sky. "It only took a week."

"You made it, nonetheless."

"I don't have to do it again, do I?"

"Not today. I've got something else for you."

Luci'oan turned toward the mountain peak and raised his hand. The stones at the base of the next cliff separated, revealing the mouth of a cave. I followed him into the torch-lit cavern. A large metal wall with a small touch screen next to it stood at the back.

"What is this place?"

"It's a tempestar room, used to strengthen elemental power."

He moved to the screen pad and tapped the options.

"How does it work?"

Luci'oan gestured toward the wall with his chin. "Hit it with your fire."

I unleashed a jet of flames onto the metal. A small green light lit up at the top, and the wall sank into the floor, revealing a second, similar room.

I looked back to Luci'oan, uncertain of what to dot.

"Now, you repeat the process. Each door you come to will require a more intense heat to open, so it may take you some time to complete the challenge."

"Anything else I should know?"

"That's for you to figure out."

I entered the next room and hit the wall with another stream of fire. This time, it met me with a loud buzzer and a red light. I looked back at Luci'oan. He gestured for me to try again.

A stronger blast of flame flew from my fingertips. The green light lit up and allowed me to pass through, but the moment I entered the next room, the wall behind me sealed. I pounded on the metal.

"Luci'oan," I called.

No answer.

Once again, I faced the wall ahead and hit it with fire. The buzzer sounded, and the light flashed red. I took a deep breath and closed my eyes, allowing my raging inferno to course through my blood. A searing blast erupted from both hands. I only had a moment to celebrate the door opening before the enigma toll seeped from my skin like steam.

My breath came in shallow waves, and I hunched over. If this was only the second level, this might be a long exercise for me.

The wall opened on a short hallway where a small basket of food was sitting, barely enough for a meal. I picked up one of the two strange red fruits I'd never seen before; it had an elongated body with three thick tendrils at its base. I put it back in the basket, deeming it wise to save the fruits for later.

When I stepped into the next room, the door behind me slid shut, locking the hallway and food behind it. I let out a frustrated groan.

38

Zaelek's room at the inn...

I leaned against the headboard of my bed and rubbed my sore bicep. After Lycaon and I had gotten the gist of enigma transfer, Arinn started our sword training sessions. My arms wouldn't go above my shoulders now without significant effort and aching. Was it possible for arms to actually fall off?

We hadn't seen Kinara for almost a week. I wondered if she was all right and what kind of training she might be doing to keep her out so long. Then again, Luci'oan had kept me for an entire day and night because I couldn't manifest my element. Maybe she just needed to complete whatever trial she was doing.

My thoughts turned to my brothers, wishing Ben and Parnikus were here with us. Then I'd at least know that they were safe.

I shut the lights off, and drifted into a deep sleep.

A Whisper of Wind

I opened my eyes to find myself alone in a black forest. *Another dream? Can't I just have one night without one of these*? It took me a moment to realize that it couldn't be a dream; I had total control of my thoughts and movements.

A small amount of moonlight filtered through the trees, outlining my surroundings. An even more terrifying howl than Lycaon's pierced the darkness ahead. I turned and ran, stumbling over the terrain. Finally, face slammed into the ground when I got tangled in a low hanging vine.

I spit out a mouthful of dry leaves and soil and caught my breath. As I lifted my head two blood-red, glowing eyes were staring at me. The eyes belonged to a volf.

Its lips curled up in a menacing snarl. Adrenaline shot through me, and a blinding light erupted from my body. The volf yipped and retreated behind a nearby tree as I rose to my feet. A ring of torches flared up around me, illuminating the surrounding forest. Light glinted off the gray suit of metal armor I suddenly found myself wearing. *What...?* I reached for a sword but found none.

The black volf stalked toward me, baring its blood-stained teeth as a female voice hissed, "Clever boy."

I snatched a torch from the ground and swung it at her while backing away.

"You're the other Daemon Lycaon told me about."

"Oh, I'm so much more than that. I'm surprised you don't remember me."

"What are you talking about?" I knew no black volves, though something about her seemed familiar, a sensation slipping along the edge of my mind that I couldn't quite catch.

The volf howled, spewing clouds of black spittle everywhere. She disappeared into the thick darkness a moment before a violent force knocked me off my feet again and pinned me to the ground. She stood on top of me, her teeth snapping inches from my face.

"Why are you here?" Her voice dared me to answer.

Why is she asking? I don't even know where I am or how I got here. Before I could respond, a flash of white slammed into her, and she yipped.

Lycaon stood between us, the hackles on his back bristling as I once again got to my feet.

"Leave him be, Yin."

The black shape grinned wickedly, torchlight glancing off those menacing teeth.

"Lycaon. I was wondering when you were going to appear."

His tail lashed back and forth as he waited for her to make a move. "Evidently, not soon enough," he snarled.

"This doesn't concern you," she growled. "Be gone."

"You're wrong. You'll jeopardize the enigma stability."

"And?"

"You know exactly what will happen. What's your plan, Yin?"

"That's none of your concern."

Lycaon threw his head back and unleashed an amplified howl.

"No!" the black volf screeched.

She charged, but a vicious wind beat her back. She attacked again and again like a maddened caged animal, but failed each time. Panting with the effort she stopped and her focus shifted from Lycaon to me. She charged again.

I reached for the presence in my mind and asked for full power. Lycaon sensed my request and fueled me with his full strength as well.

A devastating blast leveled the surrounding trees and vaporized Yin. The torches vanished as the darkness scattered and the entire forest was illuminated.

"Is she dead?" I asked.

"No, just banished back to her own realm." There was a note of satisfaction in Lycaon's voice.

"You mentioned something about a balance?"

"The balance between light and dark. She is the darkness; I am the light. Together, we keep all our elemental power in a stable state. You are the anchor that keeps Yin and me in check, that's why she attacked."

"I don't understand."

"Without you, our power would grow uncontrollably until one would eventually overtake the other. If she became the dominant power, she could take control of you."

My brow furrowed. "Like at the mine?"

"Exactly. When you chose her power over mine, she took control. Had you chosen mine, I would have let you have control of your body and could have guided you through using our power."

"Ah..."

"It was a hard lesson for you to learn. Yin is unpredictable, which makes her dangerous. With control of the anchor, she would have brought untold horrors to your realm, as you've already witnessed."

"Guess we're lucky that Elutha and Aurok showed up."

"You have no idea. Just remember, if you become strong enough to release her on your own, she can't control you and will be forced to submit. Then you'll wield her power like you wield mine."

"How long do I have before she comes back?"

"Technically, she should be sealed for as long as you need. There is a loophole, however. If you experience an extremely negative emotion, such as anger or loss, she will sense it and match them with her own. This will trigger her realm to falter, and she will take control."

The dream world shattered, and my eyes opened. Lycaon had his head on my chest. His ears perked when he felt me wake.

"Welcome back."

Arinn's sword locked against mine. We held the position for a moment, but her strength quickly overcame mine. I let her power overwhelm me as I guided the swords to the right. Just before her blow reached its endpoint, I skirted back and launched away.

"Hey, Arinn," I said, wiping a bead of sweat from my face and preparing for another assault.

"What?"

"You know that dream I had about Lycaon?"

She charged forward, unleashing a barrage of sword slashes. I parried two of them, then leapt aside.

"What about it?"

"I think I had another one."

"About Lycaon?"

"No, but he was in it. This time there was another volf."

Arinn stopped abruptly. "Did it look like Lycaon's opposite?"

"Yeah. How did you know?"

She sheathed her sword while muttering something under her breath. "You should have told me this before we started training today"

"Why? What's wrong?"

"When someone has a second Daemon, and they didn't experience the traditional way of unlocking their element, that Daemon usually only manifests itself early when there is unresolved trauma."

"Like Savvage murdering my mom, dad, and sister?"

I could see the sadness in her eyes. "Yes. If the second Daemon is not released naturally, it could fuse with your body and overtake you." She paused, looking as if she were reliving a bad memory. "Believe me, I've seen what happens to the host, and it's not pleasant. There is a way to keep that from happening, but I hope that it's not too late to keep yours in check. Follow me."

Arinn led Lycaon and me back to the village, then took us to the lake behind the massive center tree. We walked along the sand until the buildings were no longer in sight. Just ahead sat a tattered fishing shack, a variety of nets sloppily draped across the walls of its rough exterior. Various items cluttered the shoreline, giving me the impression that the structure had been abandoned long ago.

"Terdol," Arinn called.

An elderly man stepped onto the rickety old dock and squinted at us. "Arinn, is that you?"

"Yes. I need to take this young man to the Forest of Whispers."

Just hearing the name of our destination made me uneasy. "Forest of Whispers?"

"Hush," Arinn said.

Terdol paused briefly. "Are you sure it's wise to take an outsider to our holy grounds?"

"He is part of our people now. The Chieftess has declared it."

"As you wish."

Terdol disappeared into the shack, then emerged with a key in hand. He hobbled to the edge of the dock and pushed the key into the end post. The water rippled near the pier, and a small wooden boat rose from the depths. Surprisingly, the boat's polished wood showed no sign of wear and tear and the interior was dry.

Terdol reached into the vessel and retrieved a paddle, then handed it to Arinn. "Good luck."

Arinn gestured for me to get in. I hesitantly stepped into the boat, afraid that it might slip below the surface again. The vessel rocked as my weight shifted onto the backbench. Lycaon joined me, choosing to sit between the two seats.

Once settled, Arinn stretched her hand toward the shore. The back end of the boat rose, and we rode the small wave she had conjured toward the center of the lake. I looked ahead and saw a large island that I would have sworn hadn't been there a second ago.

Soon, the bow scraped against the sandy beach, and Arinn stepped into the water, pulling the boat farther ashore. Something called out from behind the wall of jungle-like vegetation. Lycaon and I followed Arinn beyond the trees to a clearing where fluorescent purple vines hung down from the canopy and gently lit the scenery. An array of luminescent blues and greens lit the stems and leaves of all the vegetation on the ground.

"This is beautiful," Lycaon said.

"I agree," I replied.

Another call sounded, but this one seemed much more like a wounded animal crying out.

"What is that?"

Arinn pulled the curtain of vines to the side. "There is something about that call you need to know. The creature it came from was once human."

A tingle of fear crept through me. "What?"

"We know them as *Bockratandem*. We must be careful here, they can turn violent if disturbed. The Forest of Whispers is a mysterious landmark that has an equally puzzling ability. It can manifest the spirits of recently deceased loved ones that didn't have the chance to say farewell."

A glimmer of hope came over me. "You mean I'll get to see my parents and sister again?"

"Possibly, but that's where I need you to be extra cautious. If the forest manifests any family members, you must promise me you won't become fixated on your loss."

"I don't understand."

"This is an opportunity for you to say goodbye, not see your family whenever you want. This forest can have either a healing effect, or it can warp your mind. Those individuals that can't let go of their family members become *Bockratandem* and are trapped here to wallow in their misery forever."

"Forever? But isn't there a way to help them?"

"No. They can only help themselves, and the longer they give in to their obsession, the harder it becomes to break the connection to this place. Some have been here for centuries."

"No one has tried to put them out of their misery?"

"Oh, yes, but the forest won't give up its residents that easily. If you kill a *Bockratandem* without provocation, whether purposely or accidentally, you will take its place."

"Why would anyone come here then?"

"It's the only way to seal your second Daemon away until you release it."

I sighed. "Of course it is." I mumbled.

Arinn guided us through the thick-leafed vegetation. She paused, put a finger to her mouth, and then pointed toward the base of a moss-covered tree. A black hooded figure knelt on the ground, its face buried in its hands. It wept heavily and shrieked.

Arinn turned away, distancing us from the creature before continuing forward. We came to a grove of trees with trunks the size of small buildings and just ahead, nestled in one trunk, I saw a stone archway. Arinn took my hand and pulled me through it.

Unlit torches hung from the hollowed-out wood. She lit the one closest to us, which systematically lit the others as if they were touching. Sparkling from the ceiling above us, tiny square crystals glimmered in the flickering flames from the torches.

Suddenly the crystals shattered, sending shining dust particles everywhere, becoming a cloud that slowly descended until it sat just above my head. The particles danced there in a circle.

"What are these?" I asked.

"You'll see."

I watched as the cloud drifted in front of me. A flash of light caused me to jump. Before us stood my mother. I felt the tears. My throat ached with the attempt to hold back the wave of emotions.

"Mom?" I squeaked.

"Oh, sweetie," she said, "look at you. I can tell how much you've grown."

Arinn touched my shoulder. "I'll give you some privacy. If you need me, I'll be outside."

I nodded, unable to take my eyes off my mother.

Mom smiled gently. "I see you inherited swords from your father and me."

"And volves from you." I gestured to Lycaon. "Mom, you wouldn't believe everything that's happened. I unlocked my element and started training under a special forces commander. I found out I have two Daemons, but one is sealed away for now." I looked down at my feet. "I wish you and Dad were here to help me master all this. It's so hard."

"Sadly, that's not how this works. Though, if he were here, I know he would be just as proud of you as I am."

Her words drew a few tears. I quickly wiped them away, embarrassed to cry in front of my mother.

"I got pure wind."

"Show me."

I extended my hands out and created the small vortex between my palms. "I haven't mastered it yet, but I'm sure I'll get there."

She laughed. "You can try, but no one really masters their element, sweetheart. There is always something else you can do with the possibilities. Just do your best, and I know you'll become a gifted Guardian one day."

I paused, taking in every second, even though I had to say goodbye. "Mom…"

I choked on the word. It was easty to understand why the *Bockratandem* had fallen into the forest's grasp. The words felt like I was letting her go all over again.

"Yes, sweetie?" Mom asked.

"I came here so I could say goodbye. Arinn said I need to accept that you, Dad, and Ari are gone."

"She is wise. It won't do you any good to dwell on our deaths. We love you, Zaelek, more than you'll ever know."

Another stream of tears coursed down my cheeks. "I love you, too, Mom."

She smiled again, then wrapped me in a warm embrace. I went to hug her back, but the particles dissipated, leaving my arms empty. My heart felt like it had disappeared with her.

Lycaon nudged my hand. "Come on. Arinn is waiting for us."

I turned and walked out of that place, never once looking back for fear that it might tempt me to stay.

Arinn came to me and pulled me into an embrace "I'm proud of you. It takes a lot of strength to walk away from that."

For a moment, I didn't hug back, worried that she, too, might disappear. However, the moment I returned the gesture, I broke down and wept until my tears ran dry.

39

In the Tempestar Room...

The red-hot metal door retracted into the ceiling, revealing the room where I had begun this ridiculous training session. Luci'oan sat meditating near the center.

One of his eyes opened. "Nice work, Kinara."

My shoulders slumped and my neck relaxed, allowing my head to bow. I sighed with relief. I had felt like I'd never reach the end of this trial, but finally, here I was. I ran my hand through my greasy hair and breathed in the fresh air of the outside world.

"How long was I in there?" I asked.

"About a week."

That sounded about right. Although, it wouldn't have surprised me if Luci'oan said I had been in there for two. I'd left my watch sitting on the nightstand in my room and there had been no way to tell time during the trial.

"What now?" I asked, hoping that he would give me tomorrow off to relax. The trial had been grueling, and I didn't want to do anything training related.

I was releived when he aid,"Now, you rest. Take tomorrow off and go to the hot springs."

My heart fluttered with excitement, hardly believing what I heard. "Really?"

"I don't see why not? You've earned it."

I sighed with relief. "Thank you."

On the way back to the village, it became apparent how deeply exhausted I was. I barely had enough reserve energy to get to the inn. Every muscle in my body ached, and a pulsing headache plagued me.

I leaned my sword against the wall of my room and removed my sweat-crusted clothes, grateful to be rid of them. Nothing sounded better to me than a hot bath. I started the water and lowered myself to the cool tile floor as I waited, enjoying the crisp freedom of the surrounding air.

A knock sounded at my door. I groaned, thinking that had better not be someone coming to tell me I had more to do today.

I wrapped a towel around myself, went to the door and cracked it enough to reveal Zaelek standing in the hallway.

"Want to…" he paused. "Are you in just a towel?"

"Yes, Zaelek, I'm in a towel. What do you need?" I said, knowing the question sounded impatient.

"I just wanted to see if you'd like to get a bite to eat."

"No. I'm not that hungry."

"Oh, okay. How'd your training go? You've been gone for almost a week."

I rested my head against the door frame and took a couple breaths. "It was fine. Hey, can I talk to you tomorrow? I'm exhausted and would really like to be by myself right now."

"Sure thing. Have a good night."

I forced a smile, then closed the door before letting out an exasperated sigh. Even that brief conversation had been draining. Though I'd been alone for every leg of my previous training exercise, interacting with anyone right now wasn't appealing.

I didn't wait for the tub to fill. The scalding water washed over me, enveloping me in its embrace. For the next hour while the heat soothed my tired muscles, thoughts came and went as they pleased. When the water began to cool, I scrubbed every inch of my body, and thoroughly washed my hair, then drained the murky water from the tub.

I dried off quickly, not even bothering to fix my messy hair, then threw myself onto the soft bed. I pulled the covers up and closed my eyes, but just as sleep came to me, I remembered my seedling on the windowsill.

With a petty whimper, I rolled out of bed and checked the pot. The soil still held moisture. A wave of gratitude flowed over me. Had Zaelek been taking care of it for me? I could kiss him! Once again, my emotions were replaced by guilt for the budding feelings I associated with Zaelek. Especially so soon after Alator's death.

40

Javelar HQ,
in the arena's platoon staging area...

I limped to the front of the formation and took my place beside Gertry and Parnikus. This would also be Gertry's last motivational speech, yet another reminder that I had no aptitude as a leader. Parnikus had always been better at things like that. Maybe he could do all the talking when that time came.

Gertry's speech sounded similar to Bluto's from my first fight. It didn't matter anyway. Parnikus and I were the only two left besides Gertry who had heard it before.

The platoon shuffled nervously. Most of them couldn't have been over the age of eighteen. The cruelty of Javelar knew no boundaries. But somehow, with every day we spent here, I discovered another new sickening twist.

A metal clang sounded in the back and the rear doors opened behind us. Six guards stepped into the room. Three carried plated suits of armor, the other three held something wrapped. They approached the front of the formation and faced Gertry, Parnikus, and me.

"It seems you have fans," one said. "They've sent gifts. Armor and weapons to complement your fighting style." The guard turned to the rest of our platoon. "Fight half as hard as these three, and maybe you, too, will earn admirers."

Fans? I didn't know such a luxury could be awarded to low-status warriors.

I whispered to Gertry, "Did you know about this?"

She shook her head. "This is the first I've heard of it."

The guard in front of Gertry said, "Hold out your arms."

She did as instructed and he placed a purple-hued breastplate on her chest, then waited as one of the other guards to cinch it up. He strapped two plated gauntlets to her forearms and greaves to her shins. The man then nodded to his comrade, and she brought forward a wrapped item. The cloth fell, revealing a beautiful spear. The woman handed it to Gertry, who examined the weapon in awe.

The guards repeated the process for both Parnikus and me. Parnikus received red-tinted armor and a black trident. Mine was dark blue and when the guards strapped it on, I felt like I was about to carry a bag of bricks into battle. Thankfully, the golden trident handed to me was nearly weightless.

The female guard who handed me the trident winked and whispered in my ear, "Go get 'em, Poseidon."

Poseidon? Do we also get nicknames?

The guards snapped back into their formation and exited, leaving a deafening silence in their wake.

Gertry looked back to the platoon. "Tork, Kima, and Disckon post." Two young men and a young woman stepped out of formation. "You three will get our other armor and first pick of the weapons. Everyone else will file to the weapon rack, starting from the front. Once everybody has a weapon, fall back in, and wait for my command."

When each platoon member had been armed, we waited until the familiar obnoxious siren blared through the arena. We shuffled into the tunnel and stopped at the metal gate. I took a deep breath to calm my nerves. Even before we'd received our gifted armor, I had worried about my strength holding up.

Another siren blared, and the gate shot open. Gertry led the charge into the arena. I followed, shielding my eyes from the harsh light glaring off the snow-covered battlefield. The crisp bite of frigid air passed through the inside of my armor, drawing a shudder from me. *We need to end this soon, or we may freeze to death.*

Gertry, Parnikus, and I moved far enough out of the tunnel to allow the platoon to form up behind us. The opposing force funneled out of their entryway. Every other arena I had fought in had at least concealed the enemy. Our clear vision of them didn't bode well for the novice fighters' nerves. I could only pray we had more experienced fighters than the red stripes.

Both platoons stood fast, sizing each other up. No one dared make a move.

The low sound of a buzzer reverberated through my bones. Ahead, the ground split in multiple places. Pedestals rose from beneath the arena, revealing four large cages.

Parnikus shifted nervously. "Are those…?"

"Sabercats," I finished.

The cage doors fell to the ground, releasing the tan, ten-foot-tall beasts from their cells. Two of the sword-fanged cats surged toward us, while the remaining three hauled off toward the red platoon.

"Hold!" Gertry shouted.

The three of us moved back toward the front line, our weapons tracking the cats' movements as they slunk forward.

A terrified shout came from behind us. "This is crazy!"

Another called out, "Hey, wait! Don't break ranks!"

Out of the corner of my eye, I saw one of our warriors running back toward the tunnel. Both cats zeroed in on the runner. I barely had time to turn before one animal pounced.

Its enormous mouth closed on the boy's head and vigorously shook. Blood spray stained the pure snow while the other sabercat snatched at the young man's lower body. Both cats snarled as they fought for the shredded flesh, ripping him to pieces.

Our platoon erupted as all of them ran in different directions.

"Wait," I shouted. "We need to stay togeth…"

A passerby knocked me to the ground in his panic. The ground shook, and an enormous paw pinned a girl next to me. I wanted to scream, but the metallic taste of blood in my mouth made me gag instead. The short-haired head of the beast dripped crimson as it tore into her face.

I felt the ground for my trident. Frantically, I looked to the right and saw it only a few inches away from my outstretched hand. My fingers inched toward it. Hot breath sent shivers through my body, and I looked up. I had gained the sabercat's undivided attention.

Before it had the chance to maul me, I rolled away from its vicious strike and grabbed my trident, using my evasion's momentum to bring me to my feet. Its leg muscles tensed when it lowered its body to the ground.

The creature stumbled and yowled in pain. Parnikus' trident stuck out of its neck. Gertry rose in the air behind the cat and drove her spear into its bony spine. The sabercat fell to the ground, thrashing wildly. A tremendous blast erupted from Gertry's spear, pushing the creature deeper into the snow and launching her up and away.

I knew what I had to do. With a battle cry, I thrust my trident into the beast's mouth, piercing its skull. The cat's body went limp. I wrenched the trident out and turned to thank Gertry and Parnikus.

She smiled. The other sabercat blindsided her, sending them both sprawling.

"Gertry!" I shouted.

She rolled, then pointed her spear at the cat and released another blast from its tip. The fury of flames propelled her away from the creature and directed the cat toward the other platoon. Parnikus and I rushed to her side.

"Mercy's breath, Gertry," Parnikus exclaimed. "Where did that come from?"

She relaxed her body and stared at the sky. "I guess the same place yours did when I first fought alongside you two."

I extended my hand. She took it, and I pulled her up.

"It's always exciting with you, boys, isn't it?"

Parnikus laughed and slapped her on the back. "Admit it. You'd be bored out of your mind without us."

For the first time since they released the sabers, I took a moment to survey the battlefield. Why were we here? What purpose did any of this serve? I silently prayed that this was just some elaborate nightmare from which I would wake, but no amount of prayers would get me out of this. Seeing the bodies on the ground made me sick. I forced myself to look away, focusing on the survival of the remaining members of our platoon.

Most of them still stood. The red stripe platoon, however, was a different story. They had dispatched the remaining sabercats, but at a high cost. Only eight of their number remained.

Gertry readjusted her armor. "Let's go get our platoon and end this."

41

Kínara's room at the inn…

I tossed on my bed. A month of vigorous training had made me restless, and it had gotten harder than usual to sleep. I threw the covers off, dressed, then headed out into the village. On nights like this, I preferred to walk around until I got tired rather than lie in bed and wait for sleep to find me.

Light from the dull street lanterns reflected off the damp cobblestone path. It looked as if it had been raining, but it was just condensation. The streets were empty but for the occasional swamprat scurrying between the alleys. Closed signs hung from every door in the market district. From what I had seen during my few nightly walks around the village, nothing stayed open this late, not even Joro's, the small pub Zaelek and I frequented during our downtime.

Taking an unfamiliar stretch of road, I walked nearly to the edge of the town. A cloaked figure stepped out onto the darkened street and looked around before continuing, unaware of my presence. Curious, I trailed the individual, ducking between roadside stands and scattered barrels. It was a perfect opportunity to practice my stealth skills.

The stranger stopped in the middle of the road to look over his shoulder. I watched from the shadows of the alleyway wall as another individual stepped into the intersection, joining my unknowing target under the dimly lit street lamp.

A male voice said, "Did *kiltay antlenop* you?"

I had picked up a little of the Altarian language while here, but not enough to comprehend a conversation.

The other man replied, "No."

"Good."

I pieced together that the man must have asked the other if he'd been followed, but that was only a guess. Nonetheless, I still wanted to follow these strangers and see what they were doing out so late. Maybe they would lead me to a tavern that was still open.

I followed at a distance, soon running out of concealment as we approached the edge of the village. I waited until the two were farther away, then slunk after them in the shadows. One man looked back, and I hit the ground, breathing as lightly as possible. After a moment, they continued on their way.

Careful not to step on anything that might give away my position, I ducked into a small grove of trees along the side of the dirt road. From there, I followed until the light of fire flickered through the leaves.

A good-sized congregation of men and women had gathered around a small bonfire. All of them wore cloaks and conversed in hushed voices.

One woman moved to the center of the group and addressed the others. "Brothers and sisters, *gientight*, we *hassay* to *hemparaigt* the outsiders."

She held the attention of everyone in the clearing. I shook my head in frustration with my lack of language.

The man I'd initially followed spoke up. "We need to *haum gealdeum.* Ailyana has *reandargelt* our *hysyst*."

Someone behind me shoved their hand across my mouth to mute my startled scream.

Zaelek's familiar whisper said, "Easy, it's just me."

I turned and slugged him in the arm. "Mercy's breath, Zaelek. You almost gave me a heart attack."

"What are you doing out here?" he whispered.

"I was following someone and happened across this."

"Why were you following someone?"

"I was practicing.... Never mind. What does '*reandargelt our hysyst*' mean?"

"Betrayed our trust. Why?"

The words were much worse than I thought. "That woman just said that Ailyana has betrayed their trust and something about us."

"How do you know they were talking about us?"

"What is this? Question hour? What else would you take 'outsiders' to mean?"

"Plenty of things."

"Not in this case. Listen."

Zaelek started to speak, then shut his mouth and listened to the group. The now full-sized volf, Lycaon, pushed through the brush and plopped down next to Zaelek.

Zaelek looked at the volf, similar to an annoyed parent whose conversation got interrupted. "Are you seriously complaining about the twigs in your fur right now? Shut up, I'm trying to listen."

Lycaon grunted and watched the Altarians. His ears perked, and he looked to Zaelek.

"What?" I asked.

Zaelek put his finger to his lips and listened for another long moment. "They disagreee with Ailyana's decision to welcome outsiders into their culture," he paused. "They keep saying *antyorsa*, but the context is hard to understand."

"What do you mean?"

"*Antyorsa* has two meanings: 'Assassinate' or 'purge.'"

"Is there something in particular about us? Maybe we can resolve this without a mess."

"I don't think we can fix this. They're mad about me taking part in the elemental awakening ritual and that we are both training now under Luci'oan."

I cursed under my breath. "We need to tell Arinn and Luci'oan about this. They'll know what to do."

"I agree."

A woman's voice came from our side. "You won't live long enough to tell anyone."

Zaelek whirled around in time to blast the woman with a

concussion of air before she could react. The noise undoubtedly gave our position away.

"Run!" Zaelek shouted.

I didn't hesitate. The vegetation slapped against my skin as we backtracked through our cover. Angry shouting came from the clearing, then something hurtled over our heads. A volley of rocks pelted the ground just ahead, making me skid to a halt.

Zaelek snatched my arm during his redirection and used his momentum to propel me around the field of sharp rocks. A faint orange glow flickered off the walls of the home ahead of us. I slammed my forearm against Zaelek's chest, forcing him to the ground with me. As we slid, a colossal fireball passed overhead and crashed against the path.

Lycaon used Zaelek's shoulders as a base and launched into the air. The volf released a gale force toward the pursuers. I went to send a fireball of my own back, but Zaelek grabbed my wrist before I could fully charge.

"No. We want to push them back, not injure them."

I couldn't argue with that either. If we attacked them with lethal force, it would make the situation that much worse. For a split second I wondered when he'd gotten so smart. A month ago, he would have let me call the shots. Zaelek wasn't the goofy farm boy I'd met in Corai anymore.

Zaelek formed a circle with his hands. A small vortex appeared in the space, and he pushed his hands forward, sending the miniature cyclone a couple hundred feet away. When it stopped, it expanded into a debris sucking monster.

Another fireball flew around the tornado's side but got pulled into the funnel. The ball of flames exploded, sending streaks of fire through the twister. I watched with horror and mild fascination, as the entire funnel transformed into a shrieking inferno.

We bounded down the path to the safety of the village.

"So much for using non-lethal attacks," I shouted.

"That wasn't my intention," Zaelek replied.

The village ambiance erupted into a frenzy of clanging bells and shouting. People ran from their homes to see what was happening and gawked at the fire-infused cyclone, barely taking notice of our dash through the streets. Just as we passed through the market district, a woman landed before us with her arms crossed. Zaelek and I came to a screeching halt.

Zaelek squeaked, “Arinn?”

Arinn dragged us into a building to our left. She shoved us onto a couple wooden stools, then slapped the back of our heads.

“Jintag moteno hyps,” she said sharply. “Are you two out of your minds? What were you thinking?”

Zaelek and I both stammered over each other’s words like children excusing their misbehavior to their mother. Arinn shoved her hands over our mouths. When we had both stopped our muffled yammering, she removed them.

“One at a time,” she said.

I looked to Zaelek, as he was the one who had understood the conversation.

Zaelek returned my look of desperation and said, “There was a group on the outskirts of the village plotting an uprising. We got caught listening before we could tell you or Luci’oan.”

Arinn placed her hand over her face and muttered something under her breath. Nothing about her reaction added up. She didn’t even look surprised.

“You knew,” I whispered.

“Of course we knew! We were just about to raid the gathering. Now, their organization will go underground. Do you two know how much trouble you caused tonight?”

We both stared at the ground—me wishing I’d stayed in bed.

Arinn turned away from us, “Unbelievable.”

“We were just trying to help,” Zaelek said.

“A fine job you did of that.” She snatched two cloaks from hooks on the wall and threw them at us. “Put these on and be quick about it.”

We did as instructed and pulled the hoods over our heads. Arinn peered out the door, then stepped through. Zaelek, Lycaon, and I rushed after her. We ducked into the alleyway almost as quickly as we had gotten onto the barely lit street. Arinn inched to the edge of the next road and peered both ways. She gestured for us to cross. Zaelek and I dashed through, only stopping to wait for Arinn once we were safely concealed in the shadows.

She joined us. I whispered, “The inn is the other way.”

"We aren't going to the inn. It's not going to be safe for you two there yet."

"Not safe?" Zaelek asked.

"We don't know who is loyal to what now."

"So, where are we going?" I asked.

"To meet Luci at the Forest of Whispers."

Zaelek had briefly mentioned that place during one of our frequent dinners together. Apparently, it was sacred ground to the Altarians, but for what reason, he didn't say.

"What if the boat keeper is part of the uprising?" Zaelek asked.

"He isn't. Trust me."

Trailing behind Aarin and Kinara...

We dodged the curious glances of onlookers as we made our way to the shoreline shanty. Arinn had us wait on the dock as she discussed our situation with the boat keeper.

Kinara looked across the lake and sighed. "Do we really have to take a boat, Zaelek?"

I cocked my head to the side. "Unless you feel like swimming tonight. Why?"

"It's nothing," she said with a hint of embarrassment.

"Don't tell me you're afraid of a tiny boat."

"No!" she stammered, "I just get seasick."

I chuckled lightly. "You're such a liar."

Kinara clenched her fists. "I am not!"

"Awe, look at you getting all flustered."

"You'd better shut it, Zaelek Khiings."

"Make me." Before I could react, Kinara swept my feet out from under me, leaving me flat on my back. "That'll do it," I gasped.

Now, she wore the smile, and Lycaon snickered to himself. She offered me her hand, helped me up, then winked and bumped me playfully with her hip. "All that training, and you're still slow."

"Well, I wasn't expecting to get ambushed by you."

She turned back toward the lake, lost in her thoughts. I hadn't seen Kinara scared like this before.

"So, what is it then?" I asked.

"What?"

"About the boat."

She hesitated for a moment. "I'm just not fond of having no idea what's underneath me."

"That's nothing to be ashamed of. Lots of people struggle with that. I thought you were going to say something dumb, like you were afraid of getting splinters in your butt."

She laughed. "You are so strange."

"I'm just glad it's a realistic fear. Arinn did say we needed to be careful about how much noise we made in the water, so we didn't get eaten by the Forest Guardian."

"The what?" When Kinara turned to me, the visible fear on her face transformed into a mixture of annoyance and anger.

Lycaon snickered again. "Keep it up, and she'll never get in the boat."

I dismissed his comment with a wave of my hand. "She'll be fine, she's tough."

"What are you two saying?" Kinara asked impatiently.

"Nothing. He's just taking your side."

"Smart volf."

We waited in silence for a few more minutes before Arinn joined us. She summoned the boat from the lake, then ushered us onto the wooden seats in the craft. When we pushed off, Kinara wrapped her arms around Lycaon's neck.

Sometimes I thought Kinara liked Lycaon more than she did me. She often came to my room to snuggle the volf rather than talk to me after a hard day of training. What a spoiled rotten beast. Whenever he sat next to her, she would run her hands through his thick white coat and scratch behind his ears. I even caught her sneaking him table scraps a few times. It wasn't like the little swinenbeast didn't get enough to eat.

The bottom of the boat scratched against the opposite shoreline and Arinn jumped out to pull us farther onto land.

Kinara looked at the mass of dark trees in awe. "I never even knew this was here."

"That's the point," said Arinn.

Arinn led us into the forest, and the darkness fled from the glow of the plant life. Kinara turned to speak to me, but I shook my head and put a finger to my lips. She nodded and followed Arinn silently. The last thing we wanted was to spook a *Bockratandem* and cause us more trouble.

We came to a small creek and followed it until reaching a clear pool near the bottom of a rock formation. Small streams of water trickled from the tops of the rocks, creating a light mist as they collided with the water's surface. The beautiful scene distracted me from the environmental noises for only a moment before I noticed a chorus of soft whispers. Was it a song or something else?

Arinn's voice startled me. "This is where the forest gets its name from."

"What are they?" Kinara asked.

"Some say they are the voices of our ancestors, but no one knows for sure."

Luci'oan stepped through the vegetation on the other side of the small pond. "I see you found them."

"Have you gleaned any additional information?" Arinn asked.

"We captured most of the traitors before they could flee, but there were a couple that managed to escape into outsider territory."

Arinn cursed under her breath. "You don't think they would turn to Javelar, do you?"

"Hard to tell. Giaanna was one that got away, so it's a possibility if she thinks they will help her become Chieftess."

With the way the Altarians seemed to adore Ailyana, it surprised me that anyone would defy her.

"I thought only those with royal blood could rule?"

Arinn shifted her gaze to me. "That's true, but Giaanna is Ailyana's cousin. The only way for her to take the throne, however, would be to best Ailyana in combat."

"Why hasn't Giaanna challenged Ailyana before."

"It's not that simple. There isn't a formal way for her to wage a challenge. She would have to declare war, win the war, then kill Ailyana. If she gets Javelar to take her side, then she will have the army she needs to declare war."

I didn't know how to feel. If Javelar attacked, there would be a lot of casualties. Still, it also meant that there would be a chance to get information about Parnikus and Ben. I shook my head to clear the thoughts. That knowledge wasn't worth the bloodshed. I also had to think about how else I might obtain that information. Anyone we captured wouldn't simply give it to us. That would mean we'd have to force it out of them. Was I willing to sacrifice a piece of my soul to torture someone?

Was this who I'd become? I shuddered to think what my parents might say if they knew how I felt. But wouldn't they have done the same thing in my place? Would they have tortured someone for information?

"Zaelek," Kinara said, "Are you okay?"

My eyes met hers. "Hmm?"

"What are you thinking about?"

I looked away from her, terrified that she might see right through me. "Nothing. It's just a lot to process."

Kinara couldn't know how I felt. She'd see me as the monster I had become in the mine.

Luci'oan gestured toward the forest. "Arinn, the Chieftess wants you to oversee the traitors' executions."

Arinn's eyes fell to the ground, and I could've sworn I saw the weight of that burden being placed on her shoulders.

"The two of you stay here," she said. "Don't leave this area, it will keep you safe."

I nodded. As our masters disappeared into the thick brush, nothing felt safe. What if someone found us, or a *Bockratandem* came to the pond? What did she mean that the area would keep us safe?

I walked to one of the larger rocks near the edge of the pond and sat down. Kinara stayed where she was, seeming lost in thoughts of her own.

Lycaon joined me. "You wanted that war, didn't you?"

"For a second. Then I realized how terrible that is."

"It's not terrible. You lost your family, and you'd do almost anything to keep your brothers alive."

"Even torture?"

"There are worse things to do to someone."

"Great. Glad to know I'm now one more step closer to being a psychopath."

Lycaon snickered. "You can thank me later."

I laughed. "I'm sure."

"Just remember that you can wish all day, but it doesn't mean anything will come of it. Whatever happens next wasn't because you wished it into existence."

Kinara joined us. "What are you two laughing about?"

I winked at the volf. "Lycaon was just telling me you could have been a blightseal with those flippers you call feet."

Lycaon's eyes widened, and his mouth dropped. "I said no such thing!"

Kinara chuckled to herself and then gave Lycaon a look that scared even me. "Is that so?"

Lycaon slowly backed toward the edge of the pond. "No! Kinara. Wait!"

I laughed, watching his complete terror as he looked for an escape route. The poor volf wouldn't make it ten feet before Kinara overtook him with teleportation.

She shoved him into the pond, laughing hysterically as he paddled back to the shore. His icy glare melted into a grin. Lycaon waited for Kinara to open her mouth to gloat before he shook his long white coat violently. Both of us screamed and covered our faces as an astounding amount of water soaked us.

I looked to Kinara, then had an idea. The corners of my mouth lifted menacingly.

Kinara caught the change in my expression. "What are you…? Zaelek, don't you dare!"

A blast of wind pulsed from my palm, sending her into the middle of the pond. My laughter filled the grove. Out of the corner of my teary eye, I noted that she no longer floated where I left her.

Her palms slammed into my back, launching me straight into the lukewarm pool. When I surfaced, she teleported next to me in the water.

"Got you," she said.

"I got you first, Flippers."

Her mouth dropped, and she splashed me with water with a light giggle. "Shut it, Sparky!"

"Make me."

She dove under the water and dragged me down by my foot. Though clever, I still had one trick up my sleeve. I sent a torrent of wind downward and rocketed out of the water like a torpedo. The moment I landed on the shore, Kinara teleported beside me and swept my feet from under me.

She rolled on top of me and pinned my arms to the ground, staring into my eyes with amusement. My heart pounded, and an ache I hadn't experienced before caused a tightness in my chest. Without thinking, I reached up and kissed her soft lips.

Kinara pulled away in surprise. Then, without warning, she returned the kiss, and with it came the rush of emotion from before. It felt like my breath had been stolen, and soon I lost myself in her intoxicating aura.

Again, she pulled away, this time with the same sadness I saw in her eyes when Alator had been taken from her. "I'm sorry—I can't do this again."

She vanished, taking my heart with her.

42

Nearby, but hidden from Zaelek...

My back rested against the base of a large tree and my arms wrapped around my knees. It was stupid of me to kiss him. I had allowed myself to be swept up by irrational emotions, and now I was headed down the same path I had been on with Alator. Was it so wrong, though?

I shook my head to quell the thoughts but they persisted: If I care about him, I have to let him go. He shouldn't have to fix something that's broken. Besides, wouldn't it be safer to settle down with someone not in the Forces?

The frustration built until I wanted to blow something up. I burst into tears. "What is wrong with me?" I whispered to myself

A familiar man's voice spoke, one that I never thought would grace my ears again. "Nothing is wrong with you, sweetheart."

I searched for the source, but saw nothing. "Alator?"

A breeze swept through the grotto. An assortment of leaves and other light debris swirled in front of me, taking the shape of a human being. A gnarled bundle of roots broke through the ground, solidifying into a man's body. Skin wrapped over the mess of roots until I stared at his completed form. He stared back at me with his amber eyes.

For the first time in a long while, no words came to mind. I didn't even know how to react. His arms opened in invitation, and I rushed into his embrace, tears streaming down my cheeks. "I can't believe it's really you!"

His hug tightened. "You're trembling…"

"Of course I'm trembling!"

A hint of sadness dulled my Alator's eyes. "Kinara, I know about your feelings for Zaelek."

My stomach knotted. "What?"

"It's okay. You need someone. Zaelek has been your friend since you were kids, so it makes sense you would choose him."

"It's not like that!"

He pulled me into an embrace again. "Either way, you can make a choice. Stay here and live a long, miserable life as a *Bockratandem* or move on and live your life with someone you love."

"I don't want to make that choice right now."

I closed my eyes and allowed myself the luxury of being in his arms again. The rage and sadness inside of me slowly fizzled out, and I found an emotion that I didn't think I would ever feel again: love.

Forest of Whispers, searching for Kinara…

I surged through the woods, searching for Kinara. She had to be out here somewhere! I hurdled over a fallen tree and skidded to a stop just in time to avoid a collision with Arinn.

She scanned me from head to toe, eyes narrowed. "What are you doing out here? I told you to stay at the sanctuary."

"Kinara ran away."

Arinn cursed. "What was she thinking?"

"It wasn't her fault!" I shut my mouth to keep myself from blurting out anything else.

She held her hand up and took a breath.

"How long has she been out there by herself?"

"Only for about five minutes. It's not that big of a deal, right?"

She slapped me in the bck of the head. "Not a big deal? Do you know how dangerous this place is if you don't know what you're doing? You'd better pray she didn't stumble onto a remnant."

"A what?"

"We don't have time for an explanation. Tell me quickly, has she lost anyone?"

"Her parents."

"When?"

"I don't know, it was a long time ago."

"*Zellimo*, Zaelek! We need to find her now!"

Arinn took off. Lycaon and I trailed her, careful not to fall behind. I didn't know how we were going to find her in this mess of tangled vines and competing vegetation.

A couple minutes later, something snatched my foot, and I tripped, bouncing off the ground and kicking up the dirt. I rolled to my back and came face to face with a hideous, shadow-like creature. Its face had no skin, only strips of the muscles that used to be human draped over its skull. One eye, attached only by its nerves, hung below its chin.

I scrambled backward and slammed against a tree trunk. The horror crawled toward me on all fours, licking its deformed lips. Lycaon latched onto its nape and wrestled it to the ground. A human sounding shriek escaped from the creature as an elongated, snake-like tongue wrapped around Lycaon's neck. He yelped as it constricted.

Arinn's sword cut through the slimy tongue and lodged in the wood of an adjacent tree. The creature bellowed and gripped its bleeding stub. Arinn launched over Lycaon, gripped the pommel of her sword, and slashed the abomination's head off.

I looked at her, then to the creature, then back to her with wide eyes. "What was that?"

"That," Arinn said, sheathing her blade with a satisfied snap, "Was a *Bockratandem*."

"We need to find Kinara before one of those things does."

Arinn offered me her forearm and pulled me up.

"Are you okay, Lycaon?"

Lycaon nodded.

Luci'oan dropped out of a void bound in front of Arinn.

"Who screamed?"

Arinn gestured toward the Bockratandem. "We'll be lucky if it didn't alert the entire forest."

Luci'oan's eyes scanned our group. "Where's Kinara? I sense a remnant nearby."

"She was the one who drew it."

"We need to split up. Take Zaelek and Lycaon with you, I'll search alone."

Arinn nodded, and Luci'oan bounded from sight.

I bounded after Arinn, observing her carefully for any hint of a direction change. Lycaon ran to the left a few hundred feet away, increasing our search radius. The severity of the situation sank in. I shuddered at the thought of Kinara alone with one of those creatures.

A low-pitched howl resonated from Lycaon. He'd found her.

Arinn and I closed in on his northern location to find Kinara lying unconscious beneath a floating entity. Its ripped grey cloak draped partly over her, and its mummified hands hovered inches from her face.

Arinn thrust her palm forward and blasted the ghoulish entity with a torrent of water. The wraith-like being shrieked and turned its deathly gaze toward us, its sunken eyes darting between Arinn and me.

It surged toward us. I waved my hand horizontally, sending a barrier of wind a few feet from my palms. The creature slammed into the wind wall and shrieked again as it bounced off. Luci'oan joined the fray, extending his hand toward the remnant. Two roots spiraled from the ground.

The roots moved with more agility than I thought possible and quickly wrapped around the creature. The moment they took hold, they slammed into the ground and pinned their catch.

"Now, Arinn!" Luci'oan shouted.

Arinn swirled her hands, then slammed the dirt with her palms. A trail of frost shot forward, overtaking the roots and entity and freezing them solid. Luci'oan formed a javelin of stone, then hurled it into the creature's chest. The rock went straight through, leaving a hole where it impacted. Two more vines shot from the soil and wove themselves through the wound. Luci'oan imitated ripping something apart, and the vines mimicked the movement. A hundred hunks of ice and tattered rags exploded everywhere.

I rushed to Kinara's side to check her pulse. A steady heartbeat rippled under my fingers. "She's alive."

Luci'oan approached from behind and studied her for a moment, then picked her up and threw her over his shoulder. "She won't survive if we don't get her to the infirmary."

43

Javelar HQ, in the Arena's platoon staging area
with Benazahg and Parnikus...

I emerged from the pit after another hard-won victory over an enemy platoon. Benazahg and Parnikus led our troops into the tunnel, instructing the new recruits where to put their armor and weapons.

"Hey, Gertry," Parnikus said to me.

"Yeah?"

"Looks like you're finally out of here for good. Congratulations."

"Thanks. Congratulations to you, too."

His brow furrowed. "What for?"

"You and Ben are the new platoon leaders."

He faltered for a moment. "Oh, right."

I clasped his shoulder. "You'll do fine. Keep fighting like you did today, and I'll see you on the other side in no time."

Parnikus smiled and started to reply, but stopped when he saw the guards heading toward us. He stepped aside as they grasped my arms and led me out of the tunnel. Once we were out of sight, I shrugged their hands off. "Get off me."

The nervous guards took a step back. “Ma’am, Commander Savvage is waiting for you in his office.”

I figured he would be. No doubt he has been eager to hear my report on the Khiings brothers.

The unwelcoming metal halls echoed with my footsteps. On multiple occasions, Javelar operatives moved to the side, saluting as I passed. I never returned their salutes. It would show respect, something I didn’t have for pawns.

When I entered the main hall, my squire, Alyssie met me. Her unkempt, curly blonde hair jiggled when she ran to keep up. “Ma’am,” she said.

I rolled my eyes. “What?”

“I thought you might want your sword for when you meet with the Commander.”

I snatched the blade from her hands, refusing to dignify her offering with appreciation. “Get out of my sight. If I need you, I’ll send for you.”

The little wretch bowed, then scurried away. I strapped my blade to my hip and felt complete once again. That stupid little poker with a knife at the end put a cramp in my style. My steps echoed in the Commander’s Stairwell. At the top loomed the familiar red wooden door painted with the blood of fallen recruits. Why Savvage had elected to keep the disgusting tradition was beyond me. I knocked and dislodged flakes of dried blood.

Savvage opened the door, and I noticed that he had slicked back his long brown hair. He’d even gone as far as combing his beard. Either there was an upcoming meeting with someone important, or he’d just had one.

“Welcome back, Zateyra. I trust you have news.”

I pulled the red wig off my head and shook out my straight black hair. “The Khiings boys have more potential than I thought. They’ve already started to call upon their elements more easily.”

“Excellent. I must commend you for how well you performed out there. If I hadn’t known you were a planter, you might have fooled even me…though, you could have shown restraint on the sabercat.”

“And became its next meal? I think not.”

He laughed. “Fair enough. I highly doubt my nephews suspect anything, so, no harm, no foul.”

"Was that all you wanted to talk to me about, Sir? I'm ready for a shower and a hot meal. Those cages are disgusting."

His eyes flickered with dark amusement. "Not quite. Our scouts have brought back a couple of Altarian defectors. I'd like you to oversee their interrogation."

"Interesting. I thought the Altarians were fiercely loyal to their leader."

Savvage sneered. "Apparently not."

"Where are they?"

"In the holding cells."

I turned and walked down the stairs.

Savvage called after me, "And, Zateyra. We only need one alive to get the information."

I smirked as my hand rested on the pommel of my sword. It had been far too long since its blade had tasted blood.

In the Forest of Whispers...

As we left the forest, Arinn asked Luci'oan to go on without us.

I found this odd. "Shouldn't we get to the hospital first to make sure Kinara is okay?"

Arinn shook her head. "No, Zaelek, there's nothing more you or I can do for her." Luci'oan resituated Kinara, then bounded toward the lake. Once we were alone, she turned to me. "I have one more thing to teach you before we leave, so the next time something like this happens, you can attempt to resolve it yourself. However, you have to promise to keep it a secret. Battles aren't won by brute force alone. They're also won by controlling what facts the enemy has access to. Now, promise me you won't tell anyone else."

"I promise."

"I'm going to teach you how to release your elemental armor. Every Guardian has armor, but the Guardian Forces usually wait until Delta rank to teach it." She held her hand out. "Hold out your hand and follow my lead, just like when we summoned Lycaon."

She drew a triangle on her palm. We made elaborate signs on

top of the triangle, then held our palms toward each other. The mark glowed bright white and spiraled up my arm. An eruption of blinding light exploded from my chest, forcing Arinn to cover her eyes. I was unaffected. When the light receded, I looked down and saw a brilliant suit of silver armor, hardly noticing its feather-like weight.

"Can I show it to Kinara when she wakes up?"

"What did I just say? She'll find out when the time is right." Arinn paused. "You need to put it in its dormant state, for now. Find it like you found your element and push it into a safe place in your mind. Remember, if you need it again, you can find it there."

I concentrated, looking through my memories for a space to store my armor. An image of my mother smiling under a grindlevast tree came to mind. As I imagined myself pushing the armor into it as if I were storing a museum exhibit in a gallery, the metal faded from my body. Arinn nodded with approval. I didn't expect that to be so easy. Maybe I was getting the hang of this stuff, after all.

"When should I use it?"

"You'll know. If you feel any risk to your life, that's when you release it. I must say though, I'm a little surprised your swords didn't change their form."

"Why would my swords change?"

"Everyone I've known has their weapon change when they release their armor. Maybe it's because you have two swords, but I don't know."

Of course. Another unique attribute that hindered my goal of being taken seriously. Now what should I tell Kinara when she sees it? She's going to think I'm defective or something.

I sat on the edge of my bed, worried sick about Kinara's unimproved condition. The doctor said she would be fine, but it might be a few days until she wakes up. *What if she doesn't?* We were lucky to interrupt the remnant, and Arinn had rubbed this in my face to prove her point. Her lecture echoed through my mind as I willed a small ball of wind into existence above my palm.

The urge to get some fresh air came over me. I slipped on a pair of pants and shoes, grabbed my swords, and silently opened the door, careful not to wake Lycaon. Outside, the hot, muggy summer air made me feel like I had just gotten out of the shower.

I took a deep breath, then started toward the area where Kinara had uncovered the traitors' meeting. Plenty of rocks, trees, and bits of nature were scattered about there for me to practice on. Even though we had been training for the last month, I still didn't know much about my element. Besides what Arinn had taught me, there hadn't been time to unravel the mystery of it.

Once far enough away from the sleeping village, I found a rock that weighed around twenty pounds and put it in the middle of the path. My enigma flowed freely in an attempt to lift the stone with wind. It shook slightly, then stopped. *I need a bit more power*. Though I had gotten the hang of manifesting my element, getting the right amount of wind pressure on the first try still challenged me. I sent a slightly more powerful torrent under the rock and watched it slowly lift from the ground. It spun lethargically and stopped its skyward movement when it reached eye level.

I closed my eyes, trying to sense the wind lifting the stone, to truly get a feel for what had been produced. Much to my surprise, something similar to a building schematic awaited me on the back of my eyelids. A thin white line extended from my feet to where the rock had been before it had risen. From this point, the route took an upward ninety-degree turn and split into two spiraling lines like a strand of DNA. They extended all the way to the bottom of the stone. The lines then disappeared, leaving a perfect, white mesh replica of its structure.

I moved my hand, also wrapped in the white mesh, in front of my face. *This is new*. Curiously, I turned my palm up and positioned it under the stone. A black line crept parallel along the white one. However, instead of following the helix formation when the white line shot up, the black prongs spiraled in the opposite direction.The stone stopped spinning.

Fascinated, I opened my eyes to see the lineless rock hovering without movement. Carefully, I dropped my hand and watched the stone begin to spin. *Okay, so what happens when the other hand up comes up?* The mesh patterns danced across my eyelids when they closed. I made the connection with my raised right hand, then lifted my left. A blue line extended from my left palm and connected to the stone in an arcing fashion. My palm pushed toward the side face of the stone. A light pressure, like touching its surface, pushed against my hand. When I put my palm down, the rock descended. The other directions worked similarly.

I opened my eyes and repeated the process, watching as the stone moved in cadence with my hand. Another idea came to me. My palms thrust toward the forest, like I intended to shove the rock. A blast of wind exploded, and the stone shot through a tree's trunk, disappearing into the forest.

"What are you doing?" Lycaon said from behind me.

My heart nearly flew out of my chest. "Don't sneak up on me like that!"

"Why didn't you tell me you were going out?"

I huffed. "I wanted to be alone for a few minutes. How did you find me?"

"Whenever you use your element, I can feel it. Think of it as a beacon for me."

"Good to know."

"Next time you want to venture off on your own, at least let me know. I'll keep my distance. It's reckless to be out here alone. What if the Altarians missed one of the traitors?"

He was right. It was stupid of me to come out here by myself. "Sorry. It won't happen again."

Lycaon looked to the tree I had blown a hole through. "What were you working on?"

"I was just familiarizing myself with my element."

"I see. Well, let's head back to the inn. Who knows what Arinn has planned for training in the morning."

I held my finger up. "Hold on. I have one more idea that I wanted to try."

Lycaon sat on the path and stared at me expectantly, but said nothing. I closed my eyes and concentrated on my body. A small torrent of wind formed at my feet and slowly encased me, then my feet left the ground. I opened my eyes and found myself hovering, slowly spinning clockwise. When I raised my left hand like I had with the stone, nothing happened. Confused, I tried with the right. Again, no results. I brought both hands up only to be disappointed.

I lowered my hands, ready to descend, but stabilized instead—

excitement pulsed through my veins. Abruptly, I fell a few inches, then the wind holding me failed. My feet hit the ground, and I looked at Lycaon with a grin. It had worked! Something seeped from my nose. I reached up and gently touched the area, and blood coated my fingertips.

Lycaon huffed. "You overexerted yourself."

I never bled while training with Arinn, so why now? "How? I thought we did all that endurance training for elemental sustainment."

"This is something different. You're lucky that a bloody nose was the worst that happened. An advanced technique requires time and practice, so you'll need to start with something smaller. Maybe something like boosting your jumps."

"I'll have to try it tomorrow after my enigma comes back. I don't want to accidentally pass out."

He turned back toward the village. "Good plan. Let's head back to the inn."

"No, not yet. I want to check on Kinara."

44

Javelar HQ,
the interrogation rooms…

The Altarian traitor's head rolled a few feet away, leaving a crimson trail in its wake. I wiped my blood-soaked sword on her garments then turned to leave while sheathing my blade.

My squire's eyes widened, "Why did you kill her, Ma'am? She could have joined our force."

I rolled my eyes. "Great plan. Offer a traitor an opportunity to betray us from the inside. She could have been a double agent, for all you know."

Alyssie ran to catch up with me. I had no interest in having a conversation with that seventeen year old brat. Why Trentir had ever considered letting her tag along with me was perplexing. She always ended up getting in the way.

"So, what now?" she asked.

The mere sound of her voice made me want to strangle her. "Now, *I* report to the commander, and *you* clean my sword." I unstrapped the weapon and thrust it into her arms. "If you so much as scratch it, I'll kill you."

Her scurrying feet couldn't disappear fast enough. If I never saw her again, it would be too soon.

Five minutes later, I stepped into the briefing room and found Savvage staring down at his holographic battle map of Alympia. The door clicked shut behind me, drawing his cold eyes in my direction.

"Ah, Zateyra," he said. "What's become of the Altarian traitors?"

"Dead, Sir."

"I see. Did you learn anything useful?"

"Where their hidden city is, and that we have an insider to help us take down their shields."

Savvage pulled himself away from the table, giving me his full attention. "Is that so? It strikes me odd that they would give you such knowledge so freely."

"They made a trade."

"Oh?"

"One traitor had royal blood. In exchange for the location and contact information, we supply bodies for a war against the Altarians and help overthrow their Chieftess. I technically haven't broken that promise. Though, I'm sure this isn't quite what she meant."

Savvage chuckled. "Excellent work. Come, show me where on the map."

I approached the table and typed in the coordinates. The map zoomed in on a mountain.

Savvage stared at the point, then shot me an annoyed glare. "Why am I looking at a mountain peak, Zateyra?"

"It's not. A cloaking device that somehow projects natural terrain on its face conceals the city."

Trentir gleefully looked at the map. "Of course!"

"They also have the other Khiings boy there."

The man's stone eyes twinkled as he grinned. "So, that's where he's been hiding. Get our troops ready to move. It's time to cross two objectives off the list."

"Two, Sir?"

He winked. "You didn't think I would risk a big chunk of our forces over one stupid boy, did you? The Altarians have a much more efficient way of unlocking elemental power, one that doesn't require a locksmith's touch after the initial awakening. That's how we'll crush Voelker's forces."

"I'm not following, Sir."

He groaned. "Must I always go in-depth on strategy for you, or will you catch on one of these days by yourself?"

Irritated, I started to answer, but he stopped me immediately with a raised hand.

"That was a rhetorical question. If we can utilize this other method, Kehndrig will have no choice but to promote most, if not all, of his forces to match our strength. What happens when a Guardian undergoes more than one rank jump at a time?"

"It takes a few weeks for them to recover." I paused, suddenly understanding where his plan was going.

His grin widened. "We can easily take them out during their recuperation period."

"I'll prepare the troops for deployment."

"Send out a few squads out immediately and have the insider disable their aerial defenses if they have any. I want the Altarians to think the advanced party is our main attack."

"Won't they see through that?"

"Not if you send a few rotabombers with them."

I smiled. *Devious.*

45

At the Altarian inn…

Lycaon and I sat on the steps of the inn, waiting for Elutha and Aurok to retrieve us for more training.

"Elutha and Aurok send their best," Arinn called from the street. "They had something come up they needed to attend to."

I furrowed my brow. "Is everything all right?"

"For now. We're just taking some extra precautions with a few more scouting units in the area. I need to get back to my duties as a commander. From now on, you'll be training at the barracks. We've put you in a squad to teach you a new set of skills. You'll follow them on their assignments and learn how each role functions."

I couldn't help feeling a tinge of disappointment there would be no more training with Arinn.

"Are you sure I'm ready to…"

An explosion sounded overhead, the light pouring in dimmed, and the ground trembled. I looked up and saw a thick black cloud of smoke in place of the sun.

An Altarian warrior rushed to Arinn's side. "Ma'am," he said, "the Chieftess needs you in the briefing room, now!"

Worry flashed across Arinn's face, and she gestured for me to follow. If Arinn was worried, I wasn't sure I'd be much help. We pushed through the chaos erupting in the streets. People were shouting and pushing, trying to get a better view of the rippling sky, children screamed for their parents, and the animals pulling carts stampeded through the street, their loads scattering and crashing behind them.

For a moment, Arinn and I wriggled between the Altarians, but we changed course and made for the outskirts of town. From there, we initiated a bound and reached the palace in minutes.

Arinn threw open the briefing room doors, revealing Luci'oan, Ailyana, and a few other people I hadn't met, gathered around the HIVE System.

"What's going on?" Arinn asked.

Ailyana waited for the current round of bombardments to pass. "Our scouts have reported multiple rotabombers hovering above our airspace."

Luci'oan looked at me. "We need you to contact your Colonel in Crete. Someone sabotaged our anti-aircraft weapons, and our shield can't take more than a day's worth of barrages."

My eyes widened. I had no knowledge of he system. "But I have no idea how to run this thing."

"We'll dial the code. You to get the Colonel on the line."

I didn't even know if Colonel Voelker would speak to me without Kinara here. The only connection I had to him was through my father. "I'll try."

Arinn placed her hand on my shoulder. "We need you to do better than try, Zaelek."

I nodded. What did they expect me to do? Force him to listen? Ailyana punched the code into the HIVE System. It only had to ring twice before a receptionist picked up. "Guardian Forces Headquarters, how may I direct your call?"

"This is Zaelek Khiings. I need to speak with Colonel Voelker. It's urgent."

"I'm sorry, Mister Khiings. The Colonel is in the middle of a staff meeting. Can I take a message?"

"No, I need to speak with him right now."

"I'm afraid that's not possible. The Colonel gave us direct orders not to disturb him."

I needed to think of something quick, but what could I do? My name probably wasn't even registered with the Forces yet. Then I had an idea. "Tell him that the son of Cronus needs to talk to him, and it's an emergency."

"Did you say Cronus, as in *the* Cronus?"

"Yes."

"One moment, please."

Music sounded over the speakers, only to be disrupted by yet another blast against the shield. Everyone in the room stared at the HIVE System like our gazes would somehow speed up the process.

The music ended, and the woman's voice came back on. "Hello, Zaelek?"

"I'm here."

"The Colonel requires you to answer a verification question."

Verification question? From what I'd discovered about my dad over the past month, I probably wouldn't know what the answer was. "What's the question."

"The nickname your father gave your twin sister?"

I let out a sigh of relief. "Ari."

Once again, the music played, but this time, it ended almost immediately when Colonel Voelker anwered.

"Zaelek?"

"Yes, Sir."

"I'm in the middle of a crucial meeting with the Generals. What is it?"

Ailyana chimed in. "Colonel, we are under attack, and most of our defenses have been disabled."

"What? How?"

"We're not sure, but we think one of our people gave Javelar our location and someone sabotaged our system from the inside."

"Give me a minute."

The Colonel excused himself briefly. When he interrupted the meeting some muffled conversation came across, but I could only make out surprised inflections in the voices surrounding him. A request to room share floated down in front of Ailyana. When she accepted it, our room morphed to match the Colonel's location. Two stern-looking men stood at the front of the room. Colonel Voelker gestured to them. "General Playato, General Yaralgo, this is Ailyana, Chieftess of the Altarian people."

Ailyana nodded. "Pleasure to meet you."

"Likewise," General Yaralgo said.

The Colonel made his way to the electronic war table that featured a map of Ulypus. "Ailyana, we need to know your location."

Ailyana worriedly looked at Luci'oan and Arinn.

Arinn touched the mute option floating near the HIVE table. "Your Highness, we have no choice. If we don't enlist their aid, our defenses will fall, and the village will be exposed."

Ailyana took a deep breath and nodded in resignation. She waited for Arinn to unmute the system then said, "Colonel, I'm sending you the coordinates to our city now."

Colonel Voelker entered the number in their system, but before he could reply, General Playato took control of the conversation. "Why should we endanger our fleet of fighters for a nation we just met?"

The Colonel looked at him in disbelief and horror.

"Sir…"

General Playato held up his hand for silence. Disappointment, confusion, and despair filled me. I thought the Guardian Forces had more honor than this.

The faces in our room reflected my worried emotions, and this time, Luci'oan muted the system. "It's a fair question."

Everyone looked at him in surprise.

"What are you saying?" the woman opposite me exclaimed.

"Think about it. If the situation were reversed, wouldn't we ask the same question? Our nation is small, so why would it affect them if we fell? We need to offer something in return that shows them our people are worth saving."

Ailyana's face flashed with horror. "Other than the fact that innocent lives are at stake?"

"This isn't an emotional decision. It's strategic," he explained. "They're fighting a war on terrorism and assisting us could compromise their defenses."

Arinn nodded. "It makes sense."

Sure, it made sense, but Ailyana's argument made sense, too.

There were many women and children here that wouldn't last the night if the Altarian defenses fell.

"What do you propose we offer?" Ailyana asked.

Luci'oan paused. "We'll teach them how to awaken their soldier's elemental powers properly."

"Absolutely not!" another man said.

"Silence," Ailyana snapped. "I would prefer *anything* else, but the awakening is the only valuable resource we have to offer." She nodded to Arinn, who unmuted the system. "Generals, I'm sure you already know about our unique process to awaken elemental power."

General Playato crossed his arms. "The Colonel may have mentioned it."

"We're willing to share our knowledge in exchange for your assistance with this matter."

"We'll dispatch a squadron to your location," General Yaralgo said, as if he'd anticipated the offer. "ETA is thirty minutes."

"Thank you," said Ailyana with a grateful sigh. The feed ended, leaving us at the main menu of the HIVE System.

Arinn faced me. "Come, we have things to do."

I followed her. "What things?"

"I have a suspicion about something. Just shut up and come with me."

And *I* had a suspicion this was going to be something I wouldn't like.

46

Behind the Altarian village central tree...

Lycaon and I gawked at the cascade of water flowing from the river running under the royal tree's roots. The mist cooled my skin with a crisp breeze and coated me with light humidity.

"Arinn..." I said.

Arinn sighed. "Yes, Zaelek?"

"This is great and everything, but why are we here?"

"The shield generators are behind this waterfall. One of our warriors failed to report in this morning. Normally, I would assume that they had just fallen asleep at their post and would check-in when they awoke, but not today. We stationed two guards at the entrance after last night's events."

I inspected the cliff's base and saw a modestly camouflaged structure serving as a gateway to the large road disappearing behind the falls. It looked like a regular powerplant. Why were we checking on some old building?

We turned off the path and followed the rocky riverbank to the base of the falls. Lycaon padded beside me, weaving between puddles.

He must have cleaned his paws last night or something. Though a wild animal, volves weren't particularly fond of getting their coats dirtier than they had to.

Lycaon glanced at me. "I don't like this."

"Me either," I replied.

If Arinn was suspicious about this situation, I had a legitimate reason to be nervous. She didn't often get antsy. Though, to most, Arinn would come across as calm and collected, I had spent enough time with her to know inner lip chewing—which she did now—wasn't one of her typical behaviors.

Arinn stopped. "Wait."

I saw nothing in our surroundings that would make us stop. "What is it?"

She crouched, running her finger along a thin line crossing the path. Is that a tripwire? How in Styx did she see that? I would have trampled against it had she not stopped. Arinn flicked one of her belted throwing knives, severing the wire. A gentle hiss passed us, but not before Arinn snatched a tiny dart from the air.

"Jehora serum," she said.

"What?"

"It's a toxin that cycles through the body in approximately thirty seconds. Good thing I didn't send any of my warriors in my stead. They may have been killed."

"So what now? There could be more traps out there."

"Yes…"

She let loose a shrieking whistle that might easily rival Dad's. I followed her gaze to the sky above and saw Aetos, Arinn's cararaptor Daemon, descending toward us.

"Can Aetos see the traps?"

"Probably, but that would take time we don't have. I'll have to send a Prowler team out when we get back. Let's not worry about that for now. Climb up on Aetos back."

There's no way we would all fit on her back! What would Lycaon do?

As if the golden cararaptor had heard my thoughts, she shuddered, then in a tuft of roiling feathers, her body expanded until she had become the size of a small home. *What?* I couldn't believe my eyes. How had she done that?

Arinn swung her leg over Aetos's bowed neck. "I'll explain Daemon expansion later, and yes, Lycaon will be able to do it, too. Get on."

I clambered up Aetos' back and wrapped my arms around Arinn's waist, becoming suddenly aware of how her soft, warm skin felt against me. Aetos pumped her massive wings and lifted us a few feet off the ground. Lycaon shot me a panicked look.

"What about Lycaon?" I asked.

A flash of brownish-orange reached out toward the volf. He yipped in surprise as Aetos wrapped the soft section of her talons around his belly.

"She's got him," Arinn said.

Poor Lycaon. That must have been startling.

It didn't take us more than thirty seconds for us to reach the camouflaged facility. When the colossal cararaptor landed, she put Lycaon down while Arinn and I dismounted. Aetos returned to her typical size before taking off again and disappeared behind the tree line. *She really isn't the most social creature, is she?*

"Zaelek," Arinn called.

I trotted over to where she knelt. The glossed-over eyes of a deceased Altarian warrior stared at me from under the bush he had been shoved under. A deep, blackened gash had been torn through his neck. I caught my breath and looked away. Though the idea of death had been running through my head during Arinn's lectures, I still wasn't prepared to witness it firsthand.

"Don't look away," she said flatly. "You need to see it."

Hesitantly, I returned my gaze to the man. He had shaved his hair save for a thin strip running from his forehead down to the base of his skull. My chest ached as I pondered who he was and what he did outside of being a warrior. He had a face that made me think he smiled often. I truly felt the loss of a brother, even if I didn't have Altarian blood in me.

Arinn stood. "Come, we must check on the other guard."

We crept up the path to the waterfall. Arinn kept our pace slow as she searched for any hint of traps, but we eventually reached two large doors that were embedded in the cliff wall behind the falls. She entered a code into the small, button-filled control pad next to the doors. The thick metal slabs slid open to reveal a hallway. Only a few of the smaller lights flickered; the rest dangled from their wiring harnesses or had been shattered. Paper littered the floor, massive, sparking, severed cables hung down like jungle vines, and scorch marks sporadically scarred the walls and ceiling. What had happened in here?

Lycaon inhaled deeply. “I smell blood. Lots of it.”

“Lead us to it,” Arinn said.

He took point and navigated us down a maze of passages. Not that it would have been hard to follow our current trail with all of the debris and destruction leading to wherever we were going. I would hate to fight in such a cramped space.

“Hey, Arinn,” I said.

“Yes?”

“How would you fight in something like this?”

She looked at the surrounding chaos, then replied, “I would avoid fighting in something like this, personally. There are too many ways to get cornered.”

I figured as much. If whoever is responsible for this mess stuck around, we’re going to have to fight them in here too. A slight tingle filled my chest, and my hands turned clammy. I don’t want to fight anyone today. How do I know if I’m even ready?

Lycaon lifted his nose from the ground to study me. “If we have to fight, remember your wind barriers. They’ll at least allow you to control the enemy’s movement.”

It was a good call; I just didn’t know how long my enigma would maintain multiple walls simultaneously. I could handle one or two for three minutes (give or take a few) but anything upward of that, and I’d be lucky to keep them up for thirty seconds. Enigma had a funny way of balancing itself. If I operated within my scope of abilities, things went according to plan. However, if I so much as lifted a pinky finger too much, it poured from me like a spillway. I guess that’s why Lycaon and Arinn always tell me “know your limits” and why Kinara is usually so cautious about how much enigma she uses.

I, on the other hand, had no issue burning enigma whenever I could. Most of the time, I just liked watching my element interact with the environment. Of course, I justified it by calling it “experimentation,” like it somehow made it seem less like a child playing with a new toy. Perhaps my messing around would pay off in a battle.

When we turned the next corner, Lycaon, Arinn, and I froze momentarily as we stared at another dead Altarian warrior. I wanted to look away from the mutilated man, but I knew if Arinn caught me, she would call me out and still make me see it. Like the first, a gash was torn in his neck, and his eyes no longer held the color of life.

"Why use a blade when you have access to Jehora serum?" Arinn asked, mostly to herself.

"Maybe they had a limited amount."

"Possibly…We need to keep our guard up. They may have rigged the halls like they did outside."

I didn't like the idea that a poisoned dart might end up sticking out of me at any given moment. My heart raced as I took the next shaky few steps, forgetting that Arinn and Lycaon had already cleared the path between them and me. *Come on, Zaelek. Don't panic on your first mission out. Just get it done and over with. Danger is part of the job. You'll get used to it.* Though I told myself that, I didn't know if I believed it. What if I never got used to it, and I cave under pressure? No, that couldn't be. Mom and Dad were so fierce. There's no way that those genes skipped over me.

The string-like web from an areightnid stuck to my arm, snagging against the hairs with its grainy texture and sending a shudder through me.

"I hate areightnids," I said, brushing the sticky web away.

Arinn crouched next to the dead Altarian warrior. "There aren't areightnids in this bunker…they can't make it past the electrical barrier at the entrance. Unless…" She gently rolled the warrior onto his side and inspected his back. Sure enough, two puncture wounds, oozing yellow liquid, blemished his skin between his shoulder blades.

"Tor'qi…"

"Tor'qi?" I asked.

"She's the only areightnid Tamer in the village."

"There's such a thing?"

I got the shivers just thinking about trying to tame those eight-legged critters. *Why would someone want to work with insects? They're so disgusting.*

"Of course. Do you think that every Tamer has a Daemon that manifests as a volf?"

My cheeks turned red, and I looked down at my feet, forgetting that *Tamer* had a different meaning now.

"I guess not."

Arinn stood. "We're close. The body is still warm."

"Why would she take the risk of attacking with her areightnid when she's the only person who has one?"

"I don't think she was anticipating we would be on her trail so quickly. Had we not followed my suspicions, she would have been long gone by the time we moved to investigate. All she would have had to do was come back, use her sword to carve the puncture wounds to look different, and sneak out of the village."

"Clever."

"She is both that and a good fighter. I trained her."

"Great," Lycaon huffed.

"Don't be alarmed. She is equivalent to one of your Epsilon rank Guardians."

My eyes widened. "Don't be alarmed? That's two ranks above me! I won't stand a chance in a fight against her!"

"Lucky you have me then, isn't it?"

I calmed slightly. If I functioned as Arinn's support in the fight, we would have Tor'qi backed into a corner. But what happens if something happens to Arinn?

Javelar HQ: the Arena...

This is it, Ben. If you survive this, you'll never have to see this arena again. Parnikus and I stood at the front of our platoon, waiting for the buzzer to start our last fight. Anxiety, fear, and uncertainty coursed through my veins. All we have to do is survive.

The buzzer sounded, and the gate opened. Parnikus nodded to me, and we surged forward into the humid jungle terrain. I halted the platoon once everyone had exited the tunnel.

Parnikus looked at me like I'd gone mad. doing?"

"This is the same arena we first fought in."

"How could you possibly know that?"

I pointed to the rotting corpse skewered by a spear. A vivid memory of the weapon piercing the young man's chest during our first battle brought on a hint of panic. "Him."

Parnikus shouted over his shoulder, "Everyone with a spear move to the front line." I heard the platoon shuffle. Once the formation finished its rearrangement, he barked, "Forward."

We moved into the thick, coarse vegetation. The broad, green leaves dragged across my sweat-drenched arm, invoking a claustrophobia-like sensation. After a minute or so of fumbling through the fauna, Parnikus stopped us again.

"What's your plan?" I whispered.

"A volley."

"That didn't work for our enemy last time."

"I'm altering it a little. Trust me." He waved for one of our spearmen to join us, then whispered to the young man, "Scout ahead but don't go too far. If you see the enemy bunched up, give the command to throw the spears, then run like Styx."

"What if they aren't bunched up?" he asked.

"Quietly report back to us."

The spearman crept forward, hunched and shaking. He disappeared into the vegetation. The command to send the volley came much sooner than I anticipated. Before we had the chance to give an order, I heard the overhead vegetation being ripped apart by our spears. Confused screaming came from behind the wall of plant life ahead of us.

"Spearmen to the back," Parnikus bellowed. The platoon shifted again. "Charge!"

We charged and I shoved my trident through their leader's neck. His eyes glossed over as he collapsed. I wrenched the weapon loose.

In the short moment that I had engaged the enemy, the rest of our platoon had split the opposing formation in half. Shrieks erupted throughout the small clearing as we commenced a massacre.

Standing at the edge of the clearing allowed me to witness the primal carnage unfold with fresh eyes. I saw men slaughtering women, women slaughtering men, teenagers being hacked to death by their elders, and vice versa. A lump formed in my throat. Why were we being forced to kill each other? What was the point of such blatant disregard for human life?

I looked at Parnikus. Blood ran off both his armor and weapon as smoothly as sweat from skin. He turned, and for the first time, I didn't recognize my own brother. A twisted grin replaced his usual gentle smile, and his eyes held a new madness.

Movement came from the right, and I barely had time to evade a spear thrust. I whipped my trident upward, knocking the attacking woman's weapon out of her hand and throwing her off balance. Her spear landed far away, leaving her defenseless. She scooted backward for a brief moment before slamming into a tree trunk. Her eyes were wide, and her breath came in shallow huffs.

I wanted to comfort her—to tell her that everything would be okay— even if it was a lie. No one should have to endure such cruelty. I didn't want to kill anyone else - I didn't want to be here anymore.

A hand grasped my shoulder, and I spun, bringing my weapon up to strike down my next opponent.

Parnikus parried my attack. "Easy, Ben, it's just me."

"Don't do that! I could have killed you."

"Sorry. I should have called your name." Parnikus nodded toward the cornered woman. "She's the last one. Finish her off so we can be done with this."

A pang of guilt settled in my stomach. I knew what I had to do, but I couldn't bear killing an unarmed human. Tears welled in my eyes. "I can't."

Parnikus squeezed my shoulder, then without a word, he drove his trident through the woman's armorless chest. I watched the life drain from her eyes, and just like that, she died, taking another piece of my soul with her.

The arena intercom crackled. "Congratulations, blue platoon. Please make your way to the nearest tunnel."

It's finally over.

Parnikus and I, alog with the remaining fifteen or so of our platoon, shuffled into the opponent's tunnel. A group of guards entered and approached Parnikus and me. "Congratulations, you made it through the arena trial. We're here to escort you to the banquet hall," one of the men said.

Was this nightmare really passed? Were things about to start looking up for us?

47

In the Altarian shield generator's central control...

More webs brushed against me as we entered the darkened control room. *This is as bad as that time Parnikus and I stumbled across that den of Areightnids in the forest.* Except we knew where the areightnids were then. Not to mention the terrifying realization that this creature could be as large as or larger than Lycaon.

Arinn flipped a breaker on the wall. A rising hum replaced the eerie silence, giving hope that the lights would brighten the room. As the fluorescent bulbs warmed to full range, more webs shimmered, creeping in every direction until they reached their shared destination: columns of webs barring the central console.

"I don't understand..." I said. "If Tor'qi wanted to hide her identity, why would she use all these webs?"

"Because she could destroy them with a snap if needed. She'd clear them away when she finished."

"Wait...that means she's still here."

"I'm aware, Zaelek."

I reached for my swords, feeling comfort in wrapping my fingers around their hilts and knowing I wouldn't be defenseless.

When had Arinn figured it out, and why didn't she tell me? Maybe she was testing my observation skills. Still, she had yet to draw her sword.

Lycaon broadened his stance. "Why aren't you pulling your sword out, Arinn?"

"What makes you think she'd attack me head-on?"

With a slight jerking motion, and her sword sat comfortably in her grip. *That's almost as fast as Dad's draw!* Arinn always drew her weapon so deliberately that I hadn't considered her true speed. It terrified me.

A robotic AI voice came over the speakers. "Self-destruct sequence will initiate in ten minutes."

"Zaelek," Arinn said while giving me a side glance, "Hit the webs with your wind."

The thought to ask *why* popped into my head, but I dismissed it. I knew the answer. Arinn wouldn't be able to use large quantities of water in this room. There were too many electronics, and accidentally taking down the shield system would result in many innocents losing their lives. That meant that I had to be careful too.

I extended my arm and loosed a torrent of wind. The webs fell, several taking pieces of the ceiling with them.

Arinn rushed to the main console and cursed. "She opened a defense program."

"That's bad, right?"

"Yes. Luckily, I was the one who taught her how to set one up and take it down. I just need a few minutes."

A clump of webs pinned Arinn's right hand to the console. Lycaon and I whirled as Tor'qi approached, an areightnid only slightly shorter than Lycaon crawling near her hip.

"I can't let you take that program down, *Master*."

"Zaelek," Arinn said. "You're going to have to fight her. I need to focus on this."

I swallowed the lump in my throat and nodded. *All we need to do is keep her at bay until Arinn cancels the self-destruct sequence.* That couldn't be too hard, could it?

Lycaon sent a tempest at Tor'qi and her areightnid, flinging them back into the hallway. I surged forward a few feet, then sealed the doorway between us with a wind wall. It wouldn't stop her advance for long, but it would buy me some time to think of something else.

"Nice work," Arinn called from behind the console. "I just cleared the first defense, only three more to go. Hang in there."

Only the first? I'd be lucky to hold the wall up beyond the second defense. The areightnid clawed at the wind, looking for any opportunity to squeeze by.

Lycaon moved closer and whispered, "We need to separate them. Let the areightnid through, then release your armor."

Would he be able to contest a stronger Daemon?

"I won't be able to hold Tor'qi back for long."

"Then we'd better kill it fast."

I released the wall just long enough for the areightnid to charge a short distance before sealing its Tamer in again. Lycaon flicked his nose upward. A blast of air sent the areightnid into the ceiling. When it hit the ground, the monstrosity was belly up, which left it open for an attack while it tried to claw its way to its feet.

"Now, Zaelek!" Lycaon called.

It didn't take me long to locate the armor tucked away in my mind. It sat in the memory of my mother smiling under the grindlevast tree. I reached for the armor, and intense energy filled my body.

"Look away, Arinn!"

A flash of light exploded around me, and the pinned areightnid shrieked. The armor's slight weight wrapped around me, starting at my shoulders and working its way down. My swords trembled, and the handles felt like they were on fire, forcing me to release them. Instead of falling to the ground, the two blades slammed together like magnets.

This didn't happen before!

Another burst of light blinded me. As my vision cleared, I saw my sword had transformed. The black and white handle wrappings ran parallel to each other and now had bright purple gems where the blue and red ones once were. Instead of one singular blade, two separate, shimmering grey blades protruded from a broad crossguard, vaguely outlining one gigantic sword. A slight gap separated the tips.

Had I not seen this transformation because my swords were sheathed the other day? Arinn had mentioned that she was surprised my blades didn't change.

I charged the areightnid, sweeping the remarkably light sword down to sever the creature's legs. A disturbance in my enigma pool signaled to me that my wind wall had dropped. Tor'qi surged in front of me, blocked me from severing her Daemon's legs, and kicked me into the primary control's back panel.

Styx, that hurt!

As Lycaon tore at the areightnid, it curled its spinneret and launched another cluster of webs at Arinn. Lycaon sent an air blast skyward, attempting to intercept the projectile, but Tor'qi caught him in the jowls with her foot, causing him to miss. Arinn ducked, and the cluster of webs exploded on the wall.

"Zaelek!" Arinn shouted.

I clashed with Tor'qi, locking her blade against mine.

"Trying!"

"Try harder!"

It didn't take long for Tor'qi's strength to overpower mine. I broke the blade lock and hit her with more wind. She stumbled backward. In the short time we had connected, Tor'qi's areightnid had flipped back over and had taken to viciously attacking Lycaon. Though it seemed like an animal, I had to remember it shared the same intelligence with other Daemons.

Lycaon dodged the latest barrage of strikes, then distanced from the areightnid. "This is not ideal, Zaelek."

"You don't say."

We didn't have the firepower we needed to stop Tor'qi. I was starting to discover that my wind had limited offensive capabilities, especially in an enclosed area. Speaking of elements, why hadn't she used hers?

"You're not using your element," I said, hoping to buy some extra time by getting her to talk.

"Don't need it."

"Not much of a talker, are you?"

Tor'qi glared at Arinn. "Not when you're trying to buy time."

I felt a tad stupid for thinking she wouldn't see through my ploy. Arinn had trained this woman.

Lycaon drove the areightnid back, then charged Tor'qi. Another cluster of web took flight just as the two clashed, leaving only me to intercept it. Remembering how my mother had fired stone shards from her blade tip, I willed my wind down mine and took aim. While Tor'qi fought off Lycaon, I swung down. The moment the wind strike left,

I felt the drain and knew I overdid it. A typhoon of concentrated air streaked across the room, intercepting the webs. It slammed into the support legs of a massive metal cylinder.

The front support legs collapsed, tilting the metal cylinder toward us. *Schleet.*

I had been so focused on the collateral that I hadn't notice Tor'qi prowling a few feet from me. Lycaon rushed between us, hitting her with another blast that forced her back. She tripped as she recovered, sprawling out and losing grip on her weapon. The falling metal cylinder crushed her from the waist down.

Her areightnid stopped all movement as if frozen in terror.

"Shree," Tor'qi called.

The areightnid limped over to her and collapsed at her side. She ran her hand down one of its legs, cooing to it as it shuddered. Though I hated areightnids, the scene conveyed a tenderness that caused an ache in my heart. Beauty is in the eye of the beholder. Though monstrous in physical form, Tor'qi's areightnid had a personality like all the other Daemons.

"Outsider," Tor'qi said. "Ailyana claims you are Altarian now. Are you familiar with *salu'ar?*"

"No," I replied with a wayward glance to Lycaon, who shook his head to say he didn't know either.

"I thought as much." She coughed, spattering the cylinder with blood. "*Salu'ar* is an Altarian mercy. You must end my suffering."

End her suffering? I knew what that meant back on the farm, but did it mean something else here? Perhaps it was some kind of last rites ceremony that Arinn could walk me through. The thought of driving my blade through Tor'qi's chest made my stomach churn. On the farm, I might've hesitated only briefly before putting down a suffering animal. Humans, however, were different.

"Kill me," Tor'qi said.

"I…I can't."

She huffed. "We were right. You're no Altarian. You're a weak, entitled little boy that…"

Arinn appeared next to Tor'qi and drove her blade through the dying woman's chest. It happened so fast that my mind took a moment to register what had happened.

"Zaelek," Arinn said. "I'm sorry."

"For what?"

"Not training you on battle customs. Altarian children learn these principles through the stories they are told in their schooling. I overlooked them and failed to prepare you for fighting our own warriors because it didn't seem plausible." She used the clean part of Tor'qi's clothes to wipe her blade clean before sheathing it. "I see your blade changes with your armor when it's unsheathed. Good to know… Come, we must report back to Ailyana. She needs to know our shields are running at full…"

A descending hum filled the room, followed by a *thunk* from inside multiple generators. Then everything fell silent again.

Lycaon immediately looked at Arinn, his eyes wide. "What was that?"

"I'm not sure." Arinn rushed to the main console, and the clicks from the keyboard echoed off the walls. "*Zellimo!* We only have a half day of shield left!"

My brow furrowed. "How?"

"We don't have time to find out. Ailyana needs to be informed immediately."

"This," Lycaon said, "was not how I expected things to go."

"You and me both," I replied.

What did all of this mean for Altarians? What did it mean for Kinara, Lycaon, and me?

I watched Arinn glare across the electronic war table at Ren'Za. "Not a chance! Zaelek is nowhere near ready to lead a squad by himself."

Ren'Za returned her glare. "Champions have always commanded our forces in battle. It is written in commandment."

"Then the commandment be damned."

"Blasphemy!"

Ailyana shook her head. "Enough, both of you."

"But, Your Highness," Ren'Za protested.

"Silence. Fighting amongst us won't help our situation."

Arinn folded her arms. "This choice is ultimately up to you, Your Grace."

"Zaelek will be put in charge of a squad. He proved to us

today that he is more than capable when he took Tor'qi down." Ren'Za shot a victorious sneer toward Arinn. "However, his squad will act as a secondary patrol after the area has been scouted by a more experienced squad."

I silently thanked the gods for Ailyana's foresight.

"As you wish," Arinn said.

"Put him under Barthol's command."

Arinn's eyes widened. "You want to put Zaelek in the special forces unit?"

"Considering he was trained by the commander of the special forces, I think it would be a fine place for him."

"That may be, but I trained him in combat, not tactics."

"What better time for him to learn? My decision is final."

"Of course, Your Highness." Arinn bowed, then stormed out of the room. I quickly nodded to Ailyana before jogging after Arinn.

"Arinn, wait up," I called.

"Ren'Za…that stubborn fool," she muttered. "Throwing you into something you're not ready for. Stupid…Stupid, stupid, stupid."

Arinn pushed through the palace front doors. Another volley of bombs blanketed the shield above. I looked up, expecting to see fire or pillars of smoke, but there were none. Those fighters should have been here by now. Did something delay them? The ground shook as more bombs struck their target. A low hum reverberated from above, and a blue wave of digital squares rippled across the rock ceiling. *What in Styx is happening up there?*

I returned my gaze to Arinn. She frowned and shook her head. "Those pilots better hurry or we're going to be…"

A hole opened in the center of the top shield. It expanded, then the entire forcefield fell, allowing the village to be exposed to the outside world for the first time. A massive aircraft hovered above us.

"I thought you said we had a day?"

"That's what the computer told me!"

Blue and green beams streaked across the sky, slamming into the side of the craft. Its colossal cylinder engines tilted, pitching the bomber sideways. *They're retreating!* The moment the machine cleared the village, multiple trails of smoke and flames closed in on it. Upon contact with the behemoth, clusters of explosions decimated its hull, sending it into a downward spiral. The craft disappeared behind the tree line, and a final blast erupted skyward, leaving a pillar of thick, black smoke in its place.

"Yes! They made it," I cheered.

"There's no time to celebrate," Arinn said. "We need to get you to your squad, so I can start giving orders."

The two of us bounded around the city, avoiding the crowded streets. We could really use Kinara's help right about now. I had been training for this moment, but the thought of fighting another enemy terrified me. The previous victory had been a fluke. What if everyone is depending on me for the next one and I lose? I cursed. What would Kinara do in this situation?

48

At the Altarian Barracks…

A group of warriors stood next to the giant stone cararaptor statue in the center of the barracks courtyard, touching their chests with closed fists when we approached.

The burly man with long black hair at the front of the formation moved toward us. "Good to have you back, Ma'am."

"Good to be back," Arinn said with a gesture toward me. "Barthol, this is Zaelek. He'll be replacing Regh as squad leader."

Barthol looked me up and down with his piercing green eyes.

I placed my closed fist over my chest as Arinn had taught me. "Pleased to meet you."

Arinn rolled her eyes. "He's new."

He grunted, then returned his attention to Arinn. "How new is new?"

Arinn smirked. "That's for me to know, and you to find out."

"Great. We're putting a pup in charge of a volf pack.

With that one sentence, Barthol confirmed my fears. These were highly trained warriors, and they were about to be led by a complete novice.

"The Chieftess seems to think so," Arinn said.

He smiled and huffed. "So, this is the Champion we've all been hearing about?"

Arinn walked toward the entrance of the brick barracks. "I leave him to you."

Lycaon snickered. "This is going well already."

"Did we expect anything less?" I asked.

Barthol sighed and shook his head, then turned and whistled at the rest of the group. They soon joined us. "Listen up. This is Zaelek, he'll be your squad leader for the time being. With Tyre out on mission right now, he'll have to meet the other half of the squad when they return." He turned to me. "Get your introductions out of the way, then come see me in my office. It's the first door on the right."

"Yes, Sir," I said.

The young man at the end of the formation stepped forward. "Sir, I'm Sejm, your first team leader. Tyre is your second team leader. The man to my right is Neejo, Joe if you prefer—next is Xeb, she's our medic, then at the end we have Apaz, and he is the support. Neejo and I are your frontline warriors, we'll keep the enemy off you."

I nodded. "Nice to meet you all. I look forward to working with you."

They saluted me in unison, but as I turned toward Barthol's office, I could feel my new team's eyes boring into my back. The unwelcoming metal doors revealed a dull, grey hallway. It felt more like a prison than a military building. Lycaon's clicking claws echoed loudly off the walls.

I walked through the open door to Barthol's office, stopping a few feet from his desk. His eyes didn't leave the document he was writing on.

"Sejm will help break you into your position. When he feels you can fly solo, he'll step back and resume his role. I will monitor your progress and decide what missions you're capable of handling. Do you have any questions?"

"No, Sir." Part of me wanted to unleash the arsenal of questions at the forefront of my mind, but the other part knew better. I didn't want to give them any more reason to doubt me.

"Then I'll put your team down for the first patrol tomorrow morning. By that time, our more seasoned scouts will have cleared the area of any dangers." He stared at me for a moment, then laced his fingers together. "One other thing. Your squad isn't going to like having someone so inexperienced leading them, but they're my warriors, so they'll behave. Show them why they should follow you, and everything will work out fine. Dismissed."

I saluted, then walked back out to my team. "Sejm," I called.

Sejm broke rank and jogged up to me. "Sir?"

"Barthol told me that you would be helping me, so what's our next move?"

"Did Barthol give you a mission?"

"No. He said we would be on the first patrol in the morning."

"Okay, so I would release the team for the day, but make sure you tell them that we have a patrol first thing in the morning. We don't want any of them to be out drinking into the early hours. You'll need to be here an hour early to receive the mission brief from Barthol. If you have any questions after that, I'll be here to help."

I gratefully extended my hand but pulled it back when Sejm looked at it with a raised eyebrow. "Sorry. In my culture, that's a way to show gratitude. Thanks for helping me out."

He smiled. "Of course, Sir."

I relayed the message to the rest of the team and watched them shuffle out of the flower-filled courtyard. Lycaon sat by my side and stared out at the village. "With Sejm assisting you, I think you'll do just fine."

I hope you're right.

The next morning I arrived at Barthol's office tired, having tossed and turned all night with with endless concerns about what the day might bring. Barthol sat behind his desk, frowning at the mountain of paperwork covering the surface.

He pulled a piece of paper and a pen from the desk drawer, then extended them to me. "Write down the information I'm about to give you."

He stood and walked to a large map of the region hanging on the wall. He pointed to an area outside the village perimeter. "You and your team will patrol the shores of lake Yakisutzi. Our advanced scouting party already cleared it for you early this morning, so you shouldn't have to worry about an enemy presence. However, if you're engaged by the enemy, you will immediately break contact. Your mission is to scout only, not fight.

"If you're pursued, find a small clearing and get a flare into the air. Once you get the flare off, keep moving, but stay in the area, even if you need to lead the enemy in circles. The moment reinforcements are on-site, get out, and return to the village. I expect a report by noon unless you're compromised. Any questions?"

I finished writing and looked up. "Where's the lake?"

"Sejm is familiar with the area, so he can guide you there. Any other questions?"

"No, Sir."

Barthol retrieved a small slip of paper and studied it for a moment before holding it out. "Take this list to the armory down the hall. They will give you everything you need for this mission. Dismissed."

The man in charge of supplies took the slip of paper and set a bag on the countertop. I thanked him, grabbed the bag, then joined my team in the courtyard.

Sejm approached and pulled me aside for a moment to go over everything Barthol had told me. He took the bag and set it on the ground, rifling through the items.

"Okay. It looks like they gave us a med kit and a flare. The medical supplies go to Xeb, and you can give the flare to Apaz if you want."

"How do I brief them on the situation?"

He held out his hand. "Here, give me your notes, and I'll show you." Once he read through the note, he called the team over. "Listen up, everyone. Our mission is pretty straightforward. We're patrolling the west shoreline of lake Yakisutzi, and that's it. If we're engaged, we'll retreat, get a flare up if we can't shake the enemy, and return to the village. Nothing we haven't done before."

I gave the med kit to Xeb and the flare to Apaz. Sejm put Neejo at the front of the single-file formation and instructed him to lead us to the lake. We exited the village and headed west. *Please let this go without any complications.*

At the palace infirmary…

I sat up in the soft, white bed. *The palace infirmary? How did I get here?*

The doctor pouring over a paper-stuffed clipboard looked over, and his eyes widened. He rushed to my side, placing his hand on my shoulder. "Slowly, Kinara. You haven't fully recovered yet."

"What happened?"

He felt my forehead with the back of his hand before moving to inspect the rest of my body. "You had a rather unfortunate run-in with a remnant."

My brow furrowed. "Remnant? Where's Alator?"

The doctor looked at me with pity. "A remnant is a creature that imitates spirits. It takes the form of someone deceased that was close to its victim."

So I hadn't actually seen my Alator. What a cruel ploy of nature. *But if that's the case…*

"If a remnant takes the form of someone close to me, how would it know all of those things about me?"

"It needs to feed on its victim while they're in a deep trance. Most likely, you saw the creature for only a moment or two before it released a strong dreamspore, rendering you unconscious. The conversation you had with whoever you saw was a figment of your own imagination."

My gaze fell to my hands. "I see."

Luci'oan pushed the door open. "You're finally awake."

Once again, the doctor checked his notes. "She'll be fully recovered by the end of the day. For now, she needs food and rest."

I looked to the green visitor's chair in the corner, expecting to see Zaelek sleeping there, but it was empty. A tinge of disappointment crept through me. "Where's Zaelek?"

"On a mission," said Luci'oan.

I cocked my head slightly. "With whom?"

He folded his arms. "His new squad."

"What do you mean, his *new* squad? How long have I been out for?"

"A few days. A lot has happened while you were taking your nap. I'll explain everything you need to know over breakfast. Get ready and meet me in the foyer."

Luci'oan pulled the doctor out of the room to speak with him privately. I grabbed my clothes that still had traces of dirt and leaves stuck to them, and hastily threw them on. Once Luci'oan had cleared everything through medical, he took me to the palace kitchen.

When we were seated comfortably by the small hearth, he said, "Do you like parnums?"

My spirits lifted ever so slightly. "I love them. I didn't know you had parnums here!"

He laughed, and I almost fell out of my chair in surprise. "We're isolated, not oblivious."

"Of course, my apologies."

He sat back in his chair. "Now, let me tell you the situation we're in."

The news came as a surprise to me. I never would have imagined that the Altarians' location could be discovered. This whole time I had allowed myself to relax under the false hope that we were safe. I shuddered. *Javelar is at our doorstep again...* It had been so easy to lose myself in our training, to forget about Savvage's ruthless campaign. Now, Zaelek was going out on patrol. Young inexperienced Zaelek. Alator had been a highly trained Guardian and still didn't stand a chance against Sàvvage and his lackeys. *Who thought this was a good idea?*

"So, that's where we're going next," Luci'oan said.

I blinked. "I'm sorry, what?"

Luci'oan frowned, clearly irritated that I hadn't been paying attention to the last minute of our conversation. "I need you to contact your Commander. We may need his assistance again soon."

"Right. But will Zaelek be alright out there?"

He paused, staring intensely into the hearth's flame. "I could give you the answer that you want to hear and tell you everything is going to be alright, but that isn't how war works. We sent him on patrol through an already scouted area, so in theory, he should be fine. That said, if anyone can find trouble on a routine patrol, it's Rodrin'dai. You know how he is."

I frowned at the unfamiliar word. "Rodrin'dai?"

"It's just a nickname Arinn and I have for Zaelek."

"Does it have a meaning?"

Luci'oan grinned. "Storm bait."

I huffed and shook my head. *Of course...* Leave it to Zaelek to find the only bad luck in a field of fortune. I stood. "Thank you for lunch. I'll contact the Colonel right away."

He nodded, and I took my leave.

When I entered the main foyer, Arinn pushed off from the wall and approached me. "Glad to see you're awake." Her eyes briefly flicked in the direction I had come before returning to me. "We need to talk about Zaelek."

My stomach tightened. *Did he tell her about what happened between us in the Forest of Whispers?*

I silently cursed. "Ma'am?"

"I'm worried that if he's pushed too hard, the entity you saw in the mine will resurface."

Though it was relief to know we weren't about to discuss the complicated development in the relationship between Zaelek and me, I almost wished that *was* the topic. That...*thing* made me nervous.

"I thought that's why you took Zaelek to the forest?"

"It is, but I'm not sure it had the effect I anticipated. Something about this creature is different...unnatural even." Arinn reached into her pocket and pulled a syringe out, holding it up for me to see. "I had the medical staff fill this with a powerful sedative. Should Zaelek lose control again, I need you to find a way to inject him with it." She extended the syringe to me. "At any cost, Kinara."

I stared at the syringe, suddenly finding it hard to breathe. My trembling fingers wrapped around the tube, and I said a silent prayer that I would never have to use it.

"I understand."

"Good. Now, go talk to your Colonel."

49

Patrolling outside the Altarian village...

Once the lake came into view, I halted our movement. I gave the order to hunker down in the trees just off the broad game trail we followed. My heart pounded against my chest. *The enemy could be anywhere out here.* There were so many trees that it was impossible to get a full view of the objective. What should we do?

Lycaon scanned the trees. "See something?"

"No," I said.

Sejm crouched beside me. "What's going on? Did you see something?"

I shook my head. "I'm just considering how to proceed."

"It's a patrol, Sir. Don't overthink it."

"I know, but I have a bad feeling."

"That's probably just your nerves talking. We really should keep moving."

I thought for a moment, then took a few deep breaths to calm myself. "Okay. Take point and lead us to the shoreline."

Sejm nodded and whistled softly. The rest of the team gave him their full attention. With a quick flick of his straightened hand, the team got back to their feet and continued forward. When we came in view of the sandy shoreline, he gave the order to halt again.

He stalked back to me. "Looks like an abandoned campsite up ahead."

"Are you sure it's abandoned?"

"Only one way to find out."

Again, a nauseous feeling churned in my stomach. I signaled, and the team moved toward the site, careful to avoid any open areas. As we approached, I caught a whiff of something savory cooking, and smoke. If the site had been abandoned, it wasn't very long ago. Sejm entered the area and pulled out a pen and a piece of paper, then scribbled something onto the page.

Xeb kicked at a foil snack bar wrapper on the ground and cursed. "Look at this mess," she muttered. "Polluting our forests… unforgivable."

She shook her head and walked toward the edge of the site. I wanted to tell her to come back and stay with the group, but maybe it *was* just my paranoia.

Lycaon padded to me. "You should trust your instincts. Don't let other people tell you that you're wrong for doing so."

"You felt it, too?" I said.

"I still do."

The knot twisted painfully in my stomach and my fingers were anxiously tapping against my leg while we waited for Sejm to stop writing. *We need to move.* The moment Sejm paused, I gave the order to move off the objective.

"I'm not finished documenting the site," Sejm protested.

"Leave it. We've been here too long," I replied.

He grumbled but took the lead. Soon, we headed for the village. Being back in tree cover helped get rid of feeling like a bullseye had been painted on my back. However, I still worried that we were being watched.

Something whistled through the air. A pike went through Sejm's stomach, causing me to jump and startling the rest of the team. Four men stepped out from behind the trees ahead.

My eyes darted to my fear frozen team. "Fall back to the lake!"

I drew my left sword and closed the gap between Sejm and me. One of the men lunged at me. I barely deflected his sword, and felt the sheer magnitude of his power behind the strike. *He's fast!* Lycaon pounced from the bushes and knocked the man to the ground. With a blast of wind, the volf launched himself up and away from the enemy.

I hoisted Sejm's limp arm over my shoulder and initiated a backward bound. Sejm's weight slowed me, and we barely reached the shoreline before the enemy launched another attack. Apaz and Neejo fought off strikes aimed at me as I half-drug, half-carried Sejm to Xeb and laid him at her feet. We had to buy her some time!

"Apaz, the flare!" I shouted, reaching toward him. If we didn't warn anyone, the city could be under attack in minutes.

Apaz dodged a blow from his opponent, then skirted away. He threw the flare in my direction, but it bounced off a log and into the rampant underbrush.

Styx! I looked back at Xeb to make sure she was safe. A stone barrier had formed around both her and Sejm, sealing them into a shell. I needed to find that flare. I closed my eyes and sent a blast of wind across the ground. My surroundings erupted into brilliant white figures, revealing a sword coming down on my head. I opened my eyes just in time to see Lycaon sink his massive fangs into the attacker's arm. The man screamed, then retreated.

Lycaon moved himself between me and the enemy. "Whatever you were doing, keep doing it. I'll hold him off."

I focused and let the air sweep over my surroundings. Come on! Where are you? Kinara's unconscious face flashed through my mind. I had to see her again.

The vegetation and ground had different textures like they were painted over with thin, transparent, white lines. A small, solid tube lay at the base of the rotting log. I immediately sent a line to the object and lifted it with a pillar of air. That's it! When I pulled it to me, the waxy shell pressed against my palm.

A torrent of wind formed at my fingertips, and exploded into the sky. The now-lit flare launched upward, leaving a thin white trail of smoke behind it. I drew my other sword and charged one of the two men Neejo had been holding off. A jet of flame shot toward me. I dove, feeling the coarse sand scrape against my side and the searing heat overhead.

With a leap, I slammed my blades into the target's metal staff.

The man sneered. "Finally wanted a piece of the action, eh?"

I attacked ferociously with both swords. Each time our weapons connected, my blades recoiled off. Soon, I had to take a defensive stance. I rolled to the ground, barely escaping the man's latest attack, and thrust both blades forward. He jumped back, giving me enough breathing room to hit him with a wind pulse and send him into the forest.

I winced as sharp pain rippled down my left arm. A blistering wave of pressure followed. Sand kicked up as I skipped across the beach. Dazed and seeing double, I looked down at my arm to see blood spilling from the wound. Within seconds the new opponent appeared above, his sword aimed to skewer me. My blades came up, and our weapons met. I struggled against the assailant's weapon before my wounded arm buckled, forcing me to shift the crushing pressure to my other side.

The enemy's sword pierced the sand, a hair's breadth away from my other arm.

A woman appeared next to me, slammed her fist into my attacker's face and sent him sprawling. She grasped my shirt and pulled me to my feet. "Take your team and get out of here."

There wasn't time to be relieved, we had to go. Holding my burning wound, I stumbled to Xeb's barrier. "Apaz, Neejo," I called to the still fighting warriors. "Get out!" I pounded my fist over the top of Xeb's rock shell. "Xeb, we need to leave."

She dropped the barrier and stared at me through tearful eyes. "Sejm's gone."

I held in the string of angry curses forming on my tongue, knowing it would only draw attention to our retreat. "We need to go."

"What about Sejm?"

"We'll come back for him when it's safe."

I hated myself for leaving him behind, but lives were still at stake. We exploded into a bound toward the village. As we passed Lycaon, I let loose a piercing whistle, and he joined us.

The village gates opened for us when we approached. There, Kinara, Arinn, and Barthol were waiting.

"I'm fine," I said.

I stumbled forward. Kinara caught me, then threw my arm over her shoulder. I realized I must have lost more blood than I thought.

"You're not fine, you idiot! Look at you, you're a mess."

Arinn turned to Barthol. "Get a medic out here now!" She helped Kinara lower me to the ground before tying a tourniquet just below my shoulder. "What happened out there?"

"It was an ambush. Sejm didn't…" The words caught in my throat before I could finish.

Arinn cursed. "Kinara, I need to go to the battlefield. You have this under control?"

Kinara nodded. "I've got him." She laid my head in her lap and stroked my hair.

The edge of my vision darkened, and I closed my eyes. *At least she's okay. I wouldn't have forgiven myself if the event in the Forest of Whispers had taken her.*

50

In the Altarian barrack's courtyard...

The medic finished up his last suture then cut the string. "You got lucky, Zaelek. Another millimeter and that blade would have torn open an artery."

My wound was the last thing on my mind. The sting of the needle piercing my skin was hardly noticeable. A more significant pain, one that could only be felt by the heart, consumed me. If only I had listened to my gut, none of this would have happened. Sejm would still be alive. The guilt threatened to eat me alive.

After taking one final look at his work, the medic slapped his leg. "Well, that about does it. Try to take it easy for the next day, you'll rip them out if you push too hard. Schnipersilk can only take so much abuse, regardless of what the manual says."

Kinara gave me a look that dared me to defy her. "Don't worry, he won't overdo it."

Barthol called to me, then gestured toward the barracks. I thanked the medic, then followed the order. The walk into Barthol's office wasn't far, but my instinct fought against it. My nerves begged me to turn and run, to lose myself in the forest where I couldn't lead anyone else to their deaths. Despite that, I pushed forward, every step heightening the fear and anxiety. I didn't even know if I could look Barthol in the eyes, let alone speak to him. They had trusted me with one of their own, and I failed them. *I should have been stronger. I should have been better.*

I stepped into the office. *Get a hold of yourself.*

Barthol leaned forward and laced his fingers together. "Close the door." I did as instructed, then walked to the center of the room. After a moment, he let out a sigh. "Tell me what happened."

Before I could finish my sentence, he slammed his fist into the table, making me jump. "Stop. You're a warrior, not a trembling child being scolded by their parent. Get control of your emotions and speak with some confidence for *feeantalo's* sake."

I swallowed the lump that had risen in my throat. "Yes, Sir."

Attempting to quell the storm raging in my chest, I recounted every part of the mission with as much detail possible. Barthol didn't interrupt again.

"That's everything?" he asked once I finished.

I bowed my head in shame. "Yes, Sir."

"Good work."

His words caught me off guard. I had expected yelling, maybe even some form of punishment. "Sir?"

His voice landed deliberately on each word as if I were deaf. "Good work."

"Good work? Sejm died, and I'm responsible."

"How do you figure?"

"I should have executed the mission differently."

He leaned back in his chair and crossed his arms. "Is that so? What exactly would you have done differently?"

Every little detail of each event leading up to the attack burned in my mind. "I could have left the camp sooner."

His brow furrowed. "Based on what? Your gut feeling?" he leaned forward again. "Kid, listen to me. You were right to doubt your gut feeling out there. You were on your very first mission, and your nerves were probably shot as is. From what I just heard, you trusted one of your more experienced men even though you were in charge. That's something that some of my own squad leaders have yet to learn. Sure, things went sour out there, but you did the right thing."

"But Sir…"

He shot an exasperated look to the ceiling. "Gods give me strength." His gaze returned to me. "Look, because you're new to tactics, I'll explain from a strategic view. You were ambushed not far from that camp. That means your team caught the enemy off guard, forcing them to rush an ambush. Had you left the camp sooner, they would have still ambushed you. Perhaps a different outcome would have emerged, but who's to say that it would have been better?"

I looked down at my feet, desperate to avoid his piercing gaze. "I understand, Sir."

He whistled to get me to look back up at him. "I don't think you do. Sejm's death wasn't your fault. Yes, you are responsible for everything that happens out there, that's just how being a squad leader works. However, you weren't the one who stabbed him in the stomach. Instead, when everything went sideways, you adapted and made the best out of a bad situation. Consider me impressed that you managed to get the rest of your team out alive. You'll return to your post as squad leader and learn from this experience." Barthol took a breath.

"Once upon a time, I stood where you are. The only difference is that I lost my entire team. I had a conversation with my squad leader very similar to this one. Whatever you do, don't start second-guessing yourself. You'll end up getting yourself killed, or worse, the men whose lives are in your hands.

"You learned a valuable lesson today, one that I wish you didn't ever have to. Men and women die, and they will continue to die, especially in a war with an organization like Javelar. Sejm may have been the first warrior you lost, but he certainly won't be your last. I pray that I'm wrong, but understand that no matter how much you prepare, something can go wrong even with the most foolproof plans. That's life."

Barthol jogged the stack of paper he held. "Now, our work today isn't done. I need you to deliver a death notification to Sejm's parents. Report back to me when you're done. We have a debriefing tonight, and I need you there as a witness to the attack, and as a squad leader. Here are the directions to get to Sejm's home."

"Yes, Sir." I touched my fist to my chest, still uncertain of how this would play out. My head swam with Barthol's words, thankful for his wisdom and uncertain of what might come next. Sejm was one of his warriors, one of their own. Even though accepted into their culture, I was still an outsider to them. When I walked out of Barthol's office, I saw Lycaon lying on the floor across the hall.

His ears perked. "How'd it go?"

"Not as bad as I thought it would."

"That's good to hear."

"Hey, would you mind doing me a favor?"

Lycaon cocked his head. "What do you have in mind?"

"Would you deliver a message to Kinara?"

"Sure, if I can find her."

I grabbed a piece of paper from the secretary's desk and scribbled a quick explanation of why I couldn't meet up with her tonight. After signing it, I rolled the paper up and put it in his mouth, hoping that his saliva wouldn't ruin it.

"Thank you," I said.

He nodded and slipped out the front door. I opened the folded directions Barthol had given me, and headed for the heart of the village.

I sat outside of the Corr'era family's home, trying to gather the courage to face Sejm's family. My heart rate steadily climbed as I approached the front door and knocked. *Please don't be home, please don't be home.*

As if on cue, a girl about five-years-old answered the door with a huge, missing-tooth smile. "Yes?"

The mere sight of her made me choke up. I cleared my throat. "Are your parents home?"

She giggled and bashfully concealed most of her body behind the door. "Yes."

"Would you tell them that Sejm's squad leader is here to see them, please?" I quickly tucked my shaking hands behind my back. *Keep it together.* The little girl darted from sight, then returned with her parents in tow.

Mrs. Corr'era looked at me with confusion. "Is everything all right? Why aren't you out on mission with Sejm and the others?"

I faltered, then remorsefully handed the letter to Mrs. Corr'era. The brief moments that passed while waiting for her to comprehend the reason behind the visit were excruciating. Her hand covered her mouth, and tears streamed down her face. She turned her head into her husband's muscular chest, sobbing uncontrollably.

Mr. Corr'era's face twisted with pain as he pieced everything together without even looking at the letter. "No, this can't be."

I looked at my feet, attempt to hide the tears threatening to slide down my cheek. *Why am I here? Why didn't Barthol do this himself?* Mrs. Corr'era's hand touched my shoulder, and I turned back to face them.

A glimmer of hope danced in her eyes. "Sejm put you up to this, right? This is all some kind of joke?"

"No, Ma'am. I'm so sorry."

Her smile shattered, and she wept harder. Mr. Corr'era ran his hand down her cascade of straight black hair as he comforted her. He looked at me and said, "Please excuse us, we need to prepare for the pass over ritual."

I nodded as he shut the door. My foot had barely struck the first step of the small porch when through the cracked window, I overheard Mrs. Corr'era tell her daughter that Sejm wouldn't be coming home. The little girl curiously asked questions about his whereabouts and the reasoning behind his disappearance. I couldn't take it anymore. The guilt and sorrow bubbled to the surface, and the tears fell, so I bounded away as fast as I could.

51

Javelar HQ, in the cafeteria…

I picked at the leathery steak on my plate with a fork, thoughts focused on Zaelek. Eerie loneliness plagued the quiet steel box they called a mess hall, leaving a feeling as if Javelar had packed up and moved on without us. Something didn't feel right about this training exercise Savvage had announced last week.

Parnikus nudged me with his elbow. "Ben, you've barely touched your food. What's going on with you lately?"

I put my fork down and looked at him. "Does something seem…off?"

He swallowed. "What do you mean?"

"I don't know. I just feel like it's weird that almost everyone went on this training exercise, but we were told to stay here and 'man the fort.'"

Parnikus mulled over my words, chewing his next colossal mouthful of food. "Yeah, I guess you have a point."

I pushed my plate over to Parnikus, whose face lit up. Though, he couldn't be blamed for getting excited. The kitchen seldom served enough food for a meal, and seconds weren't an option. Our afternoon snacks at home were bigger. *Home.* A heavy longing to return came over me like a blanket of sorrow draped across my shoulders. Saying that I missed my family was a gross understatement.

Parnikus' head came into my field of vision as he studied my face. "Hey, look on the bright side, at least we won't have to get up at four in the morning to get a seat for the arena fights."

I forced a smile, not wanting to show that I didn't really care for seeing young men and women kill each other to survive. "Yeah, there's that."

Since we'd gotten out of that forsaken pit, Parnikus had taken a liking to all of the violence. Though he hadn't noticed his personality changing, I certainly had. It felt like my brother was drifting farther away from who he used to be. He had a shorter temper, and his warmth seemed to fade with each passing day.

A man's voice barked across the room. "No sharing rations." I looked up to see the guard at the entryway making his way toward us. He stopped a few feet from the table, then pointed to my plate. "Eat your food."

"I'm not hungry," I replied.

"I don't give a schleet what you are. Eat your food, or I'll cram it down your throat."

His harsh tone didn't surprise me. He didn't care about me or my health, just like the rest of the organization didn't care. They wanted their soldiers to be combat-ready at all times, and the meals were designed to keep us at optimal strength. Nothing more, and nothing less.

Parnikus stood from his seat and squared up to him. The guard drew his lightning stick and primed it, sending blue sparks down its flat face.

I put my hand on Parnikus' shoulder and pulled him back into his seat. "You're right, Sir. My apologies for wasting your time."

The guard grunted in approval, then sheathed his lightning stick before returning to his post. His eyes bored into me, so I picked up my fork and shoved a bit of mashed seotatop into my mouth. I forced every last bite of the meal down, then stood. The moment my legs straightened, my vision blurred, and my head spun. I grasped the table and braced myself.

Parnikus stood from his seat. "Hey, you alright? You don't look so good." Just as I had moments before, Parnikus wavered and grabbed the table, too. "What the…?"

My legs buckled, and my head slammed into the table before I passed out.

Something shook underneath me, jolting me awake. I blinked a few times to clear the last of the blur from my vision and found myself looking at what appeared to be the inside of a metal tube. A loud airy growl emanated from every direction. I gingerly held my throbbing head. *Where am I?*

Parnikus slept on a cargo net bench to my right, but we were the only ones in sight. Another quake shook the surrounding tube, and light spilled in from a small window to my left. I peered out and saw the golden ground far below. *Are we flying? How did we get on a cargo plane?*

The nose of the plane tilted downward, and the machine descended. A woman's voice came over the mangled speaker in the corner of the cargo bay. "I recommend that you strap in if you're walking about."

Scared that I might float away if her instructions weren't followed, I plopped down onto the netted seat and buckled myself in. It took about five minutes for the plane to lurch to a stop. A blonde woman poked her head out of the captain's quarters and smacked a mushroom-shaped switch on the wall. "Thanks for flying with Javelar air, now get the Styx out of my plane and don't forget your weapons." The bay ramp lowered until it contacted the small dirt runway.

I looked at Parnikus, who blinked rapidly and looked around with confusion.

"Come on, we have to go."

"Go where?" he asked.

"I don't know." I helped him to his feet, making sure to grab both of our tridents that leaned against the wooden crates across from us. The moment I stepped onto the ramp, a blast of dry heat assaulted my face, bringing with it a salty taste.

Once I stood on the sand, I looked back to the impatient looking blonde as we cleared the ramp. “Where are we?”

She hit the switch again, and the metal door shuddered before beginning its ascension. “Welcome to Holus, boys.”

52

At the Altarian briefing...

Barthol leaned over during the fourth squad leader's brief and whispered, "Get ready, Zaelek. We're next."

Barthol, Lycaon, and I sat in a room similar to an auditorium. Nearly half of the chairs were occupied by various ranks of leadership, from team leaders all the way up to Ailyana. There had been a half dozen briefs concerning different assignments and missions, all of which had succeeded. At the moment, I had been the only one whose mission went sideways, and that made me even more nervous.

I tried to quell the exhausting stress and worry that had plagued me for the past hour and a half. It wouldn't have surprised me if the surrounding leaders could hear my heart slamming against my chest. I wiped my sweat covered palms on my pants.

The squad leader currently addressing us finished his report, then made his way back down to his seat. A crippling pang of anxiety pulsed through me. Barthol stood. I grabbed the map he and I had spent hours reading, marking, and studying. When we got onto the stage, I looked into the crowd, suddenly feeling dizzy. My legs shook.

Barthol introduced himself as the platoon leader responsible for our squad, then introduced me as the squad leader tasked with the patrol.

He looked at me and nodded, signaling me to begin the brief. My mind went blank for a moment. Everything that Barthol and I had rehearsed flew out of my brain like a spooked flock of carabells. I looked to the front row and found Kinara, Arinn, Luci'oan, and Ailyana staring up at me expectantly.

Lycaon nudged my hand. "Come on. You can do it."

Kinara gave me a smile and a reassuring nod, giving me just enough comfort to swallow the lump in my throat. I didn't want to disappoint her or the leaders who had placed so much faith in me. Then miraculously, the pieces of our rehearsed brief came together. The silence during the brief made me hyper-aware of my own voice. I placed the map on the projection table and indicated where the critical events occurred. On occasion, Barthol stepped in to help me, but for the most part, my presentation went more smoothly than expected. I finished the brief, and let my pent up breath slip through my lips.

Ailyana looked to Barthol. "Barthol, where was your other team during this mission?"

His feet slightly shift as he prepared for whatever onslaught of criticism was headed our way. "They were on another mission, Ma'am."

Arinn rubbed her eyebrows with her forefinger and thumb. "Why were they not acting as a supporting unit?"

"I failed to anticipate that the enemy was still in the area, Ma'am."

Luci'oan looked up from his tablet with wide eyes. "It didn't occur to you that this was a possibility?"

I felt incredibly awkward standing there while my platoon leader got grilled for my mistake.

Still, Barthol stood his ground. "To mitigate that possibility, I gave the team a distress flare and strict orders not to engage if they were compromised, Sir."

Luci'oan's face twitched. Both he and Arinn had short fuses with their subordinates, something Kinara and I hadn't experienced yet. Though, now, I had a suspicion that I would shortly discover the same fate. Even more terrifying, Luci'oan had the worst temper of the masters.

His voice rose, and his grip on the clipboard tightened so hard that I thought it might snap. "I specifically told everyone that Javelar would send at least Delta rank scouts. Why was a team of *Eta* rank warriors given a recon mission when we knew this? Who gave you your mission, and why in Styx did you not kick it back?"

"Renz gave us the mission, Sir."

Arinn shook her head. "You should have known better, given that you're a platoon leader in the special forces unit. I expect my platoon leaders to speak up when a mission doesn't make sense. You lost the excuse of blind obedience when you accepted your position."

Barthol's eyes didn't waiver from her glare. "Yes, Ma'am."

"Dismissed."

We went back to our seats without another word. Upon passing Kinara, I caught her pity filled glance. I didn't want her pity. I wanted for her to see me as a competent companion, someone she could trust to have her back. This failure painted a grim realization that I might not ever be the person I wanted her to see me as. Why did this keep happening? Every time I had a chance to prove to her that I wasn't some helpless farm boy, I somehow messed it up.

Lycaon nuzzled my hand again. "Good job. That couldn't have been easy."

I acknowledged him with a nod, not wanting to utter a sound in the silent auditorium.

The next leader got up. I recognized her from the fight, she was the one who pulled me to my feet when they first arrived. Her gentle voice addressed our leaders. "

My name is Yuta. I'm the third squad leader of the Special Forces Task Unit. It was my squad that reinforced Zaelek's team. Our squad was acting as support for first squad, and we were in the vicinity of the flare. We mobilized and went to support as fast as possible. The enemy was strong, but we overpowered them and neutralized the threat in the immediate area. One of Javelar's men got away, however. I sent first team to pursue him, but he managed to escape capture.

"The second team stayed with me. Our medic tried to aid Sejm, but he was dead by the time we got there. His body was brought back and delivered to the Corr'era family this evening."

The mere mention of Sejm's name twisted my stomach in knots. Arinn leaned back in her chair. "The man who got away, was he wounded?"

"No, Ma'am. His team provided cover for him and kept us from pursuing until they had fallen back. He had about a ten-minute head start."

Luci'oan looked to Arinn. "Well, if Javelar had their doubts about our location before, they certainly don't now."

Ailyana turned to the two masters. "How long do we have to prepare our defenses?"

"A day, maybe two,assuming we don't get bombed again."

Ailyana walked to the front of the briefing area and faced us. "The time we have is limited, so make every second count. We need to bolster our defenses and prepare for the worst. Rest to keep your strength up when you aren't on watch or helping with fortifications. The village is now under lockdown. No one leaves or enters unless given permission directly from me. Understood?"

Everyone slammed their fist against their chest. "Yes, Ma'am," they said in unison.

"Dismissed."

As Barthol and I stood up, Ailyana pointed at us. "Except you three. Arinn, Luci'oan, and Kinara, you also stand fast."

My hopes of avoiding a lecture were dashed.

Once everyone had left, Ailyana gestured for us to come forward. "After today's events, I cannot let you lead a squad into battle, Zaelek. You weren't ready, and I should have listened to Arinn over a tradition."

I hung my head. "Yes, Ma'am. I understand."

"Instead, you and your squad will keep watch over the village while the rest of us fight Javelar. You'll provide support for the people and help them evacuate should the need arise."

Arinn nodded. "I think that's the best course of action."

Luci'oan crossed his arms. "And what of Kinara?"

"Well," Ailyana said, "It wouldn't bode well if our liaison from the Guardian Forces died fighting *our* battles, now would it? She will replace Sejm as team leader in Zaelek's squad."

"I agree."

"Then it's settled. Barthol, gather all of the missions given to you by Renz and give the village-based ones to Zaelek."

Barthol touched his fist to his chest. "Yes, Ma'am."

"Dismissed."

Kinara and I left the building together. Half-way through the courtyard, she touched my arm. "How are you holding up?"

I studied her ice-blue eyes. "Not great, but I'll manage."

"Things will get better, you'll see."

I hoped she was right, but only time would tell. *I really wish you were here to tell me what to do, Mom and Dad.* Styx, even talking to Ari, Ben, or Parnikus would be helpful right now. I huffed and shook my head, knowing well enough what Ari's response would be: "Stop feeling sorry for yourself."

Why did all of this have to happen? The familiar loneliness crept in. I missed Ari so much, even if she hadn't been pleasant for the last year. My heart ached. I wish I could have told her that I loved her and she was my favorite sister—an inside joke we had come up with. I smiled to myself but Kinara noticed.

"What?" she said.

I looked into the purple-hued sky, hoping that the colors might relieve some of the pain. "Nothing. Let's head back to the inn."

Lycaon's front paws shook the side of the bed, jolting me from my sleep. His massive head loomed over me, and he stared at me with conviction. "We need to talk about the battle yesterday."

"We couldn't have talked about it last night?"

"No. You already had a lot on your mind, and I want to make sure you hear what I have to say. Also, Kinara was with us for most of the night, and we swore to Arinn that we wouldn't tell her about the armor until necessary."

"Well, spit it out." I just wanted to go back to sleep.

"You could have been killed because you didn't release your armor during the battle. That was stupid."

He was right. My armor totally slipped my mind in the heat of things. "I got so wrapped up in the battle I forgot about it."

"Next time, don't forget. It's there for your protection."

He didn't blink once as he stared at me, and I hated when he did that. I found it creepy and unsettling.

"I won't. Now, can we get out of here? We have work to do."

Satisfied, Lycaon returned to the floor. When I was ready for the day, I found Kinara waiting for us in the lobby. We walked through the lantern-lit streets in silence.

She turned to me. "We need to talk about what happened in the forest."

The memory of her soft lips pressed against mine flashed through my mind, envoking an aching chest and an overwhelming wave of anxiety. I suppressed my groan, trying to think of any way I could get out of this awkward conversation. *Not even an hour into my day and I'm getting lectured by everyone.*

I drew a deep breath. "I suppose we do."

"I just don't want things to get complicated between us. We've built a good friendship ever since we were young, and I would feel terrible if we messed it up. Then there's everything that happened with Alator, and…"

"Kinara. It's okay. I understand."

What else could I say? Telling her anything else would make matters even worse. I didn't want to lose her forever. Though, the relief of saving our friendship couldn't compare to the disappointment and hurt that I now felt.

Her beautiful eyes showed a hint of confusion and pity, which added to the emotions welling inside me.

"You do?"

"I should have been more sensitive to your situation. I'm sorry. I let my emotions get the better of me, and it was a mistake. It won't happen again."

Lycaon looked at me with horror. "You idiot! Why would you say something like that?"

I shot him a quick deathly glare before returning my attention to Kinara. Relief flooded her face, but a hint of something else was there too as she said, "Thank you."

Walking with Zaelek…

Thank you. What else could I say? I studied Zaelek's face. He tried so hard to conceal how he felt about the situation, but I could see right through him. I knew he didn't think that our kiss had been a mistake, although it didn't hurt any less to hear those words. Guilt for having any kind of feelings so soon after Alator's death threatened to tear me apart. My chest ached, and I took a few stabilizing breaths to calm the shaking in my hands.

I knew how I felt about Zaelek, I just didn't know what to do with those feelings. *I'm sorry, Zaelek, I'm going to have to let you down.*

For the rest of our walk, neither of us said anything. Though we'd both insisted everything was all right, there was a new, undeniable strain on our relationship. Upon entering the barrack courtyard, Zaelek left to receive our next mission. I looked at the orange sky.

A female voice called me from the entrance. "Good morning."

I met her deep brown eyes, admiring the length of her luscious black hair. "Good morning."

"I haven't seen you before, are you new around here?"

"You could say that."

She smiled, her eyes glinting with specks of gold in the dawn light. "I'm Xeb."

"Kinara," I said, extending my hand to her. Xeb placed her palm in mine, sending a slight warmth across my skin. She released my hand and shook her own out.

"You must be the other outsider."

"That's me. How could you tell?" A hint of amusement crossed her face as the obvious clicked. "Right, my skin."

Xeb chuckled then switched her language to Atlantean. "And your accent. You still place emphasis on some of the wrong vowels."

"Ah. That makes sense."

"I didn't expect you to be so much stronger than Zaelek," she said, studying me.

I laughed. Sometimes I forgot that I was a rank above him. With his non-traditional awakening, it was difficult to gauge exactly where he stood. "I took him under my wing after his parents died."

Her brow furrowed, and she took a moment to process what I said. "His parents died?"

"Sadly, yes." I wanted to kick myself for saying anything about it. It wasn't my place to share that story.

"Recently?" she inquired. I nodded. She took a deep breath and placed her hand on her right hip. "That explains why he's taking Sejm's death so hard."

A young man, no older than eighteen, strolled into the courtyard. "Morning, Xeb."

She saluted. "Good morning, Tyre. How did your mission go?"

"Well enough. There isn't much happening out West. Just blatar breeding, you know how territorial they get during the rut."

"Yeah. I assume you heard about Sejm?"

He nodded, and I couldn't ignore the sadness in his eyes. "He was a good man."

Zaelek peered out of the barracks. "Tyre, Barthol wants you."

Tyre turned toward Zaelek. "Well, duty calls."

I took a seat along the brick-lined, raised flower beds next to the building, and sat, letting out a heavy sigh as I recalled Zaelek's reaction to our last conversation. *I hope I didn't crush him too hard.* I was beginning to wonder if making things more complicated was one of my specialties.

The next two days were filled with non-stop missions mostly geared toward bolstering the village's defenses, but everything had been so quiet that I wondered if an attack would happen at all. My hopes were dashed when a patrolling squad made contact with a considerable Javelar force. Only one man returned from the patrol, not because he escaped, but because they let him go to make a point. The medics reported the man had succumbed to his extensive injuries a few minutes later. Not long after, the bombing commenced.

End Book 1

Acknowledgments

I wrote a whole book, and somehow, this is the hardest part for me. Not for lack of things to say, but because for once, words fail to convey my gratitude in the justice it deserves…

To my beautiful wife, Jordan, and my precious daughter, Amelia: you are the reason I have been able to finish this book. This story is for you. You keep my head above the waves in life's troubled waters, and I love you dearly, so much more than you could ever know. I can't wait to see where life takes us!

To my parents, Scott and Angela Wickel, my number one fans since the day of my birth: You taught me, loved me, and shaped me into who I am today. You have read this story as many times as I have rewritten it, yet, you never tired of hearing it. Even now, after you probably know the story by heart, you are still so eager to get your hands on it. I hope it is everything you wanted, and more! How lucky I am to have been born to such amazing parents. I'd be a fool not to see that. Thank you for being who you are.

To my AMAZING sisters and brother (plus their families): I don't even know where to start here…

Jesse: I will never forget the day that you, my younger brother, told me how poorly my dialogue was written in the early versions of this book! You were 100% correct. Because of you, my characters became human. They became relatable and lovable! Thank you for your honesty and for seeing the potential in my work. I couldn't have asked for a better brother and reader.

Kamaile: It blows my mind that once upon a time, you used to sneak into my old room to read my scribbles in a tattered old notebook. Now, here we are. You've been in this just as long as I have. Still, like Mom and Dad, you were always eager to hear the new and improved version. It's a bit odd to think we've finally come to the end. Your never-ending faith in me keeps me excited to write so I can share more with you.

Danielle: I think I was 17 when I read you my first couple of chapters. There was one particular line that Kinara said to Zaelek (at the time known as a different name) that I will never forget. Do you know why? It was because the arrangement of words sounded entirely different in my head than how it sounded when the phrase came out. You may not realize it, but at that moment, you taught me to read everything I wrote out loud before sharing it. It has saved me a LOT of time with editing and has immensely improved my writing.

Lindsey: It was you who taught me to chase my dreams and never let go. Watching you bust your tail to get where you are has inspired me to follow. You showed me that if I worked half as hard as you do, I could accomplish truly great things. There are so many things I am grateful to you for, none of which have to do with a fantastical land. The memories we have made are worth more to me than anything I could attain on this planet. If this book goes nowhere, I have been made rich with experiences and laughter, and that's good enough for me.

Shai: Your kindness and love know no bounds. You are always eager to help, always happy to be a shoulder to cry on, and one of the wisest souls I have had the privilege of having in my life. The best part? I got you for a sister! You have singlehandedly brought my creation into a physical masterpiece. I don't even want to know how much time you have invested in me. My cover is stunning, my logo is incredible, and everything in between your vast abilities and talents is phenomenal. If you never did another thing for me for as long as we live, I still don't think I could ever repay you (not that you would want that because that's just who you are).

To my family: The support you have shown me is staggering.

I have been truly blessed with each of you. Hopefully, this book offers you a brief reprieve in a chaotic world. It's the least I can do for you. My heart is full. Please accept this as a token of my gratitude.

To Callista Cox and Chris Bowthorpe, my heaven-sent Beta Readers: Without you, this book wouldn't be anywhere near the version it is now. I can't thank you enough. It has been an absolute pleasure to work with you! Your own works are awesome, by the way, and I hope to see them on the shelf one day. They really are magical. Thank you for your honest feedback, your critical eyes, and for sticking with me.

To Annette Chaudet: Two whole years… That's how long you've patiently waited to get to this point. You saw the potential in my story and helped me elevate it to a new level. I couldn't have been sent a better publisher/mentor to work with. It has been a delight to journey down this path with you, and I hope to continue our adventure. Thank you for everything. You made my dream come true, and that's no small thing.

About the Author

Aaron Scott Wickel has been a fan of the fantasy genre since he could speak. From the realm of Disney to Lucas Arts (then back to Disney when they bought the Star Wars franchise), and across a multitude of fantastical universes, he has loved the mystifying aspects of pretty much anything fiction. As a dreamer, writing fantasy has given him a unique tool to convey art through words. He believes that this art holds the key to unlocking a door to adventures not attainable in this world.

As a member of the League of Utah Writers, Aaron has had the opportunity to meet many writers that have guided his career to this point. He spent ten years honing his craft and is excited to continue his development with the future releases of the Elements series. Aside from writing, he enjoys spending time with his family, playing video games, 3D digital modeling, and composing music.

Aaron feels a very deep connection to nature and often finds the inspiration for his work while driving through Utah's winding mountain roads. Above all things in nature, however, he has a particular fascination with the elemental forces. Earth (controlled by Stone Guardians in this series) is his favorite. He loves forests and plant life in general. It's his dream to one day own a greenhouse where he can house many varieties of bonsai species. In the future you may even find a tab on his website, www.wickelwrites.com, hosting pictures of this magnificent art form.

CPSIA information can be obtained
at www.ICGtesting.com
Printed in the USA
BVHW090805200921
617094BV00015B/379/J